Over the Shoulder

Over the Shoulder

A Novel of Intrigue

LEONARD
CHANG

THE ECCO PRESS
An Imprint of HarperCollins*Publishers*

HarperCollins books may be purchased for educational, business, or sales
promotional use. For information please write: Special Markets Department, HarperCollins Publishers, Inc., 10 East 53rd Street, New York, NY
10022.

FIRST EDITION

Designed by Cassandra J. Pappas

Library of Congress Cataloging-in-Publication Data
Chang, Leonard.
    Over the shoulder : a novel of intrigue / Leonard Chang.— 1st ed.
      p. cm.
    ISBN 0-06-019839-7
    1. Private investigators—California—Fiction.
2. Korean Americans—Fiction.   3. California—Fiction.   I. Title.
PS3553.H27244 O8 2001
813'.54—dc21   00-060009

QW   10 9 8 7 6 5 4 3 2

To Cara

Over the Shoulder

Prologue

I strive to understand families. The connections through blood are mysterious to me, these accidents of birth and death binding dissimilar and often disastrous relations, and I've come to view this as a construct of convenience. My family, unified and complete for only a very short time after my birth, became a standard of comparison that to this day makes me see the tenuous and ethereal bonds parents have to one another, to their children, to their siblings. I watch others and learn.

Here is a true story: my father once tried to build a tiny pond in the backyard. He wanted to have a traditional Korean garden, reminding him of gardens he saw as a child, and bought smooth decorative rocks, pine saplings, lotus flowers, and moss. He told me a garden would relax him. The centerpiece, the pond, would have a miniature island at the center, a *chungdo*, that represented, as I learned long after his death, a respite and refuge. Because we didn't have much room in the backyard for a garden, my father wanted to install a small fountain with running water to give the illusion of depth and breadth. He wanted to hear the sound of water. He bought all the materials and worked on the pond in his spare time. But he didn't mix the cement correctly, and the concrete lining eventually cracked, leaking out the water; he also didn't have time to landscape and cultivate the earth, so the flowers withered. The pine trees thrived, however. When my father died, my aunt sold the fountain, and I helped her fill in the gaping hole, shoveling dirt mixed with decorative rocks and crumbling pieces of concrete.

Part 1

A Contrast of Mourners

Paul and I are on a typical baby-sitting job, a nine-to-fiver protecting a Silicon Valley executive, a job that is supposed to be routine. We have been with our client, Sorenson, for about a week now, and it is going more or less as planned. Sorenson needs some hand-holding after receiving anonymous threats. He and his board of directors at Integrated Communications recently laid off twelve hundred employees, and the anonymous threats, along with a rash of chip plant robberies and even an attempted kidnapping that shook up the high-tech industry, prompted IntCom to hire us at Executive Protection Services, a.k.a. ProServ. The industry is nervous.

On this job we're supposed to drive Sorenson to IntCom, stay on the premises in conjunction with IntCom's security detail, then drive him home. We do the usual things. We "rolodex" the client, checking and prepping Sorenson's daily appointments, making certain no one unexpected is allowed in without positive ID and approval; we handle the mail and packages; we accompany Sorenson wherever he goes, especially to and from meetings off the premises; and we've changed most of his and his wife's routines.

One week into the job, Sorenson has a lunch appointment at a restaurant in Monte Vista, which Paul doesn't like because it's so public. Paul Baumgartner, the supervisor for this job, tries to persuade Sorenson to change this location, have it at someone's office, but Sorenson grows annoyed, this kind of interference losing its novelty pretty fast, and tells us curtly that it's our job to protect him, that's all. He has a business to run. However, Paul manages to get Sorenson to leave early, giving us the chance to survey and prep the location. We take the Tank, a customized Chevy Suburban.

The Tank has Level III and Level IV ballistic armor, bullet-resistant tinted windows, run-flat tires that continue to roll with bullets lodged in them, and other goodies that our boss, Polansky, installed. I like the Global Positioning System with its Bay Area map display, since I do most of the driving and have a lousy sense of direction. Although at first glance the Tank looks like any other sport utility vehicle, if you examine it closely, you'll see some differences. It has a smooth belly pan—an aluminum panel covering the underside—to deter tampering. The bumpers are reinforced with extra rubber and steel.

Clients love the Tank. It's a big selling point for Polansky. I had to take a three-week defensive driving course to learn how to handle this thing, since the armor weighs it down so much. I also picked up all kinds of useful information about car bombs and bugs. At first it sounded like secret-agent crap, but once I saw the replica bombs that people have used, with detonators wired to brake lights or the ignition, mercury switches or remote-controlled explosives hidden behind the gas tank, my skepticism dissolved. I learned about heat-sensing switches near the exhaust, and detonators wired to the odometer as delayed triggers. I swept for listening devices and saw how ingenious they have become. Some long-range bugs are as small and flat as a dime.

I don't have to search for these here unless Paul and I leave the Tank unattended for too long. I usually conduct a quick exterior inspection—checking the belly pan, the tires—before letting Sorenson aboard, which I do now, and we drive off.

Paul taps his fingers on his knees and looks up and down the freeway. Though he is a decade older than me, he has the nervous energy of a kid, always moving, always antsy, his quick eyes jumping from one object to another, the slightest motion or glint in his field of vision attracting his full but fleeting attention. His splayed fingers drum at odd angles, as if he's trying to stretch them, and this constant movement bothered me at first. When we started working together almost a year ago—I had been promoted from group to paired fieldwork—I thought his impatience was a rebuke. Then I realized he was always like that. I came to see it as an advantage, his restlessness keeping him alert and wary. Paul is always *on*. I am not. My energy waxes and wanes depending on how much I've eaten, how late it's getting, how much sleep I've had. I feel myself solidifying as it grows darker out, my thoughts slowing. By the evening I turn to stone.

My nickname in high school was "the Block," given to me because of my once stocky build, the way my head seemed attached to a rectangular block of a body. I've slimmed down and have actually grown a couple of inches since then, but I earned this name as a fullback on the soccer team, barreling into opposing forwards. I still have my jersey somewhere, practically shredded with age, but it's my only proof of being part of a winning team. No, I don't think I'm a former high school athlete who relives his glory every evening with a beer and pot-belly. My high school career was inglorious in most ways, but I have so little evidence of former lives. I exist as I am. I move in the present.

We arrive at the restaurant, Florentino's, and Paul goes in ahead as point guard to check the tables, exits, and other customers, while I stay with Sorenson in the Tank. He's leafing through some papers, and he asks me, "Isn't he going a little overboard?"

"No, sir. It's what you hired us for."

"What's he doing?"

"Getting the layout." We aren't supposed to tell the client too much of what we do, since, in their curiosity, they often compromise whatever precautions we take.

"The meeting might be a while. That okay?"

I nod. Paul and I will be on our feet the whole time, scanning and appraising. Security in a restaurant is difficult—there are multiple entrances, a constant turnover of customers, unfamiliar waiters and busboys moving near the client. That it's noon at a popular downtown restaurant makes it even more problematic, which is why Paul is taking his time inside. He's probably talking to the manager, checking the table at which Sorenson will sit, familiarizing himself with the setup, the personnel.

The parking lot is busy; cars keep pulling in. Sorenson's cellular phone chirps. As he speaks into it, I see Paul gliding toward us. He walks swiftly, evenly. His dirty-blond hair rarely moves out of place, his expression cut, unflinching. Our eyes meet, but his remain cold. It's his on-the-job look. He climbs into the Tank and says, "Three exits, a dozen tables. It's small. I'll rove. You stay with Mr. Sorenson."

"Crowded?"

"Getting to be. We'll have a corner table, and the manager's assigning just one waiter."

We escort Sorenson in a standard two-perimeter zone, with me close to him and Paul on the fringe, the same pattern we'll have inside. Sorenson is still on the phone. He talks about volatile market conditions. I catch a glimpse of his gleaming gold watch, and blink at the sun's reflection.

Inside, I walk Sorenson to a large table in the corner, and Paul hangs back, standing near one of the exits. Most of the tables are filled with business suits, but there are some couples, and a family of tourists. Sorenson sits down, still talking on the phone. I move off to the side and try to be as inconspicuous as possible, though a few diners look up at me, then at Paul. The smell of Italian food makes me hungry. Paul and I won't have a chance to eat until this afternoon, when Sorenson will be in his daily staff meeting.

I scan the restaurant, getting a quick fix of the other customers, the waiters, measuring distances. I relax my vision. Scanning is similar to lifeguarding at a pool, where lifeguards don't look for anything in particular, but look for something different—splashing, sinking, fighting. I'm looking for sudden movements, hidden hands, quick approaches. Part of our training involves spotting "tags," and Polansky has all of his trainees watch hours of videos of staged and real assassination attempts. I must have seen Hinckley's attempt on Reagan at least two dozen times. One of the problems there, it seems, was that the local police had been charmed by Reagan, and had watched him instead of the bystanders.

The other executives begin arriving at Sorenson's table, and in addition to studying the new guests, I check with Sorenson and Paul, ready to intervene at any sign of trouble. Along with the others, a large man with long brown hair, wearing a sport coat and jeans, trails an executive. Both Paul and I immediately make out the gun underneath the man's coat. I move toward Sorenson and place my hand on his shoulder. I prepare to push him down as Paul intercepts the long-haired man.

"Excuse me," Paul says.

Both Long Hair and the executive stop. Long Hair notices Paul's hand on his belt. He glances at me, and a startled look crosses his face. His thick forehead and bushy eyebrows jump. "Whoa. I'm Mr. Casey's bodyguard."

Paul turns to Mr. Casey, who nods. I step back. Mr. Casey takes a seat while his security moves next to me. I can see annoyance on Paul's face as he takes in the flowing hair that spreads down past the shoulders, the cheap suit, and the badly concealed gun. Paul, and most everyone at ProServ, hates the term "bodyguard," which evokes images of dark-suited hulks with mirrored glasses and curly wires running down from their earpieces. Although this picture is often true, particularly with the President's Secret Service, these days in most commercial protection businesses the security personnel try very hard not to stand out in such an obvious way. The object is to blend in, and nothing is more obvious than a six-foot-five former linebacker bursting out of his polyester sportscoat.

Long Hair introduces himself to me—his name is Lawrence—and asks what agency I'm from.

I tell him, and he nods toward Paul. "Him too?"

"Yes. I don't think we should talk right now."

He turns to me, not sure if I'm serious. In any other situation I might chat, but this restaurant is unfamiliar, and there are too many strangers, and I know Paul disapproves of this guy who looks like a rent-a-thug. Lawrence says to me, "Whatever," and turns back to his client. He fixes his sport coat, and I see the handle of his revolver in his shoulder holster.

No one at ProServ uses a revolver anymore, even those who prefer a monster magnum for their personal use. Polansky requires us to wear interior belt holsters, since shoulder gear slows down the gun draw and requires two hands to reholster. Besides, the smaller, lighter automatics fit better in the belts. Polansky also has a deal with SIG Arms, so we are able to buy our own SIGs at a discount. I own a SIG Sauer p-230, Paul a p-226. My p-230 is compact, and its magazine holds eight instead of the 226's fifteen, but the 230 fits perfectly in my hand and has little recoil.

The restaurant is filling up with the lunch crowd. I'm getting hungrier. Paul rocks back and forth on his heels, scanning. A customer tries to flag him down, mistaking him for a waiter. Paul glares and shakes his head.

"Oh, I get it," Lawrence says. "That guy's like your boss."

"My supervisor, yeah."

"You guys have a pretty good outfit. Isn't the head of the place former Secret Service?"

I nod. Polansky was recently profiled in *San Francisco Magazine*. Business for ProServ is good.

Paul motions to me. He points to himself, then draws a circle in the air, meaning he's going to rove. I reposition myself closer to Sorenson, my back to the wall, with a better view of the restaurant.

"Why don't you guys use radios?" Lawrence asks, moving next to me.

I sigh. He isn't going to shut up. "We don't need them for two people."

"I thought it was standard target hardening."

"Who do you work for?"

"Myself. I'm a private investigator. Sometimes I do a little body-guarding."

I glance at him curiously, because PIs aren't licensed to do security unless it's relevant to a case, though this rule doesn't seem to matter; we've been getting more competition from PIs like him. ProServ is licensed by California's DCA as a private patrol operator, and though there are a few former PIs at the company, most of us come from the security field in one form or another—a few former cops, an ex-Marine, and people like me, former security detail with other companies. I used to be part of a small security team at Tronics, a computer maker, before moving to ProServ. Polansky is also licensed as a private investigator, but he never takes the standard detecting cases—no missing persons, divorces, anything like that. It's security and only security.

Paul returns to the main dining room, and I relax a bit. Although I've been doing paired fieldwork for a while now, I still don't like being alone with the client, especially in a possibly threatening public place like this. Paul has done a few solo jobs, but because he tends to be curt with clients, Polansky and Charles Swinburn, the general manager, keep him on paired work.

Some of the other executives are finishing up, leaving the table. Sorenson and two others, including Lawrence's client, remain to talk. Lawrence turns to me and asks, "Is ProServ looking for more bodyguards?"

"Not really," I say.

Sorenson and the others stand. Paul and I tighten our circle. We move with Sorenson out of the main dining room, and I hear Sorenson tell the others about the Tank. "The GPS is one of the older kinds," he says. Paul frowns at this revelation. Sometimes I wish he'd ease up a little. He stops and holds up his hand. I tense.

Paul nods toward the parking lot. Someone is trying to look inside the Tank. I ask Sorenson to wait. He barely registers me, still talking to another executive. Paul says to me quietly, "Check out that guy. I want to remind Sorenson about the nondisclosure agreement." We switch positions as I take point guard and walk outside.

It's not unusual for someone to be curious, since the Tank faintly resembles the assembly-line Suburbans, but is customized enough to invite a second look. I get a better view of the man as I walk out of the restaurant. Wearing a Raiders jacket and a baseball cap, the man is shielding his eyes from the sun, looking through the front glass. I'm surprised he doesn't set off the alarm, which shrieks at the slightest bump.

"Can I help you?" I ask.

He whirls around, then focuses on me in surprise. I study his jacket for an outline of a gun. He glances behind me, and says, "This your car?"

"My company's." I take a good look at him—ripped jeans, the jacket crisp and new, a blue cap with the insignia torn off, smooth-shaven, soft jaw—and study his eyes. He looks angry.

"What company is that?" he asks.

I hear the hostility and go on guard, suspecting he is one of Sorenson's laid-off employees. I say, "I'm going to have to ask you to get away from the car. Why don't you move along?"

He steps toward me, and I back up, surprised. I repeat my order for him to leave, and put my hand on my belt.

The man looks me over, smirks, then bows. He says, "Ah-so, do I go now? Do I reave? It velly velly good."

A warm flush passes through me. Shit. This is all I need. I remain expressionless and say, "Yeah, funny. Why don't you take off." I'm not sure who he is, but begin to think that he's just some guy wandering through the lot.

"You gonna use chop-saki karate on me?" He holds up his hands and does a few fake knife strikes.

I know Paul is watching. I need to resolve this quickly. "Do you understand?" I say. "You leave or I call the police."

"Oh, no, not the police," he says. Then, reverting to pidgin, he presses his hands together and says, "Confucius say, 'No call por-reese.'"

"Listen, asshole, I'm not going to—"

"What'd you call me? Who the fuck you think you are?" He advances. I can't believe I'm losing control of the situation. I consider pulling out my gun, if only to stop this from going further, but the man holds back. He glances over my shoulder.

"Everything okay here?"

I look back. It's Lawrence. He's staring at the man, giving him the dead-eye. I say, "I'm not sure. Ask this guy."

"Everything okay here?" he says to the man. Lawrence folds his arms and waits.

The man shakes his head. "What's this fucking world coming to?" he says to Lawrence. "You taking orders from a gook? It's not enough they own everything, they order you around too?"

Lawrence looks confused.

Before I have a chance to say anything, the man bows again, gives us the finger, then trots away. I hear him laugh, which angers me more than anything else. A quiet, nasty laugh. My chest feels compressed. I wave him off and say, "Just an asshole."

Lawrence nods, embarrassed.

Paul is still waiting in the lobby with Sorenson. I quickly inspect the Tank, then return to the restaurant. Paul asks, "All set?"

"HD," I say, giving him the coded "okay." Anything else would put him on alert.

"You check it?" He points to the Tank.

I nod.

"You all right?"

"I said everything's HD."

He tells me to wait with Sorenson, and we switch again as he takes point. He steps outside, looks around for a few moments, then relaxes. He motions for us to follow.

I escort Sorenson, who waits until Paul is out of earshot and continues talking to Lawrence's client, both of them oblivious to what just happened. Sorenson is saying to Mr. Casey, "My new car has a GPS preinstalled. . . ."

Paul lags behind and checks some of the cars entering the parking lot. He is being careful, probably agitated by my run-in. I open the rear passenger door for Sorenson, but he stops, still talking to Casey. I'm sure I could've handled the Raiders-jacket guy more smoothly. Maybe I shouldn't have mentioned the police so quickly, and I definitely shouldn't have called him an asshole. I let him get to me.

I wait for Sorenson to finish talking with Casey and don't pay attention to the purring of a motorcycle. I hear it, but I'm thinking about the Raiders-jacket man, blaming myself for not controlling him. I'm not sure how much Paul saw, if this is going in the report. The engine sound is a distinctive metallic whirring that rises to a whine as it accelerates. It floats by me but doesn't register. I'm worrying about Polansky and Charles reading about my screw-up in the daily shift report.

When Paul suddenly yells, "Take cover!" I spin toward him and see him pulling out his gun. I'm not sure what the hell is happening, but I lunge toward Sorenson, who stops talking and turns to Paul, then to me, in confusion. I grab his shoulder, knee him in the back of his leg, causing him to buckle, and I force him down. While I'm doing this I hear gunfire, and Lawrence, to my right, curses in surprise and throws his client onto the ground, immediately going for his gun. I push Sorenson toward the open door and order him to get in.

He blinks rapidly with fear, and says, "What?"

I shove him hard into the Tank, pushing his head down onto the floor, more gunshots around me, and I slam the door. I pull out my gun and turn toward Paul. The motorcyclist speeds by, his black helmet ducked low, one hand steering and the other shooting at Paul. I fire twice, but he is already hurtling away. I try to get a plate number, but he's moving too fast, and I want to run after him, shooting, but remember Sorenson. I turn back to the Tank, opening the door and checking. He's huddled on the ground, covering his head, repeating, "Shit, shit, shit," without glancing up.

My head buzzes, my hands shake, cordite in the air, and Lawrence is next to me with a nickel-plated revolver in a two-handed stance, looking wildly around. His client is on the pavement behind him, inching under the Tank. The motorcycle engine rises and falls in a scream of gear-shifting, fading away. I search for Paul, and at first think he has gone after the motorcyclist, but then I notice him lying on the ground.

"Paul?" I say and run toward him. When I see the blood, I curse, kneel down, the adrenaline beginning to pump through me. "Paul?" I ask, and with a shock I realize that his left eye is missing. I stop, then yell to Lawrence, "Call 911! Get a fucking ambulance!"

I press Paul's neck, looking for a carotid pulse, but can't find one, and bend down to listen for any breathing, double-checking his airway. Nothing. I yell, "I'm starting CPR! Tell them he's not breathing!" I give him quick breaths to start his breathing, and when it doesn't I feel the panic rising. I alternate fifteen compressions for every two breaths, and I'm getting his blood on my hands as I try to keep his nose shut; I can't stop seeing that his left eye and part of his temple aren't there. I keep my nausea down, and in between breaths I wipe the blood away from his good eye.

D eath followed me at an early age. My mother died giving birth to me, and my best friend, Chris Bruno, was hit by a car when I was eight years old. Although I don't remember my mother's funeral, I can never forget Chris's. What had seared into my memory was Chris's mother breaking down halfway through, wailing uncontrollably and shattering the subdued service. I was frightened by this, and couldn't fully grasp the consequences of death. My father hadn't been able to get off work from the shipping company, so Aunt Insook had come with me, and she seemed unmoved by the outburst. The priest paused, then continued. Mrs. Bruno let out another long, almost inhuman cry, and I heard someone trying to comfort her. "Yes, yes," the pained man's voice said to her. She was sitting two rows ahead. A chill crept up my back, my ears tingling, and I looked down at my scuffed shoes; I hunched my shoulders. The smell of cheap perfume and sweat fermented around me, and I was growing warmer as the sun shone through the stained-glass windows and heated the congregation. My collar itched; my back ached from the hard wood pews. I couldn't get the sound of Mrs. Bruno's howl out of my head, and would later hear it at night when I tried to scare myself.

When my father died two years later in an unloading accident, his funeral service at a Korean church was completely incomprehensible to me. I didn't understand what was being said, since my father had made

English the only language for me, and I could only stare at the minister as he gestured and spoke in gibberish. No one cried, not even my Aunt Insook, my father's older sister, whom I would go to live with. The service was held in the early evening, just as a reddish strip of twilight shone through the tops of the windows and constricted as the minister prayed. I watched the band of light turn into a sliver, lining the high-beamed ceiling, then blink away.

Paul's service is held at a mortuary in Palo Alto, a nonreligious ceremony with padded folding chairs lined unevenly and faint classical music in the background. A few ProServ employees including me show up. Most of the mourners are relatives, so I try to stay out of everyone's way toward the back. I see Brodie and Dunn, two older guys from ProServ who worked with Paul early on, and though they nod at me, we don't talk. I'm not sure if they're being respectful of the circumstances or if they blame me. I'm in the middle of a two-week leave of absence, and I really don't know what the others think. My boss, Polansky, walks stiffly over to me as soon as the service is over and asks me how I'm holding up. His dark suit seems a little small; he looks even bulkier than usual.

"All right," I say. "I guess."

"When you come back, I want you to take it easy. No paired work. Maybe even deskwork for a while."

"I can handle paired work."

"Allen, we'll talk about it later. And if you want to think about some counseling, our medical plan—"

"I know. You told me. I'll think about it."

Polansky, with his hard stare and silver military-style buzz cut, seemed intimidating the first few times I met him, but he tries to put people at ease. He speaks in a low, quiet voice, and despite his height, tries not to tower over anyone. During my first month of training meetings, we talked about our fathers—his had immigrated from Poland. He says to me now, "I know it's tough, but there are a couple of reporters who want to talk to you."

"Here?" The story—dubbed "the Florentino's shooting"—made all the local papers, and the *San Jose Sentinel* began running a series on crime in Silicon Valley. I refused to talk with anyone, and am still screening all my calls.

"Not here. When you get back. I've got to run. See me when you come in next week." He shakes my hand, then seeks out Sonia and

David, Paul's wife and son. I know I have to talk to them as well, but I'm not sure what to say.

Paul was shot with a hollow-point; the bullet exploded his temple and eye socket, and went through his left eye and entered his brain, killing him instantly. The other bullets went wild, hitting the building and pavement. The police interviewed me four separate times, since I was the only one who had really seen what had happened, the ambush moving so quickly that both clients and Lawrence had only noticed the rear of the motorcycle as it sped by. Polansky's contacts at the Monte Vista Police Department and the Santa Clara Sheriff's Office are saying the investigation is going slowly. No leads, no useful witnesses. They are checking all the possible suspects, but since it isn't clear if ProServ's client or Lawrence's client was the intended target, their list of disgruntled employees, potential enemies, and known gang members who might try something like this doubles. They are searching for the man in the Raiders jacket as a possible link. Lawrence and I went through mug shots for hours, but recognized no one. The police don't have much.

I keep seeing Paul's bloody face. I was too confused at the time to register what was really happening, but now, almost two weeks later, I can't stop wondering if Paul saw me as he was dying. I see myself through his one eye, my face hazing blood red as I shake him and yell for him to respond. I try to remember if I noticed some consciousness fading that instant before I began CPR. I'm not sure. Was he watching me? This thought rattles me.

I've been having strange dreams lately, dreams in which I realize I'm dreaming, but I'm unable to do anything about it. I believe it has something to do with my restlessness, an inability to bring any degree of calm to myself, and a night of sleep often leaves me exhausted.

"Allen, glad to see you," Charles says, patting my shoulder. Charles Swinburn, second in command at ProServ, was the one who suggested my promotion to paired work, and is the slicker side to ProServ. Tailored suits and gelled-back hair counter Polansky's rough edges. Charles takes off his gold-rimmed oval glasses and rubs his eyes. "Who the hell is that guy?" He points with his glasses.

Near the entrance a long-haired man corners Polansky and keeps talking. Polansky is trying to be polite and makes a small movement in another direction, but when the man continues talking, Polansky stops and listens. I recognize the hair immediately. "That's Lawrence, the other executive's security. The one with the .357—"

"The one in your report?"

"Yeah. I don't know what he's doing here."

"Drumming up business, it looks like. Allen, I want to warn you that some of the others are a little spooked by all this. Don't take it personally if some of them seem, I don't know, unsure."

"Unsure?"

"Uneasy."

"Uneasy around me?"

"Something like that."

"I knew it," I say. "Do they think it was my fault?"

Charles shakes his head and says quickly, "No, no. Nothing like that. It's just that no one has ever been killed in the field before."

"I know. Is that why Polansky wants to take me off paired work, put me at a desk?"

"No. That's for you. To ease you back in."

"So what should I do? Do they think I'm jinxed or something?"

"Give it time. We're all still a little floored by this."

I thank him, glancing around at Brodie, Dunn, and Johnson, who are talking quietly near the doorway. I make my way to the other exit. I see Sonia talking to an elderly man, nodding, and she stops when she notices me. I wave, and point to the door. She touches the man's arm and calls across the room, "Wait, Allen."

A few others turn to me. I freeze. Sonia walks quickly through a crowd, her black dress fluttering. I feel everyone watching. She asks, "Are you leaving?"

"I think so," I say. Her short blond hair is in sharp contrast to her dress, and her face seems pallid, gaunt. She has lost weight. She studies me, leaning forward and squinting. Her mascara is uneven from crying. I add, "I was going to call you later." I'm not sure if that's true.

"Thank you for coming. David wants to talk to you." She looks around. "Where did he go?"

I mumble that I don't know. I have trouble meeting her eyes.

"He had some questions," she says as she rests her black-gloved hand near her throat. She's wearing a thin pearl necklace.

"About what?"

"About Paul and you and the things you did."

"I did?" I tense.

"I mean, the things you and Paul did when you worked. He's curious."

"How old is he again?"

"Twelve."

I think, Twelve? Hell. I begin to say, "I'm really . . . I don't know how to . . ."

She shakes her head and grabs my elbow. Her bare forearm is thin and ashen, and I try to apologize again, but she hugs me. I feel her shoulder blades as I hug her back, and she squeezes me harder. Something tightens in my chest as I fight the unsteadiness, the unhinging; I force it back down. I want to say something, and try again: "I'm really sorry . . ."

She pulls away and tries to smile. She says, "Will you call and visit? David wants you to."

"I promise I will."

"Thank you, Allen."

I leave the building quickly and drive back to Monte Vista, opening my window and letting the wind whip around me. I have been at Paul's house a few times for dinner, and remember Sonia always glad to see Paul's coworkers. Paul apparently didn't like talking about work, and while on the job with me he rarely mentioned his family. So the few times I visited were a revelation for both me and Sonia, and I felt a surprising camaraderie with her that I once even mistook for a crush. But that quickly dissipated once I saw Paul and Sonia together, how easily and smoothly they spoke as a team, interrupting and prompting each other, occasionally giving knowing, sly looks of understanding that, frankly, surprised me, since Paul always seemed emotionally closed off. They even washed the dishes together and didn't know how to incorporate me into their routine when I offered to help. Relax, Paul said. Just talk to us, Sonia said.

I'm not sure what David wants to ask me, and this worries me. Does he blame me? Maybe everyone does, to some degree, but is too careful to let on. Whenever I visited Paul and Sonia, David was always a quiet, lurking presence, hovering near me, eventually withdrawing into his room after dinner. He made me nervous. Look at me, I think now. Scared of a twelve-year-old kid.

I was ten when I lost my father, and I try to remember how I felt. Stunned. Blindsided. But I didn't have much time to mourn, since I had to move in with my aunt and attend a new school in the middle of the term, and I watched everything around me being donated or discarded as my aunt efficiently, ruthlessly, cleaned out my father's house. I was allowed two suitcases of my things to survive the purge, and remember filling most of them with toys. When Aunt Insook saw this, she told me I had to pack most of my clothes. I resented her, especially after watching the garbage bags filled with my toys going into the back of a Salvation Army truck. I outgrew the clothes within a year, and was angry for giving up the toys.

David won't feel it for a while. It took me a few months, and I remember the moment of realization, occurring only after my life began to settle. I was living with my aunt and had found a new routine of watching cartoons on TV after school. I wouldn't start my homework until my aunt came home from work. One night she returned late, and I was in the living room. She opened the door, but I was engrossed in a book, the TV still on but playing the news. My aunt wiped her feet loudly on the mat, and it was the pattern of wiping that seemed familiar. Most people shuffle their feet a couple of times, but my aunt made long, slow scrapes, and I hadn't noticed it before. My father used to do the same thing, and in my inattentive state, the words of the book still lingering in my head, the newscaster's voice droning, I thought for an instant that my father had come home. The past three months vanished. I looked up, and was shocked to see my aunt. I had forgotten for just a millisecond that I was living in a new place, that everything was different. I stared at my aunt, and after a confusing adjustment realized what I had been thinking, and I knew then that my father was dead.

Morbid thoughts like these swirl around me as I return to my small apartment. I check the half-dozen messages on my machine, all of them from reporters asking for a comment or an interview. I erase them, and hope the commotion will subside now that the funeral is over. I know Polansky likes the press—he has already given a few interviews—since his company comes out looking pretty good. One of his employees, after all, took a bullet for a client.

Most of the stories mentioned me only in passing as Paul's partner, making it clear that I was not injured. Sorenson gave a brief statement describing what had happened, and he emphasized how I had stayed with him, the client, during the shooting; this exonerated me, at least in Polansky's eyes, but I can't escape the knowledge that surfaces often: I didn't suffer even a bruise.

Paul is dead. I was about ten yards away; the gunman easily could have shifted his sights toward Sorenson and me, and I could have been shot as well if Paul's quick response hadn't drawn the shooter away from us. It almost doesn't register, this proximity to death, and I wonder if I'm refusing to believe how quick and meaningless my death could be. I had never pulled my gun out during a job before, had never been shot at, and my closest encounter with death, besides last week, occurred a few years ago on the Golden Gate Bridge, when I was in a five-car pile up, two cars ahead of me crashing into oncoming traffic. My car flipped and I broke my wrist, but never really felt, despite the crunching metal and screeches, perilously close to dying. My seat belt held. I climbed out of my crumpled Toyota and cradled my arm. My current car, an old secondhand Volvo, probably wouldn't have had more than a dent, a tank of another kind.

After pacing my apartment, I go out for some air. My building is right off Main in the old part of downtown Monte Vista, a Chinese herbal store across the street, a run-down café next door. Most of the buildings, including mine, are showing their age with their crumbling and worn brick facades, though the pastel Government Center offices were recently renovated. Monte Vista is a poorer cousin to the richer surrounding towns like Palo Alto and Atherton, and it feels less suburban, at least in this area, and I like the sooty quality of downtown. Dozens of restaurants, many of them Chinese and Japanese, line Main, and a few Asian groceries and general stores with Chinese signs give my neighborhood a cozy urban feel.

I hear the bells clanging at the train crossing, the blare of a train horn in the distance. I live two blocks away from the intersection and am comforted by the sounds of activity.

Paul and I ate lunch at a restaurant down the street when I first started working at ProServ. I was still on my three-month probationary period and worried about making a good impression. Paul was a senior associate, leading group work and starting some paired jobs, and we talked about business and Polansky. It wasn't until he mentioned his son's interest in tae kwon do, Korean karate, that we both found common ground. I had learned tae kwon do as a child in the Korean churches my aunt had dragged me to, and practiced by myself throughout high school. Paul was worried about David getting hurt, but I told him it was unlikely. As a favor, I checked out the school David was interested in, and after watching a few classes was satisfied that it was legitimate. A few months later I met Sonia at an office Christmas party, and I had dinner with them shortly thereafter.

Although we didn't start working pairs together until I had been at ProServ for over a year and a half, first in group work with Paul as the team leader, we seemed to get along. Except for his grousing about office politics, which I couldn't care less about, we talked about past jobs, other security firms, and ProServ's impending expansion. Silicon Valley tech firms were booming, and we were capitalizing on the concerns of well-paid executives.

I buy ginseng tea at Wing Lum Herbal Goods—my aunt drilled into me as a child the benefits of ginseng—and return to my apartment. Two more messages are on my machine. The first one is from Polansky: "Allen? I just got another call from the *Sentinel*. Maybe you can talk to the reporter while you're still on leave. I gave her your home number. I think you should do the interview and get it over with. Don't forget to mention ProServ's expansion. Call me when you're done with it."

The second call is from the reporter, Linda Maldonado, who sounds as if Polansky has told her I have already consented to an interview today. She asks if five o'clock this afternoon will be okay, and leaves her number. I sigh. I can't ignore Polansky's indirect order, and I am more annoyed at this Maldonado person, who tried to talk to me earlier. She went over my head. I call her number, but get her voice mail, and I say curtly, "Five o'clock is fine. I'll be at the Cornerstone Café in downtown Monte Vista. I won't be able to talk for long." I hang up.

3

My name, Allen Choice, throws people off, since it is distinctly un-Korean, un-Asian, and my middle name, Sung-Oh, appears only on my birth certificate and driver's license. Upon immigrating here, my father Americanized his last name, Choi, by going through his English dictionary and looking for the word with the closest spelling. He would have chosen "choir" but had trouble pronouncing it. I'm used to the initial confusion my name causes when I speak to people over the phone and then meet them later. My appearance jars them. I see quick calculations, adjustments of expectations.

Linda Maldonado's eyes do just this as I introduce myself to her at the café. I've already found a seat, and when a young Latina woman bustles in, struggling with her oversized knapsack, I wait to see if she is looking for anyone—she is—then raise my hand and wave her over. She stops, studies me, her head jerking a fraction of an inch. She smiles, nods, and works her way around the cramped tables. She is thinking quickly even as she asks me if I am Allen Choice and shakes my hand. Polansky made sure that there were no photos of me in the various newspaper accounts of Paul's murder, and he ordered me to avoid TV cameras, since a picture of me could compromise my job. I can guess what she expected: a carbon copy of Paul, perhaps, or maybe even Lawrence, or a similarly clichéd apelike "bodyguard." Instead, she sees me: an Asian man in a dark blue suit—my "banker's suit"—

with short jet-black hair combed to the side and a smooth, unsmiling face.

I sit back down and unbutton my jacket. I say, "You didn't know I was Asian."

This stops her for a moment as she settles back into her seat. She pushes some of her long curly black hair behind her ear and says, "No, I didn't."

"My name throws people off," I say, watching her pull out a tape recorder, her nails bitten down and unevenly short. She wears a wedding band. She sets the tape recorder on the table and swivels herself smoothly, pivoting at her waist, in order to reach down into her bag and pull out a pad and pen. She shrugs off her brown canvas coat, revealing a white blouse buttoned to her neck. She seems young to be married, though I know it's relative. I'm thirty and have never had a serious relationship.

She looks up. "I just got your message a few minutes ago and rushed down here. I didn't have time to sort out my questions." She has large, dark eyes that flicker over my suit.

"I haven't changed from the memorial service," I say. "I can't stay long—"

"I know. I appreciate you doing this. Why haven't you talked to any reporters before?" She turns on the tape recorder.

"Do you have to use that?" I ask.

"Why?"

"I'm not sure I want to be on tape."

She smiles. "I don't have to, but it'll be more accurate."

A wariness overcomes me, her disarming smile possibly a strategy. "By the way," I add, "I'm not sure I appreciate your going to my boss to get me to talk."

The smile disappears, and she says, "You didn't return any of my calls."

"I didn't want to talk to the press."

"Why not?"

I glance at the tape recorder. She sighs and shuts it off. "Okay. You want to start off the record? I'm just trying to do my job, Mr. Choice."

"My job requires that I stay quiet. I'm not supposed to be noticed."

"Your boss is noticed. He doesn't stay quiet."

"He's not in the field. He's the head of ProServ."

"There won't be any pictures of you," she says. "I just want to ask a few questions." As she looks down at her pad, her hair falls over her face again. She snaps off an elastic band from her wrist and quickly ties her hair back in a ponytail. Stray wisps stick out, making her look even younger.

"The police know everything," I say.

"Maybe. But I'd like to hear it from you."

"What would you like to know?"

"Just tell me what happened."

I sigh, and tell her about that afternoon. She doesn't take notes, and stares at me intently as she listens, occasionally prompting me with a question. I suddenly become more self-conscious about my story. Her close attention is disconcerting, and I begin to hear myself as I talk; I become detached and feel a second self stepping away from the table and watching us. My voice, though low and calm, is edged with un-certainty, and I see myself trying to justify my slow reaction to the gunfire. My first thought was of Sorenson, I say. But is that true? I no longer know what my first thought was. The reporter, Ms. Maldonado, nods, but leans away at the violence in my story, perhaps even won-dering how I could talk so evenly about my partner dying. When I fin-ish, I find myself looking directly at her, and I wait for her reaction. She bites her lower lip and is quiet for a moment, then asks, "How well did you know him, your partner?"

"Pretty well. I've known him since I've been there, two and a half years, and I've been working pairs with him for a year."

"Do you know his wife?"

"A little. I've been over to their house a few times."

"What was their marriage like?"

"Their marriage?" I sit back, considering this. "Why do you want to know?"

"Just trying to get a better picture."

"They had a good marriage."

"I've been trying to talk to her," she says.

"Sonia? Why?"

"I have some questions."

"About what?"

"About Paul."

A group of teenagers come into the café and sit near the door, their loud laughter tilting the quiet balance of the room in their direction.

We turn toward them. It's usually quieter in here during dinnertime. I say, "Ms. Mald—"

"Call me Linda, please."

"What kind of questions, Linda?" I ask evenly. I hope she's not trying to smear his name for some reason. I find myself even more wary and search her face for signs.

She hesitates. "About the way he was killed. About the way he was shot but no one else was hurt."

"What are you talking about? Are you saying you think it's my fault?"

She sits back, startled. "No, no, not at all. That's not what I mean."

I try to calm myself. Too combative. I inhale and exhale slowly.

She says, "It's just that it's strange that the gunman didn't even try to shoot Mr. Sorenson or Mr. Casey. I mean, what kind of assassination attempt is that?"

"Paul had drawn his gun," I say. "He was the immediate threat."

"Well, after Paul was shot, why didn't the gunman go after the others?"

"By that time I had my gun out, and the other guy, Lawrence, did too. The gunman screwed up. Paul made him right away and forced the shooting." Her face is impassive as I say this. She has heard this before. I say, "What do you think happened?"

"Did Paul have any enemies? Was he ever in any kind of trouble?"

I shake my head. "You can't believe that Paul was the intended target."

"Why not?"

"That's crazy. Why would anyone want to kill Paul?"

She waits.

I say, "First of all, Paul and I never knew where we'd be that day until we met with Sorenson."

"Someone could've followed you."

"I doubt it. We're careful about that. Also, why would anyone hit Paul while he's at work? He's armed, alert, *looking* for trouble."

"I didn't say the gunman was smart."

Her theory is breaking down. I relax now that I know what she wants. "I can't think of any reason why anyone would want him dead."

"What about his wife?"

"That's why you want to talk to her? You think Sonia is involved?"

"I just want to be thorough."

"Have the police considered this?"

"Not really. Well, for a minute they did, but it went nowhere. They're working on the assumption that one of the clients was the target."

"And this is why you wanted to talk to me?"

"Yes."

"You think you can scoop everyone with this."

"I'm just checking all the possibilities."

"Good luck, but I doubt you'll find anything. Sonia and Paul were pretty close. They had a son. I doubt she had anything to do with this."

"Do you think you can get her to see me?"

"No. If she hasn't talked to you by now, she probably won't."

"You were just at the funeral service?"

I nod.

"How was she?"

I draw back and remain silent for a minute. Then I say, "Look, my partner and friend was killed. I just listened to his family talk about how much they loved him. Can you not be so . . . hungry?"

She looks stricken, her eyes widening. She straightens her pad and clears her throat. "You're right. Sorry."

"What's your job at the *Sentinel?*"

"I'm on staff. I work mainly on their Peninsula news section, but I'm trying to do more."

"And this would be a good start."

"It would."

"Are you the one doing that series on high-tech crime?"

"No. That's a colleague. John Yates."

"Why isn't he working on this?"

"He doesn't buy it."

I don't reply.

"I just want to rule this out," she finally says. "Even if it doesn't lead to anything. I can maybe get an exclusive interview with the wife."

"Have you tried?"

"A number of times."

"I hope you didn't mention your theory to her."

"Of course not! And it's not even a theory. It's a guess."

"And I'm sure you were considerate and respectful."

She hears my tone and sits up. "What does that mean?"

"Did you call first and express your sympathies?"

She hesitates.

"Or did you call her boss to try to make her talk, like you did with me?"

"Hey, I tried calling you a dozen times—"

"And when that didn't work you called my boss."

"If you'd returned any of my calls, I wouldn't have had to do that."

"Maybe, but you're not making me, or Sonia, eager to talk."

She frowns and taps her pen against the table, her body poised to leave. I decide to ease off and ask, "What do you think happened? What's your scenario?"

Shaking her head, she says, "Nothing definite. I just find it strange that the entire shooting seemed so directed. And I've been doing a lot of digging on Mr. Sorenson and Mr. Casey. They have some business enemies, but no one wants them dead. If you want to get a CEO, you sue him, not kill him."

"What about the botched-kidnapping theory, or the disgruntled ex-employee?"

"Kidnapping is a possibility, but no one saw another car driving away, other kidnappers, anything like that. One motorcycle kidnapper makes no sense. And a disgruntled worker might do this, but the two CEOs never had any contact with the low-level employees, the ones who were laid off. Most employees couldn't even identify them if they had to. There are too many middle layers. Maybe if one of the lower managers got shot at, it'd make more sense."

I think about the motorcyclist again, how fast everything was. Linda's word "directed" sticks in my mind, how none of the bullets came even close to the Tank. Polansky was surprised that he wouldn't have to repair anything, not a scratch. Paul had received the only assault.

Linda is waiting. I realize she has asked me something. "Excuse me?"

"Could you have been the target?"

"Me? I doubt it."

"Why?"

"I don't have any enemies. I have no money, nothing of value that anyone wants. I'm a nobody."

She smiles. "And such a big ego."

"You know what I mean," I say, and suddenly think of the unreality of this. Paul is dead and we are talking about it as if it were just a newsworthy event. I remind myself how he died. His service was with his casket closed; the meaning of that is clearest to me. I had touched his face as he died. I hope Sonia hadn't viewed him, that the police hadn't required any kind of confirming identification. I'm sure that David hadn't been allowed to see him. Maybe this is why he wants to meet me. I feel uneasy about this.

"I'm going to visit them soon," I say. "Sonia and David."

"When?"

"Soon. David wants to know more about what his father did."

"His job?"

I nod. "I promised Sonia I would."

I can see her planning quickly, and she says, "Can you ask her to talk to me?"

"Why?"

"She'd probably listen to you."

I say, "I don't think so, but I'll mention your theory—"

"Not that I think she might have anything to do with—"

"She doesn't," I say.

"I mean—"

"I know what you mean. So, this meeting was for that? You're not going to do an interview?"

"I am. Can I turn this on now?" She reaches for the tape recorder.

I shrug.

"Tell me where you were born, where you grew up, that kind of thing," she says.

I give her a brief sketch: born in Los Angeles, but complications caused my mother's death, and my father moved to the Bay Area to be near his sister; I grew up in the South Bay, but when my father died I went to live with my aunt in Oakland; I attended community college, transferred to San Francisco State, dropped out, and worked up and down California until I got the Tronics job in the city; I then moved to ProServ.

"Married?" she asks.

"No."

"What did your father do, and how did he die?"

"Drove a truck. Some kind of unloading accident. My aunt was a bookkeeper. I think she's in the East Bay."

"You think?"

"I haven't spoken to her in years."

Linda waits for more.

"We never got along that well," I say.

"Why?"

"Just never did." Our final break was when I dropped out of college.

"Does she know about the shooting?"

"No idea. I doubt it. She never read newspapers or watched the news."

She pauses. "How has the shooting affected you?"

I think about it, then say, "It shook me up."

"Will you return to ProServ, to the same kind of work?"

I must look puzzled, because she adds, "Now that you know how dangerous it is?"

"I always knew. I like what I do. I'll just be more careful."

"What's it like being one of the few Asian American bodyguards?"

"You mean there are more?" I say, smiling.

"That incident you had with the man in Florentino's parking lot, the racist remarks—does that happen often?"

"No," I say. "Not like that."

"Then how?"

I shift in my chair. "What does this have to do with the shooting?"

"Just getting a better idea of you."

I say, "Sometimes people make assumptions."

"Like?"

"Like I must know karate, or speak Korean."

"You don't?"

"Speak Korean? No."

"But you know karate?"

"Tae kwon do. Yes."

"We don't have to talk about this, if you don't want."

"I don't care," I say, glancing at the clock. "But I've got to get going soon."

"All right, I guess that's enough for now."

"It is? You got enough for a story?"

"No. My editor will probably kill it."

"You just wanted more info on Paul and Sonia."

"Partly, but I also wanted a sense of you."

"A sense of me."

"Yes."

"Did you?" I ask.

"What?"

"Get a sense of me."

"Yes."

"My boss will be annoyed there won't be a story," I say.

"Not much I can do. My editor won't want to run this, especially now that it's old news."

Old news, I think. Already. I stand up and say, "Old news about a nobody. I could've told you that."

4

That I am a nobody doesn't bother me as it might some people. I prefer anonymity, unobstructed movement through a crowd with neither a first nor a second glance in my direction. I used to think it had something to do with my job, but if pressed I'd have to admit that I was always like this. I never wanted to draw attention to myself. I never wanted to be important or special, despite my aunt's ambitions for me. She came to view me as a failure.

Bitterly disappointed in my father for marrying my mother, who had come from a poor family outside of Seoul but had managed to earn a scholarship at a small private college near L.A., Aunt Insook constantly reminded me how my father had ruined his chances for a good life by taking the trucking job and never aspiring for more. He had a degree in biology from Yonsei University and had planned to apply to medical school here in the States. But money problems as well as his difficulty with reading and writing English hindered him. After I was born and my mother died, it then seemed impossible for him to consider it any further.

Aunt Insook focused her hopes on me. Throughout high school she kept pushing the sciences at me—even, to my disbelief, buying old biology textbooks for me so I'd have a head start. At the beginning I accepted this as my taking on my father's unfinished work, but as I grew older I realized how absurd it was for me to think about medical school before I even finished the ninth grade, to consider a surgical residency before stepping on a college campus. Our fights escalated, and using a combination of guilt and money, she managed to ram me through high school and two years of college. It wasn't until I was sitting in an organic chemistry course and the professor began talking about the molecular structure of alicyclic compounds—I remember this because I hadn't done any of the readings and liked the word "alicyclic" as soon as the professor uttered it—it wasn't until this moment when I wondered how many of the students here were like me, cajoled, bribed, and whipped through these courses despite a complete lack of interest, that I knew it wasn't for me. I stood up and left the lecture hall. I kept thinking of the word "alicyclic." It became a mantra that comforted my doubts, because I knew I was never going to return.

My aunt didn't want to have anything to do with me after that. Her parting words were something to the effect that I was going to end up like my father. That didn't sound so bad to me.

This was over a decade ago, and I haven't spoken to her since. I tried at first to keep the lines open by sending her my changes of address and an occasional Christmas card, since I felt I had antagonized her by flaunting my miserable academic career in front of her, but I never heard from her. I'm not even sure if she's still alive. She would be in her mid-sixties by now.

Every so often my aunt brushes my thoughts, and today I wonder if Linda Maldonado will try to find her despite my refusal. I'm at the Monte Vista Library, only a half mile away from my apartment, and am leafing through past issues of the *Sentinel*, searching for Linda's byline. I want a better idea of the kind of reporter she is, but I'm having trouble finding anything of hers. I remember what she had said about writing for the Peninsula section, but I still can't find her name. For a moment I wonder if I was conned, if she was working for someone else. Should I have asked for identification?

But then I see her byline in a supplement, *Bay Area Life*. I stop because it isn't hard news. It's a lifestyle and food section. The title of her article is "Inger Williams's Tips for Reducing Thighs," and accompanying her text are drawings of leg exercises. I dig into the pile of newspapers and find more supplements. Her other articles include an interview with a masseuse who specializes in dog massages, a survey of Bay Area fitness centers as singles hangouts, and a "Guide to Gen-X Jargon."

This makes no sense to me. I wonder if she was recently reassigned to the news section, or if the story she's working on is going to be slanted in some strange way to fit this supplement. Maybe she's doing this outside of the newspaper. I photocopy a few of the articles and return home.

I have been creating tasks for myself to avoid calling Sonia. But I know that if I'm going to see her and David, I probably should soon. I have to return to work next week and won't have much free time then. I sit at my kitchen table and stare at the phone. It's almost noon. I didn't call last night because by the time I returned from dinner, it was too late. This morning was too early. Stop thinking about yourself. David has questions about his father. I can understand that. I find Sonia's number and call. Her machine answers, and I'm relieved. I begin leaving a message, but she picks up. "Hello? Allen?"

"Hello."

"Sorry about that. I still have to screen my calls. But the reporters are beginning to leave me alone."

"Yeah. Polansky made me talk to one yesterday. The *Sentinel.*"

"God, they've been hounding me."

I clear my throat in the following silence. I say, "Yeah, so how're you doing?"

"Okay. Thanks for coming yesterday. I know you probably didn't want to—"

"I wanted to be there—"

"It's okay. I understand. If I were you I probably wouldn't have gone."

"Does David still want to talk?"

"Yes. It's not urgent, though."

"I have time this weekend."

"Would you like to come over for lunch? Tomorrow?"

"That sounds good."

"Let's say noon. I appreciate this, Allen."

We say goodbye and hang up. She's handling this very well, and I let Linda's suspicions infect me for a second. I grow annoyed at my disloyalty and vow to avoid any more contact with reporters.

I change into sweats and head out to the gym, needing something to take my mind off all this. My membership is subsidized by Polansky, who wants all of us in shape, and I usually feel better lifting weights for a while. My needs are simple: a place to sleep, a job that's interesting, an exercise routine. Aunt Insook, who kept the books for a Korean restaurant chain, never understood my lack of ambition. I don't need to succeed. Maybe because she saw all that money passing through her books, inflows and outflows of thousands and thousands of dollars—I remember the restaurant chain growing rapidly—she had a taste of real money. She then saw her college graduate younger brother driving a rig around town, loading and unloading boxes of cheap T-shirts. She watched her nephew piss away whatever advantages he had, and she thought, What's wrong with this family?

It was the gasoline that really bothered her. Sometimes my father worked late, and when I was very young my aunt baby-sat me in the afternoons and evenings. Her bookkeeping job had flexible hours. When my father returned home, he would have grease stains on his arms and hands from moving boxes and tinkering with the rig. Lava soap only helped to a degree; for the deeply embedded smudges, he'd have to spill a few drops of gasoline onto his hands. I didn't mind the smell, since he'd usually wash a few times with soap after that, but my aunt hated it. She'd wrinkle her nose and say something to him in Korean, and he'd shake his head and shrug. She once said in English, "It's like gas station."

I'm sure her notions were partly derived from the immigrant dreams I saw in other families. And from what I gathered, my father and she came from desperate circumstances: they escaped from North Korea during the Communist takeover, stole supplies and sold them to GIs during the war. They never spoke about it, though, and my knowledge of them begins pretty much with my birth. I also suspect that my father was a different man before my mother died, possibly even more like my aunt, but I don't know this for sure.

As I drive to the gym, I catch myself thinking about all this, and look forward to returning to work. I have too much free time.

Paul and Sonia's house is a small two-bedroom in Palo Alto, the street lined with tall cypresses and a few of the yards separated by bright white picket fences. The branches of the trees meet high above the middle of the street, forming a long leafy tunnel which lets through small bursts of sunlight. I pull up to the house and notice that the blue-and-white facade seems dirtier than I remember. The lawn is overgrown with weeds. I wonder if I should offer to do a little yardwork.

I'm fifteen minutes early, so I wait in the car. Watching the pavement light up in patches, a code blinking around me, I plan what to say to David, thinking of stories that will make his father look good. The Florentino's shooting is one example of Paul's quick thinking, but there are many others. He had his share of screw-ups, though, like the time he blew up at a banker's wife because she kept asking him to retrieve something from another room. "I'm not your goddamn errand boy," he said.

I laugh at this memory. Polansky yanked us off that job the next day and put a reprimand in Paul's file.

"Allen?" a voice says.

Sonia opens her screen door and peers out at me. I wave. "Hi."

"Were you laughing?" she asks.

"Yeah," I say, climbing out. "I was thinking of something."

"Come in. What's so funny?"

I just smile. She is dressed in khakis and a black sweater, the same thin pearl necklace from the funeral swinging as she steps aside and holds the door for me. I wait for her to follow, but she leans out and stares at her lawn, her body poised at an angle as her feet remain inside. She looks as if she were in mid-dive, swanning from the doorway.

"It might be time to cut the lawn," she says. Her hair is wet, combed back, and plastered to her scalp. A few drops of water dot the nape of her neck.

"I can help out."

"What? Of course not. I'll call someone." She turns toward me and lets the screen door slam shut, the crack shooting through the house. Bare-wood and leather furniture fills the living room. It seemed uninviting the first time I saw it. I later learned that Paul had dust allergies and avoided fabric upholstery.

I ask where David is.

"He's on his way. He was at a friend's."

"What should I talk to him about?"

"Whatever you want. He might have a few questions."

"Didn't Paul tell him anything?"

"David wasn't interested until now."

The word "now" hangs in the air. Sonia claps her hands together and says, "Let me turn up the oven. Want anything to drink? Wine? Beer?"

I ask for a beer and follow her into the small kitchen. The table is set. "I hope you didn't go to any trouble," I say.

"No. Actually, I have a bunch of dishes in the fridge. My neighbors." She opens the refrigerator door and waves her hand. A half-dozen foil-covered casseroles crowd the shelves. "It will take us months to finish these. Do you like tuna?"

"Sure," I say. "You have nice neighbors."

"We didn't know them that well, but as soon as they heard, they all helped out."

I look uneasily around the kitchen, feeling Paul's absence. She hands me the beer, and I drink half the glass in two gulps. She smiles. "You okay?"

"Fine," I say.

"When do you return to work?"

"Next week. Polansky will probably keep me at a desk for a while."

"That's good."

"I prefer not to."

"Return to work?"

"Sit at a desk. That's one of the reasons I left my previous job."

"What'd you do there?"

"I sat at a console and watched TV monitors," I say. "How about you? You're on a break?"

She nods. "My boss gave me three weeks. I'm up to my neck in lawyers and paperwork." She takes out another beer and hands me the bottle. "Paul didn't leave a will."

I'm not sure what I expect from a grieving widow, though I probably have preconceptions of mourning from Mrs. Bruno, Chris's mother. Sonia seems unruffled, and I try to adjust my responses to this, not wanting to seem too morose. I must look distracted, because Sonia quickly changes the subject by asking me if I still practice tae kwon do.

It takes me a moment to remember how she would know this. "Not really. Maybe once in a while, to keep flexible. Is David still doing it?"

"He got his green belt, then stopped. He does a little on his own, though."

We hear the front screen door squeak, then slam shut. Sonia calls out for her son.

David is thin and gangly, his shaggy hair going down to his neck, which makes his face seem even thinner. He dresses in that oversized way most teens do these days: loose pants and a huge T-shirt. He stops in the doorway and nods to me. "Hey, Mr. Choice."

"You can call me Allen."

He glances at his mother, who tells him to wash up.

By the time David joins us for lunch, I've finished my second beer and refused a third. We begin eating the tuna casserole. Sonia fills the awkward silence with questions to her son about his morning. Finally, after ten minutes of this, she says to him, "So, Allen's here to answer your questions."

He nods, but continues eating.

I say, "Before I came here I was thinking about the time your dad was working for a guy who was real theatrical about the job. He kept acting like it was a game or something."

"Who was this?" Sonia asks.

"Some old rich guy. I don't remember his name. None of this came up in the interviews, but he was kind of a nut. Anyway, Paul was doing a solo job, but little by little this guy would say crazy things, like 'If there's trouble, don't let me get caught. Just put a bullet in my head.'"

"What kind of trouble?" David says.

"That's the thing. The guy was low-risk. Polansky seemed to be humoring him, if anything, since his threat assessment was so flimsy, and Paul was just doing a general screen. But this guy was always saying things like 'Don't let them take me alive.'"

I continue the story and tell them how Paul had taken this seriously at first; he worried that there was a threat that this man hadn't revealed in the interviews. Paul, being thorough, was on high alert all the time, double-checking routes, sweeping every room and car, even bringing me at one point to conduct a few action drills with the guy, so Paul and he would be prepared if anything came up. After a week of this, however, Paul began to suspect that this guy was not only exaggerating the threats but was getting off on the attention, which wasn't unusual in this business. Paul did some checking and discovered that this guy was a rich eccentric who had done this before, and even had a reputation at Black Diamond, ProServ's competitor.

"So what did he do?" Sonia asks.

"When Paul told me about this guy, I suggested he dump him. Either that or call his bluff and pretend there was a real threat, see what the guy did."

"Scare him, you mean?" David says.

"Yeah, exactly. I even offered to help. But your dad surprised me."

"How?"

"You know he wasn't always that polite around clients. It even got him in trouble a couple of times."

"More than a couple of times," Sonia says.

"But I guess he felt sorry for the guy. Instead of dumping him, your dad got to know him a little better. It turns out he was a lonely man who lost his wife a couple years back, and just had too much time and money on his hands. He started hiring security just to keep busy."

"What'd he do?" David asks.

"Your dad? He did the job—it was only a two-week thing—then hooked the guy up with some foundation, like a health research place in Chicago, and I guess the guy found his calling. He gave most of his money to the place and started working there."

"Chicago?" Sonia says. "Wait a minute. Is this Mr. Grayson?"

"That might be it."

"The ALS research foundation? Lou Gehrig's disease?"

"Yeah," I say. "He told you?"

"We get a card from him every Christmas. I didn't realize . . ."

"Yeah, that must be him. That's how they met. If it was me, I would've just had Polansky get rid of him."

Sonia says quietly, "I didn't know that. He never told me."

"But why did that get him in trouble?" David asks.

"It didn't," I say. "There was no trouble."

He looks confused, then turns to his mother. "You said he got in trouble because of his clients."

"Other clients, honey. He wasn't always that nice."

"Once we started working together, it went okay," I say.

Sonia shakes her head. "But it was his attitude that kept him from further solo work, wasn't it?"

I'm not sure I want to give David a bad impression of his father, and I say, "We worked well together. No one wanted to break us up."

"But don't you want to do solo work?" she asks.

"Not yet. Too much responsibility. Paired work suits me for now."

"Who will you work with?"

"I don't know. I haven't talked to anyone about it." I wonder if anyone will want to pair with me now. I'll have to ask Charles what the others think.

David says, "Do you like being a bodyguard?"

"Don't forget," Sonia says, "that they don't like that term."

"Oh, I don't care as much as Paul did."

"He hated being called that," she says, smiling.

"What's the difference?" David asks.

Sonia clucks her tongue. "You know your father wanted more respect for what he did." To me she says, "He used to correct our friends. It was embarrassing."

"Well," I say. "We all have these small quirks."

"He almost lost a freelance job because of it. It was pride, you know. Ego. He thought 'bodyguard' sounded too common."

I put my fork down. "Freelance?"

"He kept correcting the boss of the company. I'm surprised he eventually got the job."

"What job?" I ask. "Freelance?"

She looks up. "What do you mean, 'What job?' "

"Paul was doing freelance work?"

Sonia hesitates. "Didn't you know?"

"What kind of freelance work?"

"Paul didn't say anything to you," she says, no longer a question.

"He didn't."

"The past few months he started doing a little consulting on the weekends."

"What kind of consulting?"

"Some kind of security. He was thinking about starting his own business."

I try to remember if Paul ever mentioned this to me. He didn't. Polansky had us all sign a noncompetitive agreement, which includes prior approval for any security-related jobs outside of ProServ. I'm sure I would've known about this. "He didn't clear it with Polansky," I say.

"Why would he have to?"

I explain the contract, which would have held for six months even if Paul had quit.

"Is he going to get in trouble?" David asks.

I'm not sure how to answer this, and find it disconcerting that David speaks of his father in the present tense. "It doesn't really matter," I say. "I'm just surprised Paul didn't mention it to me."

"Maybe he was going to," Sonia says. "He just started it recently."

"What kind of consulting jobs?"

"I'm not sure about the details, but my friend's employer needed something done with their security system. My friend recommended Paul."

"To do what? Personal security?"

She shakes her head. "I think something to do with alarms."

"Was he registered with the BSIS?"

"The what?"

"Department of Consumer Affairs—the Bureau of Security and Investigative Services. In order to install alarms you need to be licensed and registered."

"I don't know."

"What company was this?"

She hesitates before she says, "General Graphics. They're in the city. You won't tell Polansky, will you?"

"No. Don't worry. I'm just surprised."

David says, "Are you carrying a gun right now?"

"No. Only when we're working."

"What about other weapons?"

"Your dad carried a telescoping baton, the kind that opens up. He was pretty handy with that. I don't carry anything."

"Nothing? Not even a knife?"

I smile. "Nothing."

The conversation wanes as we finish lunch. I tell them about some routine jobs Paul and I had before Sorenson—a short-termer during a computer conference, a baby-sitting job for a Hong Kong executive—but David doesn't seem interested. I'm not sure what he wants from me. Sonia asks if we have room for dessert, but we don't. A few more awkward silences prompt Sonia to offer me coffee.

I keep thinking about Paul's freelance work and how he kept it secret from me despite all the time we spent together. Maybe he didn't involve me because it would've jeopardized my position. But no matter how I rationalize it, Paul kept this information from me for only one conceivable reason: he didn't trust me.

When I finish my coffee and tell them I have to go, Sonia walks me to my car. She thanks me again for visiting.

"I don't know how much I helped."

"You helped," she says. "I'm sure you did."

"Do you know why Paul started the extra work?"

This change in subject confuses her for a moment. She says, "You're not going to tell Polansky—"

"I promise. I'm curious, though."

"He wanted to make more money. And I think he was going to start his own business. You know that he'd hit a wall at ProServ."

"You mean solo work?"

"Yes, and what kind of future is there? I mean, where do you see yourself in ten, fifteen years?"

I nod. I could end up like Charles, pushing papers and a yes-man to Polansky. "Why didn't he tell me?" I ask. "You think he didn't trust me?"

"No, of course he did. He trusted you with—" She stops.

"With his life," I finish. "Shit. A lot of good that did."

"No, I didn't mean that—"

"I know. It's okay," I say. "Maybe he was right not to trust me—"

"It was an expression," she says. "He trusted you. I think he didn't tell you in case it failed."

"Failed?"

"He only did a few jobs. He was probably waiting to see how they went."

I nod, unconvinced. She hugs me and says, "He trusted you. He did. He told me so."

I say goodbye, and drive away. I remember what Linda Maldonado said. What if the shooting was directed at Paul? His freelance work might be connected to that.

General Graphics. I wonder what kind of business they do.

6

I try to imagine myself in ten years, but can't see anything different from the way things are now. This worries me. I'm not sure if it's my lack of imagination or if my life has actually stalled. Fifteen years from today I'll be forty-five years old, close to the age my father was when he died. I'll be living in the same apartment, working at the same job, and possibly even driving the same car. My Volvo never seems to break down. I don't see a family, a house, a life like Paul's, and am not sure why. I'm in a holding pattern, hovering, waiting, though I'm not certain what exactly I'm waiting for.

Recalling what little physics I took in college, I used to think I was in inertial rest, a body at rest remaining so. Once an outside force applied itself to me, I would be in motion. I liked this idea. It freed me, relieving me of the responsibility. I just had to wait for an outside force. But I soon realized that this was an illusion. Even more than an illusion, this was a deception. By leaving everything to inertia, I was avoiding free will. I had the ability to choose and act, and found the concept of inertia dangerous. If I really believed in it, I'd just sit in my apartment all day. I decided to call it the *inertial deception*. I can't succumb to it.

I'm driving into the city with these thoughts confusing me, heading toward Japantown, where General Graphics is located. They are a small graphic design firm that produces annual reports, brochures, posters, and corporate logos, and it is their expansion into web page design that led them to increase their security. They recently invested thousands of dollars in new computer equipment, and Paul helped upgrade their perimeter alarm system. I learned this on the phone with their office manager, Sonia's friend, who bought my story of following up on Paul's work as soon as I mentioned Sonia.

I decide that the least I can do is check Paul's freelance work, if only to rule it out. Linda Maldonado's suspicion coupled with Sonia's news about Paul digs at me. I can't dismiss this. But I don't see any reason to tell Linda, or the police, yet. I don't want Paul in trouble with Polansky, who would also suspect my previous knowledge of Paul's moonlighting. I'm curious to know how Paul set up these jobs. I call the DCA to see if Paul was licensed as an alarm agent, but he wasn't, so his work was possibly illegal as well.

Traffic in the city is backed up, and I inch up Van Ness. I'm certain Paul never gave me any indication of his extra work. The only clue I can think of was when I asked him about his weekend once and he simply answered, "Had some business to take care of." I assumed he meant personal business, and now I wonder if that was my opportunity to ask him more. Instead, I let it drop.

Once I make it up past the Civic Center and toward Geary, I begin looking for parking, which takes another half hour. By the time I walk to General Graphics' office on Laguna, I'm irritable, unsure why I'm going through this hassle. The office is on the second floor of a small brick building, and I can see why they wanted to upgrade their security. The front door of the building is unlocked, the lobby empty, and anyone can walk in and take the elevator, as I do, to any floor.

I see the cardkey entry system next to the General Graphics door, a card with a magnetized strip and an access code required to unlock it. I knock, and a harried-looking woman, her hair mussed, her face shiny with sweat, opens the door abruptly. "What?" she asks.

I step back. "I'm here to see Noreen, the office manager."

She turns and yells for Noreen, leaving the door open and walking away. I enter, and turn toward another woman approaching from a different room. I hear the first woman say, "I'm not the receptionist. You should get all callers."

Noreen frowns and rolls her eyes at me. She asks, "Are you Allen?"

"I'm a little late. Parking trouble," I say.

"You just missed my boss, but if you're here to check things out, I can help."

She's in her late forties, her blouse and skirt meticulously ironed and straight, her graying hair wound tightly in a bun, and she smiles pleasantly, unconcerned. I say, "Don't you want to check my identification?"

"Right. Sure."

I show her my BSIS Private Patrol license and my ProServ ID. "I could be anyone casing this place," I tell her. "You should be more careful."

She shrugs. "I recognized your voice, and frankly couldn't care less if someone robbed this place."

I smile. Nothing like company loyalty. "Okay. How long ago did Paul install the alarm?"

"About two months. Were you his partner?"

"At ProServ. The alarm work he did himself."

"You were there when he was shot?"

I pause, then say, "Yeah. I'm following up his jobs. Any problems with the alarm?"

"I don't think so."

"How long did he work on this?"

"Just one weekend. I can check the records if you want."

"How much did he get paid?"

"I don't remember. Let me check." She goes to her computer and opens an accounting program. She says, "He was paid nine hundred and ninety dollars for seven hours of work."

"Really? That include expenses?"

"One sec," she says, scrolling down the screen. "No real expenses. We had the equipment, but I just needed someone to install it. My boss got a deal on the system."

"You know, you need a licensed alarm company agent to install these things."

"The place where my boss got this wasn't licensed."

"A retailer doesn't have to be. The installer does."

"That's what Paul said, but that doesn't make sense. Anyway, he knew what he was doing, and I know Sonia."

"She suggested Paul."

"Right."

"Do you know if he worked other places?"

She says, "You don't know?"

"Not really. He kept this sideline quiet. Sonia doesn't really know either."

"Just one other place, Harbor Associates, another design firm. They called us for a reference. And actually, he might have mentioned a chip place or something techie. My boss might know."

"Noreen!" a man calls from down the hall.

"When can I talk to your boss?"

"He'll be out for a few days. You might try calling later, though. I'll let him know."

"You mind if I take a look around? He did the alarm, but did he do anything else?"

"Noreen! This goddamn fax isn't going through!" the man yells.

She ignores him and says to me, "He set up special locks for the computer equipment and reinforced the locks and alarms on the windows. Go ahead. You're not charging us for this, are you?"

"No. But I'll leave my card and home number in case you need to contact me." I realize I'm jeopardizing my job by doing this. I'm taking over for Paul.

I inspect some of Paul's work, particularly the perimeter alarm system—mercury switch motion detectors on the windows, the double contact breakers on the door—and find that this is more than enough security. Maybe too much. If she hadn't told me that the equipment had already been purchased, I might have suspected a little padding. I can't imagine how working here would get Paul in any trouble. Linda's suspicions seem far-fetched. I have to admit that I almost want her to be right; if Paul was the target, it would've been a hit, not a bungled job on our part. My part.

Before I leave I ask for the phone number of Harbor Associates, and thank Noreen. She promises to call me if there are any problems. Is it this easy to moonlight? Paul made almost a thousand bucks for less than a day's work. That's almost double my weekly take-home, after taxes. I see why Paul risked his ProServ job. Just working a few weekends would add a nice pile to my bank account, although there isn't anything that I really want to spend it on. I could upgrade my gym membership to include aerobics, which I don't like. I could buy a new stereo for my Volvo, which I don't really need. Maybe I could go away on vacation. I have two weeks saved up. But where would I go? What would I do?

When I return home I call Harbor Associates. I speak to the owner, using Noreen's name and my story about following up Paul's work. I discover that Paul simply recommended which security system to buy, leaving the installation to a licensed agent. I ask if he needs me to come by and check on the installation, but he says it isn't necessary.

"I was wondering if you know of any other businesses Paul consulted for. I'm trying to follow up on everyone, but I don't have a complete list."

"Besides General Graphics?"

"Yeah. Did he give you other companies as references?"

"Not as references. He mentioned a couple others, telling me about the different kinds of alarm systems."

"Do you remember the names?"

"Uh, one of them was some kind of silicon chip place. He told me about some robberies they had. It was three letters, like DSM or AMD."

"Advanced Micro Devices?" I ask, surprised. That place is huge.

"No. I know them. This was different. Something Silicon Makers or sounding like that."

I jot this down. "Any others?"

"A nontech place. He told me about wiring up a warehouse. Some import/export place. It's near the airport, I think. I wasn't paying attention. I just wanted to talk to the other design place."

I give him my number in case he needs any work done, and thank him. I'm becoming more convinced that Paul's freelance work was unrelated to the shooting, and debate whether or not to drop this whole matter. Yet I'm curious, and to rule out Linda's suspicions completely I know I should check all of Paul's jobs.

As if she senses my hesitation, Linda calls me that evening. I'm eating dinner and watching the news. When I pick up the phone, I recognize her voice immediately, and I say, "I was just thinking about you earlier today."

"Good."

"Good?"

"You haven't forgotten me."

"No," I say.

"I was wondering if you were able to talk to Sonia Baumgartner."

"I was."

"And did you get a chance to mention me? I mean, for a possible interview."

"She's not speaking to any reporters. Not for a while."

"But didn't you tell her how harmless I am?"

I smile. "No. I forgot that part."

"Oh, well. Listen, I'm at that café we met at before. Do you have time right now?"

"You're there right now?" I ask. I hear the low murmur of background voices.

"I happen to be in the neighborhood."

"Right," I say, unable to keep the skepticism out of my voice. "But I'm in the middle of dinner."

"We can meet when you're done. I'm going to get something to eat first."

I consider the new information I have and wonder if she might be able to make more out of it. I say, "An hour from now?"

"Really? Great! One hour."

After I hang up I look for the photocopies of her old articles.

D owntown Monte Vista at night is usually busy, with most
of its bars and restaurants open late, music swelling onto the
street, customers crowding out of doors while waiting for tables. Many
of the customers are office workers still in loosened ties and wrinkled
shirts and blouses; their sleeves are rolled up, their slacks and skirts
creased and crushed from sitting. The punk-clad teenagers come out
and gather near the bus stop benches, sprawled on the curbs with their
cigarettes and skateboards. Most evenings I'm too tired from work to
go out, but this past week I've been restless in my small apartment and
have been bringing a magazine to the coffee shops up and down Main.
The movement and noise around me are comforting. The signs of life
are encouraging.

I walk off dinner before meeting Linda and stop at the Asian grocery for some sweet rice cakes, a childhood dessert I've been craving.
The grocery is busy with crashing shopping carts and beeping cash
registers. I browse the aisles for a few minutes, still unused to having
this much free time, this much energy at the end of the day. As I walk
to meet Linda, I debate with myself whether freelancing is a smarter career move. Maybe Paul had the right idea.

Sometimes I wonder if I should be doing more. More what? I don't
know. It's a vague uneasiness, a sense of always being unsettled and off-
balance, of looking around me and feeling disconnected. I attribute it to

guilt and shock over Paul's death, but I've sensed it for a long time now. It's more than unease with everything around me. It's more than a reaction to externals. In a way it's a *dis*-ease with my life and my self. It's internal and viral. Perhaps Paul's death heightened these concerns. Perhaps I'm imagining it. Perhaps I just need to get back to work, and soon.

Linda is sitting at an outdoor table at the Cornerstone Café and waves me over. She is sipping coffee, a newspaper open in front of her. "You're early," she says. She is dressed in jeans and a thin black leather jacket. When she stands, her jacket hangs open; underneath is a white T-shirt and a small iron cross that swings on a leather string. I stop. I can't remember what she wore yesterday. She flips her hair back as we shake hands, and she notices me staring.

"You look different," I tell her. She's wearing dark lipstick, and when she smiles her teeth seem brighter.

"I'm not in work clothes."

"Ah. I didn't know reporters had dress codes."

"We don't," she says. "What's in the bag?"

I show her the small, sticky squares packaged in plastic and Styrofoam. "It's a dessert."

"Korean?"

"The packaging is Chinese, but it's pretty common everywhere," I say. "Did I tell you my background is Korean?"

"You mentioned it."

"I did?"

"You did. But you never told me where your last name comes from."

I explain my father's attempt to Americanize the name Choi. She finds this amusing and says, "But there are so many Chois out there. It's not like Americans don't know how to say it."

"This was over thirty years ago. There weren't many Korean immigrants back then."

"So you could've been Allen Choir, the choirboy."

I shrug.

"So what did she say?" Linda asks.

I study her. "I looked up some of your articles."

She remains still, then settles slowly into her seat, watching me as I pull out the photocopies.

I say, "I found them at the library."

"You copied them?"

"I did. I thought you did Peninsula news."

"News about the Peninsula, yes," she says, her voice tighter.

"But isn't this lifestyle? I thought you meant—"

"It's Peninsula news. News is news."

When I hear the edge to her words, I push the copies aside. I sit back, unwrap a rice cake, and take a bite; it's sweet and chewy. I offer her one, but she shakes her head. I change the subject and say, "So, I found out some interesting things about Paul."

She hesitates. "About Paul?"

"When I spoke to his wife, Sonia. I learned something I didn't know before."

"What?"

"Should I drop this?" I ask, pointing to her articles.

"What's to drop? I write lifestyle, as you say, and am trying to do harder news."

"It's just that I'm not sure why you misled—"

"I didn't mislead you, Allen. I just didn't think it was relevant."

This is the first time she uses my name. It sounds strange. I wonder if it's a strategy. I ask, "You don't like lifestyle?"

She sighs. "There's nothing wrong with it. But it's not why I became a reporter."

"So, you want to do this story—"

"To write what I've wanted to since graduate school."

"You went to graduate school?"

"Journalism school. I got my master's at Ohio State," she says.

"How old are you?"

"Twenty-six."

"Pretty young to be married," I say, pointing to her wedding band.

"What? Oh, that. I'm divorced. I wear this to make me seem older." She nods toward the articles. "Look, that was the only opening in any Bay Area newspaper. You have no idea how competitive it is."

"How long were you married?" I ask.

"Two years. It was a mistake. Tell me about Sonia."

"Okay," I say. "But are you allowed to do this story on Paul?"

"I haven't pitched it yet."

"So you're just doing research?"

"Yes." She pushes her coffee cup aside and pulls out a pad and pen. "Are you going to tell me what you found out?"

I want to ask her about her divorce, but instead tell her that Paul was moonlighting.

She looks up, raising an eyebrow.

I tell her about my meeting with Sonia, and my conversations with General Graphics and Harbor Associates. She interrupts me. "Wait. You already talked to these places?"

"Yeah."

"Why didn't you call me?"

"Was I supposed to?"

She is about to reply, but changes her mind. "Okay, what did they say?"

"They told me what he did for them, that kind of thing. The second place he just consulted. The first place he installed a security system. They were both small design firms, and I can't see how working there could put him in any danger."

"Maybe not, but if he worked there, he could've worked at other places."

"He did," I say.

"Where?"

I mention the two possibilities, the silicon chip maker and the import/export firm. Linda jots these down as I recount the phone conversation with Harbor Associates. She is getting excited and says, "A chip plant? You're kidding."

"No."

"You know how big the stolen-chip business is these days? What if he saw something? It's obvious."

"The guy at Harbor did mention that the chip place was robbed."

"Three initials? Something Silicon Makers?"

I nod.

"What about that import/export place? A name?"

"No, he just said it's a warehouse near the airport."

"In Burlingame?"

"I guess."

She taps her pen against the table. "How did you get them to tell you so much?"

I say, "I told them I was following up Paul's work, taking over. That's not a complete lie."

"You're thinking about doing the same thing?"

"I'm not sure. I can get fired for moonlighting, but Paul seems to have made some good money."

She says, "He might have gotten killed over it."

"I don't know. Just because he was doing outside work doesn't mean anything. What about the police investigation?"

"Last I heard they're still going through possible suspects who had grudges against the CEOs. The two companies are establishing a reward fund, which might move things along."

"Maybe we should tell them about Paul's freelance work."

"They won't bite," she says. "Not yet. I'm going to find out more first. Will your story hold up?"

"My story?"

"That you're taking over Paul's work."

"Why?"

"We should pursue this. Your status as Paul's partner will get us in."

"Us?"

"You got a problem with that?"

I think about this, then say, "My boss can't know about this, for Paul's sake, for my sake. If he thinks I'm going to moonlight—"

"He won't know."

"What if you do the story?"

"I can leave that part out."

"But you don't have approval to write this yet. Your boss doesn't even know."

"The news editor. I can bring him the story once I have enough. He'll let me go with it."

"What if he doesn't? What if he assigns it to someone else?"

"It'll be mine. I'll make sure of it." She stares at me defiantly. "First we need to find out more about Silicon Makers, then we'll visit them."

"What about the warehouse?"

"We need more information. You know how many import/export warehouses there are in Burlingame?"

I shake my head, trying to think of a faster way. "I wonder if Paul kept any records," I say. "If he was making money, he'd have receipts or something."

"Even a check stub," she says. "Of course. How much did Sonia know?"

"Just the first place, General Graphics. But she must know if he kept records." I'm not sure how to ask Sonia this without stirring things up. "I don't want to keep reminding her of Paul."

"Just use your story. Tell her you're thinking of following up on his work."

I don't reply, uneasy at the thought of grilling Sonia. "Maybe we should look into the chip place first," I say.

"What's wrong?"

"I don't want to keep bothering her."

Linda sighs. "You'd think *you'd* want to get to the bottom of this."

"What the hell does that mean?"

"Never mind."

I stare at her. "No, what are you saying?"

"Nothing."

"You think I don't want to find out about Paul's death? You think I was involved in this?"

"No, just forget about it."

I push back my chair. "I think I will." I grab my bag and begin to leave.

"No, no. Wait, wait. Please." She stands up. "I'm sorry. That was stupid of me to say. Please stop."

I stop. She immediately adds, "I'm not sure what I'm doing. It's all very frustrating. I'm really sorry for that remark."

I turn around and say quietly, "We'll talk later. Now's not the best time."

"When?" She looks anxious.

"Call me when you find the chip maker," I say, and leave, heading down Main. I'm not actually that angry—a little annoyed perhaps—but find myself not wanting to talk to anyone. This has been happening more often. I'm easily switched into a mode of antisocial behavior; suddenly, with a word, a look, or just my realization of where I am and what I'm doing, I'll be sick of other people and have to struggle to keep from getting rude. I wonder if it's the dis-ease. Maybe that's why Paul and I got along in paired work, since he often seemed the same way, though instead of walking away he might actually say something scathing.

Sonia. I know I'll have to call her, follow up on Linda's questions about Paul's work. I ought to do it right now, before it gets too late, but I can't bring myself to head home. Something is wrong with me. I feel tense, agitated. I try not to think about Linda, who surprised me with her news about her divorce and graduate school. I used to tell myself that getting my degree is simply a matter of taking more credits at SF State, but too much time has passed. I can no longer picture myself in a classroom.

I eat another rice cake. As a kid I used to let them dissolve in my mouth, and I do this now.

Two kids on skateboards swerve down the sidewalk, contorting their bodies as they avoid a parking sign. Their jackets with reflective logos shimmer as they coast beneath a streetlamp. They jump off a curb. Their wheels scrape the cement as they land and plow around a corner. The sound of them pushing off in faster, competing rhythm mixes with salsa music coming from a restaurant. There's a momentary stillness, a pause in the tape, a red light, a silence. Then, after this brief respite, the light changes to green, new music begins, and the cars drive on, people chatter, and the music swells.

I'm going back to work in a few days. Although I'm probably not ready for fieldwork, I'm certainly not looking forward to sitting at a desk. This has been the first extended break I've had since coming to ProServ, and I find myself eager to return. But is it ProServ or another kind of work I want to do? I've had too much time to think. I feel the seductive pull of the inertial deception. It's so easy to drift. Perhaps it's work that will shake me from my dis-ease. Maybe I need to overwork, like Paul, with extra hours on the weekends. No wonder David has questions about his father. When did he ever see him?

Once, when Paul and I were waiting at SFO for a client, we sat at the arrival gate for two hours, the plane delayed at a stopover in Chicago. We read four newspapers and three magazines, Paul becoming more impatient at each new delay announcement. I was used to his jumpiness, but found his newspaper rustling and page-snapping irritating. Finally, I said, "Will you take it easy? The plane's not coming any faster by you getting more pissed off."

He turned to me, surprised. A brief look of annoyance passed across his face, then he smiled. "Jesus. You sounded just like Sonia."

"What?"

"I think she said the exact same thing a few months ago when we were picking up her friend."

I wasn't sure how to respond. I didn't like being compared to his wife. He watched me, then laughed. "All right, all right. I'll take a walk." He stood. "This goddamn job. You know, I spend more time with you and our clients than I do with anyone else? Even my family, for chrissake."

"Great," I said. "Perfect."

"I need a new life," he said, and left.

At the time I ignored this and went back to my magazine. Now it makes more sense. He was tired of his job. He had been there for almost ten years by that time. I hear Sonia's voice: where do you see yourself in ten, fifteen years? That question keeps surfacing, and I keep trying to swim away from it.

I head back to my apartment. I see a man across the street in a business suit, a newspaper tucked under his arm. He is walking briskly toward the train station. A breeze flutters his jacket and flips his tie over his shoulder. He tucks it back in and buttons his jacket, hunching his body in the cool evening air. It's almost ten o'clock and this guy still has to take the train home. This goddamn job, Paul says, stalking off. For a startled instant I imagine that the man now crossing the street is Paul. I think, Where is his car? Why is he taking the train?

I shake this off, disturbed. Sometimes my mind wanders too much. The man hurries through the yellow lights of a streetlamp, then flashes off into the darkness.

I count cars when I drive, a technique I picked up from the defensive driving course. Whenever I glance in the rearview mirror, I count the cars behind me, not just in my lane, but in all the lanes.
It isn't a conscious count, though it was at first when I was learning
this, but is a snapshot of the cars trailing me. This forces me to look at
the cars themselves, if only for a millisecond, to register their presence.
Most drivers rarely acknowledge the cars behind them. They check to
make sure no car is too close, or maybe they gauge the merging distance before moving into another lane. But I learned that by counting
cars—a quick one-two-three-four that soon becomes automatic—I can
track who is behind me, because when I go back to count again, I'll
usually notice commonalities, or, as my instructor put it, "marks." The
marks stick out, especially on city streets where cars are constantly
turning and changing lanes. So, if there is a car following me amid the
confusion, I have a better chance of registering it. It's not foolproof,
and when I'm on assignment, especially in the Tank, I'm much more
conscious and vigilant about being followed.

When Linda mentioned her theory of Paul as the possible target,
and the gunman following us, I immediately discounted it. Paul and I
have always been careful, especially with clients. And if there was a
motorcyclist, we would've almost definitely seen him. Two pairs of rov-
ing eyes can't miss a motorcycle.

It's during my usual habit of counting cars that I notice a mark, a blue sports car. I'm driving to Sonia's, thinking of the best way to ask her about Paul's files. On the phone I said only that I had a few questions about his freelance work. I don't want her to think I am actually investigating anything. I don't feel I am. I particularly don't want her to worry about any trouble with Polansky. I want this to look casual.

I'm not on the job, my attention focused on other things, so when I look in my rearview and check the cars behind me, it takes a few minutes to register the blue car. I must have counted it at least four or five times before I do a double-take. Wait a second. I stare at the car more closely. A light blue coupe, hidden behind a minivan, keeping pace with me. How long has it been there?

I don't worry too much about it. If I were driving the Tank with a client I'd immediately begin altering my course, but now I just watch the car carefully. I'm on Camino Real, taking a longer route to Palo Alto, and I move into the slow lane, allowing the minivan to pass. The blue coupe stays behind, slowing and letting a sport utility overtake it.

Shit. I continue watching it. I have to try a few more tests. I see a gas station a few blocks ahead and turn into it. The coupe drives by. I see a figure inside, one driver, though the glare from the sun makes it difficult to identify much else. The taillights go on, the driver tapping his brakes. I try to get a license plate, but the car moves too quickly. I pull up to a pump, and keep watching the car as it turns at the next intersection.

As I fill my gas tank I try to keep my paranoia in place. I could be wrong, and the car might not be sitting around the corner waiting for me to drive by. I ought to check again before doing anything drastic. I top off my tank, pay the clerk, and continue toward Palo Alto. The blue car appears three cars down, keeping its distance.

It could be the police, wanting to keep tabs on me for some reason. It could be a colleague of Linda's, since she might not completely trust me. It could be someone interested in my current activities, my recent visits and queries about Paul's jobs tipping off someone.

I want to see the driver, so I slow down. A few cars pass me, but the blue coupe keeps at least two cars behind, also slowing. I put on my hazards and pull off to the side. The car has no choice but to continue. I see through his front windshield that the driver is a balding man in a jacket and tie, but the man keeps his eyes forward. The passenger window seems tinted, so I can't get a better look. After the car drives by, I catch a fleeting glimpse of the license plate. When the car continues down the road, I'm not sure if I'm imagining all this or if the driver has given up.

Maybe I'm wrong. The car could be heading to Palo Alto, like me, and could have pulled over earlier for some other reason. I merge back into traffic and continue to Sonia's. Unsettled, I count cars more deliberately, making sure there isn't a backup. I'm annoyed for not being more alert.

By the time I reach Sonia's neighborhood, I've taken a few detours to be sure I'm not being followed. I begin doubting the entire incident. This is the problem with working solo: there is no one to double-check your instincts.

Sonia is waiting by her car, and she glances at her watch as I pull up. She is dressed in a beige suit and smooths her skirt. She looks at her watch again and frowns at me.

"I'm late," I say. "Sorry. I took a longer way—"

"I told you I have a lawyer's appointment. What couldn't be done over the phone?"

"I'm following up some of Paul's freelance work."

"Why?"

"I'm thinking about maybe doing the same thing."

"But you said it's not allowed."

"I know. I might try to do it the way Paul did, which is why I wanted to talk. I'm wondering if Paul had any contacts I could look up."

"I told you about General Graphics."

"Yeah, and I appreciate it. But there were more, and I'm having trouble finding out exactly who."

"I don't know anything more than what I told you."

I say carefully, "Do you think Paul left some records? Does he have files on this?"

She sighs. "I'd have to check." But she moves toward her car door, opening it.

"I'm just following up his work, to know where to start."

"I really have to run. But I'll look tonight and give you a call, okay?"

I know when I'm being brushed off. She's already climbing into her car. I thank her and say, "Please do. Sorry I'm late."

She flashes me a small, polite smile and pulls out of the driveway. I return to my Volvo as she speeds down the street. I sit heavily with my door still open and wonder who might have been following me. Polansky always says that paranoia is a good thing. Harness your instincts, he says. Paul and I used to make fun of these pronouncements by making up our own: harness your jock. Listen to your body gases. Stay attuned to your TV.

What would Paul do now? He might break into the house if he thought it was the only way. He'd be too impatient to wait for Sonia's call. I stop thinking about this. It was that blue coupe. Why would anyone care what I'm doing, where I'm going? I'm a nobody, and this possible interest in me is alarming.

I begin driving back home, but see David walking toward the house a few blocks away. He has on a knapsack and is listening to a Walkman. I make a U-turn and pull up beside him, leaning over and opening the passenger window. "Hey," he says when he sees me. He takes off the headphones. I can hear the distorted music from where I am.

"Don't you still have school?"

"I'm cutting the afternoon classes," he says. He nods toward the house. "Is she gone yet?"

His bluntness surprises me. He looks around and repeats his question.

"She had to meet her lawyer," I say.

"I know. I was hanging out until she left."

"Are you sure this is a good idea?"

He smirks. "Are you going to turn me in?"

"No," I say. "I've probably cut more classes than you."

"Oh, yeah?" he says. "Were you visiting Mom?"

"I was going to, but she was in a hurry. Need a lift?"

He looks toward the house. "Sure."

I take him to the house, parking in the driveway, and tell him, "I wanted to check your father's files for something."

"For what?"

"I'm looking into his freelance work and need to know the other companies he worked for," I say. "Hey, you want to check for me?"

"I don't know what to look for."

"All you need to do is find some receipts with the names of companies."

"Why don't you do it?"

"Your mother's not home—"

"You can come in. I have the key."

I pause, then say, "I'm not sure if your mother would like that."

"Why not?"

"Because it's your father's personal things."

David thinks about this. "But he's . . . he's dead. What does it matter?" He opens the door and climbs out, but waits for me. I follow him to the front door.

"She was going to show me if I wasn't late," I say, more to myself.

"My mom likes you," he says. "I don't think she would care." He unlocks the door and lets me in. I glance back at the street, then enter his house. David dumps his knapsack on the floor and turns on the TV.

"How often do you do this?" I ask.

"Whenever."

"Doesn't your school call your mother?"

"I forged a note. A doctor's appointment. They only call if there's no note." He sits on the sofa. "My mom put most of my dad's work stuff in boxes. It's in the hallway."

Already? She's packing away Paul's things a week after the funeral? I move toward the hallway and find three cardboard boxes stacked against the wall. The top box is crammed with manila folders, crinkled and creased papers sticking out unevenly. I check a few of the pages and recognize copies of ProServ shift reports, some of them a decade old. The reports are now filed online, but most of us still keep hard copies, since we don't fully trust the server. I hear David watching a talk show, and consider warning him about cutting school. But who the hell am I to lecture? I check the second box and find books and pamphlets; most of them relate to alarms and perimeter systems. I'm not sure what Sonia is going to do with these.

"Find anything?" David asks from the living room.

"Just ProServ stuff," I say. I check the third box. "Why are you cutting classes?"

"I never miss much."

"You doing okay in school? Grades okay?"

He doesn't answer. I find more manila folders filled with blank ProServ stationery and notepads that Paul must have stolen. Everyone does this, but it occurs to me that Paul could've used the stationery to solicit clients. Polansky can't know about this. Then I find a small pack of yellow credit card receipts rubberbanded together: purchases for tools and small hardware—screws, wire, nails. I dig further into this box.

There are handwritten timesheets with figures added up next to the hours worked. When I come across an invoice for Harbor Associates, I take out the folders and lay them on the floor. David is moving about, and approaches with a bag of potato chips.

"What's that?" he asks.

"I think it's what I'm looking for. Receipts for his freelance work."

He nods, and holds up the bag of chips for me. I smile and shake my head. I skim the various receipts and say, "I did lousy in school, and regret it."

"Yeah?"

"I even dropped out of college, which I think was a mistake."

"Why?"

"You need a degree to do anything."

"But you're working as a bodyguard."

"I could be doing other things, though."

"My dad went to college and he was a bodyguard."

"True, but he was already thinking about moving on." I find an invoice for Advanced Silicon Marketing, ASM. This must be the chip company. I also find a sheet of scrap paper with an itemized list of electronic supplies. A scribbled name, WestSun Imports, is listed at the top, a note at the bottom reading "Dblchk current trembler/garage." The piece of paper is dated about a month ago, and I can't find any other reference to it in the files.

I realize it has become quiet, and I look up. David is watching me, a potato chip in his hand. "Sorry, what'd you say?" I ask.

"Nothing. You find something?"

"Yeah. The companies your dad worked for. Now I can follow up better." I examine the rest of this folder, but find more receipts for hardware. I begin putting it all back, including the ASM invoice and the WestSun list. All I need is the names. "What's your mother going to do with these boxes?"

"I don't know. Throw them away?"

I glance at him. "I'll have to talk to her about that."

"You can't say I let you in."

"Why not?"

He frowns. "She can't know I cut school."

"Ah. So this never happened? You never saw me?"

"Yeah," he says.

I feel uneasy about this, but say, "I can do that."

"Cool. Hey, do you think I can see ProServ sometime?"

"Haven't you been there before?"

"No."

"Your father never took you?"

"Nope."

"All right," I say. I guess Paul wanted to keep the lines between work and home clear. I can understand that. "I'll clear it with Polansky. Show you around."

"Cool."

"Tell your mother I'll call her tonight."

"I can't. Remember? We didn't see each other."

I smile. "You're good at this, but don't make it a habit. You'll regret all this cutting come finals time."

He walks with me to the door. "So you'll show me around?"

"Yeah, I promise."

He stands in the doorway, watching me leave the house and climb into my car. As I back out and drive away, he holds up his hand in a goodbye. I feel sorry for him and wave back. The kid is lonely.

9

When I return home, Charles calls to confirm my return to work in two days. I tell him I'm ready. Then I call Linda, and she tells me that she has found out the name of the tech company.

"ASM," I say. "Advanced Silicon Marketing."

"Yes. It's the only one with those initials in the area. How did you know?"

"I was at Sonia's and looked through Paul's files."

"Did you find anything else?"

"Not really."

She clears her throat. "Sorry about yesterday."

"I can be touchy."

"No, it was my fault. I'm hoping this gets me out of my career rut."

"Rut? You're twenty-six."

"Rut," she says.

I make a face, which I'm glad she can't see. "How did you find ASM?"

"Just went through a corporate directory. There is no name with the last two words as 'Silicon Makers.' There is a Silicon Valley Marketing, but they never heard of Paul Baumgartner. ASM did."

"You called?"

"I did. It's not a chip plant. It's a marketing and PR firm. And the robbery they had was of their office computers."

"What did Paul do for them?"

"Nothing really. The man I talked to said Paul checked and tested their new alarm system. He was referred to them by General Graphics, which works with them often. I talked to General Graphics, and the owner confirmed this."

I realize I should've spoken to the owner of General Graphics, since it would've saved me some time. The office manager, Noreen, mentioned that the boss knew the names, but I didn't follow up. Sloppy of me. I say, "You don't think ASM is important?"

"It's a three-man company that does press releases and ad copy for computer places. I don't see how Paul's working for them for an afternoon could mean anything. In fact, I'm beginning to wonder about this whole thing. It's looking like a dead end."

"I found out the name of the import/export place."

"What's the name?"

"WestSun Imports."

"I guess we should talk to them," she says.

"You don't sound optimistic."

"Even you said this whole thing was unlikely."

"That was before I learned about his moonlighting." I remember the blue car, and add, "Also, I might have been followed earlier."

"What? Are you sure?"

"No. There was a car staying pretty close, but it left."

"So you don't know—"

"No."

"You could've imagined it."

"Yes."

She is quiet, then says, "I don't know. I think we might want to see something here."

"This import place might be important."

"Import/export? I don't know. A warehouse?"

"All right. I might talk to them to see what kind of work he did."

"Let me know what happens. I've got to get back to work."

"To your rut," I say.

She is silent. Then she says, "I told you I was sorry."

"I know. Maybe I'm in a rut."

She says. "Maybe you are. I'll talk to you later."

We hang up, and I immediately find out WestSun's number from the information operator.

"WestSun Imports. Front office," a woman answers when I call.

I ask to speak to the owner.

"Who is this?"

"My name is Allen Choice. I'm following up the work of Paul Baumgartner."

She asks me to hold, and after a minute a man picks up. "Hello? Who's this?"

I repeat my opening, and add, "I just wanted to make sure that there were no follow-ups needed for Paul's work."

"Who?"

"Paul Baumgartner."

There is a pause, and the man says, "What is this about again?"

"Am I speaking to the owner?"

"Yes. This is Roger Milian. Who are you?"

I repeat my name and say, "I was Paul Baumgartner's partner, and he . . . recently passed away, so I'm double-checking all his freelance work. I believe he consulted with you about a month ago."

"Mr. Choice, I'm sorry, but I don't know what you're talking about. I didn't meet with any consultant. Are you trying to sell me something?"

"No. Paul Baumgartner consulted on your security. He was probably updating your alarm system."

"Security? For this company?"

"This is WestSun Imports, isn't it? Burlingame?"

"Yes."

"You didn't hire Paul Baumgartner?"

"Not to my knowledge."

"You're the owner?"

"Look, obviously you're mistaken. I've got another call. Thanks, anyway." He hangs up.

I try to remember that scrap of paper, and am certain that I have the name right. I wonder if I haven't made myself clear. I dial the number again, and hear the same receptionist's greeting.

"Hello, this is Allen Choice again. Is there a general manager or office manager there?"

"Which one?"

"Not the owner, but a general manager."

"Please hold."

I write down the name of the owner, Roger Milian, and wait. The receptionist returns and says, "Mr. Durante is in a meeting. Can you leave your name and number?"

I do, and ask, "Is Durante the general manager?"

"Mr. Durante is the vice president and chief operations officer."

I write this down as well, and ask, "Is there anyone else I can talk to who would know about hiring outside consultants?"

She says, annoyance creeping into her voice, "You'll have to ask Mr. Durante."

"What about an office manager?"

"No. You'll have to speak with Mr. Durante. Thank you."

She disconnects me. I stare at my notes. Something doesn't seem right. Perhaps Paul hadn't gotten the job and was going to make a pitch, write a proposal. Maybe he wanted to point out flaws so they'd hire him. Was he inspecting the place without their knowledge? But "double-check" meant he had already been there once before. Also, if you want to make some money, you pitch to a tech firm, not a warehouse, and surely the owner would have remembered him. Perhaps Sonia knows more. I'll talk to her about this soon. I hope she's not annoyed with me for making her late. She reminds me of Paul in that way, though in his presence she usually was the patient one.

I think of the Christmas party at ProServ, the last time I saw Paul and Sonia together. Of the spouses, Sonia was the most glamorous, wearing a long, tight-fitting black velvet dress, and she drew a few glances, including mine. Paul and Sonia stayed at each other's side for most of the evening, moving from group to group, couple to couple, and I could see Paul's attention waning, his irritability growing. Sonia took over the conversations, occasionally bringing him in but more often than not mercifully leaving him out. I watched them dance through a few songs, then Paul sat morosely at a table and nursed his drink. I sat with him and we stared at the others in silence. Sonia would look in our direction every few minutes until finally she swept over to us and said, "You two are having a wild time. All right, honey, let's go." She wrinkled her nose at me and drew her husband to his feet. Paul nodded in my direction. Sonia linked her arm around Paul's, kissed him on his cheek, and guided him out. The party seemed spiritless after her departure, so I left. I marveled at married life—spouses saving each other.

Reminded of ProServ, I sort through my laundry. I need to have some shirts and slacks dry-cleaned for my return. The prospect of these mundane details and an extended amount of deskwork ahead depresses me. I have to clean and oil my gun. I have to check my e-mails and the messages on the conference boards. My list of errands and tasks grows as I begin moving into work mode, and I feel the low hum of stress rising within me, something that I had forgotten about during my break. I wonder how my coworkers are going to react to me, if Polansky is going to make a big deal of my return. I hope not. My thoughts begin spiraling like this, imagining difficult scenarios, worrying about being snubbed or avoided, until I finally shake this off and head to the gym. Freelance work doesn't sound so bad.

10

By the next morning I have called WestSun twice more, but Durante still hasn't returned my calls. He's obviously avoiding me, and my confusion about them grows. All they'd have to say is he tried to offer his services, but they turned him down. I want to finish this up by tomorrow, when I'll be busy at ProServ and loaded down with paperwork, so I call Linda and tell her what has been happening. She agrees to visit WestSun with me, both of us hoping the presence of a news reporter will get their attention. She isn't convinced that this is a real lead—she suspects as well that they genuinely don't know or don't want to be bothered—and when I meet her to drive up to Burlingame, she adds that they might be even more resistant to talk because of me.

"How so?"

"A partner coming to follow up a pitch. Maybe they think you two were working together in the freelance work. So, you're a persistent salesman."

We are driving north on 101 in my car, Linda having left hers at my place. "Should I explain the situation better?" I ask.

"No, but this time make it clear that I'm there to do a story about you and Paul. And even if you can't talk to the manager, you can still talk to the other employees."

"Why?"

"You never know. It also might have the effect of bringing out the higher-ups. They'll want to control the information."

"You've done this before?"

"I interned with an investigative reporter during school." She glances at her watch.

"What did I take you away from?"

"I have a five-o'clock deadline, but I'll make it."

"What's the story?"

"Nothing really." She waves it off.

I turn to her, and she shrugs.

"No, really. What is it?" I ask.

"Just a profile of a chef."

"That could be interesting."

"If I cared about cooking, which I don't. I eat microwave dinners." She leans back and crosses her legs. She tugs at her skirt. I glance at her legs in pale stockings, then look back at the road. "What else did you find in Paul's papers?" she asks.

"Old shift reports, work-related files."

"But nothing that would lead you to believe he might have been involved in something illegal?"

"Illegal? Other than working in security-related businesses without the proper licensing? No."

She makes a "hm" noise through her nose, and I try not to look down, her skirt pulling up every time she moves. I notice for the first time her well-defined calves. She says, "So Sonia was already packing up his things?"

"Yeah."

"Doesn't that seem pretty quick?"

"It was just his work things."

She doesn't reply. We approach the airport, and I turn off the freeway. I say, "Can I ask you a personal question?"

"Not too personal."

"You were married for two years?" I ask.

"I was. Married in college."

I wait.

She says, "Divorced right before grad school. And you? Ever married?"

"No. Not even close."

"Lucky you."

"Why?"

"Marriage sucks."

I glance at her, but she doesn't elaborate. I drive onto South Airport Boulevard and begin searching for WestSun. I say, "It should be along here. It's past a parking lot."

"There's a lot up ahead," she says. "Why did you want to know?"

"Just curious."

"We were married way too young. Neither of us was ready."

"Ah."

"I blame myself for getting married in the first place. I was just a scared kid. He wasn't such a nice guy." She points ahead. "There are a bunch of warehouses."

We read off the numbers, and as we approach the right address, she says, "Not a nice guy at all. There it is."

WestSun Imports is a huge hangarlike building with a loading dock to the side. An eighteen-wheeler is backed up against the dock, men dollying crates into the semitrailer and unloading them with booming thuds. The sidewall is blank, except for a few gray spots covering graffiti, and I look for logos of WestSun, but can't see any. I park the car near the main entrance, a tall garage door pulled halfway open, and ask Linda how we should do this.

"We ask to see the top, and talk to whoever we can." She pulls out some business cards. "I'll introduce myself as needed."

We walk through the entrance and see a few offices to the side, small rooms with large windows facing the warehouse floor: crates and boxes on metal and wood shelving that reaches as high as the ceiling, almost three stories. Near us is a forklift with its front prongs rising up twenty feet with a hiss; its pneumatic columns elongate far beyond its center of gravity, and both Linda and I watch in surprise as the driver maneuvers the forks under a crate and slowly backs it off the top shelf, the vehicle beeping in reverse. Looking around, I see that the warehouse is wired up with motion detectors, a trembler switch on the garage door entrance. When engaged, the switch will activate an alarm at the slightest movement. Two video cameras are stationed in the far corner. I point out to Linda the trembler switch and remind her of Paul's note to double-check it.

She turns to me. "Are they common?"

"The switches? Yes, but my guess is that he wanted to double-check it because every time someone slams that garage door, it jars the sensitivity. Over time, it could malfunction."

She nods.

My nose itches. The smell of sawdust and chemical solvents surrounds us. Through one of the office windows I see a woman stand and watch us, the fluorescent light above her making her seem pale, her face shrouded. The other office windows have their blinds drawn. Thin slats of light leak through unevenly, with jagged, bright holes where the blinds are bent or broken. I notice movement behind these slats— quick shadows travel along the bright bars.

"Can I help you?" the woman in the first office asks as she steps out.

"We're here to see Roger Milian," I say.

"Do you have an appointment?"

I recognize her voice. She is the receptionist who was stonewalling me. "I've called a few times, and thought we'd drop by."

This registers, and she frowns. "You're the one. Look, I passed your messages along to Mr. Durante, but—"

"My name is Linda Maldonado, and I'm here with the *San Jose Sentinel*." Linda hands her card to the woman. "I think your boss should talk to us."

"The *Sentinel?*" The woman reads the business card and glances at Linda. She hesitates.

"You'd better tell your boss we're here," Linda says.

The woman asks us to wait and returns to her office. After a few minutes she comes out and tells us to go to the area in the back, behind a wall of crates. We follow her directions, our shoes crunching on more sawdust, and find ourselves heading through a maze of storage shelving. Linda says, "I hope he doesn't call and check with my editor." We turn a corner and see another row of similar offices, the one to the right with Milian's name on the door.

Roger Milian is heavyset, in his late sixties, with white hair and a short, well-manicured beard. He studies us from his desk, his window blinds pulled up. This office has an adjacent meeting room. Part of a large conference table shows near the doorway behind him. He stands slowly and impatiently waves us in. The sleeves of his white button-down shirt are rolled neatly to his elbows; his silver watch digs tightly into his fleshy arm.

"Yes," he says when we enter. He looks from me to Linda, back to me. He scratches his beard and rests his palms flat down on his desk, leaning forward. When we don't respond immediately, he says, "Well, what is it?"

"My name is Allen Choice, and I'm here following up Paul Baumgartner's—"

"Yes, yes, I remember your call. I told you I don't know any Baumgartner or anything about security consulting." He turns to Linda and asks, "Why are you here?"

"I'm working on a story about Mr. Baumgartner and am accompanying Mr. Choice as he follows up Mr. Baumgartner's clients."

"But we weren't a client of his. I keep telling you this. That man never worked here."

"I'm fairly sure he did," I say. "Maybe your Mr. Durante knows—"

"Are you implying I don't know my own company? I told you you're wrong." His face seems red because of his white hair and beard.

"Well, he made notes about your setup, so I'm pretty sure—"

"Do you have a work order or contract with us?"

I think about this for a moment. "I'm not sure."

"Well, then. Anyone can write up notes about us. Maybe he was going to rob us. You're wasting my time here. I checked our records after you called, and he did not work for us in any capacity."

I'm about to ask to see those records, but Linda says, "Thank you, Mr. Milian. We appreciate this. Will you call us if you find out otherwise?"

"Certainly."

I look at her with surprise, but she motions for us to go.

"What're you doing?" I ask as we walk toward the main entrance. "Something didn't seem right."

"I know. We were making him nervous."

"Could this be him worrying about Paul's death?"

"Does he know?"

"I think I mentioned it to the secretary."

"But why would he worry?"

"I want to talk to this Durante guy," I say.

"Yes. But we need to find out more about this company. We need better footing."

"One sec," I say, seeing a man with a clipboard walking toward the front offices. I run over to him and ask, "Is Mr. Durante here?"

"Out back, with the rig."

Linda and I leave through the front but circle around to the loading area, and when I see two men talking, I call out, "Mr. Durante?"

They stop and glance at me. The younger one, dark-haired with babyface cheeks and mirrored sunglasses, seems startled, his body freezing. He's dressed like Milian, his sleeves rolled up neatly, his tie loosened at an angle. He says something to the other man and turns toward the doorway. I call out again, "Durante!"

But he slips through the door and closes it behind him.

"Was that Mr. Durante?" I ask the second man, who turns to me, bewildered.

"Yeah."

"What did he say?"

"Nothing. He had stuff to do."

"What the hell?" I ask Linda.

"Let's go," she tells me. The other man looks her up and down.

I point to the door. "That was—"

"I figured. We'll come back."

"Something is really strange—"

"I know. Let's go."

I don't want to leave, but when I meet Linda's eyes, she shakes her head a fraction, then nods toward the front. We walk back to my car in silence. Once we climb in and I start the engine, she turns to me and says, "I think we might have found something."

"What?"

"I'm not sure."

"He took off as soon as he saw me."

"He was caught off-guard," she says.

"Why?"

"We'll have to find out."

I pull away from the WestSun lot, hearing a beeping of a truck in reverse. I picture Durante surprised at the sight of me; it was more than just having his name called out. He recognized me. He knew me. I try to remember if I've ever met him before, and I'm pretty sure I haven't.

11

inda's story about the chef appears in the next day's *Bay Area Life* supplement, which I read during lunch. The chef, a Thai immigrant, opened a tiny three-table restaurant in San Jose that serves only one dish a night. He is the sole employee—maître d', chef, busboy—and has a three-month reservation list. I enjoy the immigrant-does-good angle to the story, but see why Linda might be getting frustrated. The first sentence reads, "Reservations three months in advance? Your elaborate entreé—the only one on the menu that night— served by the chef himself? No, you're not in the fanciest restaurant in Nob Hill, but in the wildly popular Lei-lai Kitchen in downtown San Jose." It just doesn't sound like her.

She is supposed to call me tonight with more information about WestSun. I spend the day preparing for my return to work. I'm doing my laundry in the basement, waiting for my clothes to dry. I read the *Sentinel* twice while I sit on a dirty lawn chair, the rhythmic humming and stifling warmth making me sleepy. I have two suits and a few shirts waiting for me at the dry cleaners. I still have to clean and oil my gun and look over the office memos about new security procedures.

I called Sonia earlier today, hoping to find out if there are any more of Paul's files that I might have missed, but she wasn't home. I left a message, even though she was supposed to call me last night. My day consists of waiting to hear from everyone.

By the early evening I've finished most of my chores, and Linda calls. She is still at her office, and she tells me, "I've found a listing for the company—it's been around for a while—and I had an intern here look into Milian and Durante."

"And?"

"And she's still working on it, but the company's been around for three decades, in different forms."

"Why don't you come by? Have you had dinner?"

"Not yet. I guess I should finish up here."

"I'll order some take-out Chinese."

"Okay. You live near that café?"

"Next door. The brick building. Apartment 2C."

She says she'll be by in thirty minutes. I call the Chinese restaurant down the block and quickly clean my apartment, folding the rest of my laundry and throwing away old newspapers and magazines. I look around and realize how dirty everything is, a grunginess that has settled over the countertops and tables, dustballs in the corners, the wastebaskets overflowing. I haven't even folded up the futon; my sheets are bundled up in a ball.

Linda arrives early and rings the downstairs intercom. I buzz her up, still cleaning. I'm wiping down the grimy kitchen table when she knocks on my door.

"It's a mess," I say as she walks in.

She takes off her jacket, looks around, then sits down on the futon with a sigh. "You mind? My legs are killing me."

"I have to pick up the Chinese food."

"Oh," she says, sitting up slowly. "Should I go with you?"

"You can wait here."

"By myself?"

"Sure."

She smiles. "What if I steal the furniture?"

"A secondhand dining table and a broken futon? Be my guest."

She leans back her head and says, "I'll just rest here."

"I read your story today, the one about the chef."

Covering her eyes, she says, "Please. Let's not talk about that."

I tell her I'll be back in a minute and slip out. I see her leaning her head back as I close the door.

The Chinese restaurant is at the end of the block, and I jog there, noticing the streetlamps flickering on, darkness descending. A few others are waiting near the entrance of the restaurant, also picking up their dinners. We mill around and wait for our names to be called. When my name comes up, I pay the cashier—a young Chinese American woman with green contact lenses who recognizes me and smiles— and I hurry off.

On my way back to the apartment, I think about buying a bottle of wine, but decide against it. This isn't a date, after all.

I reach my front entrance and take out my keys. I hear someone behind me, possibly another building resident, and I begin to turn around. But this person grabs my neck, then forces something hard into my back. "Stop. Don't move," a man says quietly.

"Oh, shit," I say. Mugged at my front door?

He pulls me away from the entrance and pushes me toward the side alley, his hand still on my neck. I hear another set of footsteps behind him. Two of them.

"Is that a gun?" I ask.

He pushes it harder into my spine, hurting me, and he says, "Quiet. Walk."

"Just take my wallet. It's in my back pocket," I say. I'm getting jittery, and begin thinking of fighting back. The gun is the problem. The second man. Another gun? There is supposed to be a light in this alley, but it's dark. I slow down, worried. If they took the light out, then this was planned. I stop. "Wait a minute. Don't you want my wallet?"

The hand leaves my neck, and he punches me in the kidney, the pain thrusting through my back. I drop the food and stumble forward. I feel the pull in my stomach as I twist and try to avoid another punch, but the man jumps toward me, his hand grabbing my shoulder and throwing me hard into the wall next to the Dumpster. I cushion the impact with my arms, yelling, "Wait—" but there's another punch to my kidney.

"Fuck," I say, my legs crumpling, but he pushes me up. I start to turn to protect my back, but he digs the gun behind my ear.

"Turn and I shoot."

I keep still. I cough, and have trouble breathing. "What do you want?" I manage to say.

He pushes my head into the wall, and the darkness flashes with light, my forehead scraping against the brick. "Goddamn—"

He presses the gun into my neck. I shut up.

"Stop," he says.

"What?"

"Stop what you're doing."

I know instantly what he's talking about, but say, "What do you mean?"

I hear movement, the hand loosening its grip on my neck. A sudden coolness. I hear a whistling, the sound of something buzzing through the air, and for an instant I feel someone hitting the back of my head, and my forehead slams against the wall, ricocheting off it, and I can't stay on my feet, my body losing its coordination, and as I feel myself blacking out, the world falling away, I grab the wall for support, my fingers clutching at crumbling brick. I fall heavily, and protect my head. Something wet on my face. I feel better on the ground. I rest my cheek against the cool concrete. I look up, squint, and see two darkened figures hurrying away. Their footsteps click on the pavement. A piece of wood clunks onto the ground. A quick murmur and an answering whisper. Rustling plastic. Everything blurring. A car honking in the distance. A TV show coming from an apartment above. Canned laughter.

I can't move at first, my limbs stiffening with pain. I call out for help, but my voice cracks, then fails me. Slowly, I try to sit up. I take deliberate, deep breaths, not wanting to lose consciousness. I wipe my cheek. The strange thing is that I immediately look for the Chinese food—eighteen dollars' worth of dinner—hoping it's okay. But I can't see the bag. It's gone. I falter. Dizziness sweeps through me. Where's the bag? I touch my forehead lightly, but can't feel anything. The numbness travels to the back of my head. I look around for my food. I'm having trouble focusing. My dinner is missing. They took it. My hearing pulses, the beating of my heart loud in my ears. A whooshing sound. I crawl to the Dumpster and lean against it.

Part 2

The Physics
of Movement
and Rest

12

A voice echoes around me as I feel cold metal against my cheek; I'm still leaning against the Dumpster, trying to keep myself from falling over. The smell of rotting garbage envelops me. Someone calls my name again, and I realize it's Linda. I yell out to her, but need to hold my head in my hands to keep the pain down. I yell again, and Linda approaches slowly, her shadowy silhouette crouched and tentative. When she sees me she rushes over, and I ask her about the Chinese food. She tells me it's not here. I ask her again, confused. She repeats her answer and tries to help me up. "Did you fall?" she asks. There is something familiar about the way everything looks around me—blurry, fractured, with streaking lights—and I remember my accident on the Golden Gate Bridge. I climbed out of my car at the time, and saw the smoking, smashed cars piled around me, millions of tiny glass shards strewn about and glistening in the sun; I thought for a dazed moment that a jewelry transport had overturned, and diamonds were laid out before me. I thought, Get the diamonds. Then I began to realize what had happened, and how my wrist seemed crooked.

"Just like the diamonds," I mutter to Linda as she helps me up.

"What?"

I concentrate. "The Chinese food. It's here somewhere."

"I don't see it. Did you drop it? Jeez, did you fall?"

She walks me into the building and up to my apartment. I have to stop a few times and wait for the dizziness to subside. I keep asking about the Chinese food. Linda sits me down at my kitchen table and asks me again what happened. "Were you mugged? Should I call the police? Did you fall?"

"I didn't fall," I say. I look up at the lights. She checks the scrape on my forehead, and lets out a quick breath when she sees the back of my head.

"Oh, man. We should go to a hospital."

"Why? It doesn't hurt." I'm beginning to focus. "My forehead hurts more."

"How did this happen?"

"Someone hit me."

"Hit you? Who? With what?"

I remember hearing something clunking to the ground. I say, "A piece of wood."

"You've got a nasty bump. Does this hurt—"

"Ah!" I yell, and pull away.

"Sorry."

The throbbing dizzies me, and my stomach lurches. I shuffle toward the futon and say, "I'd better lie down for a second." The kitchen light hurts my eyes, which Linda notices, and she turns it off. The small lamp next to the futon is on, and I aim it away from me. I sit down heavily, causing the lamp to shake; shadows waver on the wall. Bending over, I take a deep breath and fight down the nausea.

"Are you passing out? Should I call an ambulance?"

"No. I'm all right. Just dizzy."

"I have to call the police, though, and you should call your credit card company. If they took your wallet—"

"It wasn't a mugging. They didn't take my wallet." I check my back pocket.

She stops. "What?"

"I wasn't mugged. Nothing was taken, except for the Chinese food. Are you sure it wasn't down there?"

"It wasn't. You were mugged for the Chinese food? Was it a fight?"

I shake my head. "They warned me."

"About what?"

"The guy warned me to stop what I was doing."

Her body straightens, her full attention on me. She says, "What?"

I nod. "He told me to stop."

"Stop what?"

"Whatever. He must have meant my poking around."

"He didn't mention Paul?"

"No, but what else could it be? I start asking questions, and now someone uses my head as a baseball."

She sits down next to me. The lamp shakes again. I inhale and say slowly, "There were two men. They were waiting for me. I should've known, since the alley light was out. I was stupid."

When I look at her, I see her eyes shining. She sits up. "A warning. We were right. There's something going on."

"Maybe," I say. "Or someone really wanted some Chinese food."

"Will you stop talking about that? This is important."

"My dinner is important. It was almost twenty bucks."

"Allen, I'm serious."

"I can't believe they took it."

She studies me. "You're in shock."

"Maybe." I look at my palms—dirt is embedded in my callouses.

She asks me if I was able to identify the voices, and I tell her that only one of them spoke, and I didn't recognize him. I didn't get a look at them, which embarrasses me. I was caught completely off-guard. I'm getting soft. Maybe it's this two-week leave. Maybe I'm getting lazy.

"But he didn't mention Paul or WestSun or anything specific?" she asks.

"No."

"So the police won't have much."

"Unless we tell them what we've been doing."

She hesitates.

"It could also be something unrelated," I say. "I might have run across something at one of the other places."

"Maybe, but this happened after our visit to WestSun. Something's going on over there."

"We don't know that," I say.

"I have a feeling."

I remain quiet, my bearings coming back, my sense of embarrassment rising. Why didn't I notice anything? Because I was thinking about having dinner with Linda. I was thinking about buying a bottle of wine. They had a gun. I could've been shot. Could it have been the same way when Paul was hit? Was I distracted then?

I'm suddenly not so sure I'm ready to return to work.

Linda is watching me. "What're you thinking?"

"Nothing. I have to be more alert."

"Should we call a doctor?"

"I don't think so. I'll just have a headache."

"You sure? What if you have a concussion?"

"I'm pretty sure," I say. "What about WestSun? Didn't you bring some info?"

She looks at my forehead again, and sighs. "All right. If you think so." She gets her bag and pulls out photocopies, laying them out for me. I notice that I have dirtied the sheets. More laundry. The copies are short entries of private companies in some kind of corporate listing, the information about WestSun only a few lines long. Roger Milian is the owner and CEO, with sales of its imports estimated at fifteen million a year. WestSun was originally called Western Imports, and about twenty years ago merged with Sunrise Goods to form the new company WestSun Imports.

"It's not much," she says as I leaf through the other pages, which are older listings and entries for Western Imports and Sunrise Goods. "They import cheap clothes from Asia, mostly the Philippines and Korea, though they're apparently working on a deal with China right now."

"How'd you find that out?"

"The business editor hooked me up with one of their competitors."

I read an old entry on Sunrise Goods, which Milian had owned before the merger, and I notice a subsidiary named Shilla Shipping. "Hey. I know this company. My father used to work for them."

"Shilla Shipping?"

"Yeah. Well, Shilla's a common name, but Shilla Shipping sounds very familiar."

"How common?"

"I know a couple of restaurants named Shilla."

"But Shilla Shipping? Are you sure?"

"Pretty sure. But it was a long time ago."

"Your father wasn't in management?"

"Not even close," I say. "He drove a truck."

"Could he have known Roger Milian?"

"I have no idea." I suddenly realize that I might have met my father's boss when we went to WestSun, and this unsettles me. Maybe Milian remembers my father. "It just might be a strange coincidence."

"Can you find out?" she asks. "Can you know for sure?"

I think about this. "My aunt might know."

"The one you haven't spoken to in years."

"Yeah."

She doesn't say anything, but her question is clear. She waits. I'm not even sure if I still have Aunt Insook's number. "You think it'd help?" I ask.

"Yes. You can get some background on the company."

"I don't know."

"This could be important." She looks at my forehead. "It stopped bleeding."

"Good." I'm still thinking about Milian as my father's boss, and try to picture him twenty years younger. I imagine him with darker hair, maybe without a beard, but don't recall anyone like that. Could I have seen him when I visited my father at work? Once in a while my aunt, baby-sitting me, would bring me to Shilla as my father's shift ended. She'd leave me near the entrance as she wandered through the warehouse. I was awed by the mammoth trucks, frightened by the sounds of machinery, gears grinding, pneumatic dollies hissing. The people were faceless, formless, just bodies moving back and forth, buzzing around boxes.

Pain travels from my temples to my neck. I steady myself.

Linda hurries to the freezer and empties my ice trays into a plastic bag. "At least put this on the back of your head. That bump will swell." She looks inside the refrigerator and checks the shelves before bringing me the ice.

"Thanks." I take the bag and place it gingerly on my head. "You're hungry."

"A little."

"I'm sorry. Let me order a pizza."

"No," she says. "Can I just find something in here?"

"Whatever you want."

She looks through my cupboard. "All you have is cold cereal."

"I know. It's easy to eat."

"For dinner?"

"For everything. My father and I used to do that a lot when I was a kid."

"All right. That's fine," she says, and takes down a box of cornflakes. I sit at the kitchen table as Linda prepares her cereal dinner. She holds

up a second bowl for me, but I wave it away. She moves slowly and deliberately, her attention distracted. She drops some extra flakes on the
counter and pops them into her mouth. She turns to me. "You and your
father ate cereal for dinner?"

"Sometimes he'd bring home fast food. He rarely cooked. TV dinners were common too."

Linda sits down across from me and mixes her cereal. She spoons in
a mouthful. "Your aunt?"

"Never stuck around to cook. She'd watch me when my father
needed her to, less as I grew older. I don't even know if she's still alive."

"Why did you two fight?"

"Who knows?" I say. "I think she resented having to take care of
me. All that responsibility." I wave this off. "Your family is in the
area?"

She shakes her head. "In L.A."

"What about your ex?"

"No idea."

"Really? What about alimony?"

She snorts and almost drops her spoon. "Are you joking? Alimony
is for people with money."

I wait for more.

She sighs. "He was a loser. I married him when I was young and stupid, and scared, and he took advantage of me. He was . . . mean. I
heard a rumor that he might be in the Bay Area. You keep asking me
about it, but I'd rather not get into it."

"Okay."

"This cereal isn't bad." She grins.

"The sound of crunching cereal always reminds me of having dinner with my father in front of the TV." My hand is getting numb from
holding the ice bag. I switch hands. "This is helping. It doesn't hurt as
much."

"Good," she says. "You and your dad ate in front of the TV?"

"Almost always."

"You didn't talk?"

"He wasn't a talkative guy."

We fall silent, and I worry about my attack. I say, "You don't think
we should go to the police."

"We don't have much. A couple of guys jumping you? A weird vibe
from WestSun? It's not a lot."

"What if they come back? What if they warn you?"

She looks up.

I say, "We have to be more careful. We don't know what's going on."

"You should be my bodyguard."

I shake my head, which hurts. I close my eyes. "I'm not very good, as you can tell." I remember that tomorrow I have to start working, and feel a nervous pulse.

She finishes her cereal and points to my head. "How is it?"

"Better."

"You need some more ice?"

"No. It's not that bad. It was just a shock."

She puts her bowl in the sink. "You sure you're okay? I guess I should get going."

"I'm okay."

"Thanks for dinner."

"It was supposed to be Chinese."

"Enough with that. This was fine."

"I still can't believe they took it."

"Are you going to talk to your aunt?"

I sigh. "I have to find her first."

"If you do?"

"If I do, I'll decide then."

She stands up. I say, "You can hang out here for a bit. I don't mind."

"I have work to do."

"How about some coffee? I have coffee."

She says, "All right. Some coffee."

"Sit. I can do this."

She sits. I move to the counter and watch her open her planner, checking her list of items to do. She pulls out a pen, jots a few notes, chews on the cap, then taps it against her chin. She catches me staring, smiles for a moment, then returns to her notes. I find myself glad for the company, which is strange. I usually don't like company.

13

The mood at work is subdued. I receive a few concerned greet-ings, but for the most part I am left alone. My head feels squeezed; a low, insistent throbbing distracts me. My forehead is ban-daged, and I tell everyone who asks that I took a spill while jogging. They make sympathetic sounds, but their eyes flash Bad Luck and they stay away.

My cubicle, in the large room along with most of the others, is filled with stacks of shift reports and protectee files, and I'm separating them into piles for shredding and piles for inputting. Polansky wants to have everything on the server and databases, but there was a transition pe-riod of almost a year when some people worked on the server, others on hard copy, and it's my job to get everything sorted out and entered into the computer. It is, without a doubt, busywork. Most of the in-formation is outdated, and I can see no reason for anyone wanting the old shift reports. They are important while the case is active, but two years later they're useless. No one will see this work I am doing now. No one will care, and yet I feel obliged to carry out my tasks. Once I start typing in the data, I continue doing so. Inertia. I try to resist this. I stop and look around. I take breaks.

Last night I had trouble sleeping. Linda stayed for about an hour while we talked about her work, though I was tempted to ask her per-sonal questions, especially about her ex-husband. After she left, the coffee and my headache kept me awake well past midnight, and I paced my apartment in the dark, occasionally looking out my window and watching the Walk/Don't Walk sign blinking with no pedestrians in sight. The sounds of the apartment were amplified, and my leaky faucet irritated me; I had to put a beer bottle underneath the spout so the drops would run quietly down the side of the glass rather than splash into the sink.

I tried to pinpoint my sense of dis-ease. I came up with this: *re-movement*, the state of being removed from everything. It's also a variant of "movement," reflecting the tendency toward inertial deception. It's not enough to move when moved, rest when already at rest. Re-movement is the awareness of this deception.

My fingers cramp up on the keyboard. Obviously I had way too much time to think last night. I stop typing and squint at the computer screen. I'm not even sure what I've been inputting. When I finally fell asleep last night, I had those waking dreams. I know they can't be good for me, since I'm exhausted after a series of them.

ProServ is housed in a complex on Shore Drive, among accounting and financial offices, and across the street from a computer company with a long row of shiny commuter vans in front. I find myself staring at smokers leaving the building and standing near the curb, flicking their butts into the street. One man in a yellow tie appears every half hour. He takes almost ten minutes to finish his cigarette. That's twenty minutes every hour. One-third of his time devoted to inhaling smoke. I wonder if his boss knows about this.

"How's it going?" a voice behind me says.

I whirl around and see Charles standing there. Pain vibrates through my back from turning too quickly. "All right," I say. "Working my way through this crap." I wonder how long he has been watching me, how long I was sitting idly.

"You think you'll finish that in a week?"

"I don't know. It's a lot of inputting."

"Doney is putting together a team for next week, a software convention. Interested?"

"Group work? But I've been doing paired—"

"You have to ease back in, Allen. Besides, we need time to figure out the new rosters."

"You want an answer now?"

"No. But soon. Doney is working up a list."

I nod. Before he turns to leave, I say, "By the way, I'd like to bring David, Paul's son, to show him around. I promised him I'd give him a tour."

"Of this place?"

"Yeah. That okay?"

Charles frowns and pushes his glasses back with his finger. He says, "I don't know if I want some kid hanging around."

"Not some kid, Paul's kid. And it's just a quick look."

"How about after hours, when it's quiet? How's he doing?"

"Seems okay. Both of them."

"But the kid is handling it?"

"I think so," I say. "I got a question for you."

"Shoot."

"Has anyone been fired for moonlighting?"

"Oh, yeah. Remember Harry Arkin?"

"Arkin. That guy from a while ago—"

"Right around the time you came. He was doing corporate protection on his own. Then he started talking to Triumph, and once Polansky got wind of it, he fired him on the spot. Why?"

Triumph Associates is another one of ProServ's competitors. I reply, "Just curious."

"You're not thinking of that, are you?"

"No. Just wondering."

He studies me, then says, "If it's unrelated to us, then Polansky might not mind, but you need his okay."

"I'm not planning anything."

I return to my data entry, but after a few minutes grow bored. I pull out my old address book which contains Aunt Insook's phone number—I found it this morning—and leaf through the names of high school friends, names I no longer connect to faces. I find my aunt's number and dial. Not surprisingly, I get a wrong number. She must have moved a while ago for this number to be reassigned.

I rest my hand on the stack of files in front of me and return to the phone, calling information in Oakland. My aunt's name isn't on record. I start calling other cities in the East Bay, then the South Bay, then the city, and it isn't until I call information in Marin that her name appears, which surprises me. The North Bay is affluent and generally Anglo; I can't see my aunt fitting in there.

I call her number and listen to her phone ring a few times. When

she answers, her voice distinctly older but her accent immediately rec-
ognizable, I freeze. I recall her sharp features, angular chin and cheekbones, and am suddenly a teenager again.

"Hello? *Yubuhseyo?*" she asks, trying the Korean greeting.

"Aunt Insook?" I say. "This is Allen."

"Who?"

"Allen. Sung-Oh."

Silence. She says, "Sung-Oh?"

"Yeah, it's me. How's it going?"

"What do you want?" she asks.

I'm not sure how to answer that. I say, "Sorry to bother you, but I
have a question about my father."

"Your father?"

"Do you remember the name of the company he worked for, the one
where he drove the rig?"

"Why you want to know?"

"Because I'm looking into a few things."

"What things?"

I sigh. "Nothing important. Do you remember?"

"That was many years ago, a long time ago. I don't remember." A bit
more of her accent comes through, and I wonder if she's being difficult
just to spite me.

"Wasn't it Shilla Shipping?"

"Maybe it was Shilla. It was years ago."

"You hated his working there. You don't remember the name?"

"Maybe it was Shilla."

"Is this a bad time? Should I come by? When did you move to
Marin?"

"Few years ago."

"Where are you? Sausalito?"

"Mill Valley."

I wonder why she has moved there, and remember some boxes she
had put in storage. "Do you still have any of my father's things? Didn't
you have a few boxes—"

"*Aigoo,* that was many years ago. I don't have anything of his."

I take this in. So everything of my father's is now gone. I say, "Was
it Shilla Shipping? Were they ever taken over by another company?"

"Sung-Oh, why you ask this? So long ago."

"I know. I'm curious."

She's quiet, then says, "What you do now? Where are you?"

"Monte Vista. I'm in security. Are you still a bookkeeper?"

"No, no. I retire years ago. I'm old woman, Sung-Oh."

"You're not that old," I say, recalling when she used to declare these kinds of truths about herself. I'm smart woman, Sung-Oh, she said many times when she lectured me at the dinner table as a teenager. It's a strange habit that I concluded grew out of her solitude. I wonder if I'll start doing that in a few years. "You're what, sixty-six? Sixty-seven?"

"Still old," she says. "What kind security? A policeman?"

"No. Executive protection," I begin saying, but know she won't understand. "A bodyguard, for businessmen."

She doesn't reply.

I say, "Do you remember the company? Is there someone who would? Did my father have any friends in the area?"

"Why you want to know? How many years ago, twenty years?"

"Aunt Insook, this is important."

"You shouldn't worry about that. Past is past."

Her resistance is typical—she doesn't want to help me if she doesn't understand why. I ask, "What about Roger Milian? Do you recognize that name? Was he my father's boss?"

I hear static on the line, and she says, "I can't remember. Too long ago—"

"Milian? Even the name of the company? Shilla?"

"Sung-Oh, I don't think of that time for many years."

"But you must have some idea if it sounds familiar."

"I'm tired woman, Sung-Oh. I need to rest."

"I understand. How about a name of one of my father's friends?"

"I can't remember. We talk some other time, okay?"

"Are you hanging up?"

"We talk soon."

I hear a click. The static fades. "Hello?" I'm not surprised that she hung up on me, but I wonder if she's getting senile. I replay the conversation in my head, knowing that I flustered her by pressing my questions.

Charles walks down the hall with a prospective client. I'm not used to being here when it's so still, when the loudest sound is the hissing of the air conditioner above me; I'm usually only here to file reports, interview clients, or meet with coworkers. I like the late afternoons best,

when Paul and I would come in and find a handful of others already filing their shift reports, the relief of the end of the day palpable as voices
grew louder, moods lighter. Some of us might go to the bar and restaurant down the block for a drink, though Paul and I often drifted home;
he was sick of the others, and I was usually exhausted.

Another smoker stands on the curb across the street. Hearing my
aunt's voice was oddly comforting. She hung up on me, but even this
abruptness is familiar. She was never one for polite entrances or exits,
and I remember her talking to one of my teachers when I had just
transferred to a new school after my father's death. We came in one
morning before the first bell, and Aunt Insook demanded that I get special attention to catch up with the other students, since I had already
missed half a year with this teacher. Mrs. O'Hara, befuddled by these
demands, barely had a chance to reply, since my aunt, after announc-
ing her mandates, turned and left. I stood there as surprised as Mrs.
O'Hara. Aunt Insook hadn't even said goodbye to me. "Well," my new
teacher said. "That was interesting."

The sound of Charles's laughter jars me. He is escorting the client
out of the lobby, and when I glance at the clock I see that I have wasted
almost an hour. I return to the files and continue inputting. I wonder
what Aunt Insook looks like now.

14

A unt Insook looks surprisingly the same. She has clearly aged, of course, but I'm not sure what I expected. Although her hair is now streaked with silver and the wrinkles around her eyes and mouth have deepened, she is slimmer, even physically fit, but I can't imagine her doing any kind of exercise. When she blinks up at me in surprise, at my sudden appearance, I find myself smiling uneasily, tentatively, because I know I have changed much more than she has. Does she even recognize me?

"Sung-Oh?" she asks, studying my face. We've never really resembled each other; my features tend to be smoother, whereas hers are prominent: high cheekbones, a more Anglo nose, larger eyes. Maybe more prominent features means they resist aging better.

It has been almost eleven years since I have seen her, and I remember again that last angry fight about my dropping out of school. Her face was red, her lower jaw jutting out as she told me in a deep, threatening voice that she had done her best with me, and if I left school I would have to leave her house and her life. She had that familiar hands-on-her-hips confrontational stance, and as she said those words I felt a release, an opening up within me. Thank you, I said. I might have even smiled. That's just what I wanted to hear, I said.

My aunt's house is hidden up a winding, unnamed road, and to find it I had to drive through the maze of streets behind Mount Tamalpais

High School, the only real reference point I could locate on the map. I eventually backtracked and parked my car at the foot of a hill, and began walking up a dirt road with huge potholes and jagged rocks lying along the side. The farther up the hill I went, the better the view of Richardson Bay, the high school, and Mill Valley.

I drove up here almost impulsively, getting Aunt Insook's address from the information operator. As I crossed the Golden Gate Bridge, nervous because of my accident there, I found myself strongly curious to see where she lives and what she looks like.

And she looks more or less the same. When she opens the door and stops at the sight of me, I recognize her instantly. She squints at me with suspicion, her thoughts of turning away a salesman clear in her expression. The quickness in her eyes hasn't changed. I tell her it's me, Sung-Oh, and recognition flashes across her face, her mouth pursing in surprise. She repeats my name and peers closer. Her movements are smooth and swift, and again I wonder if she has been exercising.

"This is a nice place," I say, stepping back and pointing up to her house and the area. She lives in a gray-and-white A-frame, the back facing the school football field and the marsh beyond, and the flaws— a few patches of peeling paint, a torn window screen—are shrouded by sprawling pines, long arching branches brushing against the shingles.

"What you doing here?" she asks.

"You said we could talk. I thought I'd show up."

She blinks, still taking this surprise in. "How you know where I live?"

"You're listed in the phone book." I point to her mailbox with her name on it. "Not too many Insook Choices around here." I step farther back, not wanting to seem threatening. I don't remember being this much bigger than she is, and I feel lumbering and brawny.

"Why you didn't call first?" she asks.

"Do you want me to go?"

She hesitates.

"Why'd you leave Oakland?"

"Too dangerous for old woman."

"You don't look old at all," I say. She left Oakland for here, prime real estate. She must have done well. She seems to be debating what to do. I say, "Should I go?"

She steps back and opens the door farther. "Come in."

As soon as I walk in I see the large bay window at the back with a view of the school field, a soccer game in progress, yellows versus blues. Beyond that I see the marsh with joggers and bicyclists inching along a trail. I stare, and say, "Nice view."

"Why you come? We can talk on the phone."

"You hung up on me."

"I was tired." She sits on the sofa, and I move to the chair across from her. She says, "What's wrong with your head?"

I touch the bandage. "I bumped into something. Have you thought about what I asked?"

She seems so tiny. Why did I imagine she was taller than me? I remember our fights and how she loomed over me, pointing her finger and scolding me from above. Even at the dinner table, when I was close to flunking out of high school, she appeared to fill the room with her harsh voice as she peered down at me and warned me about my future. Now, as she settles into the sofa, smoothing her silk blouse and picking lint off her slacks, I see her for a moment as others probably did during that time: as an attractive middle-aged woman with more responsibilty than she wanted. I feel a twinge of guilt. She says, "Shilla is right. I think it was Shilla."

"Shilla Shipping? My father worked for Shilla Shipping?"

She nods. "Why you want to know?"

"I knew it sounded familiar," I say. "I'm looking into a few things."

"What things?"

The light from the bay window fills the living room and reflects off the shiny hardwood floors. My aunt waits for an answer. It's a strange, familiar sensation sitting across from her, and I recall the times when in her Oakland condo she'd sit in the living room listening to a Korean soap opera on tape while I was supposed to be doing my homework, though my mind would wander and I'd find myself lulled by the meaningless chatter floating around me. She made me do my homework in front of her, but I had perfected the pose of attention and diligence when I was really falling asleep.

"What things?" she asks again.

"Shilla Shipping. Do you remember anything about it? Who ran it, and that kind of thing?"

She sighs. "I try not to think about it after your father died."

"Tell me how he died again."

"You know."

"All I know is that he was killed unloading his rig. Some kind of accident."

"Yes."

"What was he unloading?"

"I don't know."

"Tell me what you do know."

She thinks about this, then says, "Your father work late, behind schedule. So he probably rushed. He unloaded truck and something fell on him, and he had a heart attack."

"Did he have life insurance?"

"No, but the company paid for everything, and gave us settlement. I spent for your college."

And I wasted it. The accusation hangs between us. I say, "Was Roger Milian the head of Shilla Shipping then?"

She shakes her head slightly and says, "I don't know. Maybe. The names from so long ago."

"Have you heard of that name?"

"Maybe. I don't know."

"What about Sunrise Goods?"

She rubs her eyes, then nods. "Yes. I remember that name."

"Shilla owned them, right?"

"No," she says, frowning. "Other way around. Sunrise had *meeguk-saddam,* had white owners, and took over Shilla."

"So it wasn't a Korean company?"

"No."

"So my father was the only Korean guy there?"

"Oh, no. There were many Korean workers, but the owners were white."

"Did my father have any friends?"

She nods. "Yes. I think so."

"Are they still around?"

"*Aigoo,* I don't know. Why you want to know?"

"You have no idea?"

"I don't know," she says, talking slower, her voice tired. "I don't know who they are. What you looking for?"

I'm not sure how much she wants to know. I say, "My partner was recently killed, and I'm looking into some companies he worked for."

"Killed?"

"Murdered. Shot. It was in the newspapers."

"He work for Shilla?"

"No. Shilla isn't around anymore. He worked for a company that took over Sunrise and Shilla. WestSun Imports."

She looks confused, and I add, "It was a coincidence, this connection to Shilla, but I figured I'd get some more background."

"Why was he killed?" she asks.

"No one's sure. He might've just been in the way."

"Be careful, Sung-Oh."

Startled by her concern, I lose my train of thought. I wonder if she's genuinely worried. I say, "Are any of my father's coworkers still around?"

"I don't know."

"Isn't there someone from back then you know of? Another Korean worker? Someone my father might have mentioned?"

She brightens and says, "Maybe. Korean driver. He goes to Korean church in Sunnyvale."

"You know him?"

"No. My friend Grace know him. I think he was driver like your father."

"For Shilla?"

"I think so. Grace once tell me long ago he did."

"What's his name?"

"Kim . . ." She closes her eyes. "Kim . . . Junil? Junil Kim?"

"Can I have your friend's number? Can I call her?"

She looks for a pen and pulls one out of a drawer, jotting a number on the corner of an old envelope. "Her name is Grace Park," she says. "I don't know Junil Kim, but she knows."

I glance at the number. "She's in the South Bay?"

"She lives near Sunnyvale."

"I appreciate this," I say.

We are quiet for a moment, then she says, "How you been?"

"All right."

"I look for your father's things. I couldn't find anything."

"Threw them all away?" I ask. This comes out sharper than I intended, and she glances at me.

"Twenty years ago, Sung-Oh. I don't keep many things."

"I remember when I had to move in with you. You made me throw away all my toys."

She rolls her eyes. "You have too many toys! There was no room in my house!"

"But I didn't have to throw everything away."

"I live in small one-bedroom, and all the sudden I had young boy and his things. Not enough room for all your toys."

"I know," I say. "I wish I could've saved just one or two things." I remember small mementos, like a good attendance award from Mrs. Fromm's third-grade class, and my walking stick that my father had helped me carve from an oak branch. He had shown me how to burn designs into the wood with a magnifying glass and the sun, tiny white dots browning beneath a thin trail of smoke. I burned the figure of a winding snake, and then dotted my initials near the top. The whole process had taken me over three hours in the hot afternoon sun.

Aunt Insook asks me if I want any coffee. I say I do and she breezes into the kitchen. Looking around her living room, I see some photos over the fireplace mantel. There is one of me and Aunt Insook at the Monterey Bay Aquarium, taken when I was about twelve. I appear sullen and annoyed. My aunt, in a flowery summer dress that I don't recognize, is smiling into the camera, laughing, I think, at the stranger whom she asked to take the photograph. Her hand is motioning the cameraman to stop kidding around. I remember being embarrassed by this. The man took the photo while my aunt was speaking just to tease her. There's also an old black-and-white photo of my father and my grandmother in Korea—my father appears to be in his twenties. The other photographs are of people I don't know, mostly older Korean women, a few couples. I look for a photo of my mother, but there isn't one.

"Do you remember the fish?" she asks, nodding toward the aquarium photo. She holds up two mugs. "Instant coffee."

"That's fine," I say. "I remember being tired from the drive down there. And we fought about something."

"You saw some boys by themselves. You wanted to look without me."

"I did?"

She smiles. "You didn't want to be with your mean aunt."

"Oh," I say, not remembering. I don't doubt her, though. By that time I was growing more defiant, and knew she had no real hold on me. "I was pretty determined to do what I wanted."

"You were so mad," she says.

"Mad?"

"Mad at me and everything."

"I was just a kid."

"I took off a day from work for you," she says. "I try to spend time with you, and you don't want to be with me."

She leans back against the wall and blows on her coffee. I feel a faint stirring of resentment. I am about to tell her that she tried to control everything I did, and I hated it, but I let it go. I sip my coffee and say, "Yeah, I guess I was an angry kid."

"You live in Monte Vista?" she asks.

"Downtown, near the train station."

"How come you don't call me?"

"Call you? You never called me."

"I don't know where you are."

"I sent you change-of-address cards, even a few Christmas cards. You never wrote back."

"*Aigoo,* that was years ago."

"And you moved without telling me. The only number I had was your Oakland number."

"I don't know how to tell you!" she says, her accent stronger.

"Well," I say. "I called you now. I'm visiting you now."

"Just for information."

I sigh. Oh, man.

After a moment she asks, "You have girlfriend? You're married?"

"No."

"Why not?"

I shrug. "Why didn't you ever get married?"

"No time. I had to raise you—"

"Whoa, whoa," I say, holding up my hand.

"I had to work so much—"

"You can't blame *me* for that—"

"Your father left little money—"

"All right, that's enough," I say, shaking my head. "We don't need to do this again." I put down my coffee and stand up.

"Do what?" she asks.

"Argue about how I messed up your life."

Her expression hardens, her lips pressed together. She doesn't say anything, and I feel like I'm a teenager again. Nothing changes. I clear my throat and say quietly, "Thanks for the coffee and the information. I should get going."

"Already?"

"Yes, already," I say.

"Why?"

"I don't feel like arguing."

"We won't argue," she says.

"I should still get going."

She nods. I move toward the front door. She remains on the sofa.

"Thanks again," I say, holding up Grace Park's number.

"You come visit some other time."

I pause at the door. "Why?"

"Because I'm your aunt."

I nod, and slip out the door, closing it softly behind me. Kicking up the dust on the dirt road, I hear cheers from the soccer game carrying up these hills. I climb on a small embankment and look out toward the school, watching the blues and yellows running up and down the field, the bleachers filled with parents.

15

I am seven years old. My father comes home from work with dinner. Sometimes he brings McDonald's, meaty pizza, or takeout from a dingy Korean restaurant that serves cafeteria-style, plastic trays and all. For a while he experimented with TV dinners, the kind with salty beef entrées and bubbly apple pie sections, but these took too long to prepare, and they were never enough for him; he usually ended up eating two. Since he doesn't return until later in the evening, I snack on cornflakes, our cupboard filled with industrial-sized boxes my aunt gets through her restaurant connections. Tonight my father brings home *bibimbap*, a mixed rice, vegetable, and beef dish that I like, and we sit down in the living room in front of the TV, the news on. He eats with the disposable chopsticks that come with the dinner, the cheap kind that splinters, while I use a spoon, and neither of us talks. He watches the TV huddled over, his Styrofoam bowl in one hand, the chopsticks in the other, his eyes fixed on the screen. I barely listen to the news—unemployment, stagflation, malaise—while I read my comic books.

I can never finish my dinner, since my snacks have filled me up, and my father empties my bowl into his, barely breaking his eating rhythm. When he finishes, he leans back and opens his beer. "What's that stick in kitchen?" he asks.

"I found it today."

"For fighting stick?"

"A walking stick."

He nods. "When I was boy I use walking stick. I walk up mountain path. But you got to carve bark off."

"I need a knife."

"Tomorrow I show you. You use my knife."

"Tomorrow, when?" I ask. He usually works on Saturdays.

"Afternoon. I try finish early. You got magnify glass?"

"I think so. Why?"

"I show you tomorrow."

I am pleased. The next day when he begins demonstrating to me how to carve off the bark, I feel shy with him. I watch his thick, dense hands whittling an end; two of his fingernails are black. After he uses the magnifying glass on the whittled portion, burning two dots, I ask him what I should draw. "Anything," he says. "Your walking stick."

It takes me almost three hours in the hot afternoon sun, and my eyes sting with red dots from staring too long at the tiny focused beam of light, but I finish. When he sees my snake design, he notices the way I shaded the top of it by varying the time I kept the magnifying glass in the sun. His leathery face wrinkles into a grin, and he tells me mine is nicer than the one he made when he was my age.

I haven't thought about this in years, and as I return home after my visit to my aunt's, I realize that the Salvation Army would have thrown out the stick. Most of my things would have been discarded, since beat-up toys and old branches wouldn't have interested anyone. I can't help feeling that familiar twinge of resentment toward my aunt, the childhood anger at having to give up so much, but there nevertheless, two decades later.

I try to call Linda from my apartment, but she's not home. I then call Grace Park, who says that Junil Kim doesn't have a phone but he'll be at church tomorrow. She can introduce me then.

"Where does he live?" I ask, not wanting to go to church.

"Milpitas. I'm not sure about the address."

"He doesn't have a phone?"

"He's a little strange. But he always goes to church."

After I take down the church address and hang up, I debate whether I need to do this. I'm straying further away from Paul's free-lance work, but find myself compelled to continue. I want to meet one of my father's coworkers. I call Linda again, but still can't reach her. I'm a little worried. I feel the tenderness in my lower back where the man punched me.

I know I was lucky. This morning, before driving up north, I went to the gym but couldn't do many reps. Any lifting that involved my lats and lower back was painful, and when I tried some sit-ups, the sudden movements gave me a sharp headache. I ended up riding a stationary bike for fifteen minutes, thinking about getting beaten up.

Instead of a couple of punches, the man behind me could've used a baton, a sap, brass knuckles, or worse, a knife or gun. I still don't want to carry my SIG outside of work, since Polansky has done a good job of convincing us to secure our guns when we're off-duty; the statistics for accidental discharges and guns being used unnecessarily are persuasive, though all of us know Polansky is more worried about bad press from a vigilante-type shooting or an accident involving his employees. Still, I can't help imagining the meeting with the two men differently: me pulling out my SIG and shoving it down the guy's throat, slamming his head into the brick wall. I'd beat the one who used the wood on me, maybe giving him a taste of the back-head slam. I grew angrier while fantasizing about this on the stationary bike. I wanted revenge. I had to stop pedaling to calm myself.

In the evening, as I'm eating a late dinner, Linda returns my call. My first question is "Are you okay?"

"Yes. Why?"

"I couldn't reach you. I was a little worried."

"You were?" She sounds amused.

"Yeah. I mean, after my run-in, I thought . . ."

"No, no. I'm fine. I was out."

"You weren't at work, though."

"No," she says.

"What were you up to?"

She says, with a slight hesitation, "Oh, just hanging out."

"With friends?" I ask.

"Yes, a friend."

"Ah. A date."

"Excuse me?" she asks.

"A date."

"Yes," she says.

"Sorry. I don't mean to be nosy."

"It's okay."

I tell her about my meeting with my aunt, and tomorrow's plan to see Junil Kim.

"You actually met with her?" she asks.

"I drove up there, yeah."

"After all these years?"

"Yeah."

"What was she like? Did you get along?"

"Not really."

She waits for more, and I say, "I was only there for a few minutes."

"I see. Did she know about the company?"

"Not a whole lot. I don't know if this Junil Kim will be helpful, but I'm interested in meeting one of my father's friends."

"I'll know more about Milian on Monday," she says.

I want to ask her about her date, but am not sure how. I say, "Where'd you go this afternoon?"

"Lunch and a matinee. Nothing much."

She isn't going to tell me anything. I smile. "All right. I won't pry. I'll talk to you tomorrow if I get to Junil Kim."

"No, I didn't mean—"

"It's okay. You hardly know me, after all. But be careful. We don't know what we're stirring up."

She says, "Call me after you talk to him."

"I will."

"And thanks."

"For what?"

"For worrying about me."

We hang up. I stand by the phone, feeling a small pang of jealousy. I shake this off and return to my dinner; my cornflakes have turned soggy.

16

The church in Santa Clara, off Camino Real, is shared by a Korean and a white congregation, the sign in front "Second Santa Clara Methodist" in English with Korean lettering underneath. When I attended a Korean church with my aunt in Oakland, we often arrived early as the changeover was occurring—the white congregation leaving as the Korean congregation arrived—and I found this racial shift bizarre, groups of black-haired Asians streaming in as light-haired whites climbed into their cars.

I arrive at the Santa Clara church in the early afternoon, making sure I miss the main service, which is in Korean. I'm not here to worship. At most Korean churches, there is a long lunch and social period after the service, members of the congregation bringing food, buffet-style, while the kids take Korean language and culture classes. This was the way I learned tae kwon do as a teenager. As I suspect, Santa Clara is no different, and when I walk into a main hall adjacent to the chapel, I see dozens of tables filled with well-dressed Koreans eating and talking. The voices—speaking mostly in Korean—mingle and merge, rising up to me on the staircase. I take in the view, and wonder for a moment what I believe in. I don't know.

Not much has changed since I last entered a church. A mix of young and old around the tables, some older women in *hanboks,* traditional Korean garb with overlapping gray canvas fabric, but most everyone dresses in suits and Sunday bests. A few people look up at me curiously. I eye the food—fried dumplings, *kimchi,* rice and vegetable dishes, soups in huge pots—and realize I'm hungry. The smell of broiling spicy beef fills the room. A young man in a suit approaches and asks me something in Korean.

Shaking my head, I say, "I don't speak Korean."

"Are you visiting us?" he says in English.

"I'm looking for Mrs. Grace Park."

The man smiles and points to one of the older women at a nearby table. They all look toward me, and the man says something to them in Korean. Mrs. Park stands up. "You're Insook's nephew?" she asks.

"I am."

She tells the others at the table something, and they nod. "How is Insook?" she asks, walking toward me. She is a tall, regal-looking woman with expensive gold jewelry and careful, subtle makeup. Everything about her—her short, stylish hairdo, her gray suit—seems to have been meticulously prepared.

"My aunt seems fine," I say. "Is Junil Kim here?" I glance at the other tables.

"He teaches calligraphy."

"Calligraphy?"

"He taught himself when he retired," she says. "Korean calligraphy. He's very good."

"How do you know my aunt?"

"I met her when she lived in Oakland."

"You live in Oakland?"

She nods.

"Were you there when I was there?"

She says, "Yes, but I didn't know Insook then."

"But you did later."

"Yes. Why do you need to talk to Junil?"

"I want to ask him about my father."

"Come," she says, motioning to another set of stairs. "We'll go upstairs to see him. He should be finishing up now."

As we walk up to another level, she asks me how I hurt my forehead. I mumble that I had an accident. I ask her if she knew my father.

"No. He died long before I met Insook." She leads me down a hallway and points to the door at the end. "Junil's a strange man. You should be nice to him."

"Nice? Why wouldn't I be?"

She smiles. "Insook said you can be pushy."

"You talked to her?"

"I called her after you called me."

I nod. "All right. I'll try not to be pushy," I say. "If you live in Oakland, why do you go to this church?"

"I have friends here." She peers through the doorway and stops, turning to me and holding her finger to her lips. I look in. Five young Korean Americans sit at a table with brushes and inkstones, carefully copying figures from a book. At the head of the table is a gnarled old man with massive shoulders, his face leathery and wrinkled. He is speaking in Korean, and the kids listen while they work.

"What is he saying?" I ask Mrs. Park.

We step away from the doorway. Junil Kim's scratchy voice carries into the hall. Mrs. Park whispers to me, "He's telling an old folktale. I think they're writing scenes from it." She continues listening, then says, "It's the one about the blue frog."

I shake my head.

She turns to me, surprised. "You don't know it?"

"No."

She listens, then translates: "A young blue frog never listened to his mother. She told him to stay away from the caves, where the snakes lived, but he didn't. One day he was fighting with a snake and she came to help, but she got bitten. Before she died she told her son to bury her near the river. She thought that he wouldn't listen and bury her in the mountains. But after she died the son was so unhappy that he listened to her, and buried her near the river. Every time it rained the river flooded and the frog worried that his mother would be washed away. That's why blue frogs cry when it rains."

She opens the door and enters.

Junil Kim looks up calmly as Mrs. Park speaks to him in Korean, and I hear her use Insook's name. The students stop what they're doing and watch us. Mr. Kim speaks to them, and they begin packing up. Mrs. Park says to me, "I'm going back to my lunch. You say goodbye to me when you go."

I thank her. The students file out. Mr. Kim stays seated, watching me, and I can't help noticing his thick forearms and hands, his knuckles and joints enlarged and bulbous. He caps a red ink pad and carefully places a stamp into a velvet case. His clawed, thick fingers and hands are out of proportion with the rest of his body. Finally I say, "Mr. Kim? I'm Allen Choice."

"I know," he says in his raspy voice. "Sung-Oh. I remember you."

"You do?"

"You were small kid. Nose always running. Sniffy." He looks me up and down. His unkempt hair needs combing, and his lower lip is swollen, jutting out. He has stubble growing along his chin. "You look like your father," he says.

"Do I?"

"No?"

"I don't know. Maybe."

He finishes packing away his brushes. When he stands, I see that he is shorter than me by a few inches, and we shake hands; he crushes mine. I try not to flinch. He says, "You eat yet?"

"No."

"Come." He lumbers toward the door, and says, "You were allergic to chemicals in clothes and dust. So when you come in, you kept sneezing, runny nose."

I realize he's talking about Shilla Shipping, but I don't remember this. "I must have been really young. How long did you know my father?"

"I work there two years before your father come."

I glance at him, but don't repeat the question he misunderstood. We enter the main dining hall, where the kids have now taken over a few of the tables, dozens of them filling their own corner of the room. Most of the adults are finishing their lunches. I see a few kids wearing tae kwon do uniforms. Two older men greet Mr. Kim in Korean, and he grunts in return. We fill up our paper plates with food and sit down at a small folding table away from the kids. He shovels large chunks of sticky rice into his mouth. I say, "You were friends with my father?"

"Friends? We work together many years." He chews.

"But you weren't friends?"

He thinks about this. "We were friends."

Up close, I see that the skin on his face has been damaged by the sun; there are discolored blotches along his cheeks and nose. I say, "Did you know Roger Milian?"

The name jars him, and he looks up from his food. "Our boss."

"So he was your immediate boss? My father's too?"

He nods. "Why you want to know?"

"I'm trying to learn more about Milian's current company. It might be a coincidence that he was my father's boss. How long did you stay at Shilla?"

"I laid off after company bought."

"Western Imports."

"You know?"

"It's called WestSun Imports now, and Milian is the head of it," I say. "What did you do after you were laid off?"

"I work at other trucking company. Then I join my brother-in-law at landscaping."

"Do you remember my father's accident?"

He turns to me. "I remember."

"Were you there?"

"He working alone."

"What happened?"

"Your father try to unload too many things without help. He rushed. Use a pulley block but not secure, so it fall and hit his head, and everything fall on him."

I've never heard the full details, and am startled by the violence of this. I say, "Then he had a heart attack?"

"What?"

"My aunt told me he had a heart attack."

He shakes his head. "No. He crushed."

"No heart attack?"

"Maybe, but he die from the crush."

I try to figure out what I missed, and Mr. Kim says, "Your father rushing. He should've wait until morning."

"Why didn't he?"

"If not unloaded in time, we get trouble."

"Why was he late?"

Mr. Kim shrugs and continues eating. He is already half finished with his lunch, so I start with the dumplings. He says, "Why you wear patch?"

"What? Oh, the bandage. I was in a fight." I ask, "What was Milian like back then?"

"Fight? I used to be good fighter," he says, a small smile appearing and disappearing. He finishes his rice. "Milian was hard man."

"How'd a white guy run a company with a Korean name and Korean workers?"

"He had Korean partner, but bought share. No one really liked Milian."

"Why?"

"Think only of money. And we know many will be laid off. We know he talks with another company to merge. Who you fight with?"

"I don't know. Two men—"

"Two? Two against one?"

"Yes. They told me to stop looking into this."

Mr. Kim stops eating. "Into what?"

"I don't know. That's what I'm trying to figure out." I tell him about Paul, and how I only recently started asking questions.

He listens, then says, "I don't know much. I was just driver. But you talk to Louis . . ." He pauses, trying to think of the name. "Larry? No, Louis. Louis Stein. He was weekend manager. He knows more about company and Milian."

"How do I find him?"

"He used to run restaurant in Palo Alto," Mr. Kim says. "Japanese restaurant near post office downtown."

"How long ago?"

"Long ago."

"Restaurant? I don't understand."

"Milian laid off. Louis become manager of restaurant. He hated Milian."

"He's not Korean, though."

Mr. Kim smiles. "Not Korean. He come to work after Milian bought full company."

The restaurant is probably no longer there. I say, "How'd you like my father? You two got along?"

"Got along? We do our work."

"So you didn't spend any time together outside of work?"

He shakes his head. "He busy taking care of you."

"Are you married? Any children?"

"No," he says. "You?"

"No." I watch two kids argue over a package of *kimbop,* a Korean version of vegetable sushi. The dining hall is quieting down, many of the adults moving outside into the parking lot, some driving off. The sink is running in the kitchen; someone washes pots and pans. I ask, "Do you need a ride home?"

"I take church van."

"So you really didn't know my father that well."

"We took coffee break together. Sometimes we eat lunch. But your father very quiet."

We finish eating, and I thank Mr. Kim. I ask him if I can call him with more questions later.

"I don't have phone."

"Why not?"

"I live in trailer. Don't need phone."

"Can I visit you then, if I have more questions?"

He nods, and tells me his address, a trailer park in Milpitas.

"By the way, where'd you get that story about the blue frog?"

"You understand Korean?" he asks.

"No. Mrs. Park told me."

He smiles, and says, "Everyone know. Teach kids to listen to parents."

I thank him again. He crushes my hand goodbye, and disappears outside. I look for Grace Park, but she seems to have already left.

On my way home I think about what Mr. Kim told me. Yes, my father was very quiet. I used to wonder if he was that way with just me, since he and my aunt talked, even argued, often, but he rarely spoke more than a few sentences to me. I figured that after my mother died, he didn't know how to deal with a child. Sometimes I'd catch him looking at me as if I were some kind of strange animal, uncertainty in his eyes. Once, when I was engrossed in digging up an anthole in the sidewalk, I imagined ants yelling "mayday" at each other, and I began talking in an ant voice. "Look out, here it comes again!" I said as I dug my stick into the dirt. I was about six years old. I looked up, and was surprised to see my father standing on the front steps, watching me. He had a baffled look on his face, and said, "Dinner." I was embarrassed, even more so when he didn't ask me what I had been doing.

At my apartment I call my aunt and tell her I spoke with Junil Kim.

"You see Grace?"

"I did. She's fine," I say. "Do you remember how my father died?"

"I told you. Accident when he was unloading."

"Yeah, but you said he had a heart attack during the unloading, and that was what killed him."

"Yes."

"Junil Kim said that a pulley block fell on him, and then he was crushed. He didn't have a heart attack."

"People told me he had a heart attack," she says. "He didn't?"

I hesitate. I didn't realize that maybe she had been told this to lessen the shock. She sounds genuinely surprised, and asks again, "He didn't have a heart attack?"

"I'm not sure. He might have. But his death was from being crushed."

"*Aigoo,* I don't know that."

"Who told you about the death?"

"Someone from the company. I don't remember."

"Roger Milian?"

"I don't remember. It was long time ago."

"Junil Kim told me that my father was rushing, that he was late. I was wondering if you remember why he was rushing. Was he usually late with things?"

"Your father? No. He was very good about time."

"So do you know?"

"Know what?"

"Why he was late."

She breathes loudly. "You don't remember the day?"

"Me?" I say uneasily. "Why would I?"

"You had chicken pox. You were very sick."

"Chicken pox?" I do remember the itchy scabs all over my body, surprising me whenever I looked in a mirror. I couldn't resist scratching and ended up with a few scars. I say, "What about the chicken pox?"

"You had it around that time."

I begin to understand what she is getting at. "How sick was I?"

"You had bad fever. We had to call doctor."

"And that's why my father was late?"

She sighs. "Sung-Oh, it was long time ago."

"So, my father was late because I was sick."

"He worry about you."

I wait for her to tell me more, but when she doesn't, I say, "Funny, I don't remember that."

"It was long time ago."

"You keep saying that."

"It true."

I look at the scar on my forearm, a small pockmark that I remember always being there. I once filled it with my aunt's makeup to see what a smooth forearm would look like. I say, "Do you know a man named Stein? Louis Stein?"

"No. Who is he?"

"No one. Never mind. I've got to go."

"You come visit me again. Okay?"

I say I will, and hang up. I sit down. I always thought I had the chicken pox after my father died. I remember my aunt taking care of me for most of the time, not my father. Yet I know she is right. What I picture is my aunt giving me some medicine while I recovered, my aunt yelling at me to stop scratching my scabs. My father was a hovering presence during my fever, a disembodied voice asking my aunt how I was. I can't remember the exact night he died. Was he there with me for a short while? Was my aunt there? I see nothing. I do see hazy images of a doctor. A cold compress on my forehead. The curious feeling of scaly bumps as I ran my fingers across my arms. A twenty-year-old memory surfacing.

17

My father smoked unfiltered Pall Malls. He liked to pinch and loosen the burning end before lighting up, because he believed it helped the flavor. He rarely smoked in the house, since I began to develop an allergy after spending too much time in closed, smoke-filled rooms, my sinuses clogging, my eyes watering. He started sitting on the patio to smoke, and would return inside with a strong, bright smell that would settle and turn stale after a few hours. It was never unpleasant, just a distinctive odor lingering around him, and I watched the rusty coffee can outside slowly fill with brown, crushed butts, my father throwing it out only after a weed sprouted among the rotting filters.

Junil Kim's memory of me sniffling at Shilla triggers these old images, and I do recall my head stuffing up whenever I visited my father. But I have trouble remembering what his workplace looked like. The only things registering are a sense of vastness and rumbling noises, and cracked, oil-stained cement under me. Someone told me not to sit on the ground. I couldn't understand why.

It's Monday afternoon, and I'm meeting Linda for lunch in downtown Monte Vista, glad to get away from ProServ. All morning I have been entering data onto the server, and the office is busy with a transition team for three Japanese executives visiting the Bay Area, headed by Brodie and Dunn. Polansky himself is checking up on the details, and the activity is distracting. A few coworkers visited my cubicle, asking me how I was doing. I wasn't feeling talkative. I still feel their awkwardness around me. One of the younger agents, Johnson, seems spooked by my presence and averts his eyes whenever I look at him. Because of this I decide to take Charles's offer to do group work. If I don't go in the field soon, I'll be branded. I told Charles before I left for lunch that I'll finish the paperwork by Friday, when Doney will be briefing his team and running through the following week's target-hardening strategy.

Linda arrives fifteen minutes late, and I'm already eating an appetizer. "I wasn't sure if you were going to show up," I say as she sits across from me. She swings her bag off her arm and looks down at my soup and spring rolls.

"I know. Sorry. Been busy." She reaches over with her fork and stabs a roll. "Do you mind? I'm starving."

"Go ahead." I motion to the waiter. I tell Linda, "I tried calling last night a few times, but your machine kept picking up."

She nods. "I was out."

"Ah," I say, realizing that she must have been on another date. "I'm glad you called this morning. What did you find out?"

She stretches down into her bag and emerges with hair in her face. She flicks it away and skims her notes. "Let's see. Milian is pretty rich. WestSun's assets make him a millionaire, but the company has a lot of debt. He almost sold it a few years ago, but the deal fell apart. He's divorced, had some tax problems, and lives in Los Altos Hills."

"What kind of tax problems?"

"Underpayment, that kind of thing. Nothing too serious. But his manager, Durante, is more interesting. He has a criminal record. Grand larceny, trafficking in stolen goods, assault. He was involved in some kind of stolen computer scheme. He had a juvenile record that was going to be sealed, but was reopened after he was arrested again. He stole cars as a teenager."

"And now he's a manager?"

"Milian hired him soon after San Quentin, while he was on probation. Kind of strange. They must have known each other before."

"I don't get it."

"Maybe he's a family friend, or a relative."

"How'd you get all this?"

"Most of this is public record, from superior and municipal court clerks, but WestSun's financial position was tough. My intern and I had to hound WestSun's competitors to give us some dirt. Milian tried selling the company because he wants to retire soon."

"Does he have any children?"

"I don't think so. Divorced a long time ago, never remarried."

"I talked to an old employee," I say. "Milian was my father's boss twenty years ago."

She raises an eyebrow. "A connection?"

I tell her about my meeting with Junil Kim and the lead for Louis Stein. "I'm going to look for Stein tonight, maybe tomorrow."

"But does this connect with your partner? Is this a coincidence?"

"I have no idea. Maybe it means nothing."

"It means something," she says. "Otherwise you wouldn't have that bruise on your forehead." A waiter finally arrives and Linda orders Thai noodles. I ask for curried chicken. She says to me, "You have to go back to Paul's wife and try to find out more. He must have provoked someone. It must be at WestSun."

I mention that I'll be bringing David for a tour of my office soon. "I'll talk to her again."

"Try to find out if Paul did anything that would connect him more with WestSun. Maybe he got involved in something illegal."

I don't reply. I have trouble imagining this. Linda keeps eyeing the rest of my spring rolls, so I push the plate toward her. She grins shyly.

"Go ahead," I say.

"It's just that I skipped breakfast . . ."

I wave it away. She finishes the rest of the rolls in two bites, then asks, "What was it like meeting your father's coworker?"

"He remembered me as a kid. He told me more about my father's death." I recount the story my aunt told me and also what seems to be the truth about the accident. "She was surprised by what Junil Kim said. Maybe she was told it was a heart attack to lessen the shock."

"Or she made it up and started believing it herself."

I say it's possible. The restaurant is filling up with more office workers. The people at the table next to us are getting louder, bursting into laughter every few minutes. Someone is telling a long story. I feel a sense of dislocation, the everyday lives of these people unreal and beyond my comprehension. My partner is dead. I'm looking up my father's old coworkers. I'm in the middle of entering useless two-year-old data into a computer. I'm eating curried chicken while talking about my estranged aunt.

Philosophy of removement. Am I being subjected to the inertial deception? Am I doing these things because I have already started doing them? I wonder if I can stop right now, if I can stand up and tell Linda it was nice knowing her, but I want to go home and lie down. I stare at her eating. She smiles. She is the prime mover. She put me in motion. My life seems to be a response to prime movers. It dawns on me that if I am not careful, I will be a living example of the physics of movement and rest, pushed and prodded and acting by outside forces alone. Perhaps my entire existence is built on the inertial deception. If I question it too much, I will cease to exist.

Our dishes arrive. Linda says, "You're spacing out."

I look up. "Do you ever get the feeling that you do things just because you're already doing them?"

She tilts her head, studying me. "Everyone does."

This surprises me. "Really? You feel like that?"

"Of course. The trick is to be able to step back and look at yourself objectively."

Removement, the awareness of the deception. "Do you?" I ask.

"All the time."

I am impressed, and want to say something nice to her. "You're great."

She looks startled, then laughs. "I keep forgetting you had a nasty hit to your head."

We continue smiling. I say, "How did your date go?"

She breaks our eye contact and begins eating her noodle dish. "Okay."

"Was it both nights? Saturday and Sunday?"

"Yes."

I wait. She doesn't elaborate. I ask, "Where did you meet him?"

"On a story I was working on."

"Which one?"

"The chef story."

"The one-man restaurant?"

She nods.

"You'd rather not talk about this?"

"Nothing to talk about. Yet."

"You're going out with the chef?"

"No." She is concentrating on her noodles, trying to twirl her fork. I notice she isn't wearing her wedding band.

"Are you having fun?"

She looks up, her cheeks flushed. She seems uncertain, then says, "I think so."

"Good." I change the subject, telling her about my memory of the chicken pox and how this might have made my father late the day he died. She's interested, and I give her Junil Kim's version of my father's accident: he was late, rushing to finish, and was careless.

"But you can't really think it was your fault," she says.

"No. I was a kid. I wasn't even fully conscious. I think I had a bad fever at the time." I watch the people at the noisy table split the bill and leave the restaurant. I turn to Linda, curious about her two dates, but hold back. What does she talk about with other people?

"You're staring," she says without looking up.

"Sorry. I was trying to imagine you on a date."

"Do we have to get into this?"

"What?"

"My romantic life."

"Your romantic life?" I can't help smiling. "That sounds exciting."

"Believe me, it's not. This weekend was my first date in months."

"It must have gone well to happen two nights in a row."

She gives me a heavy-lidded, deadpan look.

"All right," I say. "I won't ask about it."

"Thank you."

"But you know I'm curious—"

"Allen," she warns.

I hold up my hands. "Never mind."

"How will you find this Stein?"

"I'll go to Palo Alto and look for a Japanese restaurant near the post office."

"And you think you'll find him?"

"No. But I might find someone who knows him, or knew him."

"Do you want company?"

"Are you offering?"

"I am."

I say, "Of course I want your company. But do you have time?"

"I have time."

"From your busy dating schedule? From your romantic life?"

She frowns. "Funny guy."

"It might be a waste of time. I'm just checking to be thorough."

"I know. It's a good idea."

"All right," I say.

"I lived there for a couple of years before moving to San Jose."

"Why'd you move?"

"It became too expensive," she says.

We finish our lunches and order Thai iced coffees, neither one of us in a hurry to return to work. She asks me how I'm doing at ProServ, and I tell her I'll be in the field next week.

"Already?"

"I can't stand deskwork. Also, the longer I wait, the more jinxed I'll become." I remember Johnson's uneasiness around me and wonder if it's racially motivated. I try to recall his attitude toward me before Paul's death. My guard tends to be relaxed with younger people. I need to watch him more carefully, especially if he'll be in Doney's detail. It's tiring to think about this.

We pay our bill and walk to our cars, Linda agreeing to meet me in Palo Alto at six. She slips on a pair of small sunglasses and smiles at me. I blink, almost not recognizing her, since I'm not used to seeing an attractive woman smile at me. Did I really call her great? I shudder at the thought of this. She waves. I wave. I watch her drive away.

18

When I first started at Tronics, I kept seeing a beautiful Asian woman arriving late for work; she rushed through the doors, shuffling in a skirt and high heels. She'd call out to hold the elevator, and I, at the security station in the lobby, would watch her slip around the corner and hear the elevator hiss closed. I had the morning shift, four a.m. to noon, and looked for her during the lunch break. I timed her: she was usually late on Mondays and Wednesdays, and skipped lunch on Thursdays and Fridays. She wore sharp black skirts and slacks with cropped jackets, an occasional dress in the summer, but always seemed crisp and linear and smooth. She carried a brown leather briefcase. I noticed that her long black hair always drew looks from others, men and women, and she probably knew it too, the way she ran her fingers through it, flipping her head back.

Of course, I didn't have a chance.

But I'd smile and say good morning. I even wore my name tag, which all of us had but usually never attached, and checked her eyes when I said hello, noticing that she'd glance at my tag for a moment, then nod to me. I was part of the infrastructure, as meaningful as the small sculptures standing in the lobby, but I couldn't help myself.

Once, when I was filling in during the weekend shift, she came in and had to sign the off-hours log. I introduced myself and learned that her name was Christina. The next few days I'd say hello and her name, which surprised her, and she'd have to glance at my tag to respond. Sometimes I felt her looking past me when she said hello.

One afternoon as I was finishing up my shift I saw her near the mail drop, talking to a coworker. I steeled myself and approached. She saw me coming but didn't register me until I asked her if she had a minute. Her friend did a double-take after she saw my uniform. She glanced at Christina curiously. Christina eyed her friend, then said to me, Sure, what's up? Her friend stepped away, but remained within hearing distance.

I asked if she wanted to go out for lunch, since I was getting off work. As I was talking I saw something shift in her eyes. It was hard to know exactly what I saw, but it was something akin to dread and realization. I could almost read her mind: Oh, no. The surprised look moved from discomfort to pity. She said, Oh, I don't know. I don't think so. Thanks anyway.

I said, Sure, no problem. Have a good day.

As I walked away I heard her talking to her friend in a low voice, and I waited for laughter, but thankfully heard none. She no longer smiled at me after that, and never used my name. I stopped saying hello, since she seemed annoyed when I did. When all of the Tronics security team received memos that told us to avoid fraternizing with the employees, I knew immediately who had complained, and couldn't look in her direction after that. I dismissed any notions of romance from my life. I focused on work. I got back into shape. I went running often.

I used to run almost every day. I liked to run as a teenager, and remember more than anything else of those days with my aunt my sweaty, blurred view of the streets of Oakland, near the Piedmont border, as I jogged up and down the hilly sidewalks, dodging dogs and illegally parked cars. I liked hearing only my heartbeat in my head. I liked feeling the burning ache in my legs. I steadied my breathing, timing it with my heart, and pushed through the heavy evening air with rhythmic pleasure.

As I walk through downtown Palo Alto, I remember those runs and want to return to that sense of movement and freedom. I tried the treadmills at the gym a few times, but it feels strange to run in place. I tell myself to start running again. I think about Christina from Tronics, and am surprised that I still remember her name. That was almost four years ago, and I've tried not to dwell on it. It surfaces only when I start feeling sorry for myself.

I don't see any Japanese restaurants near the post office, which I expect, and I walk up and down the street, double-checking. Although a parallel street, University, has more restaurants and stores, I stay on Hamilton, looking into the few coffee and gift shops, wasting time, since Linda isn't supposed to show up for fifteen minutes. I ask a waiter at the Caribbean Café if there is a Japanese restaurant nearby. He mentions two restaurants on University, but doesn't know of anything else along this strip. I ask what the oldest store on this street is, and he shrugs, pointing to the cleaners directly opposite us. "That's been there ever since I can remember," he says.

Royal Cleaners is busy with a line at the counter. A humming, mechanized mass of hanging clothes wrapped in soft plastic feeds in from a back room. I watch the clerk, a tired-looking woman with a Stanford T-shirt, taking orders and retrieving clothes from the rotating rack. I wait until the customers are gone, then approach the counter. She yells for someone in back to sweep the floor, and a teenager's voice answers, "In a sec!"

The voice reminds me to call David tonight. I ask the woman about a Japanese restaurant that used to be next to the post office, about twenty years ago.

She smiles in surprise. "Do I look that old?"

"No. Not at all—"

"Let me ask my uncle. Hold on." She goes into the back. An older man in his fifties walks out.

I ask him what I asked his niece, and he thinks about it. "I remember a Japanese restaurant. It wasn't very good."

"It's not there now," I say.

"No. It was there for a while, and moved about eight or nine years ago. It did well."

"It moved or closed down?"

"Moved. Just a few blocks away, off University. A bigger place. Next to the kitchen store." He points farther down Hamilton.

I thank him and leave. It's past six now, so I hurry to the post office and find Linda leaning against the front railing, watching cars pull up to the curbside mailboxes. I stop before she sees me. One of her legs is hooked behind her on a lower rung, and she is resting on her elbows, her body leaning lazily back. Her hair partially hides her face, but when she looks up at the dark orange-and-gray sky, her body set against the streetlights, I study her profile, the collar of her leather jacket falling back and exposing her slender throat.

I call her name. She straightens, and unhooks her leg. She waves.

"I found out where the restaurant is," I say. I continue looking at her smooth neck.

"It's still around?"

I look up. "Yeah, but it moved. I don't know if it's the same owner or anything, but it's supposed to be this way." We begin walking, and I say, "Thanks for coming."

"I want to."

"Even if it's a dead end?"

She nods, but doesn't seem to be listening. She says, "Look, I'm sorry about this afternoon."

"About what?"

"About being curt with you, when you asked me about my weekend."

"Oh, that."

"I know how it looks. I ask you a whole bunch of personal questions, and as soon as you ask me something, I get defensive."

I shrug. "You're just doing your job."

"Still."

"So you're saying you're going to tell me about your weekend?"

"What do you want to know?"

"Who's the guy?"

She turns to me. "A friend of the chef's. He was hanging around the restaurant, and we got to talking. He's an investor."

"And you saw him two nights in a row?"

"It went well."

"Are you seeing him again?"

"Yes."

We turn the corner and I see a restaurant. "That might be it," I say. The Samurai is a sushi bar with a dozen small tables. We peer through the window—only a few customers inside. I ask, "How should we do this?"

"Have you eaten yet?"

I shake my head.

"Let's eat here. We can ask more casually."

"I haven't eaten out this much in years."

"My treat," she says, opening the front door and walking in. The sushi chef behind the bar greets us and motions with an open hand to take a seat anywhere. We sit at a window table. The smell of barbecued beef rolls in from the kitchen. A young Asian waitress hurries out of the back with two menus and asks us if we want anything to drink.

"How about a couple of beers?" Linda asks me.

I agree. The waitress jots this down and returns to the back. I look around. There is an air of exhaustion to this place; the menus are frayed and creased, the table unsteady, and along the grimy walls are sun-faded photographs hanging next to a few framed and yellowed clippings of good reviews. Even the music piped through a small pair of speakers crackles with age.

"What's the name of the guy?" Linda asks.

"Louis Stein."

The waitress is returning with our beers. She asks us if we are ready to order. Linda decides on chicken teriyaki, and I choose a small sushi platter. Before the waitress leaves, Linda asks, "By the way, do you know a Louis Stein?"

The waitress stops. "Oh, you know Lou?"

"Is he here?"

"He's at his other restaurant, but he should be dropping by soon."

"His other restaurant?" I ask.

"The Samurai at the mall."

"He owns them?"

She nods, checking her watch. "He'll be by in an hour or so."

She gives my order to the sushi chef and disappears into the back. Linda says, "You said he knew your father?"

"Probably. But he definitely knew Milian."

"We'll wait, then. Eat slowly." She sheds her jacket and leans back with the glass of beer in her hand.

I say, "You're not wearing your wedding band anymore."

"You noticed."

"You stopped after this weekend."

"Well, well," she says. "Not much gets by you." She holds up her hand and looks at her bare finger. "It seems unnecessary."

"Did the guy say something?"

She smiles. "No, but he noticed it."

"And you told him you weren't married."

"I did. I realized I didn't like what the ring meant."

"You did at work."

"People already know there that I'm divorced. I guess I was just used to wearing it."

"You never told me why you got divorced."

"I know." She stays quiet.

I don't ask again. A couple walks into the restaurant, and the waitress appears, directing them to a table near the sushi bar, then hurries to us with our miso soup. As soon as the waitress leaves us, Linda sighs. "It's a boring story. I was a dumb college kid. He began to get mean."

I look up. "Mean?"

"He was older than me. I was young and stupid. We met when I was in high school and continued dating."

"And you married . . ."

"When I was a sophomore at Cal State Long Beach. It was a very stupid move."

I'm not sure what else to ask, if this is too personal. "What'd your parents say?"

Rolling her eyes, she says, "They were pretty mad. Actually, I heard from my sister that he's trying to contact me."

"What?"

"I think he called some old friends down in L.A." She waves it off. "I'd rather not think about it. It's just so ridiculous."

The waitress approaches with our dinners, and Linda looks grateful for the interruption. She asks me about ProServ as we start eating, and though I know she's trying to change the subject, I don't press the issue. I mention my impending move into the field, and when she asks me about how I feel. I admit I'm nervous. "I'm so used to working with Paul."

"Do you think I can go with you when you work sometime? Maybe I can do a story about it."

"I don't know. My boss is pretty strict about fieldwork."

"I'll ask him. It could be good publicity."

"You'd also have to clear it with the client."

"You don't want me there."

I stop. "I don't."

"Why?"

"You'd make me self-conscious. And I'm not in the right mind-set. If I was still working with Paul, it'd be fine."

She nods.

Another customer comes in, a skinny man wearing a short-sleeved T-shirt and khakis. But the sushi chef gives him a glance and doesn't greet him. "It's him," I say.

Linda turns and watches him as the waitress appears, then talks to him. She motions toward the back, explaining something, and Louis Stein replies. I try to remember if I have ever seen him. His thin, bare arms are taut and knotted from physical work. He glances at us as the waitress continues speaking.

"Good evening," he says to us as he approaches. "You were asking for me?"

"Louis Stein?" I say.

He smiles. "How can I help you?"

"Did you work for a company called Shilla Shipping a while ago?"

He looks mildly puzzled, then cocks his head. "A long time ago, yes. What's this about?"

I notice the web of wrinkles around his eyes, and despite this and his thinning, graying hair, he could pass for his mid-forties, though I know he must be older. I say, "You might have known my father, John Hyung Bul Choice? My name is Allen."

His face remains impassive for a moment, then recognition washes across it, his eyes sparking. "You're John Choice's son?"

"So you remember him?"

"I do. My God, how old are you?"

"Thirty."

He presses his hand on his chest, his biceps flexing, and lets out a whistle. "I'll be damned. I knew your father pretty well. I was the third-shift floor manager."

"Would you like to join us for a second?" Linda asks.

"Oh, this is Linda Maldonado, my friend," I say.

She says hello to Stein. He smiles at her but continues shaking his head at me.

"Junil Kim told me about you," I say.

"Junil? You're kidding." He laughs. "He's not still working there, is he?"

"No, no. He's retired. We didn't talk long. He's in Milpitas."

"How's your aunt doing?"

"You knew her?"

"Through your father."

"She's okay. Have a seat," I say.

He hesitates. "I don't want to interrupt—"

"I came here looking for you."

He considers this, then pulls up a chair. He asks me what I'm doing, and when I tell him, he says, "You weren't involved in that Florentino's thing, were you?"

"I was."

"Christ. I couldn't believe something like that could happen."

"Actually, that's what this is related to," Linda says. "The man that was shot, Allen's partner, was moonlighting for Roger Milian—at least we believe so—and we were wondering what you could tell us about him."

Stein kept still. "Milian's mixed up in this?"

"We don't know. It's a guess," I say.

"I thought it was a kidnapping attempt or something."

"It's just that whenever we try to talk to him, he stonewalls," Linda says.

"That's not unusual," Stein says. "He's a paranoid, secretive bastard."

Linda grins. "Don't hold back now."

"Yeah," Stein says. "He gets me going."

"And after we kept trying to talk to him, two men came by my place," I say. I point to the bruise on my forehead.

"Really? I'm surprised. He's lost his subtle touch. I don't remember him sending a goon squad around."

Linda mouths the word "goon" a few times, trying it out. Stein keeps looking at me and shaking his head. "John's son," he says quietly.

I ask, "So you didn't get along with Milian?"

"No. He eventually canned me. Best thing to happen, though, since I ended up in a new business. But he was a bottom-liner and didn't give a crap about anyone."

"Bottom-liner?"

"Money man. Profits. He'd keep cutting our benefits, overtime, to boost his profits."

Linda asks, "Was he involved in illegal activity?"

Stein turns to her. "Are you a cop?"

She shakes her head. "I'm just helping Allen."

Stein says, "It wouldn't surprise me, but I don't know for sure. Unless you mean workplace violations and hiring illegals."

"He did that?"

"Sure. And he pushed us into longer shifts. Tried to set us against each other with bonuses only going to one guy. It was a poisoned place to work."

"My father never mentioned that," I say. "No one liked working there?"

He sighs. "Your father was an honest, hardworking guy. He took a lot of shit."

"Like what?"

Stein grimaces and sits back. "I'm real sorry about what happened to him. I was going to go to the funeral service, but someone told me it was going to be in Korean."

"It was."

"Your aunt took it hard."

"She did?" I ask. My memories of that time are of movement and action, of bustling to and from my old apartment to my aunt's place.

Linda says, "What kind of things did his father have to deal with?"

"Milian seemed to go extra hard on him," Stein says to me. "Maybe it was the education thing—Milian never went to college and your father had a fancy degree and was studying for some kind of test."

"Test?" I ask. "What kind of test? You don't mean for medical school?"

"Right. Milian loved the fact that your father was driving a truck around."

"I don't get it," Linda says to me. "Why?"

"It was a language problem. He could never get his English into any shape."

"That's right," Stein says. "He had a lot of trouble." He glances out the window as a young couple passes by. He says, "His death was . . . bad."

"Were you there?" I ask. "During the accident?"

"No. Someone should have been there, which was strange—"

"Why?" Linda asks.

Stein turns to her and says slowly, "Why? He knew better than to unload a rig by himself. He never did anything like that before. And I never got it why he came in after hours."

"He was running late," I say. "He had to unload something that day, but was taking care of me because I had the chicken pox. And wasn't that merger happening soon? So maybe he was worried about his job."

"Our parent company was merging, but no one really knew if our jobs were in trouble," Stein says. "Maybe you're right. I don't know. I never liked the way that whole accident was hushed up."

We become very still. Linda finally says, "In what way?"

"No real investigation or inquest. Cal-OSHA dropped by and called it human error without a real review. Milian probably kept it all quiet because of the merger. Maybe worried about a lawsuit. Who knows?"

"I think he gave my aunt a settlement."

"Probably a lot less than if she had sued."

"You don't think there was anything unusual about his death, do you?" Linda asks, her tone softened.

"Unusual?" Stein says. "Sure there was. He wasn't supposed to be there, he was never that careless, and everything was hushed up? Of course."

"I mean, would you have any reason to suspect that his death wasn't an accident?"

Stein's mouth opens, but then closes. He thinks about the question, looking up at the ceiling. Linda and I wait. There is something about the hardening of memory that has kept me from imagining other possibilities; the stories and explanations told to me when I was younger quickly became accepted fact. Even Junil Kim's new information hasn't quite registered with me. An accident or a heart attack—they are both failures of mechanics, of systems whether man-made or man-sustaining. After a minute, I say, "Could Milian have wanted my father dead for any reason?"

Stein turns toward me. "Son, I don't know. Your father never bothered anyone to my knowledge."

"Was a man named Durante there when you were?" I ask.

"Allen," Linda says. "He would've been a kid then."

"Right," I say.

Stein is confused by this, and says, "No, I don't know that name."

Linda asks, "So, could Allen's father's death have been intentional?"

"I really don't know. A cover-up? Maybe. But you mean murder? I don't know."

"Is there anyone else we can talk to about WestSun and Milian?" Linda asks. "Either current or former employees?"

"Current? I have no idea. I haven't been near Shilla in twenty years. And you spoke to Junil?"

I nod.

Stein runs his finger along his lips and says, "I can't remember a single name."

"What about Milian? Is there anyone close to him we could talk to?"

"I was third shift: nights and weekends. You can try and find the first- and second-shift floor managers." He sounds doubtful, and adds, "Though there was a high turnover because Milian was such a hard boss. And I never really met any of them."

"Who would you suggest we talk to?" Linda asks.

"To find out more about Milian?"

She nods.

He cracks his knuckles while thinking. The waitress comes over and asks if everything is all right. He smiles and says it is. To us he says, "Maybe his wife?"

"Ex-wife," Linda says. "I believe they divorced some time ago."

"Even better," Stein says. "I didn't know that, but an ex-wife is always a good place to start."

"What more can you tell me about my father?" I ask.

They turn to me. Stein says, "A real plugger, a nose-to-the-grindstone kind of guy. I always believed he'd make it out of there, the way he hit the books."

"Are you sure he was studying for med school?"

"I think so. Textbooks and all that."

I always thought he had given up on that after my mother had died. A decade had passed and my father had been thinking again about returning to school, perhaps his finances improving, perhaps my aunt helping with me enough to ease his responsibilities. As I grew older I required less baby-sitting, and spent more time by myself; maybe this helped my father too. And yet I can't remember a single time at home when he had studied or even opened a book.

Stein pushes out his chair and begins standing. "Well, I've got a lot of work to do. It was great talking to you, but I have to get back to the mall."

"Thanks for helping us out," Linda says.

"Don't know how much I helped. Come by again." To me he says, "Good to see you."

"Can we call you if we have more questions?" Linda asks.

He nods and hands her a business card. He says, "By the way, dinner is on me. Order up anything else you want."

I say, "We couldn't—"

"I want to. And if you see Junil again, give him my best."

We thank him and he disappears into the back. Linda watches me and says, "You okay?"

"I'm fine." I listen to the rapid chopping of the sushi chef, the crackling, hollow music in the background. I keep thinking about my father studying textbooks.

"I'll try to find out more about Milian's ex-wife," she says.

I nod.

"He seems like a nice guy."

I agree. It's dark out, the headlights of cars flashing by the front window. Linda seems to read my mind. She says, "Let's go. You've had a long day." She smiles. I'm surprised by her look of concern. I remember her word "mean" to describe her ex-husband, and this with all the incomplete information about my father makes me feel uneasy. Too many variables. Too much uncertainty. I touch the back of her hand lightly and thank her.

The next evening I wait for David at ProServ, the entire day a blur since I rushed to finish the paperwork before the end of the week. I met with Doney for a few minutes today to talk about the team. I'll be second, with Johnson and Lauren Alexa as the third ring. Alexa is one of the newer members of ProServ, and Johnson, the one who seems nervous around me, has been here for a year. I mentioned to Doney how I haven't done group work in a while, and that I'm getting a strange feeling from Johnson. Doney dismissed this. "It'll iron out in a day or two. This will be routine. We'll start the threat assessment Friday morning, nine a.m. sharp."

ProServ is almost empty. Polansky stays an hour later, and stops by my cubicle before he leaves. "Group work on Friday?" he asks.

"Looks like it."

"You okay about it?"

I say I am. He glances at the paperwork on my desk, and I say, "I'll be done by tomorrow."

"I know. Is the kid coming by now?"

"Yeah. Charles cleared it with you—"

"He did. It's fine with me. You'll be the last out, so make sure you activate the alarm."

I nod.

"You ever take up the counseling I told you about? It's free."

"No. I appreciate it, but I don't think I need it."

"All right," he says. He turns to go.

"What did your father do for a living? When you were growing up."

This stops him. He smiles. "My old man? Why?"

"I've been thinking a lot about this kind of stuff lately."

Polansky rests his arm on the top of the divider. "I guess all that's happened . . . Your father died a while ago, right?"

"Yeah. Remember, we talked about it—"

"Of course. When you came in. My old man did a lot of things, but for a long time he owned a couple of shoe stores."

"Really?"

He smiles. "Women's shoes. I hated it, seeing him kneel in front of old rich hags and kissing up to them. But he made a decent living. He wanted me to take over, but no way."

"You went into the Marines."

"You bet I did. My kid brother took over for my old man, but then soon sold out to some chain. Made a bundle."

"I didn't know you had a brother."

"He's in New York now, managing for Wal-Mart or Kmart or one of those places," he says, waving his hand. "But what's going through your head?"

"What? Nothing. Just thinking."

"How old are you now?"

"Thirty."

"You're still young. Wait until you hit the big five-oh. Fifty. That's when you really start thinking about those things." He hears something and turns toward the door. "The kid might be here. I'll get out of your hair."

"You can stay and—"

"No. I gotta run. I'm already late." He gives me a quick, casual salute, and says, "See you tomorrow, Choice."

I watch him slip out, and wonder if he's uneasy around David. I set aside my paperwork and walk toward the front entrance, looking out into the parking lot. David hasn't arrived yet. I plan to show him around, maybe pop in one of Polansky's assassination videos—nothing too gory, of course—and talk about what Paul did. Then I'll buy him some dinner. Maybe I'll take him to my gym. What the hell do kids do?

Cars speed by on Shore Drive. Everyone is racing home. I think about Polansky's father fitting shoes, handling feet all day. That doesn't sound too bad. At least he didn't have to move tons of boxes and drive an eighteen-wheeler six days a week. I want to ask my aunt about my father's studying. Could he really have been thinking about going back to school?

An image of my father comes to me. He is hunched over a book, a large book. Not a textbook. He flips a cardboard page, plastic crackling. It's a photo album. I'm very young. Five years old? He is completely absorbed, and when I approach he doesn't look up, and lets me sit next to him. I'm wearing pajamas and one of my pant legs pulls up to my knee as I try to settle in next to him. He glances at my bare shin and tugs the pant leg down. He smells of stale cigarette smoke. In the album there are photographs of him and my mother, sunny shots of them individually and together at the beach. My mother, in a black bathing suit, is very pale, and my father has a farmer's tan: his forearms and half his biceps are dark, his face and neck brown, but his chest is glaringly white. "That's you?" I ask.

"When I younger." He is about to flip to another section, but I point to my mother. He nods and says, "Yes. Your mom." He waits until I have seen enough, then his thick and calloused fingers delicately turn the pages. I eventually grow bored. It isn't until the next year that I realize he is following a ritual—he goes through the photo album, adding pictures that he might have taken that year, reviewing older pictures, on that particular day, my mother's birthday.

I plan to ask my aunt for that photo album. I'm fairly certain she wouldn't have thrown it away.

Sonia's Toyota pulls into the ProServ parking lot, and I return to my desk, turning off my computer and tidying up. I hear the front door opening. I stand, and am surprised to see only David. He waves.

"Where's your mom?" I ask.

"She just dropped me off. Is it okay for you to drive me home? If not, I got to call her."

"It's fine," I say, suspecting that she's avoiding me, that my showing up late that day I wanted to check Paul's files annoyed her. "How about a quick tour, and then we can decide what you want to do."

He shrugs. I lead him around the office, trying not to feel nervous. He's just a kid. He keeps throwing his hair back, and nodding with sleepy eyes as I tell him what we do in the different rooms. He turns to me with interest when I show him the video room and mention the assassination tapes. "I can show you one, if you're into it."

"Cool."

We sit down at the conference table and I load a tape I know well. The amateur video, taken by a tourist and subsequently broadcast on Mexican TV, is of a kidnapping. Five masked men, believed to be members of a drug cartel, pulled a typical "plug and stopper" maneuver, where a stopper car, driving in front of the victim, either stages an accident or simply stops. The plug car, directly behind, traps the victim. In this video, the victim is a high-ranking Mexican judge, apparently pushing a drug prosecution case forward. Before I play the tape I tell David that it's a little violent.

"Cool."

The shaky, slightly blurred video begins of a parade, but quickly pans away at the sound of a crash. A compact car, its front end crumpled against a lamppost, is smoking. I begin narrating for David, explaining that this is the stopper car and the two masked men, jumping out and running to the target car, are the point team. "The car behind is the plugger. See how it's making a U-turn?" Another two men climb out of the plugger car. All of them are armed with handguns. Although I turn down the sound, we can still hear the person with the camera saying, "Oh my God. Do you see that?"

I pause the tape. "Now this is where it gets a little violent. You sure you want to see this?"

"Yeah."

I press play, turning the sound all the way down. The woman who is taping it will yell, "They shot him! They shot him!" and someone else will tell her that they have to get out of there. The two men from the stopper car move to the driver's side of the victim's car and shoot the driver and another man, who turned out to be the judge's personal security. As this is happening, the two men from the plugger car yank the judge out. All four men drag the judge to the plugger car. They get in, then drive off. Everything is finished in under two minutes.

"Damn," David says as I stop the tape and rewind it. "That was real?"

"Yeah. Maybe I shouldn't have shown that."

"No, it was good. My dad had to protect people from that?"

"It's not as bad here, but we definitely have to prepare for it."

"Man," he says. "But that's not what happened with you guys."

"No. We don't know. Basically, your father was so quick and alert that he caught that motorcyclist off-guard, and was shot because of it."

"Man." He thinks about this, then nods toward the TV. "What happened to the judge?"

"Killed. The Mexican authorities refused to deal."

"Man."

"Hm. Maybe you shouldn't tell your mother you saw this."

"Yeah. She wouldn't like it too much."

"How's she doing, anyway? Is there a reason why she didn't come in here?"

"No," he says, looking at the row of videotapes on a bookshelf. "She's working a lot right now."

"She's working tonight?"

"Not tonight, but other nights," he says, reading the labels on the tapes.

"You have dinner yet? How about some pizza?"

He looks up. "Pizza. But what about another tape?"

"They're not going anywhere. You hungry?"

He says he is, and I motion for him to follow me.

We spend the next two hours at a pizza place downtown. David doesn't have many questions for me, but I tell him about the jobs Paul and I had. It isn't until we finish up dinner and start heading out that the conversation moves to tae kwon do, which seems to loosen him up. He wants to start practicing again, but doesn't like the school system.

"How so?" I ask.

"The belts and the test. And I got to pay every time I take a test. It's kind of a scam."

"You could do it yourself."

"I never know if my form is good."

I tell him about my own training, how I started at Korean churches, and then taught myself. I offer to help him, though I can't give him any official belt rankings.

"That'd be great. All you got to do is tell me if I'm doing things right."

On the drive home, David is quiet, and I ask him if everything is okay.

"Yeah. I got a bunch of homework to do."

"You're not still cutting classes, are you?"

"No. They called my mom at work."

I head into Palo Alto. As we approach his house I ask, "What happened?"

"I'm grounded, except for this." He points to us. I pull up in his driveway next to Sonia's car. The light over the front door flickers on and David says, "Don't tell her about the tape, okay?"

"I won't if you won't."

"Can we see more some other time?"

I nod. Sonia opens the front door and walks out toward us. She's wearing jeans and a gray sweatshirt. I kill the engine. David climbs out and ignores his mother as he walks by. Sonia studies him, then turns to me. She sighs and comes to my window. "How'd it go?" she asks.

"Fine."

"Come in for a drink?"

I hesitate. "David says you're pretty busy these days—"

"Come on. I'm making coffee." She stands back and waits for me to climb out. I wonder why she hasn't returned any of my calls. She doesn't seem annoyed at me.

"Did you get my messages?" I ask as I follow her into the house.

"Oh, yes. Sorry. I've been putting in a lot of overtime."

"I just wanted to ask about Paul's moonlighting—" I stop when we walk inside. The boxes of Paul's things that were in the hallway are gone. I'm about to ask where everything is, but remember that she doesn't know I was in here. I say, "Did you get a chance to look through his things?"

"I checked a little, but it was mostly junk. I threw a lot of it away."

"You threw it away?"

"He had reports from years and years ago."

"It might have been important," I say, disturbed. If David hadn't let me in, I would never have found the further connection with WestSun.

"Why?"

"I'm looking into one of the companies Paul freelanced for, and I have some questions."

"What kind?"

"For one thing, they're denying Paul ever worked for them. You might have thrown away any evidence of it."

"It might be a legal strategy," she says. "I'm beginning to see how things really work now. Did you know Polansky retained a lawyer in case I decided to sue?"

"What?"

"I just had some questions about Paul's 401(k) and a life insurance policy through ProServ, and Charles directed me to a lawyer."

"I didn't know this."

"It was just a question, for crying out loud." She pours me a mug of coffee and sits with me at the kitchen table. "I'm sure they're worried about me suing for some kind of wrongful death or workplace compensation."

"Can you?"

She looks pained, and rubs her eyes. "I just want this to be over. I can't take much more of this."

"I'm sorry," I say. I'm not sure how to mention Paul's notes again.

"You have nothing to be sorry about. You're the only one from ProServ who showed any kind of class, talking with David and everything." She stares down at her coffee, then nods toward the living room. "Did he tell you he's grounded?"

"Yeah."

She turns to me. "He did? He seems to trust you more than either me or Paul."

I don't know how to reply. She studies me, tilting her head and resting her chin on her bony fist. "How're you doing? How're you holding up?" she asks quietly.

"I'm all right."

"Are you really?"

The way she says this, almost unbelieving, makes me think. I pause for too long. She says, "One of these days I'll make you a real dinner. Paul said you live on TV dinners and takeout. Is that true?"

"More or less."

She smiles. "You're not touching your coffee. Would you rather have a drink? Beer?"

I say, "This is fine. I should get going soon. I've got a long day tomorrow."

"At ProServ? They don't deserve your concern." She pulls out a bottle of rum from the cupboard and pours a shot into her coffee. She says, "No, I don't mean that. Charles is just a little slippery. Stay awhile. I could use the company."

"I have to finish up all my filing tomorrow. I'm going on group work on Friday."

"Group work? Why not paired?"

"They want to ease me back in."

"Are you sure it's not a demotion?"

"Yeah," I say, though I'm suddenly unsure.

"Be careful with them. They weren't very straightforward with Paul."

"You mean solo work."

"Especially that. Not paying him enough. And I probably don't know the half of it. But it sure didn't help our problems."

"What do you mean?"

She says, "You didn't know?"

"About what?"

"We were having problems. Marriage problems."

I stare. "What?"

"Nothing too serious," she says quickly. "We were just wrapped up in our own things, and had trouble talking. We were thinking about separating for a short while, to get things straightened out."

"He never said anything."

"Of course not. He never does. Did."

I try to see this, but can't. "I was just thinking about that Christmas party where you two seemed fine."

"Oh, that," she says, waving her hand. "I can't believe he dragged me there. I did the best I could. You should've heard the fight we had that night."

I don't like hearing this, and stand. "Well, it's been a tiring day—"

"It's still early," she says.

"I could crash right now."

"Please," she says. "A little while."

I nod, and bring my coffee to her, motioning to the rum. She smiles and pours some for me. The bottle gulps out too much. I hold up my hand. "That's good."

"You can hardly taste it."

"I want to be able to drive home."

She raises an eyebrow and says, "We'll be good."

I hear something more in her voice, a teasing that makes me uncomfortable. She raises her mug in a toast, and we clink them together. "To friendship," she says. The rum taste is too strong. Sonia watches me with a small grin. I realize that she might have been drinking before David and I arrived. I ask where he is.

"Probably in his room, doing homework."

"I like him. He's a good kid."

"Is it true what Paul once said about you," she asks, "that you live like a hermit?"

"Did he say that?"

"A long time ago, when he first got to know you."

"I live alone, but I don't know if I'm a hermit."

"Are you seeing anyone?"

I shake my head and move back to the dining table. She pulls out the chair next to me, angles it toward me, and sits down. I say, "How long were you and Paul having problems?"

"Not long. That's why I didn't know a lot about his extra work."

"Why did you throw out all those papers?"

"Every time I looked at them I felt terrible. I felt worse."

"Why?"

Her jaw tenses. "I feel guilty."

I wait for her to explain. Footsteps from another part of the house approach. We both look toward the living room, and David appears. Sonia smiles tightly. "Yes?"

"I'm beat," he says, glancing at me. "Can I finish my homework in the morning? I'll get up early."

"How much do you have left?"

"Just a column of math problems. That's it."

"Okay. Kiss me good night."

David hesitates, then walks to his mother and pecks her on the cheek. I shake his hand. He thanks me again for dinner. "And maybe you can check out my forms?" he asks.

I nod.

Once he leaves, Sonia looks puzzled. "Forms?" she asks.

"Tae kwon do," I say.

"Really? I thought he'd lost interest."

"In organized classes. Is that clock right?"

"Is it ten already?" she says. "God, it feels like I just got home."

I clear my throat, and ask, "Why do you feel guilty?"

"What?"

I repeat the question. She sighs, finishes her rum and coffee, and finally says, "We'd been having problems with money. His extra work started because of that. Sometimes I wonder if he was tired from working too much, and maybe he wouldn't have gotten killed . . ." She looks down into her empty mug.

"No. He wasn't tired. He was completely on. It was his alertness that saved us."

"That's what your Mr. Polansky said. But I don't know."

"Believe me. If it had been me, it would've ended up even worse."

"Is that true?"

I nod. "I didn't hear the motorcyclist until the firing started. Paul was five steps ahead of me."

Sonia rubs the back of her neck and hits one of her earrings. "God, am I still wearing these?" she says. She unclasps the swinging gold pendants, laying them on the table. She looks down at her sweatshirt and says, "I look like a frump."

"You look fine."

"I didn't realize you were coming."

"I've been here too long," I say, pushing my chair back. "I really should leave."

She grabs my arm. "Allen. Stay awhile."

I keep still, staring at her hand. I feel the warmth passing through my shirt. My past attraction to her is strong, and her touch reminds me of the times I watched her with Paul, here in this house, how affectionate she was with him, laying her fingers on his shoulder. She kissed his ear. Were they having trouble even back then? Maybe this is why I haven't been invited over for dinner the past few months.

Sonia moves closer to me and puts her other hand on my thigh. She says, "Stay awhile."

"I don't know," I begin, almost stuttering. "Paul . . ."

She pushes our mugs away and stands slowly, resting her hand on my thigh, then sliding it off. She looks at me without moving, and keeps her right hand locked on my forearm. Then, after a full silence, she lets go, holds my gaze for a moment, then walks out of the kitchen, past the living room, and disappears down the hallway to the bedroom. My face is flushed, my neck sweating. I exhale. Shit. My heart is beating so fast that I press my palm over my chest. Shit.

I think about David and remember that his bedroom is only a few steps away from his parents' room. This is Paul's house, for Christ's sake. His bed, his family.

Sonia is waiting for me. I can't decide what to do. I stand up, and wince. I haven't been this excited in a long time. I turn off the lights in the kitchen and walk toward the front door, listening for sounds coming from the bedroom. I hear a clock ticking. I turn toward Sonia's room, turn back toward the front door, then turn around again and walk slowly through the house, trying to keep my steps quiet. I keep thinking, What are you doing?

In the hallway I stop and examine a row of small paintings hanging at eye level. Sunflowers and daisies. I hear the swish of fabric on fabric coming from Sonia's room, and exhale slowly. Can I do this? Sonia is moving around, the floor creaking. For a moment I wonder if I misinterpreted her and if I am about to make a mistake. A huge mistake. I move toward her doorway and peer in.

Sonia is wearing a paisley satin bathrobe, and stops throwing dirty clothes onto the floor when she sees me. I'm about to say I don't think this is such a good idea, but she puts her finger to her lips and shushes me. She motions to David's bedroom and pulls me in, closing her door. She leans in and whispers in my ear, "We have to be very quiet."

"I don't know about this," I say in her ear. I smell coffee around her, and for some reason this makes me more excited.

She touches my shoulder. "You can go if you want to."

We are only a few inches apart. Her cheeks are red, and I see that she has just washed her face. She is waiting for my response. I move closer to her, resting my arm around her waist, our legs pressing together. She touches my neck, and we lean in to kiss. This seems to shut off the resistance in me, and I pull her tightly into me, the feeling of her closeness a shock, and I have to touch her arms and cheek as we pull apart. "I can't believe this," I say, touching her cheek again. She smiles. She walks to the door and turns off the main light. A small reading lamp beside the bed is still on, casting shadows around us. I pull her toward me, tugging at her waist belt, which comes undone; her robe falls open and I see that she is naked underneath, her breasts partially hidden in the semidarkness, smooth skin along her stomach. She presses up against me, and when I touch her warm skin, my fingers running up her stomach and along her breasts, she becomes still and closes her eyes. I stop.

"No. I like that," she says.

We move to the bed and she lies back, opening her robe further. I run my fingers over her skin, lingering around her nipples, dragging my nails lightly over her arms and legs, and she sighs. In the dim light I memorize the contours of her body, her breasts still marked along the sides from her bra, indentations that I stroke, her nipples hardening; as I begin kissing them, I feel her hands reaching across my back, pulling me closer, tugging at my shirt. I move away and undress. She watches me.

I crawl up along the bed, kissing her legs, and stop when I reach the soft fluff of hair that tickles my forehead. Her legs move farther apart, and when I kiss her there, she says, "Oh," in a startled, low voice. I continue kissing her, pushing myself against her and tasting a sharpness that I can't define, amazed that here I am and here she is and we are together in her room, her bed. She lets out a quick breath as I press further into her, trying to taste all of her, and after a few minutes she grabs the back of my head, signaling me. I wince as she presses the healing bump where I was hit, but I don't say anything.

I kiss a trail up her stomach, along her breasts, then slowly rest on top of her. She reaches toward the night table and points. I'm not sure what she means until I pull open the drawer and find a package of condoms. I nod and put one on.

We continue kissing as I rub myself against her, the condom making it more difficult to feel the warmth. I try to push harder and feel myself slipping into her. She stops and says, "It's been a while."

"What?"

"It's been a while." She looks uncertain.

"It's been a while for me too," I say. I start to pull away, but she grabs my waist tightly and holds me there. We begin moving in rhythm as I bury my face in her neck, my disbelief of where I am and what I am doing almost making me giddy. I stifle a small laugh, and she stops. "What?"

"Sorry," I whisper. "I can't believe we're doing this."

She wraps her legs around me, tightening her grip and forcing me deeper inside her. "Believe it," she says. She closes her eyes and leans her head back. I begin moving more slowly, and ignore a sting of conscience as I hear her mumble "Yes" to me, our bodies so tightly hugging that I feel her quick heartbeat against my own, our chests hot and slick with sweat, and she feels so good engulfing me, squeezing me against her, that I say, "Thank you," and she grins without opening her eyes.

20

Ernest Doney is the lead, and he runs through the threat assessments and primary locations for the software executive. We are going to spend all of today—Friday—and most of tomorrow preparing for Mr. Yin's arrival, scheduled for Sunday afternoon. Pro-Serv was hired for around-the-clock attention, seven days, six nights, while Mr. Yin attends the convention during the days and meets with other company executives and analysts in the evenings. When Doney shows us Yin's schedule, we groan. Very little downtime. Yin is going to squeeze in as much as possible during his visit here, and that means ProServ has to be a day's prep ahead of him throughout the week.

Doney will coordinate everything and will be the liaison with the security at the convention hall; I'll be the contact with the Bartley Hotel; Alexa and Johnson will work with the various software companies and brokerage analysts who will be meeting privately with Yin. This, along with two of us on Yin twenty-four hours, means a lot of overtime this week. I don't mind. I'm paid time and a half.

All morning Doney lays out the itinerary and goes through the possible threats, particularly in light of the Florentino's shooting. At one point in the talk Doney asks if I have anything to add about off-premises security. I reply that although the leak for the location at Florentino's could have come from the other executives, I can't rule out a tail, despite our caution.

"You couldn't mark a motorcycle?" Johnson says.

"Of course we could," I say. "We didn't see one. A tag team could've just as easily come through."

He frowns, and I see Doney watching us. Johnson is young, maybe only twenty-two or twenty-three, and I recognize the brashness. I see his affected five-o'clock shadow, his double-breasted jackets, his platinum pens, and I see "hotshot." He thinks Paul and I screwed up the Sorenson job, and there isn't anything I can say to make him believe otherwise.

Alexa clears her throat and asks, "Do you think the Tank is too easily identified?"

"Yes," Doney says. "But try and tell Polansky that."

"No more identifiable than an armored limo, which Triumph uses," Johnson says.

Alexa nods. She recently had a tattoo added on her upper arm, a rose with barbed wire wrapped around the stem, and with her sport jacket off, the bottom spikes of the wire peek out from her T-shirt sleeve. We are all dressed casually today, since it's an unofficial rule to wear comfortable clothes during the long and tiring prep sessions.

Doney waits for another response, and when there isn't one, he goes on about the airport security checklist, which isn't a high priority but will become one from now on. I am to work out the general advance security checklist, making sure everyone else receives copies. I have to interview the Bartley Hotel manager tonight, with a possible follow-up tomorrow, and appoint and inspect Yin's room. The list of things I have to do is growing, and after yesterday's rush to finish the paperwork, I am worn out.

I still haven't spoken to Sonia since our meeting two nights ago.

That our evening together was a mistake became clearer with each day. The awkwardness with which we spoke to each other as we dressed that night, as I stumbled across the floor trying to keep quiet, was painful. "Do you want to stay?" she asked quietly, though from her tone I knew she didn't want me to. When I didn't answer immediately, she said, "You'd have to leave before David wakes up."

"No, I should go," I said. I was dressing in the dark.

"Are you okay?"

"Yeah. You?"

"It was nice."

Dread filled me. I only wanted to get out of there fast. I finished dressing and looked for my shoes, feeling along the floor.

"What are you doing?"

"I can't find my shoes."

"Cover your eyes. I'll turn on a light."

"No, no. They should be right here." I knelt and swept my arms around me, straining my sore back. I hit a shoe and grabbed it, finding its mate. The silence extended and I said, "Found them."

"Shh. Not too loud."

"Sorry." I stood. "I should get going." I heard her getting up and I said, "You can stay put. I can lock up."

"Allen . . ."

"Yeah."

"I don't think we should tell anyone about this."

"I know."

"It's just that it might not look—"

"I know," I said. "I know what you mean."

I hesitated, then felt along the wall for the door. "I should go. Thanks."

"Good night."

I left her bedroom and walked quietly toward the front door. Once I made it to my car, I shivered in the evening chill, buttoned my shirt, and grimly mulled over what had just happened. Idiot. I started to drive away, glancing back at the house, and thought I saw a face hidden behind a curtain. Startled, I couldn't tell if it was Sonia. The face disappeared. What worried me was that it might have been David.

Once I arrived home I called Linda, wanting to talk to someone, but either she wasn't answering her phone or she wasn't there. It was eleven-thirty. Was she on another date? I took a long shower, paced around my apartment for an hour, then tried to sleep.

Doney is now explaining a few points on the threat assessment forms we have in front of us, and I try to focus. I feel guilty for not calling Sonia yesterday, and know if I don't call her today, it will look even worse. I still haven't talked with Linda either. Doney is asking me a question, and I catch the tail end: ". . . interview on Sunday before checking in?"

I nod. "You mean briefing the client?"

He looks alarmed. "What? I'm talking about the hotel manager."

"Oh, right. All that will be taken care of."

Doney stares at me for a moment, then continues talking about a group briefing on Monday morning with Yin before the beginning of the convention. He says, "All right. That's enough for now. Break for lunch, and then take the rest of the afternoon setting up your individual assignments."

We stand and head out. Doney says, "Allen, can you hold up?"

I stop. Alexa and Johnson glance at each other as they leave the conference room.

Doney walks to the door and closes it slowly. I sigh.

"How's it going?" he asks.

"All right."

"Are you here? Is everything back to normal?"

"More or less."

"What does that mean?"

I say, "I rushed yesterday to finish all that paperwork Charles gave me. I'm trying to get back in work mode."

Doney straightens his tie and erases the notes he made on the marker board. He has the rumpled, formal look of a tired teacher. He says, "Allen, are you ready for this?"

"I am."

"I lost you at the end of this meeting. Where were you?"

"Thinking."

He folds his arms and shakes his head. "You know, Charles was thinking about bringing in Brodie as second."

"What? I've been here—"

"It's not about seniority. It's about getting the job done. Hell, Johnson asked to second this job."

"Johnson?"

"I know. I laughed. But you got to admire his balls."

"Goddammit."

"I told Charles you'd be fine as second. Don't fuck up, Choice." His eyes turn cold, and he waits for my response.

"I won't fuck up."

"All right. Check in with me this afternoon when you've set up the Bartley Hotel."

I leave the conference room, my temples pounding. I don't need this crap. I think about Paul freelancing, his own problems with Polansky and Charles probably worse than he revealed to me. Paul didn't tell me anything, especially about his marriage. I didn't know a thing about his life.

I skip lunch and call the hotel manager at the Bartley. They've worked with ProServ before, so we set a time to meet this evening to take care of the initial details of Yin's arrival, which include choosing his room, preapproving the surrounding rooms, and talking with the head of security. On my own I'll survey the area and map out the routes to and from the convention hall. I'll have to drop by again on Sunday, right before check-in, to do a last-minute sweep as well. My "to do" list grows. I start typing up my own advance security checklist, skewing it for the hotel.

My phone rings. When I answer it, Linda says, "You busy?"

"A little," I say. "I tried calling you last night and the night before."

"I know. I was out late."

"One of these days I'm going to meet this guy."

She says, "I found Milian's wife."

"How?" I ask. Milian. All that seems so distant.

"Divorce records at the county clerk. She's living in the city."

"Will she talk to us?"

"I called her and she seemed okay about it. She didn't care. You have time tonight?"

"No. I have to work. Tomorrow?"

"I'll check. Let's say tomorrow afternoon."

I agree. "How are you?"

"Fine. The other night you called late. My machine said almost midnight."

"Yeah."

"Something happen?"

I look around. Charles is at the copy machine. Although he is out of earshot, I don't want to say anything. "I'll deal with it. I did something stupid."

"What?"

"Yes," I say, raising my voice. "I'll talk to the head of security tonight, when I drop by."

"Huh?"

"Yes."

"Oh, I get it. Okay. Can't talk."

"Yes," I say.

"When will you be done tonight?"

"Maybe nine o'clock?"

"Hm. I won't be around."

"Oh, really?"

"Yes, really. I hear you smiling. I'll talk to you tomorrow, then."

"All right."

"Are you okay? Is something going on?"

Charles stops his copying and is leafing through some papers. I say, "We'll talk later."

"Be good," she says.

This stops me. "What? What do you mean?"

"Nothing. Just an expression. I should go now."

I say goodbye and hang up. Be good. That's a strange thing to say to me. I return to my advance security checklist, but keep thinking about Linda and her new boyfriend.

21

Linda drops into the passenger seat with a smile and says, "To the city, Jeeves." We meet in Monte Vista and agree to take my car to Mrs. Milian's home in the Marina district. Linda laughs and jokes at my driving, saying I deserve my Volvo for handling it like an old lady. She is in a good mood, and I say, "You took too many happy pills today."

"Ha. Ha. Did you see that? A ninety-year old guy in a Yugo just sped by."

"I'm a careful driver."

"A kid on a skateboard just passed us."

"Boy, you're pretty high today."

"Such a nice day." She looks out the window. "Weekends are nice, aren't they?"

"Well, I've got to work tomorrow."

"What're you doing?"

I tell her about the new assignment with Yin. Last night I met with the hotel manager and the head of security, and tomorrow all of us will be preparing for Yin's arrival.

"This is for the software thing?"

"Are you covering it?"

She snorts. "They won't let me get within a mile of that place, unless it's about the diet of the conventioneers."

"Ouch."

She turns to me. "You're looking kind of worn-out. Is it from working?"

I say it is, but immediately think of how my schedule is out of sync because of that night with Sonia. The guilt feels worse with Linda right next to me. I say, "So when will I meet the mystery man?"

"The mystery . . . oh, him."

"Yeah, him."

"Soon, I guess. He's in Seattle for the weekend on business."

"So it looks like I'm the second string, then."

She winks. She remembers something and says, "Tell me what was so important that you called the other night."

"Never mind."

She sits up. "What do you mean? Yesterday you said you did something stupid."

"Did I say that?"

"You certainly did. What, was it something about your aunt?"

"My aunt? No."

"Tell me."

"It's nothing," I say. "I was tired and wanted someone to talk to."

She rolls down the window. Her hair flies back and her blouse flutters. She closes her eyes for a moment to feel the wind. She turns to me and has to raise her voice: "What'd you want to talk about?"

I can't tell her. I know how stupid I was. I know how she'll look at me. I say, "Why did you think it was about my aunt?"

"I figured our meeting with Stein made you want to talk to her again."

We head into the city off 101 and up Van Ness, the wind from Linda's window blowing around us. It's cooler here, and the closer we come to the Marina, the more chilled I get. I promise myself to call Sonia soon, knowing each day I wait makes what we did seem worse. My excuse to call will be David; I promised to practice tae kwon do with him.

"It's a left on Bay, and then two blocks," Linda says.

We find Krista Milian's townhouse easily, a two-story stucco building with dark green shutters. I'm surprised by how clean everything looks around here. I can't see any litter. The pastel colors on the facades are bright and pristine. "She knows we're coming?" I ask.

"Yes. She was curious about the whole business."

We approach the front door. "You'll do the talking?"

She says, "We'll play it by ear. She sounded easygoing enough."

When Mrs. Milian answers the doorbell, she welcomes us in with a wave of her hand and immediately offers us drinks. Her eyes bounce between Linda and me, taking us in. She relaxes her expression, the corner of her mouth rising into a smooth smile. We introduce ourselves and accept her offer of coffee. She calls out to the kitchen, "Sara, could you bring three coffees?"

"Yes, ma'am."

Linda suddenly looks uncomfortable. We are in the main living room, with vaulted ceilings and a skylight high above, a second level sectioned off with a low wall and winding staircase, rooms hidden from view. A few paintings lit by recessed lights glow on the walls. Mrs. Milian asks us to sit down and directs us to a sprawling U-shaped sofa with dozens of throw pillows.

"We don't get the *Sentinel,* but it looks like a very good newspaper," she says to Linda.

"Thank you."

Mrs. Milian, in her mid-fifties, has a leanness to her face that belies her heavy frame, her loose slacks and blouse deftly concealing her thick arms and thighs. She sits down facing us, clasps her hands together, and says, "I trust nothing we talk about will end up in the paper."

"It won't. This is strictly background."

"I don't mind if you crucify Roger. But I don't want my name anywhere near it."

I smile.

A young Latina woman in a light blue uniform walks out of the kitchen with a mahogany tray and three small porcelain mugs filled with coffee. Mrs. Milian is saying, "But I don't know what I could tell you. I haven't seen or spoken to him in seven or eight years."

Linda nods, and glances at the woman serving us. The woman bends forward with the tray and lets us take our mugs; she then places on the coffee table a tiny pitcher of cream and a small bowl of sugar, a teaspoon dug into the mound. I try to catch the woman's eye to thank her, but she keeps focused on the coffee table. Linda turns back to Mrs. Milian. "How long were you married to him?"

"Only for about six years. After we divorced I remarried and stayed married for eighteen years. Edward passed away over a year ago."

"I'm sorry."

"Thank you, but he'd been sick for a while. Sara, that's all for now."

Sara nods and withdraws into the kitchen. This is the first time in my life I have ever seen a real maid. I say, "May I ask why you and Mr. Milian divorced?"

Linda cringes. I realize I've been too blunt. "Oh, that's very personal," I say quickly.

Mrs. Milian laughs. "It's all right. He was having affairs, and was quite unpleasant to live with."

"You kept his name," Linda says.

"I did, didn't I? Actually, my name now is technically Milian-Barney, my late husband's addition. But yes, I kept Roger's name. At the time it seemed logical, but now, of course, I'm not sure why I did it."

"Paperwork," Linda says. "I kept my ex-husband's name as well."

"Ah, yes. And my maiden name was Stark, which I never liked." She stirs her coffee and turns to me. "What's your interest in Roger?"

"He was the employer of my late father."

"Oh, really? Who was your father?"

"You wouldn't have known him. John Hyung-Bul Choice?"

She thinks about the name for a moment, then says, "Choice. It sounds familiar. He wasn't the one who wanted to be a doctor—"

"Yeah!" I say, surprised. "I can't believe you remember that! You knew him?"

"Not really. I believe he was over at our house a couple of times back then."

"Your house? But he was just a driver."

"Was he? I don't remember."

"He drove a rig."

She shakes her head slowly.

Linda asks, "Was your husband ever involved in any activity that might be considered . . . illegal?"

"Illegal. He rarely told me about his work. But he was in trouble with the IRS for a while."

Linda continues asking questions about Milian's work, which Mrs. Milian doesn't know enough to answer. I'm still amazed she knew about my father. "Did you actually meet him, my father?" I ask.

"I believe so. Once or twice. A nice young man. Very quiet, intelligent."

"How did you know he wanted to be a doctor?"

"I think Roger made some joke about it."

Linda says, "Do you know anything about the accident?"

"Accident?"

I say, "My father's accident."

"What accident is this?"

Linda and I glance at each other. "My father died in an unloading accident," I reply.

"At Shilla Shipping?"

"Didn't you know that?"

"Back then? He died in an accident back then?"

"Almost twenty years ago," I tell her. "When he was unloading a rig."

Mrs. Milian frowns, the wrinkles around her mouth deepening. "I didn't know this. But I might not be remembering. Roger never told me much."

I study her, wondering if she's lying. She doesn't seem to be.

"Do you remember any other employees?" Linda asks. "Especially the names of any shift managers?"

"It was quite a while ago," she says. "I hardly remember my own name." She turns to me. "Did Roger pay your family any workmen's compensation?"

"I think he paid my aunt something."

"Your mother?"

"She died when I was born," I say. "So you don't know why my father would be at your house?"

"I guess it was work-related, though now that I think about it, Roger would never have had a driver at the house. Maybe it was something else. I can't believe he never told me about your father's death."

"We spoke to one shift manager who said that the accident was covered up," Linda says.

I add, "It might not even have been an accident—"

"We don't know that," Linda says quickly. "It's completely hypothetical."

Mrs. Milian says, "So is this about your father?"

"Yes."

"Partly," Linda adds. "It's about Allen's partner, who worked briefly for your ex-husband, and who was then killed. Mr. Milian has refused to talk to us."

"You think Roger had something to do with it?"

"We don't know. We're just trying to find out as much about him as possible."

Mrs. Milian turns to me. "Do *you* think Roger is involved?"

I pause, weighing my words carefully. "He seems to be lying to us about my partner's connection to him. He has since refused to talk to us. It feels . . . suspicious. After we kept trying, two men visited me and warned me to stop asking so many questions." I point to my forehead.

"Oh, my," she says, staring.

"Can you help us?" I ask.

"Who was the shift manager you spoke to?"

I say, "Stein. Louis Stein."

"No, I don't know that name. There was someone else, a man who was fired and sued, but lost. He was a manager. It was in the newspaper at the time. He accused Roger of all sorts of things."

"Do you remember the name?" Linda asks.

"No, but I believe it was around the time that the Son of Sam killer in New York was arrested. I remember that news story also."

"This man suing your ex-husband was in the papers?"

"Yes. It made Roger so angry."

"We'll look it up."

"And Mr. Choice . . ." she says to me.

"Call me Allen."

"And Allen, I'm sorry about your father. I didn't know." She presses her lips together and looks at me with pity.

"It's all right."

"I suspect your father was at our house for personal, not work, reasons. Roger liked keeping the boundaries sharp."

"I can't imagine them being friends."

"Neither can I, but this news is disturbing. There must have been a reason for his concealing your father's death."

"For covering up the entire accident."

"Perhaps your Mr. Stein wasn't completely wrong."

"What do you mean?"

"My ex-husband could be a cold, ruthless man. Frankly, I was frightened by him. My divorcing him was more a matter of his divorcing me, and I was glad for it." She looks at my forehead. "And I am not surprised by his use of violence. I am not surprised at all."

"You don't think he could've been involved with my father's death, do you?"

"I don't know. But I think you might be wise to be more careful."

Linda asks if it would be all right to call again if we have any more questions. Mrs. Milian says it would be fine. We thank her for the coffee, and she shows us to the door. She looks hard at me and says, "I am very sorry about your father. You were left an orphan at a young age."

"My aunt took care of me."

"Nevertheless, it's unfair for a child to be deprived of his parents."

This digs into me. Linda thanks her again. In the car I drive back to the South Bay, and I say, "He must have done it. He killed my father."

"Allen, we don't know that."

"Look at it. Milian killed him, or had him killed, and covered it up. He paid off my aunt to keep quiet."

"Allen, take it easy." She knits her eyebrows and studies me.

I say, "Just look at it."

"We can't make that leap yet."

But the thought clings to me and grows.

Part 3

The Block in Motion

22

Mr. Yin, a tall, lanky man with heavy horn-rimmed glasses, is constantly baffled by our presence. His company insisted on protection that he feels he doesn't need, and although he listens to our instructions with interest, he always has on a disbelieving, amused expression. He stares at us with the corner of his mouth rising up into a half-smile; his eyes, already magnified by thick lenses, widen even more. At one point during the initial briefing on Sunday, when Doney is describing the target-hardening procedures, especially when Yin will be outside of the hotel or the convention hall, Yin says, "You're kidding. Someone is with me always?"

"It's for your own safety, Mr. Yin," I reply. "We'll be as discreet as possible, but we need to maintain constant surveillance."

"What about the bathroom? What if I have to go to the bathroom?"

Johnson says, "Then Alexa here will go with you."

Yin looks shocked, then realizes that Johnson is kidding. We laugh. Doney explains that there will always be someone in the vicinity, but of course he'll be alone in his hotel room and at other times. "But whenever you're in any public location, we'll be near you."

"And we check out public bathrooms before you enter them," I say.

"When I'm in my hotel room, where will you be?"

"Next door," I say. "And possibly in the hall."

"Jeez." He studies me.

"You're important to your company and therefore to us," Doney says smoothly, and we go on with the briefing.

By Tuesday we establish the twelve- and six-hour shifts, depending on where Yin will be and who is leading the security. Only one of us needs to be at the hotel during the graveyard hours, and we alternate six-hour shifts, but during the days Yin has two of us on him at all times, the pairs rotating the central location. Doney is usually on Yin at the convention hall, Johnson or Alexa during the private meetings in the afternoons, and I work at the hotel in the early evenings. Ideally we would have one or two more agents with us, but Yin's company is already paying over fifteen grand per week for the four of us.

Doney's detail is the most difficult, because of the sheer number of people in the convention hall and the lack of organization with the daily events. Although there are seminars and lectures at scheduled times, most of Yin's activities consist of wandering up and down the aisles, visiting booths, and talking to company representatives. Yin's job requires him to know of any new applications and search for possible competitors and alliances. He is apparently well known, since he is constantly running into old colleagues and friends, and is invited out to lunch and dinner every day. He declines most of the invitations. The few he accepts cause us more work.

Doney has an appointment book that he is continually updating, adding lunch and dinner meetings and reassigning us to scout the locations. We urge Yin to have his meals at the hotel restaurant, but he smiles and shakes his head.

At the convention hall I meet a former Tronics coworker, now doing security at Sun, who has heard about the Florentino's shooting. We speak briefly, but Doney gives me a look that tells me to move on. Working with a new team leader is always difficult, since everyone has a distinct style. Paul gave me enough credit to know not to speak for too long with someone.

Doney has the inner perimeter, sticking to Yin, while I take the outer perimeter, circling them as they move from booth to booth. There is security everywhere, including a contingent from Triumph—I recognize one of the small triangular lapel pins they use for quick identification—who seem to be with a group of three conventioneers. ProServ rarely uses lapel pins since Polansky never takes on jobs that require a dozen of us changing shifts. He keeps it small, and makes sure there is always a ProServ point man who will instantly recognize Pro-Serv people and direct the assignment.

I notice a man walking quickly toward Yin. Doney does too. He intercepts, and I begin scanning for other threats. But the man is a friend of Yin's and is greeting him. I relax.

One of Triumph's security is watching us, and he smirks at me. He isn't sure at first what we are doing until Doney and I go back to our perimeters. The man then nudges his partner and says something; they both study us before returning to their detail. Triumph is larger and better-known than ProServ, though the Florentino's shooting raised our profile a bit. We consider ourselves their rivals, but to be frank they probably don't think twice about us.

The noise level in here is growing, voices rising as computer demonstrations and music from the booths compete for attention, and I focus on the dozens of conventioneers streaming near Yin, watching the fringes for any unusual activity. It feels good to be back at work, real work, with all my thoughts directed toward one thing, Yin.

A river of people rushes by, parting around Yin and Doney, then merges behind them; Doney puts his hand on Yin's shoulder and draws him away from another approaching crowd. Everyone is getting too close, and I quickly become point guard, hurrying ahead of them and forcing an opening. The Block in motion. Doney and Yin follow. We work our way to a quieter aisle, and Yin begins talking with a woman in a Management Software booth. I back up, trying to get a better overview.

In midafternoon my shift is over. I am exhausted. Alexa and Johnson take over for Yin's meetings, but I have to return at nine tonight at the Bartley. I have enough time to eat, shower, and nap. I drive to my apartment and don't bother with any of the first two tasks—I fall onto my futon and go to sleep. I haven't even taken off my suit, so when I awake three hours later, my tie chokes me, and I'm sour with sweat and the stale smell of the conventioneers' cheap cologne. My answering machine is humming, rewinding, which means I've just missed a message. I pull myself up and replay the tape.

It's Linda telling me we need to talk. I call her back.

"That was fast," she says.

"I was asleep."

"Already? Did I wake you?"

"I was on all morning, and have to go back tonight. What's up?"

"I found the name of the manager who sued Milian. Noah Garvey. But I'm still looking for more information about that lawsuit and where this guy is now."

"How'd you find the name?"

"An old *Chronicle*. But it didn't have that much information about the lawsuit itself, so I'm going into state court records."

"I should help."

"Well, that's why I called. You need to talk to your aunt again. We have to find out more about your father's death. When did he die?"

"When I was ten."

"And you're thirty. Something is strange here," she says. "Everything was happening around then—the merging of the company, the lawsuit, your father's death."

"They might be related," I say.

"They might be."

"Should I call her now?"

"No. Talk to her in person."

I think about my schedule. "I won't be able to until tomorrow night. Will you come with me?"

"Me? What can I—"

"You're better at this. I can use your help."

She is quiet for a moment, then says, "All right."

"How does this connect with Paul?"

"I don't know. I'm beginning to wonder if it does at all."

"It has to. There has to be a link."

"Allen, random things happen. It might be a coincidence."

"I don't believe that."

She sighs. "Well, it's still too early to tell."

"Thank you," I say. "For doing all this."

"It's not just for you," she says. "Remember, if we find anything, the story is all mine."

"All yours. I promise."

"Even your story."

"Your exclusive."

We agree to meet tomorrow after my shift is over. I take off my clothes and fall back to sleep. I have another waking dream, and watch myself get shot. I feel the bullets hit my chest. I wake up, wipe off the sweat on my arms and neck, and drift off again. This time it's better.

When I show up at the Bartley Hotel, I am rested and alert. Johnson is in ProServ's room, reading a newspaper. "Yin's going to bed," he says.

I nod, and check my watch. I'm fifteen minutes early. "You can go."

Johnson snaps the newspaper closed and throws it on the night table. "Alexa went to get some coffee. Will you tell her that I'll do the shift report tonight?"

"Yeah. How'd the meetings go?"

He shakes his head. "Boring." He loosens his tie and checks himself in the mirror by the door. He pats down his thinning hair, rubs the stubble on his cheeks, and turns to me. "So they catch the guy who hit Paul?"

"Not yet."

"You know, your stock is up right now."

"What's that?"

"Your stock. Triumph has heard of you. Black Diamond also. You can probably ask Polansky for a raise. Hazard pay or something."

I take this in. Johnson wants second position for this job, and now he is giving me career advice. I say carefully, "Maybe I'll mention that in the next review."

"The annual review isn't for, what, seven or eight months? By then everyone will have forgotten."

"Not everyone. Not Polansky."

"Suit yourself. You'll just be doing paired work forever."

I study him. "I doubt that, and I've only done paired for a year or so. There's time."

"But now you're doing group again."

I try to keep my voice steady. "Thanks for your interest, but I can take care of myself."

"Suit yourself."

"You should be careful of the hard sell, Johnson."

He stops and turns. "What?"

"The hard sell."

"What're you talking about?"

"Even if I left group and paired work, there are four or five others who'd move into paired before you."

"So?"

"You're pushing too hard. You're too obvious, trying to get second in this job and now hustling me out. Your strings are showing."

His face closes up. "I don't know what you're talking about."

"Yeah, sure," I say. I smile and add, "Just do your job, and you'll do fine."

Annoyance flashes across his face. He is about to reply, but stops himself. He turns and walks out, mumbling something under his breath.

"What was that, Johnson? You say something?"

He turns and says, "No." A dead expression.

I smile. "I think you've forgotten. As second I do your and Alexa's performance evaluation."

From the way he tenses, he must have forgotten.

"You have a nice night," I say. "You think about that."

He leaves abruptly, and I hear Alexa say, "Where're you going?" She walks in with two large cups of coffee and glances back out the hallway. "What's with him?" she asks me.

"Nothing."

"He didn't want his coffee."

"I'll take it. You can go on. He said he'll do the shift report tonight."

She puts down the cups and glances at her watch. "I still have fifteen minutes."

"That's okay," I say. "Anything happen tonight?"

"Nope. Yin asked about you, though."

"What about?"

"He wanted to know what kind of name Choice is and what your background is."

"Background? You mean ethnic?"

"Yeah. I had no idea."

"Korean," I say. "How is Johnson doing? You working well with him?"

"He's okay. Kind of pushy. Young." She fixes her belt holster. "Are you wearing body armor?"

I shake my head. We've all been issued Monarch vests, but wearing them is up to us. Most of us don't unless there's a definite threat, like a known stalker, but even then the Monarchs are rated midlevel protection, and with the armor-piercing bullets out there, there's a mood of skepticism. There are higher-rated vests, but they're expensive, heavy, and hot. And Paul, even if he had been wearing a vest, wouldn't have been any better off. Not with a bullet in his head.

I ask Alexa, "Why?"

"Just curious. Johnson said you must be spooked after Paul."

Goddamn that kid. I say slowly, "Yeah, I'm more alert, but unless the threat assessment changes, I'm going do it the way I always do."

She sips her coffee, then says, "Am I on at three a.m?"

"You are."

"I'll get going."

I nod, and watch her leave. I settle back in the chair, the door propped open, and look over the floor plan: Yin is in the next room; across the hall is a couple; the room on the other side of Yin is empty for now; and, for the next five nights, the rooms diagonally across from Yin and me are occupied by conventioneers. The Bartley Hotel security guards patrol the halls every hour, and I've met all three of them in person, making sure I can recognize them easily. Their Polaroids went to the others.

I hear Yin's door opening and jump up. He steps out of his room. I quickly intercept and say, "Mr. Yin, can I help you?"

He's in a robe with an ice bucket in his hand. He looks at me sleepily, trying to focus without his glasses. "I just need some ice."

"Let me get that for you. Stay in your room and lock the door."

"Is everything all right?"

"Yes, of course. But you should let one of us take care of things like this." I take the bucket from him and wait until he has gone in and locked up. I sigh. I hope he hasn't done this earlier. I'll have to mention it in my report and ask the others about it. Doney should reemphasize our roles to Yin, that we ought to be with him if he ever leaves his room. I hurry down the hall to the ice machine.

On the way back, my senses heightened by the silence around me, I feel different working this job, especially here, alone, in the hotel. Some might consider this the boring part, the long isolated watches with nothing to do, but I prefer it to the crowded, bustling, high-alert shifts like in the convention hall, where there are too many things going on. Here, with my protectee in one place, the variables are fixed, the conditions constant, and I focus on externals. I'm in control.

Interesting. I don't seem to feel the dis-ease.

I knock on Yin's door, telling him who it is, and hand him the bucket of ice. He thanks me, and I hear the sounds of the TV news as he closes the door and locks up. I look up and down the hall, smelling cigarette smoke—possibly one of the conventioneers—and return to ProServ's room. I sit on the bed, the TV on but the volume off, my door propped open, and I listen to the faint sounds of traffic outside, the creaking of people in rooms, the mini refrigerator humming. I focus on the hallway, waiting for footsteps, voices, movement. Waves of me emanate out, encircling Yin and his hotel room. I feel good. What should I call this? I've temporarily escaped the inertial deception because of a purposeful and meaningful task. I'm connected, functional, and alert. I need to name this, and decide to call it the *engagement,* since this seems to stave off the deception through work. It's a form of battle. I'm at war. Skirmishes.

As the hours pass, however, I begin to get distracted. I try not to think about Paul's death. How would he work with me on this job? He'd double-check the stairwell doors, making sure they're locked outside but unlocked inside. He'd reinspect the windows and Yin's balcony. He'd go over tomorrow's schedule. I'll do all that soon. I need more worthy tasks. I still have four hours to go. My mind wanders to my father and what I've learned so far. I think about Linda and wish I had told her about Sonia. Now it's too late. Missed chances. I force this out for now. I have to concentrate on my job. The dis-ease begins to creep back in. I do some push-ups, finish Johnson's cold coffee, and rove the hallway.

23

Aunt Insook is expecting us, but still blinks in surprise at Linda's presence. She steps back to take us in, her eyes flickering between us. She straightens herself and buttons up her thin sweater. I have to remind her that Linda is a friend who is helping me out.

"Helping what?" she asks.

"Find out more about Shilla Shipping, or WestSun Imports."

"You are girlfriend?" she asks Linda.

"No. I'm a reporter and am working with Allen on this story."

"What story?"

"About WestSun."

My aunt nods and leads us to the living-room sofa. It's only eight o'clock in the evening, but she seems to have been heading to bed, the lights off here but on dimly in her bedroom. She turns on a few lamps and says, "You stay short. I had a tiring day." The bay windows are uncurtained, and with the interior lights filling the room, the glass reflects our images against the darkened sky.

"Of course," Linda says. "If this is a bad night, we can come back another time."

I glance at her. It's a long drive up here.

"No, you're here already," Aunt Insook says. She sits down. I notice

Linda sniffing, and realize that the house smells vaguely of Korean food, hints of garlic and peppers. I associate these smells with childhood.

I turn to my aunt. "Did you know that my father was studying to go back to medical school?" I ask. "A couple of people mentioned it."

"Your father? Before your mother died, he wanted to be a doctor."

"No, I mean later, at Shilla. He was studying to go back to school."

She shakes her head. "I don't think so."

"That's what people said."

"What people?"

"Louis Stein, one of the shift managers, and even Krista Milian, the ex-wife of Roger Milian."

Aunt Insook looks uncertain. "He never said to me."

Linda and I are standing over my aunt. I move to the side and lean against the armrest."Were you two fighting a lot?" I ask. "I seem to remember that."

"Not a lot. We argue a little."

When I recall the few dinners with my aunt and father present, I hear either silence—or more accurately the clinking of silverware and the drone of a radio—or heated arguments in Korean, harsh guttural sounds flying across the table with only a word or two having any meaning to me. My name, Sung-Oh, occasionally pierced through the blanket of noise, and it was jarring to register any references to me; for some reason I had believed that because they spoke English to me, any conversations about me would be in English. I soon suspected otherwise. Right before my father died I began getting a better sense of what he might be saying, not from the words themselves but from his gestures, tone, and inflections. I knew when he was talking about me not just from my name, but from a timbre of concern that usually crept into his voice, a faint undercurrent of apprehension.

I ask my aunt again, "Are you sure? I remember fights at the dinner table."

"I hardly have dinner with your father. I go home after he comes home."

Linda sits down next to her and says, "So how long did you know Roger Milian?"

"Not long. I met him just a couple of times."

I turn to her. "I thought you said you didn't remember him."

"I didn't," she says. "But I thought about it more. I remember him now."

"What do you remember?" Linda asks.

Aunt Insook sighs. "He was Hyung-Bul's boss. He made everyone work hard."

Linda says, "When did you meet him, Roger Milian?"

"When? I can't remember that. It was so long ago."

"Didn't you meet him when Allen's father died?"

"No. I met with lawyers."

"How much was the settlement?" Linda asks.

I can see Aunt Insook bristling, her lips pressed together, and she shakes her head. "I don't remember." She never liked revealing how much money she had.

"But it was a lot, wasn't it?" I ask. "Enough to have paid for me."

She replies, "No. It paid for father's funeral expense, and for college, but that's all."

"But I never finished college. Is the money still there?"

"No. I use for your regular expense."

I'm about to question this, but a sharp look from Linda silences me.

Linda says, "Were you told to keep quiet about your brother's death? Was that a condition for receiving the money?"

"Condition?"

"It was a settlement, but did you have to promise not to talk about the accident? Did you sign release forms?"

She thinks about it. "Maybe. I signed papers, yes. I don't know if I wasn't allowed to talk about it."

"Did you ever think there might be something suspicious about your brother's accident?"

"Suspicious? Why?"

"You noticed that your brother and his boss didn't get along, didn't you?"

"No. I didn't notice."

"But," Linda says, confused, "didn't you and your brother argue about that? His boss?"

Aunt Insook looks startled. "I . . . maybe sometimes."

"You argued about his boss. What in particular?"

"It was so long—"

"But there must be something you remember."

Aunt Insook hesitates, then says, "Maybe he puts his job in danger."

"Yes," Linda says. "He jeopardized his job. Was it over the working conditions?"

"I don't know."

"Why did you think he was jeopardizing his job, then? Did he do or say anything?"

My aunt tries to remember, and I'm amazed that Linda is getting this much. Aunt Insook says, "He just didn't care about his job. He wasn't careful."

"How so?"

"He was friends with troublemakers."

"Noah Garvey?"

Aunt Insook, dazed by the rapid questions, stops for a moment. "I think so. I don't remember. I'm getting tired."

Linda nods slowly, then says, "Of course. I'm sorry. We'll get going. You've been helpful."

"It's late," my aunt says.

"It is." Linda stands up to leave.

I ask, "Do you remember that photo album my father used to have? The one with pictures of my mother?"

Aunt Insook stares at me, her expression distracted. "Album?"

"Photographs of my mother."

"I don't think so." She walks us to the door.

"Thank you again," Linda says. "If you think of anything that might be helpful, any memories of Roger Milian or your brother, I'd appreciate hearing from you." Linda hands her a business card.

"All right," Aunt Insook says, pocketing the card without looking at it. She turns to me. "Good night." She rubs her eyes and squints.

As Linda and I return to my car, I say, "Damn, you're good."

She looks down with a small smile.

"She's hiding something," I say.

"Yes, but I don't think it's what you're thinking."

"What's that?"

"I think she's feeling guilty."

"About my father?"

"No. Not directly. You know what I think?"

"Tell me."

"I think she used the money that was supposed to go to you."

I stop walking. "How do you . . . ?"

"You dropped out of college, right?"

I nod.

"If Milian gave your aunt enough money for your college, and you dropped out and went to work, where did that money go?"

"She said—"

"Did she provide for you after you dropped out?"

"Hell, no."

"That could be a lot of cash."

I tally up tuition for four years. "But where could the money—"

"You said she was a bookkeeper, right?"

"Yeah."

"She could've invested it, then used it to help her retire."

"Or buy a house."

"Or buy a house."

"Damn," I say, not sure if I should be angry. "I wonder if I can get that money back."

"I doubt it. It sounds like Milian paid her off, but not officially. She probably signed a release that silenced her, but the money wasn't legally required to go to you or anything, like a trust. You would've known about it when you turned twenty-one if it was a legal trust."

"Just 'Here's the money, keep quiet, and use it for your nephew.' "

"And 'Sign here, please. If you talk about this publicly, we can suc your ass.' "

"So my dropping out of college probably helped her," I say.

"Maybe."

"Oh, that's sneaky."

"She probably would've paid for your college if you had stayed in."

"What if I decided to go back?"

Linda smiles. "That'd be interesting. You should ask your aunt."

I turn to her. "You are really good."

She punches my arm lightly. "Shut up."

"I'm serious."

"Let's get going. I'm starving."

"Dinner?" I ask.

"Yes, but not cold cereal tonight, if you don't mind."

"My treat. I'm getting a lot of overtime this week."

"Well. Big spender."

We climb into my car, and she says, "To the restaurant, Jeeves. And step on it."

"I'll try."

"And don't drive like an old lady."

"I like driving like an old lady. What's wrong with old ladies?"

She grins and punches my arm again.

24

After dinner, Linda returns home to finish up an article and I head to my apartment. Although I don't have the graveyard tonight, Doney and I will be driving Yin to the convention hall at eight-thirty tomorrow morning. Today I was on duty twelve hours, six to six, and after the drive up to Mill Valley I'm having trouble concentrating. I give up on the idea of going to the gym or trying a short run, and limp up my stairs, collapsing on my futon. My feet are tender, the heels rubbed raw. Yin did a lot of walking today.

I explained this at an Italian restaurant to Linda, who is very curious about my work. She had conducted a quick search at work of Yin's company and found that with his stock in the company, Yin is on *High-Tech* magazine's list of the five hundred wealthiest technology-related business-men in the country. "Number four seventy-eight," she said. "Not bad."

"Funny. He doesn't seem rich," I said.

"How does he seem?"

"Normal."

We shared two pasta dishes and talked about trying to find Garvey. Although I wanted to learn more about my aunt's settlement from Milian, Linda didn't see the purpose. "Consider it gone. Maybe she used it to pay for the house."

"I know, but it bothers me that he bought her off, that she took the money."

"She might not have had many options."

"I'd still like to know more."

"Unless she's willing to talk, I don't know . . ."

"We have to get to Milian. He has the answers."

"Not a chance."

"We should try again. What if we get him outside of work?"

Linda watched me carefully. She said, "I don't think he's going to say anything, especially if he's the one who sent the two men to warn you."

"I have to do something. I can't just sit around."

"All right," she said. "Maybe you should go back to that man who knew your father—Kim. Find out if he knows anything about Noah Garvey and the lawsuit. Also go to Louis Stein and ask the same thing. We need to piece together what was going on at the time. Your aunt said your father was friends with troublemakers. We have to find those troublemakers."

I knew I was getting tired because I had trouble following her. Junil Kim. Louis Stein. I nodded.

"And we can forget about Paul's connection, if there is any," she said.

I didn't like this, but couldn't think of a response.

"We might not get to Milian," she said, more to herself now. "But maybe we can get to the other guy, his manager . . ."

"Who?"

"The guy who ran when you called him."

"Durante."

"Right. Maybe through him we can find out about Paul and what he did for them." She rubbed her temples. "This is getting to be a handful."

"Still think there's a story here?"

"There's something. Maybe more than a story."

"Like what?"

"A book. A long magazine article." She sighed. "Anything but a few inches by a lifestyle writer."

"We'll make it work," I said. "Newspapers will be begging for you when you do this."

She gave me a small, indulgent smile.

"I'll try to follow up Kim and Stein tomorrow," I said.

"What about your job?"

"I'll fit it in." I then tried to cheer her up by asking about her boyfriend.

She looked up at me. "I wouldn't call him that quite yet."

"Oh."

"I haven't seen much of him lately. I think he's tiring of me."

I thought of Sonia, guiltily reminded that I hadn't called her yet. I was too embarrassed to tell Linda. It would've sounded awful. I had taken advantage of a grieving widow. My partner's wife. What an idiot I had been.

Our moods dampened, she told me she had some work to do. Before we said goodbye, I said again, "I thought you handled my aunt really well. You got information I could never have."

She tilted her head, checking my expression, then said, "Thanks."

Now, as I go over this conversation while lying on my futon, I wonder if I should have asked her more about her boyfriend. Maybe she wanted to talk about it, but I kept conspicuously quiet after her opening; I must have missed a cue.

The thought of Sonia pushes me toward the telephone. The longer I avoid calling, the worse it looks. I dial her number, and David picks up. Relieved, I say hello and ask, "Things have been busy the past few days, but I haven't forgotten about our tae kwon do."

"Good," he says. In the background I hear Sonia's voice. He says, away from the phone, "It's Allen."

"I'll be finishing up on Sunday," I tell him. "We'll try after that."

"What should I be working on?"

"Getting back into shape, especially if you haven't stretched in a while."

I hear him talking again to his mother. He says, "Okay. Here's my mom." I hear movement.

"Hello, Allen," Sonia says.

"Hey. I'm sorry I haven't called—"

"I haven't called you either."

I hesitate. "Right."

"I think we need to talk. I think it was a mistake."

"You do."

"I've been thinking about it, and that . . . that wasn't too smart."

"No."

"Maybe we should just forget it." She lowers her voice. "Forget it ever happened."

"Maybe."

"It was stupid."

I clear my throat. "I guess so."

"So can we just forget it?"

"Yeah," I say. "I'm sorry about all—"

"No. I'm sorry. It was quite pathetic of me—"

"Wait, no. I should've been more . . ." I search for the word.

"More level-headed?" she says. "Both of us, yes. I just want to make sure this doesn't change our friendship."

"It won't."

"David is looking forward to seeing you."

"I know. Maybe some evening after work. I can take him to my gym."

"That'd be great."

We say we'll talk again, and hang up. I let out a breath of relief and think, I keep dodging all kinds of bullets. I wonder how long my luck will hold out.

I feel uneasy that she regrets the whole incident so readily, that I have so little effect on her. Then I laugh this off. I wish I were a Casanova. Instead I'm a mistake.

I call Louis Stein and leave a message, and then find Junil Kim's address. Tomorrow I'll drive into Milpitas and search for Kim's trailer park, fitting him in between shifts. I shower and prepare for bed; I review Linda's interrogation of my aunt. I'm not sure how I should feel about the money. Somehow I can't muster up anything but mild surprise. All Aunt Insook's talk about my wasting her money was lies. It was my money from the beginning. There were times when my aunt, upset over my lackluster year in college, was so angry that she followed me around the house yelling at me. None of the bedroom or bathroom doors in her house locked, for some reason, so it was useless to close a door. She'd just open it and continue her sentence. I soon installed a simple bolt on my bedroom door, which she promptly ordered me to take out.

Now that I think about it, the same thing used to happen with my father and my aunt. My father, apparently not a very good debater, would sputter a few words, throw up his hands, and try to shrug her off. But Aunt Insook would never let an argument drop. Maybe that was why we had only a few dinners together. After one argument I remember, one in which my name definitely came up a few times, my father grew more frustrated as Aunt Insook kept interrupting him, her responses and rebuttals quick and cutting. My father's face became red, and at one point he slammed his hand sharply onto the table, making the glasses shake. He saw me jump. They both seemed surprised by my presence. My father took a deep breath, patted my head, then left the table. I continued eating, and after a few minutes, I could see that my aunt wasn't finished with the argument. She frowned to herself, then stood up and went after him. I heard them in the living room, their voices lower but anger still lacing their words. I had no idea what they were arguing about. I couldn't remember doing anything that might have caused the tension. I also wondered if they had fought like this as kids. I had trouble imagining them as young brother and sister. I still can't picture it.

I know nothing about their childhoods in Korea. I never met my grandparents, and had only once seen a tissue-paper-thin aerogram from Korea, the Korean letters pressed hard on the paper, indentations from the other side of the world. Oddly enough, I felt almost no curiosity about the letter, about any possible connections I might have had in Korea. I still don't. I'm too far from the language and culture to feel anything but a vague impression of lineage. Hell, I never even met my mother. Why would I feel connected to her family? I hardly knew my father. Except for my aunt, I'm not sure if I have any relatives.

I lie down slowly, my body so drained that I have to ease myself into sleep. With the unsettling thought that I might be alone in this world save for an aunt who cheated me out of my inheritance, I close my eyes and listen to the train-crossing bells ringing, a familiar and soothing sound.

The next afternoon I'm working with Alexa. We accompany Yin to his meetings with brokerage analysts. I have to drive the Tank into the financial district of the city, but because we head against the rush-hour traffic—it's four p.m.—we make good time. Alexa has already cleared this meeting at the Bainbridge Building and is watching the cars around us. Yin is in back, flipping through his folders.

"How long have you been doing this?" Yin asks.

Alexa and I aren't sure whom he's talking to. Alexa says, "I've been with ProServ about a year, and was with the San Francisco Police Department for three years."

"You were?" I ask. "I didn't know that."

"How about you?" Yin asks.

"ProServ for three years, other security firms before this for about the same."

"Is it a good living?"

Alexa and I glance at each other. She waits for me to reply. I say, "Well, it won't put me at number four seventy-eight, but it's not a bad line of work."

Yin laughs. "So you know about that."

"About what?" Alexa says. "What's four seventy-eight?"

I explain to her Yin's ranking. Her nose twitches and she is about to look at him, but stops herself.

Yin says, "That's all bullshit. It's not like I can actually sell off any of my equity. As soon as I did, it'd start a run and I'd be worth nothing."

"Not nothing," I say.

He is watching me in the rearview mirror. "You know, I was talking to someone and mentioned ProServ. He told me about that shooting."

Alexa says, "That was Choice's gig."

"Sounds like a dangerous way to make a living."

"That kind of thing is rare," I say. "Never happened to me or Paul before."

"Paul?"

"The guy who got killed. My partner."

"Sorry," Yin says.

We're silent for a while. Yin asks, "So they haven't found the guy yet?"

"Not yet."

"And no one knows why it happened?"

"No."

"And since this much time has passed," Alexa says, "it's probably heading for the dead case file."

"Already?" I ask.

"Well, soon. After a couple of days the leads dry up. And since there's no pressure—unless Polansky or Paul's family starts yelling— there are other murders happening all the time."

"Christ," I say.

We drive up Market and onto Front. I park at the Bainbridge Building garage, and Alexa does outer perimeter as we leave the garage and enter the main lobby of the building. Alexa speaks with the guard at the kiosk, and we take an empty elevator up to the twenty-third floor. Yin still reads his folders.

Because we're early, Yin and I wait in the lobby of the offices while Alexa roams. Yin sits on the overstuffed sofa. I stand near a window. The sounds of telephone rings and the soft clacking of keyboards filter into the lobby from a main room next door with tall dividers hiding its workers. Yin says, "Have you ever worked for a software company?"

I shake my head but mention my stint at Tronics.

He smiles. "They're heading for bankruptcy."

"I didn't know that."

"Most people don't. If you own any of their stock, you should bail."

"I don't."

Yin nods, fixes his glasses. "We always need good security people. Have you thought about going back to working in-house?"

I blink. Is this a job offer? I say, "Only for the right company."

"You don't see a lot of Asian Americans in your line of work."

I shrug.

"Would you consider relocating?"

"I might," I reply. "But maybe we should talk about it after this job."

"Make sure you get my card before I leave town."

A secretary appears in a doorway and asks Yin to follow her. I motion to Alexa, who returns from the hall. Since she prepped the analysts earlier, she'll take over from here. I remain in the lobby, resting. I'm on until three a.m. again, so I try to pace myself. I wonder how he knows about Tronics. Inside information. It's a world that I guarded, but have no real access to. I'm not even sure what it means to bail from a company—sell its stock? I wonder why I never bought shares of Tronics. I should be thankful for the company, since it moved me from generic security to personnel detail. I went from standing around and looking menacing to coordinating in-house security for Tronics' executives. It was that experience that got me the ProServ job.

When Yin finishes, Alexa and I accompany him back to the hotel. I feel myself slowing down. I'm glad Yin is turning in early tonight, having his dinner sent up to his room.

I call Linda from the hotel room to check if she found out anything about Garvey.

"I'm not sure how helpful this is," she says. "The guy was kind of a kook."

"How so?"

"Are you at home?"

"No. I'm still working."

"He tried to sue Milian for wrongful termination, but brought in all kinds of strange accusations, like the use of illegal immigrants, even having secret deals with the South Korean government."

"Oh, man."

"I know. The case was thrown out of court, and everyone dismissed him as crazy."

"Where is he now?"

"He died about fifteen years ago. An apparent suicide."

"Apparent?"

"It was deemed a suicide by the medical examiner. He finished a bottle of whiskey and ran a tube from his exhaust to his window. No note, though."

"You don't think . . ."

"I don't know. This just gets more complicated. Have you talked to Kim or Stein?"

"Not yet. I'll try tomorrow."

"Ask them about this Garvey and also about his accusations."

"I will," I say.

"We should try to get to Milian. Like that Durante guy or someone else at the company."

"That might be tough," I say. "I'll work on it."

"Do you have time for dinner? When do you get off?"

"Three o'clock."

"In the morning?"

"Yeah."

"Oh," she says. There is something different about her tone.

"Are you okay?"

"I'm okay. I just wanted to talk with someone."

"Something happened?"

"No, no. Nothing really. Thomas, that guy I started seeing. He just dumped me."

"What? You're kidding. Why would he do that?"

"I don't know," she sighs. "We probably started out too fast."

"Sorry. It's his loss."

"You sure you can't take off an hour?"

I consider this, then say, "I don't think so. I can't really leave my post."

"You're . . . on duty or whatever?"

"Yeah, but it looks like the client will be turning in early."

"How about I drop by? Just for a second. Where are you?"

"The Bartley Hotel," I say. I want to see her, but am unsure about Yin. "Room 214."

"Just to hang out. A short break. Did you eat? I can bring you some dinner."

I hear the sadness in her voice, and suspend my work concerns. I was going to order room service for a snack, anyway. I say, "If it's for a short while . . ."

"Room 214? I'll be by in thirty minutes," she says.

I hang up. I walk to Yin's door and listen. The sounds of a TV murmur through the door. I stand in the hallway, hoping Charles doesn't decide to drop in. He has never done that, at least not with me, though I can imagine it happening—him walking in and seeing me with a woman. But I'm not going to miss another one of Linda's cues. She wants to talk, so we're going to talk. I feel an anxious beat in my chest and ignore it. I return to my room and wait.

L inda brings Chinese food, joking that she should be the
one buying it from now on. "No one wants to steal it from *me*,"
she says, placing the bag on the bed. She hides something behind her
back and grins. I wait, puzzled. She steps in front of me, straightening
her posture with her feet slightly apart. Her leather jacket falls open
and I see a different necklace—a polished arrowhead. She says, "Guess
what I have."

I shake my head.

"Guess."

"A check for a million dollars."

"Fat chance." She holds out a package of sweet rice cakes.

"How did you know . . ."

"I remembered."

I look up at her, pleased. "Thanks. Thanks very much."

We sit at the desk next to the TV and lay out the food. I make sure
I can still see Yin's door, even though I know it'll be a quiet night. We
don't have plates, so we eat straight out of the white containers, and I
fumble with my chopsticks. I ask Linda for the details about Garvey.

"He was his own lawyer, which was his first mistake, and whatever
semblance of a real case he might have had was lost in the bizarre
charges he made against Milian. As soon as he went public, everyone

pretty much knew he was unstable. Most newspapers ignored him after a few days, which is why I had trouble finding more information."

"And my father was friends with him?"

"I don't know. You'll have to find that out."

"What about the secret deals with the Korean government? What's that about?"

"It sounds like paranoia."

"A dead end?"

"I don't know. None of these things are making sense. I think Paul's connection to Milian and to your father is pure coincidence. We're looking for links that aren't there."

I resist this. There has to be a reason why I feel the connections. Although I believe in coincidence and the randomness of events, I also am suspicious of anything too easy. I stare at my uneaten rice cakes divided into rectangular pieces, and think, I must consider this in small parts, and wait for the larger truths to emerge. I can't demand order and integrity before it's time. I must accept incomplete knowledge for now.

"Don't you worry about falling asleep?" she asks, looking around.

"All the time. I'm usually loaded up with coffee." I hear voices down the hall and stop. The voices move away and continue toward the elevators at the other end.

"Why are you still wearing your tie?"

"I should be wearing my jacket, but I can't do push-ups in a sportscoat."

"Is that your gun?"

I look down at my belt holster. "Yeah," I say. I finish the fried rice. "You haven't told me what happened."

Her smile slackens. "You mean Thomas."

"Did it happen tonight?"

"There were signs a few days ago," she says, staring at the soundless TV. "But tonight we had drinks and he told me he wanted to back off a little."

"A little."

"A lot. These things are never clean. We have vague plans to get together next week, but either he or I will cancel. By answering machine. Same old story."

"What happened?"

"Who knows, and who cares."

I glance up at her. "I never got to meet him."

"Good."

"You're okay with it?"

"Better be. I just have to accept it."

I wait, and when she doesn't explain, I ask, "Accept breaking up?"

"Accept . . . solitude."

"Solitude isn't so bad," I say, knowing this isn't the best answer. I can think of nothing else.

"Oh, I know. I would've given anything to have this when I was married." She lets out a small laugh, thinking of something. A commercial comes on the TV, and she watches it absently.

"What's funny?"

"I just heard myself whine. 'Poor me, poor me.' Promise me you'll shoot me with that gun if I start whining again."

I smile.

"I did the same thing to my sister, who's probably sick of hearing it. Oh, and get this: my ex-husband called her, asking for my number."

I straighten up, remembering her brief description of her marriage. "Why does he want your number?"

"Why else? Probably to hit me up for money. He is such a goddamn snake."

"Did she give it to him?"

"My number? No."

"Does she know him?"

Linda looks at me. "Yes, she knows all about him. She never trusted him."

"He'll probably find you if he really wants to."

"You don't think I know that? You don't think I haven't thought that?"

I remain quiet.

She says, "Sorry."

"It's all right. It was a stupid thing for me to say."

"It's like my old self is creeping back into my new self."

"Old self?"

"Weak and scared," she says, shaking her head. "A dumb teenager." She waves this off and says, "Change the subject."

I think of something else and nod toward the other door. "Yin might have floated a job offer to me."

"The client?"

"Yeah. It was just a hint, but I think it was legitimate."

"Here in the Bay Area?"

"No. I think the headquarters are in New York, but Yin came from Portland."

"Would you do it?"

"I don't know."

"What would you do?"

"I don't know. Head up security?"

"That sounds nice."

"I don't know. I'm not sure what I want," I say. We sit quietly for a few minutes. Linda tries a piece of a rice cake and makes a face. I laugh. "It takes getting used to."

"It's like dense gelatin."

More footsteps in the hallway. I check the clock and see that it's probably hotel security doing their walk-bys. One of them, Vinnie, looks into the room and waves. He stops when he sees Linda.

"A friend," I say.

"Howdy," he says, and pulls his head out. He continues down the hall.

"He's not ProServ," she says.

"No. Hotel security. They roam the halls every hour, looking for unlocked doors, things like that."

"So your client is pretty safe."

"I think so."

She rests on the bed, bouncing slightly. "What would your father say about your job?"

I have to think about this. "Why?"

"I'm trying to get a better sense of him. It sounds like he was ambitious."

"It does, doesn't it? I didn't know that," I say. "I have no idea what he'd think of me now. He wasn't like my aunt, who's clearly disappointed."

"What was that photo album you asked about?"

I say, "At my aunt's? I was thinking about an album my father used to look through. It had pictures of my mother."

"How come you don't have it?"

I explain how confusing and hurried my move was soon after my father's funeral, how most of my personal things had been donated to the Salvation Army. "I remember being blitzed by decisions—my aunt asking me all kinds of questions—and I began withdrawing, leaving everything to her. It was too much for me." As soon as I say this, I know I can't really blame her for getting rid of so many of my belongings. I wanted someone to take charge, and she did. She was probably overwhelmed by the sudden responsibilities, by my father's death, and attacked it all as if it were an accounting problem: coldly and clinically.

"What about your friends? Did you have to leave them when you moved?"

Chris Bruno, my childhood pal, had been dead for two years by that time, but I don't tell Linda about him. I'm not sure why. I say, "Yeah, once I moved I pretty much kept to myself."

"Like now."

I hesitate.

She smiles and says, "You don't think you keep to yourself now? Have you seen your apartment, your lifestyle?"

I shift in my chair, and remember Sonia mentioning something about this. Why is everyone bringing this up?

"It's not a criticism," Linda says, watching me. "Just an observation."

I shrug.

"Your aunt's a little like that too, I think. Was your mother?"

"I have no idea. I don't know much about her. I should probably ask my aunt more, but she didn't like my mother."

"Why didn't your father ever remarry?"

"I don't know. Me, probably. Work. He could've met some Korean woman—it might even be protocol for a widower with a kid to find a new mother—but he never did."

"No women friends?"

I shake my head, and picture him watching the TV news in the evenings, a can of beer on his knee. His eyes were usually half closed from exhaustion, but he refused to go to bed until the eleven-o'clock edition was over. He needed his routines. I required less sleep than he did, and often heard him turn off the TV and walk slowly to his bedroom. Once in a while he'd fall asleep on the sofa with the TV on. I'd creep in and watch old sitcoms or bad late-night movies. He'd snore behind me, and sometimes I'd study his face, the rough stubbled skin so unlike my own. He'd smell faintly of gasoline. After I was sure he was asleep, I'd sit very close to the TV and keep the sound low, giddy with freedom. My neck would start hurting, my eyes smarting, but I loved it.

"What about your family?" I ask. "You said they're in L.A.?"

"My mom and stepdad are in L.A. My younger brother still lives with them and is sucking them dry. My sister, my stepsister technically, lives in Walnut Creek."

"East Bay? Do you get to see her?"

"Not often."

"Your brother . . ."

"Never. He's taking advantage of my parents. He's too lazy to get a job, so he lives at home, hangs out with his friends, and steals their money."

"Where's your other father?"

"Divorced a long time ago. We have no idea where he is. He might have gone to Mexico."

"Is that where your parents are from?"

"My mom. My stepdad is Anglo."

"What does your sister do in Walnut Creek?"

"An administrative job. She has a family." Linda smiles. "Twenty questions over?"

"Sorry. I'm interested."

"It's funny. It feels like you already know this stuff, but of course you don't." She stands up, takes off her leather jacket, and stretches. The arrowhead necklace swings to the side of her blouse. "I don't know how you can do this all night. Don't you go crazy?"

"No. It's quiet, but nice." I am careful not to stare at her as she leans back.

"You don't listen to the TV," she says, motioning to the screen.

"I can't. But I'll read newspapers or something."

"The *Sentinel*?"

"Yeah. You have anything in there?"

"Not today. On Friday I'll have a piece on permanent makeup." She turns to me. "Don't say a word."

"I wasn't going to say anything."

She studies me. "Okay."

While I go out to check the hallway, Linda uses the bathroom, and she comes out with the complimentary lotion. "Can I take this?"

"Go ahead."

She looks around the hotel room and nods. "This isn't so bad. This stakeout."

I don't correct her. She checks herself in the closet mirror, touching the corners of her eyes and squinting. She leans closer. Her white short-sleeved blouse, untucked, hangs forward, and I see some of her bra through her sleeve.

"It's late," she says. "I should get going."

"Thanks for dinner, and the rice cakes."

"The least I can do, after the last time you bought takeout." She looks at my forehead and says, "It's much better."

"And my back doesn't hurt anymore."

"Good," she says. "You'll talk to Stein?"

"And Junil Kim. I'll ask about Garvey."

We stand there for a moment, then she smiles. "Have a good night, Allen." She leaves, and I listen to her quick steps moving down the hall, the faint smell of almond hand lotion lingering. I listen for her elevator, which rings and closes. I then turn to the silent TV and sit down on the floor in front of it, trying to find the same position I used when I was a kid, craning my neck. I haven't thought about that in years. The TV in my father's living room was smaller, but positioned at a similar height. I raise the volume just a fraction, so that all I hear is whispers from the news anchor.

Yes, this is it. I remember watching the tail end of newscasts, waiting for the bad sitcoms. This was how I sat, cross-legged, my hands pressed together in my lap, my torso leaning forward and my head angled up. My neck begins to hurt. The room is still. It was exactly like this. If I turn around, I'll see my father sleeping.

The next morning I head to Milpitas, searching for Kim's trailer park off 680. I drive a little too fast, missing my exit, and end up in San Jose. I circle back, and soon find the small fenced-off area with TV antennas jutting up from the dilapidated rows of trailers and campers. Rusted corrugated tin fences separate the small plots, and as I walk down the main thoroughfare, counting off numbers, I think about Linda's comment about how I keep to myself. It bothered me more than I admitted. I don't always keep to myself, and sometimes it's not a choice. But even if it is, what's so wrong with it? I don't know. I look around the trailer park. Am I going to end up like Kim, holed up in a trailer and separated from others by a piece of rusty tin?

Number 27. Kim's trailer is small, with a green plastic hood hanging over the entrance and an aluminum lawn chair in front. One of the screen windows has a deep tear sewn clumsily back together in a cross-stitch with what looks like dental floss. I listen for any sounds inside. Nothing.

I knock. Although it's ten-thirty, it might be too early. I knock harder. "Mr. Kim? It's Allen Choice. Are you there?"

"I haven't seen him around," a voice behind me says.

I turn. A muscular young man in a tight T-shirt stands there, a newspaper in his hand, his chest and biceps bulging. He studies me. I ask, "Do you know where he is?"

"No. He's usually sitting right there, drawing his stuff. I haven't seen him in a couple of days."

"You don't think something's happened to him, do you?"

"To Junil? That tough old dude? No. Maybe he went to visit family."

"He has family?"

"I don't know."

I knock again, and ask, "Is there a landlord or someone around?"

"No. He comes by on Mondays."

I check the door handle. It's unlocked, which surprises me. I turn to the man, who says, "Are you a friend?"

"He's a friend of my father's. You want to check inside with me? I just want to make sure he's not hurt or anything."

"You don't know Junil that well. That guy's like a freakin' iron man."

I open the door a fraction and nod toward it. "Just in case?"

He shrugs as I climb into Kim's trailer. Cramped and hot, the interior has dozens of sheets of paper with calligraphy hanging all along the walls and cabinets. I say, "Mr. Kim?" but see he's not here. There's a staleness in the air that's made worse by the heat. The plastic hood outside casts a greenish shadow onto everything, and the man in the doorway says, "Christ, it's muggy."

"When was the last time you saw him?" I ask. I look at the tiny kitchen area, but don't see any evidence of his eating recently.

"A few days ago. He was sitting out here doing the drawings."

"Does he ever go away like this?"

"Except for Sundays, no."

"What about shopping or something?"

"He got people from his church coming by. Also he does most of his stuff on Sundays."

I climb out of the trailer and shut the door after him. I ask, "Will you tell him that Allen Choice dropped by? I'll see if I can meet him this Sunday."

"Gotcha."

"In fact," I say, pulling out my card. "Can you give me a call if he doesn't show up here by tomorrow? That's my home number on the back. You can just leave a message."

"You worried about him?"

"A little."

"Gotcha."

I thank him and drive to Palo Alto, wondering where Kim could have gone. I don't like the idea of returning to his church, but I'll have to.

The Samurai is open for lunch, and the waitress, who recognizes me, says that Mr. Stein is in the back room. His door is ajar. I knock and look in. When he sees me, his face tightens.

"Mr. Stein, do you have a minute?"

"Did anyone see you come in?" he asks, standing quickly.

"What?"

"Goddammit, did anyone see you come in?"

"The waitress," I say, stepping back as he rushes to the door and looks out. He motions me into the room and shuts the door.

"Listen," he says angrily. "I don't want you coming by again. Do you understand?"

"What happened? What did I—"

"Someone tried to set fire to my other restaurant. It was contained in time, but I got a call warning me I wouldn't be so lucky next time."

"What? But why—"

"He mentioned your *name*," Stein says, grabbing my arm tightly. His grip is strong. "Now, leave before anything else happens."

"Wait," I say. I look down at his hand.

He hesitates, then releases me.

"Do you know who it was?" I ask.

"Who do you think?" he hisses. "He didn't leave his name and number, if that's what you're asking. I want you to leave now."

"Mr. Stein. I'm here already. As soon as you answer my questions, I'll go and won't bother you again."

"Jesus," he says, turning away and shaking his head.

"Did you tell the police?"

"Are you joking? The police can't do anything until after I'm ruined."

"Was it Milian himself?"

"No. He wouldn't be so stupid."

"What did the person say?"

Stein sighs. "He said my talking to Allen Choice was a mistake. If I do it again the fire won't be so small."

"I'm sorry. I'll be out of your life in a few minutes. I need to know about Noah Garvey."

"Who?"

"Noah Garvey. He sued Milian. He was a shift manager."

"Jesus. You're still digging up dirt on Milian? Just let it go already. Move on with your goddamn life."

"Noah Garvey."

Stein closes his eyes and pinches the bridge of his nose. "Noah Garvey. I think I remember that name. He made that big stink after he was fired."

"What do you remember?"

"Some kind of lawsuit that was thrown out of court."

"What can you tell me about him?"

"I didn't know him. I heard he was bizarre, an erratic manager. That's why he was fired."

"What about his lawsuit? He made claims of illegal labor, of deals with the Korean government."

Stein turns to me. "I don't know about that. But Garvey's lawsuit looked like an attempt to scuttle the buyout."

"How so?"

"Look, if you're about to buy a company and all sorts of allegations come out, wouldn't you stop, especially with the uproar over the Korean lobbying scandal?"

"The what?"

He says, "You don't know about that?"

"Scandal?"

"My God, where is your history? Don't you know about that? A Korean lobbyist was indicted for bribing over a dozen congressmen. It was all funded by the Korean CIA. So of course Milian was worried about his company. Anyone doing any kind of business with Korea was suspect."

"Did my father know Garvey?"

"I think so. They must have worked together."

"Were they friends?"

"I don't know," he says, lowering his voice. "Look, you have to tread more carefully. Milian is dangerous. Why are you doing this? Just move on."

"What do you know about Garvey's suicide?"

"He committed suicide?"

I nod. "Apparently."

Stein looks shaken. "When?"

"Fifteen years ago."

Stein rubs his hands and says quietly, "Suicide? You don't get it. You cross Milian and you end up dead. I want you to go now and I don't want to see you again."

I say, "I appreciate your time—"

"Just go, please," he says. "Please. Go out the back way."

I leave, circling around the block to get to my car. Before I drive off, I try to think how Milian would know about my visit with Stein. I must have been watched. My shoulders tighten. I'm probably still being watched. Yet I couldn't have been followed—I've been counting cars around me and would have noticed a mark. Then I realize that my car could be bugged, and that I've been very sloppy. I haven't swept my car at all.

I drive back to Monte Vista, but head straight for ProServ. I park inside the garage space usually kept for the Tank and walk into the equipment room, pulling out one of the RF probes. This hand-held device with a small antenna can detect wideband, low-level radio frequencies from 200 Hz to 3 GHz, essentially covering the entire spectrum that a transmitter might use. The meter on the display registers background frequencies as well, but any spike as I move the device around the car will mean there is something transmitting a frequency. I'm looking for two things: a tracking transmitter that sends out signals for a receiver to monitor my location, or a simple bug. I suspect the latter, since a tracking transmitter is usually large enough to be spotted, and a quick inspection underneath the car and under the hood reveals nothing. I start scanning the interior and immediately see the meter fluctuate. I bring the probe closer to the dash, and see a spike.

Shit. I pinpoint the location, beneath the radio. I climb underneath my dash and see something strange. The bug is there—a one-inch-square exposed circuit board—but it's attached to a step-down transformer, stealing electricity from my car battery. Whoever did this would never have to replace a battery, typically a nine-volt. The bug will continue transmitting as long as it goes undetected. I have no idea how long it has been there. I haven't done a sweep of my own car since I took that defensive driving course, almost two years ago.

"What are you doing?" Charles asks.

I look up. He is watching me from the garage doorway and sees the probe in my hand. I back out of the passenger seat and shut the door, putting a finger to my lips. He raises an eyebrow. I point to the door.

We walk out of the garage and shut the door. He says, "What's going on?"

"Could you do me a favor and check the bug underneath my dash? It's beneath the radio housing."

"Is it active?"

"I assume so."

He's about to ask me more questions, but his curiosity pulls him away. He takes the probe and I follow him into the garage. He climbs under my dash and sees it immediately. Looking up to me, he motions with one hand, pointing down below, clicking his finger. He wants a flashlight. I nod and hurry back to the equipment room.

After he examines the transmitter with a light, we walk out of the garage. He says, "Why is someone bugging you?"

"I'm not sure."

"You're not in any trouble with the law, are you?"

"The law?"

"That's law-enforcement-grade, and judging from the power supply, it has a range of about a mile."

"A mile!" I say. "Shit."

"Allen, what's going on?"

"I'm sure it's not the law. Don't worry." I have to think quickly.

He asks, "So, who is it?"

"I have a friend who's an investigative reporter. During my time off I was going with her as she worked on a story. I think my presence made some people curious."

"What kind of story?"

"Just corporate espionage."

He studies me. "You can't jeopardize ProServ in any way—"

"I'm not. It's probably old. Since I started back here I haven't had time to help—"

"I have to tell Polansky about this."

"I know."

"As a precaution we'll have to sweep everything, the office, other cars. You should do your place."

"I know."

"Hell, Allen. What're you doing? Helping a reporter?"

"I was just hanging out with her."

He frowns. "Her. Your girlfriend?"

"Nothing like that. Just friends."

He lets out a tired breath. "Polansky's not going to like this."

"I don't like it either."

"I want you to take the tap detector for your phone lines."

"All right."

"You want to disable this bug?"

"Not yet."

He turns to me. "Why?"

"I want to see how extensive this is. And I want to tell my reporter friend, maybe check her place first."

"If we find anything here, it's coming out. You know that."

"I know that."

"Hell, Allen. Why're you doing this?" He stops. "What if it's Triumph? What if we're being investigated by the feds? Goddammit."

"No, it's not the feds. It's not Triumph. I'm sure it's just me."

"How do you know that?"

"I just do."

"Christ. What the fuck are you getting into?"

"Nothing. I told you it's nothing."

"It's not nothing. You know that."

"I didn't plan on this, you know."

He waves me away and walks back into ProServ's offices. I'm annoyed that he blames me. I find the telephone line meter and take along a VLF—very low frequency—probe, sign all three devices out, and drive home, wondering if I'm being listened to right now. I turn on the radio.

If Milian knows about Stein from bugging me, then he also knows about Junil Kim.

Once in my apartment I immediately conduct a sweep and find a similar transmitter glued underneath my futon, a nine-volt attached. It's the same kind of FM bug as in my car. I stare at it in shock. They got in, and I didn't notice a thing.

I plug the telephone line meter into my phone jack and tune the voltage meter to a steady reading. This device allows me to test for current flow in the telephone line, detecting a drop in voltage or a change in polarity if a listening device is activated when I pick up the phone. There is a steady current always running through the phone lines, and if I pick up, the change will register on my meter, as well as on a listening device. The device, sensing the voltage change, will then turn on, and this will appear on my meter as a second spike.

I pick up the telephone and see the first spike, then, a fraction of a second later, the needle spikes again. I hang up, and test this a few more times. There's a tap on the line. I begin following my telephone line around my apartment—there is another jack in the kitchen area—but can't see any splices. I walk out into the hall, follow the line, then walk downstairs. I search for the main telephone switch box. It should be either down here or outside. I find the cabinet next to the laundry room. It isn't locked, so I know the tap must be somewhere around here. I open the cabinet and study the grids of wires, looking for my connection. There. 2C. I follow the two lines connected to my terminals as they snake into a clump of tangled wires, then disappear into plastic tubing. No splices. I trace the wires along the wall, figuring they follow the electrical outlets, and when I see an old broom closet, I suspect where the tap will be. I go into the closet, push aside a mop and bucket, and find a hole punched into the lower part of one wall. I reach in. A small tape-recording device is connected with alligator clips to two wires, my telephone line. It must have taken them a couple of hours to do this, punching this hole and finding the right wires. I glance at the tape recorder, which is set on a slow speed—at least a few hours of recording time per tape. It then hits me: they have to replenish the tape. I check to see how much they've already recorded and gauge that about half of the tape is finished. I pop out the cassette. The first thing I have to do is erase this.

I return upstairs, worried by how professional all of this is. When I play the tape on my stereo, listening through headphones, I realize it's set at the wrong speed; I don't have the right kind of tape player. It doesn't matter. These are just my conversations. I tune the radio to static, turn down the volume, then press record.

The phone rings. As I go to answer it, I glance at my futon. That bug is still transmitting. "Hello?"

"It's Charles. Everything's clear here. Can we talk?"

"Not my end."

He is silent, then says, "Not you?"

"Not me."

"Your end is still transmitting?"

"Yes."

"Not a phone tap?"

"Not at the moment."

"So you're loaded?"

"Completely."

"Fuck. I don't know what the hell you're—" He stops himself. "All right. Tomorrow morning, nine o'clock, we're having a meeting."

"I'm on at nine with Yin."

"Not anymore you're not."

"What?"

"You heard me. Polansky's orders. You're off that detail for now."

"Shit."

"Nine o'clock," he says, and hangs up.

I'm about to call Linda, but stop. I'll have to leave the apartment and use a pay phone. I check my stereo, the tape still recording static, erasing hours of phone conversations. I sit down and wait; every bit of noise I make is known to someone out there.

28

W hat?" Linda says, quickly lowering her voice as people turn. "In your car and apartment?"

"And my phone. We need to check your place, and your car. And we need to think of what to do."

"You're serious. We're being bugged?"

"Pretty sophisticated job, too."

"Stein was warned," she says. "So they heard us talking about him?"

"Him and Junil Kim, who I can't find."

"We've been stupid."

We are at a café in downtown San Jose. I met her here after calling her at work from a pay phone. "I was thinking of making sure who's doing this, maybe pretending something's wrong with the phone, and they'll think it's their tap."

"So they'll come to fix it or something."

"Then we'll know for sure."

"And then what?" she asks.

"We follow him and find out who he's working for."

"Then what?"

"Then we have confirmation. We have yet to find any direct links to Milian or Durante."

She nods. "With that we concentrate everything on finding out what they're so worried about."

"Maybe we should just call the police," I say. "They're breaking the law now."

"I don't think Milian would let anything lead to him. And none of our questions will get answered."

"I'm worried about Junil Kim."

She asks me if he has any family or relatives. I don't know. I tell her that I'll call the woman from the church, Grace Park, and ask if she's seen him.

"Do you want to try the trap?" she asks.

"Yeah."

"When?"

"We can do it this weekend. They'll probably try to check it as soon as we say something. We'll have to stay up and watch."

"Don't you work the weekend?"

"I had to tell them about the bugs, and they're concerned. They took me off my detail."

"Why'd you tell them?"

"In case the office was bugged."

"Oh." She frowns. "Right."

"I'm going in tomorrow morning to get grilled."

"You can't reveal too much. It might—"

"Don't worry. All I'm saying is that I was helping you out on a story."

"Good. That's good. You can tell them to call me for confirmation."

I point to my knapsack. "Let's check your car first. If there is a transmitter, then just talk carefully."

"And my apartment."

I don't even have to use the equipment. The transmitter is exactly the same as the one in my car, positioned farther back but still tapping the car battery. I also find a transmitter underneath her bed, and another one underneath her coffee table. I use the telephone line meter and see the voltage spikes, and follow the same procedure as I did for my telephone; I find the tape recorder spliced into her telephone line outside her building, the main telephone console housed in a wooden cabinet near the garage. The cassette inside is the same as the one I have with me—I haven't returned the static-filled tape yet—so I simply switch the two, intending to erase Linda's conversations as well.

We walk around her block as she tries to take this in. "I can't believe this! How long have they been there? Can you tell?"

"No."

"Under my bed. My goddamn bed." She seems stunned, her face flushed, and she keeps shaking her head. "How did they get in? They were actually *in my apartment?*"

"Probably sometime when you were at work. They picked the lock."

"I can't believe this. They could hear everything?"

"Probably."

"Oh, this is great. Just great. They heard me in bed." She presses her forehead with the palm of her hand and says, "How do we turn them off?"

"We can't yet. Then they'll know."

"God, Allen. So you just want them to listen?"

"We have to think carefully."

"Oh, man. I feel kind of sick."

I then realize why she keeps mentioning her bed. She might have had that guy Thomas over. In her bed. This image shakes me. Linda stares down at the sidewalk, her hands balled into fists. I say, "We should both be in my place, and either you or I will pretend to make a call. We'll say something's wrong with the line—we hear static and a bad connection—and that I'll have to call the phone company in the morning. Either that night or that morning they'll probably try to check."

"What if they don't?"

"I don't know."

"You said it looked professional. How professional?"

"The range of the transmitters is pretty wide, and the installation is well done. We should check your office, but chances are they left it alone."

"Check it anyway. Check it now."

"Lead the way."

After sweeping her office and finding nothing, I return the equipment to ProServ, and leave before I see Charles or Polansky. At home I immediately head to the phone, intending to call Grace Park, but stop. The bugs. I write myself a quick note—"CAREFUL!"—and tape it to the phone. I then call Mrs. Park from the pay phone at the café. She tells me she hasn't seen Kim but expects him at church. I tell her I'll call her back.

Back in my apartment I pop Linda's tape into my stereo, set to record over it with static, then replace it into the recorder downstairs. I can't stop thinking about her and that guy in her bed, having sex. What's on this tape—her phone calls to him, to everyone? I plug in a pair of headphones and play the tape, but as before, the speed is wrong, the voices chirping and rushing by. Searching through my closet for the old handheld recorder I once used for notes, I find it and connect it to a lower-power supply meant for a portable reading light. I then play the tape, the motor running slower. Although not quite the right speed—the voices are still slightly fast—it is slow enough for me to understand and recognize the voices. Linda is speaking, and I recognize her inflections. I stop the tape and use my headphones. I rewind the tape for a few seconds, then play it. I hear something unclear, odd silences, and raise the volume. I then hear Linda crying and saying, *But I didn't do anything.* Another voice, a woman, says, *Forget him. He's a bastard. A stupid bastard. Just forget him.* Linda cries again, staccato gulps. *I really liked him,* she says. *He was nice.* The other voice says, *Forget him.*

I stop the tape. A chill runs through me, and my heart tightens. Her crying reverberates in my head. I take a deep breath. I eject the tape and put it into the stereo, rewind it, and begin erasing over it with radio static.

29

I walk into the ProServ conference room with Charles and Polansky waiting for me at the table. Charles motions for me to close the door. They both appear grim. I sit down across from them, already knowing what they're going to say. I ask, "How long?"

"What?" Charles says.

"How long?"

"What do you mean?" Polansky asks.

"How long am I suspended?"

Charles turns to Polansky, who remains fixed on me. Polansky says, "You understand the situation we're in."

"I understand."

"We have no idea what we're dealing with, and what our exposure will be," Charles says.

"There's no need to double-team," I say.

"It's just that we have to be clear about our possible liability," Polansky says.

"All I want to know is how long."

"We'll start with two months."

"Two," I say.

"And we'll want to talk to the reporter."

"She won't say much," I tell them.

"Who's doing this?" Polansky asks. "And why?"

They are only concerned about their company. I say, "I don't know."

"Two months until this clears. Longer if it doesn't. Could it be the feds? You're not mixed up in anything . . ."

I shake my head. "No. This seems related to the reporter."

"You're a security risk," Charles says. "We can't be worrying about you while you're with a client."

"I know."

"We're going to have to block your access to our server and change the security codes."

"I'm not going to do anything—"

"We know, but if someone's been watching you, they're getting all your information."

I nod.

"It's temporary," Polansky says. "Come to us when the story breaks. But we have to protect ourselves."

I ask, "It's an unpaid leave?"

"Allen, we can't realistically pay you—"

"Just checking," I say. "But what if the story doesn't break? What if nothing changes?"

They glance at each other. Polansky says, "We'll see in two months."

"Look," Charles says. "What if this company, or whoever, decides to sue the reporter or you? The fact that we deal in countersurveillance and you're helping the reporter—it exposes us. Don't you see that? We could be seriously hurt, not just financially, but what clients will want to come to us? The publicity would kill us."

"All right. I get it," I say, and stand up. "Is that it? I'll take my things."

"That's it," Polansky says.

"You made a good impression on Yin," Charles says. "He was disturbed we took you out."

I remember Yin's job offer. Hell, I don't need ProServ. I shrug them off and clean out my desk. A two-month unpaid leave is as good as being fired. They don't want to terminate me outright, since it might look bad for them, the dead hero's partner being let go. I can't muster much anger, though, since they are obviously only protecting themselves. But it was foolish to let Charles know what is happening. I should've lied.

I get my SIG from the locker, holster it, and consider for a moment stealing body armor. I decide against it.

I put what few personal items I have—a small cast-iron paperweight grenade, a few security manuals, a stainless-steel pen we all received as gifts last Christmas—into a plastic bag, and check the drawers again. Charles is hovering nearby, watching but not watching. I turn on the computer. Charles says, "Uh, Allen. What're you doing?"

"I want to check if I have anything saved in here."

"I'm sorry. I can't let you do that."

"What?"

"I'm afraid I'm going to have to ask you not to go into the computer."

"What are you talking about? I just want to see if I have any personal—"

"This computer and everything on it belongs to ProServ. You shouldn't have any personal files on it."

I stare at him. "You're not kidding. I can't even check?"

He shakes his head.

"Oh, shit," I say. "You think I might sabotage something? Erase something? You're going to search this as soon as I leave?"

Shifting on his feet and avoiding my eyes, he says, "Allen, it's office procedure—"

"Fucking hell!" I say. "What a load of crap! This is how you treat your coworkers?"

Polansky steps out from his office. I turn to him, give him a disgusted look, and grab my bag from the desk. Brodie and Dunn, near the copy machine, watch me. The news will travel quickly. I mutter a few things about company loyalty and trusting their employees, then leave.

I drive back to my apartment, even though I have nothing to do there. I go over the confrontation a few dozen times, thinking of better ways I could've handled it. I imagine threatening a lawsuit or cursing them out. I imagine alluding to bad publicity or being completely cool and stoic and telling them it was nice working with them but they aren't worth my time. I imagine anything but muttering to myself and slinking out as I did.

I really liked him. He was nice. Linda's quiet voice stings me. I should never have listened to that tape, and now I can't get her crying out of my head. Who was the other woman? Her sister. Linda mentioned speaking to her sister. Whining to her sister, she called it. I have trouble picturing Linda as she says these things, seeing her crying, and then I try to push this away; I don't want to see her crying. I want to help her. Stop thinking about it, I tell myself.

When I enter my apartment, I am feeling depleted. I move to sit on my futon, but see the blinking light on my machine. I'm about to play the message, but see the "CAREFUL!" sign on my phone. I turn on my stereo, aim the speakers at the transmitter under my futon, and tune the dial to a talk radio station. I then turn the volume down on my machine and play the message, putting my ear against the speaker. Junil Kim's neighbor says that Kim still hasn't shown up and that he doesn't know what to do. Then I realize that the bug probably picked this up anyway when the call first came in. Sloppy of me. I want to call Mrs. Park, and even though I haven't put the newly erased tape back into the recorder, I decide to be absolutely safe. I call her again from the café pay phone, telling her I'm a little concerned. She says she'll call friends and check. "But he might be with a relative," she says. "I don't know everything about him. Still, he never misses church. He likes teaching that class."

I call Linda at work and tell her that I was suspended from ProServ. She doesn't sound surprised. "Was it the bugs? They got scared."

"Yeah."

"What does a suspension mean?"

"Pretty much fired."

"Oh," she says. "Where are you calling from?"

"Pay phone."

"I'm having trouble finding out more about Garvey's lawsuit, except for what was reported in the papers. I have to go to the county clerk and do more digging at the superior court level. Do you know if Garvey had family?"

"No. I should ask, though. I'll ask my aunt, maybe Stein."

"Try," she says.

"We should do that trap, with the phone."

"When?"

"Tonight," I say. "I have no work tomorrow."

"I do."

"I can do this myself."

"No," she says quickly. "I want to be there."

We agree to meet for dinner. After I hang up I am about to call my aunt, but stop. I don't want to talk to her yet. I don't want to talk to anyone. *I really liked him. He was nice.* I head to my car, intending to go for a long drive, but remember it's bugged. Goddammit. Everyone listening to what I'm doing. I begin walking down Main, recalling my long runs as a teenager, the world jostling around me, my breathing and my heartbeat the only sounds that filtered in. It was best going out in the early evenings, right before my aunt would return from work, as the sun drifted low in the sky and the air cooled, the feeling of the world settling. My days at school were uneventful—I moved through them robotically—and my nights were filled with homework, reading, TV, and my aunt lecturing me. But the runs were all mine. One of my favorite routes was a convoluted series of zigzags from my aunt's place to Lake Merritt, where I stopped to rest before the run back. By that time the sun would be setting behind some buildings, the shadows long, the reflections on the water rippling orange. I felt peaceful, calmed.

The urge to run fills me now, and although I'm in slacks and a dress shirt, I begin jogging slowly down a side street. I unbutton my collar and try to shake everything away. Without my job I worry about losing the engagement, and what that means. The dis-ease brushes against me. I think about my father struggling with medical textbooks in his spare time, his boss making fun of his aspirations. I think of Linda crying. I think of my aunt sitting alone up in that house, hoping for company. I think of Milian listening in on everything about my life. I think of my now unemployed state. I think of Paul and Sonia and David.

I run harder.

30

I speak with my aunt from the pay phone in the café. Aunt Insook doesn't remember much about my father's friendship with
Noah Garvey. "Was he married?" I ask.

"Maybe. I didn't meet him much."

"How friendly were they?"

"He was a troublemaker. I keep away from him."

"When you did see him, where was it?"

She says, "Just once or twice, not sure where. Maybe at warehouse?"

"Why was he a troublemaker?"

"He make trouble."

"Yes, but why? What did he do?"

"I don't remember. He argue all the time."

"About what?"

"I don't remember. Long time ago."

I sigh. Another wasted call. I remember what Stein mentioned, and
ask, "Do you know anything about some scandal in the seventies with
the Korean CIA?"

"Scandal?"

"Something about bribing congressmen."

"Yes! Park Tong Sun! He was in the news everywhere. He pay

money to Congress to get better treatment for South Korea. The Korean CIA help fund. He was arrested. They call it Koreagate."

"Could that have made it hard for Milian?"

"Hard for anyone who deal with Korea. Everyone worry what people think. Everyone think Koreans bribe and get secret deals."

"So Roger Milian would've been worried about any kind of bad publicity, since he was an importer dealing with Korean goods."

"Maybe."

"So you don't remember anything about Noah Garvey?"

"No."

"If you do, will you let me know?"

"Okay."

I hang up and return home, where Linda is waiting for me. We have already worked out how we will set the trap, including our script to prompt whoever is listening to check their equipment. I have already disconnected the transmitter in Linda's car, which she parked in my lot. We know this might not work, especially if no one is listening at the right moment, but if it does we'll know exactly what our focus will be.

In my apartment, Linda is standing by the window, looking out onto the street. She turns. Her body is tense, her mouth drawn, and she gives me a questioning look, asking me if we're going to start as planned. I nod. Linda moves near the futon and says, "You want to see a movie or something tonight?"

"When's the next showing?"

"An hour."

"Yeah. I can use a break."

"Can I make a call? I want to check my messages." She walks to my telephone and lifts the handset. She presses the hook a few times. "Something's wrong with your phone. No dial tone."

"Again? Let me see." After a few tries, I say, "It's been giving me trouble lately. I already called the phone company, but let me call again. I'll use a pay phone." I leave the apartment and pretend to use the pay phone at the café. When I return, Linda asks me what they said.

"They don't know what it is. They're sending someone over tomorrow morning."

"Shall we go? We can get a drink or something before the movie."

I agree, and we leave the apartment. Linda taps me on the shoulder and whispers, "We're terrible actors."

We walk to her car, and she drives us around the block as I check to make sure we're not being followed. After it seems safe, we park near my building, with a view of my lot, and settle in.

"It's not . . ." she says, pointing underneath her radio.

"I disconnected it. I also checked for others, though just visually. I don't have the probes. I think it's fine."

"What if they weren't listening?"

"Then we have a long wait. If they were, then they'll come while we're at the movies."

"So give it three hours?"

"Yeah. Or else we'll have to think of something else. Maybe I can create interference with one of the car bugs, and we can set a similar trap."

She lets out a sigh and sinks back into her seat. It's beginning to get dark, headlights passing us, reflecting off the chrome bumper of the truck parked directly ahead. Linda has a better view, and I tell her to keep watch for anyone entering the building through the side door. "It's locked, but residents don't have keys to it."

"Then how can they get in?"

"If they're professionals, and from the bugs they might be, then they'll pick it."

"Why not just wait at the front for a resident?"

"No. Because of burglaries, no resident will let anyone in without a key."

After a few minutes she asks, "What did your aunt say?"

"She remembered the scandal, the one Stein told me about. It was called Koreagate, though that sounds like a joke." I fill her in.

"I can do more background on that at work. But it makes sense. Milian was worried about the buyout."

"And Noah Garvey was going to screw it up, so Milian went on the offensive, having the case thrown out."

"And your father's role?"

"Friends with Garvey. Maybe he had something, or knew something. And then he had an 'accident.'"

"All around the same time," she says. "But we need evidence."

"We need more information about Garvey."

She leans her head against the window but keeps watching the lot. Although I can make out her figure in the dim interior, it's now too dark to see her expression. She folds her arms, and I hear the heavy beat of music coming from a passing car, the pitch rising, then falling as the car speeds away. Then, sudden silence.

Linda says, "I'm sorry about your job."

"To hell with them. I'll find something else."

"You're not going to wait it out? Maybe it's really a temporary suspension."

"No. I'll look into other firms."

"I guess this is my fault, starting all this. You wanted to forget it."

I pull down the sun visor, angling the mirror so that I can see behind me. "No. If my father's death was suspicious, I want to find out."

"Are you mad at me?" she asks.

"What?" I say, turning to her.

"Are you mad? You seem . . . curt."

"Do I?" I stop and consider this. "I'm not mad. I'm worried about this whole thing, but I'm not mad."

"Okay. You seem mad."

I try to see her face, but it's too dark. Maybe I am a little mad, though not at her. I think about Charles hovering over me as I cleaned out my desk. That's what got to me. I wasn't allowed to turn on my computer? What kind of crap was that? If I wanted to sabotage the place I could do a pretty good job of it, not some pansy hard-drive crashing. I could screw up their security system, kill the Tank, zap their server. No wonder Paul wanted to leave that place. I'm sure Black Diamond will give me an interview. I don't know about Triumph. There are a few other smaller security firms I can try. Maybe I'll contact Yin. But I never got his card. What's the name of that magazine? *High-Tech?* I can track him through there.

"My sister just got a promotion," Linda says.

"What kind?"

"She was an administrative assistant at an investment firm. Now she's office manager. She oversees the other admins. And her daughter is really smart."

"Smart?"

"She's going into a special gifted program."

I nod, wondering why she's telling me this. "How old is she?"

"My niece? Five."

"Young."

"Yes. They're all doing well. Even Julie's husband. He makes so much money."

"How much?"

"You really want to know?"

"Of course."

"Two hundred grand a year."

"Jesus. Doing what?"

"Something to do with computers and credit cards. I never under-stood it."

"Man, that's . . . I don't know. Man."

"So," she says. "Am I a loser or what?"

I laugh.

"What's so funny?" she says, an edge to her voice.

"Not you. I was just thinking that I've lost my job, I've got barely any savings, and I'm sitting in a car waiting for who the hell knows what. You're not a loser."

She laughs now. "What a pair."

"And you're only, what, twenty-six?"

"Twenty-seven. It was my birthday last week."

I sit up. "What? Why didn't you say anything?"

"No big deal. But Julie's thirty. By the time she was my age she al-ready had a family, a great house, a good job, and all that."

"That's right," I say. "Rub it in."

"You know what I mean."

"I know."

We grow quiet. I say, "Well, at least you have me."

She snorts, and I glance at her. She says, "I'm kidding. Just kid-ding."

This bothers me. But I let it go.

"I was kidding," she says.

"Okay."

After a long silence, Linda stretches and yawns. I say, "We can take shifts. Let's switch seats. You can nap for an hour."

"That would be great. I could use a quick nap." She pushes her seat back and says, "Should I get out?"

"Can we do it without walking around the car?"

She lifts herself and moves as close to the windshield as she can, propping herself up with one arm. I try to slip behind her, but our legs get caught, and her head hits the roof of the car. "Ouch," she says.

"Almost there," I tell her. I flatten myself in the driver's seat, my legs still against hers, and she moves farther toward the passenger seat, her back pressing against me. She rubs along my legs as she slips aside, pulling herself from underneath the steering wheel, and at one point as she frees herself from my legs and the steering wheel, her knee brushes against my groin. I wince.

She says, "Sorry," and settles into the passenger seat.

"I'll keep watch. You can rest," I say.

"Thanks." She pushes her seat back and closes her eyes. I look up at the apartment building. Someone on the fourth floor is watching TV in the dark, the curtains flickering. The parking lot is quiet. My legs are sore from my unplanned run earlier, and I remember going for miles as a teenager without any hint of stitches or cramps. Today I had three cramps, and had to stop running after fifteen minutes. I feel old.

Linda breathes steadily, and I turn toward her, watching her silhouetted profile, and I think about her ex-husband. I can't imagine her with anyone mean, and realize how little I know about her. It unsettles me, this weak grasp on the truths around me. I wish I were smarter.

"What's wrong?" Linda asks.

I can't see her eyes. "Nothing. Just checking if you're awake."

"I'm just resting. Long day."

I watch the parking lot. After forty-five minutes pass, and I have gone over the day's events dozens of times, worrying about my job prospects, I see an unfamiliar van pull up into the parking lot. A man climbs out, looks around, and kneels in front of the side door. I say, "Linda."

She clears her throat, sitting up. "You see something?"

"I think so." I can't make out what the man is doing, but he must be picking the lock. He opens the door. "Jesus, that was fast. He's in."

"Maybe he has a key."

"Maybe." I start her car. I time the man, figuring he'll need less than five minutes to check the line tap. "The van is what they need. They can monitor the bugs from anywhere, and stay mobile when we go by car."

"But you never saw any vans following us."

"They can be up to a mile away. As long as they know where we're going, they don't have to be near us."

The man reappears, and he is carrying something. "I think he took the whole thing. He can't tell what's wrong with it."

"He's going to replace it," she says.

The man climbs into the van and starts it up. I say, "Here we go."

The van pulls out of the lot and speeds down Main. I stay far behind, the height of the van easy to follow from four or five cars back. I'm not used to the quickness of Linda's Honda, and ease back on the accelerator. She says, "What do we do when they stop?"

"I'm not sure. I just want to get a fix on who we're up against."

"Don't we know?"

"We need to be sure."

The van drives onto the freeway, heading north, and as we pass the Palo Alto exits and San Mateo, Linda says, "We're going to WestSun."

The Burlingame exits are approaching. "Yeah."

We follow the same route Linda and I took when we visited West-Sun from South Airport Boulevard. Both of us are quiet, since there is no doubt now. It's almost a letdown, since I expected something more revealing. The van pulls into an open garage at the side, a few lights on inside. Everything else is dark. I park at the edge of the lot, and say, "Not a whole lot of security out here."

"Now what?"

I stare at the garage. "I'm going to take a look."

"What? Inside? That's trespassing."

"I know that they have two cameras, a motion detector, and a trembler switch. The switch will be off because the door's open. The motion detector is probably off because they just drove in. And the cameras—look, it's dark in there."

"How do you remember all that?"

"It's my job. Or was my job." I open the door and quickly turn off the interior light. "You want to wait here?"

"No. I'm coming too."

"You just said it's trespassing."

"I want to see." She points to her car. "Is this safe here?"

I stop. "No." I close the door and repark the car down the block, in front of a small office complex. We climb out. "We're not really prepared for this," I say. "But we have the opportunity."

"All right. Let's go."

She has more to lose than I, but she is already walking toward the parking lot. I check my pistol and replace it in my belt holster—I'm not about to take any chances, not after the incident in my alley—and catch up to her. I say, "We'll slip inside behind the van and see who's around. If there are too many people inside, we turn back. Okay?"

"Okay."

We hurry toward the warehouse, searching for any signs of activity. A security light by the front entrance is on, but the garage light isn't. I consider the possibility of a trap. Linda slows her pace and whispers, "Are we crazy?"

"We're just going to look. That's all. They bugged everything around us. They're worried."

She nods. We move along the wall, and I try to get a fix on the two cameras up in the corners. Since it's dark inside, I wonder if they even work—some places use dummy cameras. We approach the van. "Ready?" I ask.

She says she is, and we enter the building. I peer into the van. Newspapers, magazines, and candy wrappers lie on the passenger seat. A pick gun. That's how he opened the lock so fast. Possibly one person monitoring us. The key is still in the ignition—he'll be returning shortly.

A few lights are on in the front, toward the offices, and Linda moves in that direction. I catch up and whisper, "Slow down."

She glances at me, her face tense, and says, "Let's hurry."

We walk along an aisle, huge crates looming above us, and approach the offices. One is lit up; there is movement behind the blinds. We're about to walk to the offices next to it, but I wonder if the front office is the right place. I whisper, "What about Milian's office in the back?"

She nods quickly.

We detour around these offices, walking toward the back where we met Milian. There's a loud slapping sound near the garage entrance, and we stop. Voices emerge from the office near the front. I see the sweeping beam of a flashlight and say in Linda's ear, "Keep still."

They are walking in the aisle next to us. "You leave the door open? Close it," someone says.

"I thought it'd take a second."

"Sounded like one of the plywood sheets."

Their voices move toward the van. Linda and I hurry in the other direction, toward Milian's office. We crouch behind the wall of crates, and Linda is about to try Milian's door. I stop her. "Slowly. Let me make sure there are no alarms."

We hear the garage door being closed, the rumbling filling the warehouse. Linda whispers, "How will we get out?"

"There must be other ways."

"Let's go. This isn't working."

"We're here," I say, and kneel in front of the door to check the door handle. I look for any wires around the door. I peer through the window, searching for a blinking light, an armed alarm, but don't see anything. I turn the door handle slowly, but of course it's locked. Linda stands up and looks out toward the aisles, then crouches back down. "We're safe. How will we get in?"

I glance at some of the crates around us, and know they must use a tool to open them. I say, "Look for a pry bar near any of the open crates."

She nods, and we search in separate directions. I find a flathead screwdriver, which might be useful, and continue looking. Linda picks something off the floor and waves me back to Milian's door. It's a twelve-inch pry bar, a flat piece of metal with a nail claw. I say, "I'm going to pry the door from the frame. When there's enough room, use this screwdriver to push the latch bolt—"

"The what?"

"The part that sticks out into the slot. Push that in and we should be able to open the door."

We position ourselves next to each other, and I begin prying the door from the softwood frame carefully. I don't want the bar to slip. Linda sits ready with the screwdriver. After I make a quarter-of-an-inch gap, I ask her to try, but there isn't enough leeway. I have trouble pushing any farther, and I put more of my weight behind the bar. The door makes a sharp cracking sound.

We freeze. Linda holds her breath. Everything remains quiet. I continue opening the gap in the door and ask Linda to try again. This time she manages to force the screwdriver in and pushes the bolt open. The door swings in. I look quickly for any alarms on the mat or around the frame, but find nothing. We walk in and I shut the door. The drawn blinds make it very dark.

"I can't see," she says.

"I'll use this." I grab a jacket that hangs on the chair and cover the desk lamp. I turn on the light and make sure only a sliver leaks out.

She says, "I'll check this file cabinet."

I look through the second cabinet and find carbon copies of work orders and shipping forms. I then move to his desk, turn on his computer, and leaf through some papers. While the computer boots up, I find his desk calendar, where Milian has jotted some notes. "Pinewood

Investments—K. Frankel" is scribbled and underlined. The computer monitor shines brightly, and I quickly dim it. I see that the computer requires a password to continue. "Shit."

"I'm not finding much," Linda says.

I turn off the computer. "Same here. Maybe we should look in—"

She holds up her hand, turning toward the door.

I whisper, "What's—"

She says, "Shh." I listen, but don't hear anything. It's too quiet. I stand up slowly, uneasily. I wave Linda to come to the door. She slides the file cabinet closed, turns off the desk lamp, and throws the jacket back onto the chair. She follows me out of the office. I lock the door and check the damage to the wood. It might not be noticed. We listen. A soft scrape—the sound of a shoe against cement—comes from a far aisle, then stops. I grab Linda's arm and motion for us to go in the other direction. We hurry away from Milian's office and slip into another aisle, crouching down behind some crates. Both of us breathe hard. I listen for any more movement in the other aisles, and hear whispering. Damn. They know something's going on. I reorient myself. The best way to escape is back through the garage or the door next to it. The front entrance is too exposed.

"To the garage door," I whisper in Linda's ear.

We walk swiftly toward the exit. Linda bumps into me when I slow down. I try to listen for their location, but they're being quiet. I pull out my gun, and Linda, seeing it, whispers, "What're you doing?"

I put my finger to my lips.

"Oh, Jesus."

We hear the sound of someone's footsteps racing in a nearby aisle, so we run toward the exit; Linda kicks a metal container by accident and sends it booming across the concrete floor.

"Aisle four! Aisle four!" someone yells from the other end.

As we emerge from the aisle, a dark figure jumps out at us, grabbing my arm, and I immediately lash out with a front kick, connecting into his stomach. My shoe digs in. He curses and lets go. He then tries to tackle me, but I swing the butt of my gun into his head. My hand jolts as I hit him dead on, and he stumbles away with a grunt, clutching his ear. Linda seems frozen, and I yell, "Move!" which she does, running toward the door next to the garage, trying to unlatch the bolt.

"Here! Here!" yells the man as he leaps after me again, grabbing my shirt. He pulls me down, but I yank myself away and swing my gun again. I hit his elbow, feeling bone. He exhales sharply and falls back. "They're fucking here! Right here!"

The other person runs up the aisle, and I say angrily, "Screw this," and point the SIG toward the ceiling. I fire two shots. The man on the ground curses and leaps away. I hear someone else diving for cover, the sound of crates crashing over. Linda pulls the latch free and throws open the door. We run out, but I pull her along the side, wanting to avoid being exposed in the middle of the parking lot. She keeps saying, "Oh man, oh man." The lights attached to the warehouse suddenly burst on, the parking lot flooded. I'm glad we're on the fringes, running through knee-high weeds. I keep expecting to hear gunshots, and have my pistol ready to fire back. But there's nothing. I glance back and see one man peering out toward us, but we're now out of the floodlight range and rush farther into the darkness. We reach her car and jump in, and I ask for the keys.

"What?"

"The keys!" I yell, alarmed that she might not have them.

She reaches into her pocket and says, "You've got them!"

I check my pockets. She's right. I fumble with them and start the car, keeping the lights off, and we speed away.

Linda folds her arms, squeezing her hands in her armpits. I check the mirrors and make sure we aren't being followed. I head straight for the freeway. I ask, "Are you okay?"

"No."

Still tense with adrenaline, I breathe deeply, calming down. My mind buzzes, and despite the danger of almost being caught, I'm excited.

"Why did you shoot your gun?" she asks.

"We were about to get caught. The gunshot bought us some time."

"You could've killed someone."

"No. I aimed up. I just wanted to scare them."

"Jesus. What we did was stupid."

"We got away."

"Jesus."

I let out a small laugh, and she turns to me, her eyes startled. I say, "They didn't get a good look at us. They're not sure if it was us. We've put them on the defensive."

"What's going to happen now? Are they going to come after us?"

She balls her hand into a fist and presses it against her thigh. "Will they call the police?

"I doubt it. They must have something going on. But we're going to have to be careful."

"They're going to listen in," she says. "They're bugging us."

"*Were* bugging us. I want to disconnect everything."

"Then they'll know."

"Yeah. No more screwing around. I'm going to find out what the hell's going on over there."

"You're going to antagonize them."

I make a gun with my fingers and shoot up into the air. "Pow. Too late."

31

Linda finds Noah Garvey's daughter living in Berkeley. She surprises me with this information when we meet the next evening. Although I disconnected all the bugs, we are still wary of talking in our apartments, so we are at a bar near her place. She says, "I didn't think of the smaller newspapers. I was looking in the *Chron* and the *Examiner,* but it made more sense to look in the small Oakland papers, the *Tribune* and the *Post.* The extended obituary was in the *Post*, which doesn't exist anymore, but the Oakland library has it on fiche."

"When did you do this?"

"Today. After I found out that Garvey has a wife and kid, I looked them up in a few databases. The daughter is a grad student at UC Berkeley."

"The wife?"

"In New York. Garvey was divorced from her when Arianne, the daughter, was two."

"You've been busy."

"We see her tomorrow afternoon," she says. "And you found Frankel, the name in Milian's calendar? Who's that?"

"Kyle Frankel is a partner of Pinewood Investments," I say, telling her briefly about the calls I made. I contacted a few different businesses named Pinewood and soon found Pinewood Investments in Foster City.

"They're an investment group that buys and sells companies, more or less. He wouldn't tell me much, but it seems that they're interested in WestSun."

"To buy?"

"He wouldn't say. They also invest money in companies, become silent partners, but I don't know."

Linda says, "We can find out more. My business editor will know."

"I also called around for Junil Kim again."

"And?"

"And I'm worried. He hasn't been home, and I talked to a friend of his, Grace Park. She doesn't know either. She's been checking with relatives. If he doesn't show up at church tomorrow, she might have to call the police."

"You don't think . . ."

"They warned Stein. I'm sure they warned Kim. I'm planning to go to his church to check myself."

"Tomorrow? But we have to talk to Garvey's daughter."

"I know. I'll call Grace Park tonight. Did you get anything more about Koreagate?"

"Yes. It was apparently big news. A Korean lobbyist was funneling money from the KCIA."

"How much?"

"Over a million bucks to eighteen congressmen. They tried to cover it up, which made it worse. There was even a *Doonesbury* comic strip about it."

"What happened?"

"People wanted to sever some ties with South Korea and impose trade tariffs."

"Did they?"

"No. The lobbyist was indicted and expelled, and it died down."

"But Milian must have been sweating. If there were tariffs or worse, some kind of trade sanctions—"

"He could've been ruined."

"And any hint of illegal doing—"

"Would've messed up that merger."

I say, "But would Milian have killed my father to keep everything stable?"

"Good question. And what exactly did your father do?"

I shake my head.

We sit quietly. Linda says, "I'm worried about last night. I'm still waiting to hear from the police."

"They won't call the police."

"Why not?"

"They don't know what we found out," I say.

"I'm worried about getting a visit, like you did in the alley. Or like Stein."

"I know. We have to be careful."

"Careful? They already got into my apartment without me knowing. In my car too! How careful can we be?" Her voice rises a pitch. She takes a deep breath.

I say quietly, "Tonight I'll reinforce your locks, put in a simple alarm. We'll think about safety."

"Tonight? You going somewhere?"

"I have to buy some of the equipment."

"I'll go with you."

"You don't have work to do?"

She says, "I always have work to do."

"Let's go."

We drive to my apartment, where I pick up a door handle alarm I never use and some tools. David calls as we leave, asking if I'm still interested in doing tae kwon do with him. I have forgotten about that, and set a time tomorrow night to go to my gym.

"That's nice of you," Linda says when I hang up.

"I promised him."

"Where to now?"

"Hardware store."

We find a small store on Camino, buy window locks and a deadbolt, then drive to Linda's apartment. When we walk inside it takes me a moment to realize that she has rearranged her furniture. I look around, and, seeing my confusion, she tells me that she was making sure there were no more bugs. "I couldn't sleep last night unless I checked again," she says. I see indentations in the carpet where the tan sofa and glass coffee table used to be. Everything in the living room is now close to the window. In the bedroom, her bed is shoved into the corner. I add sliding bolts to her two windows and replace her deadbolt with a newer, stronger Medco. Then I show her how to use the doorknob alarm, a mercury motion-sensor device that hangs securely on the doorknob—if anyone moves the knob a fraction of an inch, the alarm will screech. The only way to turn it off is to use the key or destroy the alarm, which is housed in reinforced steel. "There's a five-second delay when you turn it on, so you can leave it hanging inside when you go out. But when you come in, it'll activate, so be ready to use the key to turn it off."

"Can I hang it on the outside?"

"You can, but then it's easier to tamper with."

"Why do you have this?"

"When I first moved to my place, one of the ground-floor apartments was broken into. But I don't use it anymore. I don't have anything to steal." I glance at my watch. It's past eleven, and I haven't realized how long the installation has taken. "Whoa. It's getting late."

"You want to crash on the couch? It's a hassle of a drive."

I hesitate.

She says quickly, "No big deal."

"Okay. I'll take off early in the morning, though."

She nods. "Great. I have some extra work to take care of anyway."

"Are you sure? I don't want to be a—"

"Of course. The couch is pretty comfortable. I've fallen asleep there many times."

"Thanks."

"I'm going to take a quick shower. Turn on the TV or whatever. Have a beer."

"Perfect," I say. I relax on the sofa with a beer and flip through the channels. I settle on the late news. I hear Linda in the shower, and try not to read anything into tonight. She's just being polite. She begins humming, her voice carrying into the living room amid the sounds of splashing and the steady drumming of water on the plastic curtain. I check the new locks on her window and door and turn on the doorknob alarm. I return to the couch and have trouble staying awake.

I open my eyes and see Linda spreading a blanket over me, her hair wrapped in a towel. She's wearing pajamas. She says, "You fell asleep."

"Your shower sounded like rain."

"Do you want pajamas or something? I might have old sweats."

"That's okay." I sit up slowly and stare at Linda's face, her cheeks pink and soft. "You look so clean."

She laughs. She leans her head and body to the side, then ruffles her hair with the towel. "What's new?" she asks, pointing to the TV.

"Not much," I say, watching her.

"I was wondering in the shower if you had any other relatives or your father's friends around. Someone who would've known him back then."

"I don't think so."

"Maybe Garvey's daughter will know."

I can't think about that right now, my head muddled. I say, "What do you do to relax?"

"Relax?"

"When you're not working."

She stops toweling her hair. "I read, go to movies, take walks," she says. "You don't want to talk about work."

"Not really."

"All right. Do you want me to leave you alone?"

I shake my head. "No. Tell me something new about yourself."

"New?"

"Something I don't know."

"Like a secret?"

"It doesn't have to be," I say. "I just want to talk about something else."

She smiles and sits down on the sofa, continuing to dry her hair. "Okay. No work. You want to hear something about me personally, or something that you just don't know about me?"

"What's the difference?"

"Well, you don't know what I do with my hair after I dry it, but that's not very personal."

I look at her wet, curly hair and watch her try to comb it with her fingers, pushing it back. "What do you do with your hair after you dry it?" I ask.

"You only get one question. You sure you want to waste it on that?"

"Only one?"

"Only one. Then it's my turn."

"Okay, I don't want that one," I say. "I want something personal." I remember her crying on the phone to her sister. I add, "Not too personal."

She thinks about this, then says, "Something about me as a kid?"

"Sure."

"All right. You ready?"

"I'm ready."

She says, "I was really fat as a kid."

I sit back. "You're kidding." I look her over, and can't see it.

"Stop that," she says. "I know what you're thinking. Stop looking at me like that."

"Like what?"

"Like you're trying to imagine me fat."

I laugh. "Okay. But how fat?"

"Really fat. When I was thirteen and five-four, I weighed one-fifty."

"How tall are you now?"

"Five-six. I'm one hundred and three pounds."

"That doesn't mean much to me."

"Let me give you an idea. My mom sent me to doctors she was so worried. Kids used to call me 'Lean-da' to torture me."

"Linda?"

"Lean-da." She spells it. "I thought they were using the Spanish pronunciation of my name until someone told me what they were really saying."

"Oh."

She shrugs it off. "I lost most of it when I got to high school. I started taking diet pills and lived off diet soda and crackers. So of course I became anemic."

"Man."

"Anyway, that's my secret. What's yours?"

I think about this for a while, knowing it's something to do with living with my aunt.

"Come on," she says. "No stalling."

"I'm thinking."

"Something bad you did? Some secret you have?"

Then I remember something. I look up. "I haven't thought of this in years, but I killed my aunt's cat."

"You what?"

"Yeah, I was kind of screwed up. We were fighting a lot, because my father never used to tell me what to do. He always left me alone, but then when I went to live with my aunt she was always ordering me around. I couldn't stand it."

"So you killed her cat."

"We had a huge fight," I say, nodding. "I was so pissed off. She controlled everything. I ran out of the house, and I saw her cat. She pampered it more than anything. I remember thinking how she gave her stupid cat more freedom than me, so I picked up a rock and threw it at the cat. It was a lucky shot. I nailed the cat right in the head. I must have cracked its skull or something. It went down right away."

"Jesus, Allen."

"I know. I was shocked that I'd done it, but there was no way I could tell my aunt that. So I buried it under some bushes and pretended I knew nothing about the lost cat. I think she thought the cat just ran away or got picked up by some kid."

"Are you sure it was dead?"

"Yeah. It was dead. I checked its heartbeat and it wasn't breathing."

"What a nasty little kid you were."

"Yeah. Nasty and angry."

"Did she get another one?"

"No," I say. "But it's not like I would've done it again."

"She never found out?"

"No."

Linda shakes her head and looks at me with interest. "I wonder if we would've gotten along as kids."

"Maybe."

She stands up and says it's getting late. "I should get some sleep."

We say good night, and I watch her return to the bathroom. I hear the blow-dryer humming for a few minutes. The toilet flushes. She brushes her teeth, spitting into the sink. She walks quietly into her bedroom and shuts the door. I turn off the TV and lie still, thinking about burying the cat. The ground was hard, and I used a screwdriver to loosen the dirt, a hammer to dig the hole. My aunt didn't have a shovel. I had actually liked the cat, and although petting it sometimes triggered my allergies, I used to scratch its neck, feeling it purr. Almost two decades later, I feel an unexpected sense of remorse. At the time I was more concerned about my aunt discovering what I had done, and geared my energies toward hiding the crime. I covered the burial spot with leaves and dead grass. I left the deadly rock as a grave marker. I didn't give myself any time to think about the cat. What was the cat's name? I picture my aunt standing on the back steps, calling out to the cat. I see her clearly, stepping out through the back door, peering into the darkness, but I can't hear the name she calls out. Her frowning expression is a mixture of annoyance and concern. She leaves the screen door wide open, waiting for the cat to streak through. The back light attracts insects, and I see a moth flutter into the kitchen. She calls out the name again. I know she is going to turn to me and ask me if I have seen the cat. She does. I shake my head. She calls out the name again. Why can't I remember the cat's name? This bothers me, and I fall asleep trying to hear the name my aunt calls out into the night.

32

Arianne Garvey's shaven head has a layer of blond, wispy fuzz that glows in the late-morning sun. She wears four different earrings in each lobe, and despite her militant garb of army pants, a camouflage T-shirt, and regulation boots, her face and bare arms have a softness that don't quite fit, her skin pale and oily, a product of indoor living. She immediately whips out a pack of cigarettes and begins chain-smoking when we sit down at an outdoor café off Fulton. Linda told me that Arianne is a perpetual grad student, in her mid-thirties and on her second master's degree—this one in anthropology. I have trouble imagining this woman in a classroom. "So what's this about?" she asks Linda. Smoke leaks out of her.

"Just a few questions about your late father."

"But for what? A story?"

"Possibly, but we're looking into some things involving Roger Milian and WestSun."

"Who're you?" she asks me.

I tell her my name and that my father used to work for Milian.

She asks me my name again. When I tell her she repeats, "Choice? Choice? Why is that familiar?"

"I understand that my father knew your father."

She looks up, her eyes registering this, and she says, "Oh, shit, you're his son? The guy who died for my dad?"

Linda and I look at each other. I take a deep breath, my nose itching from her smoke. "What do you mean? Did you know my father, Ms. Garvey?"

"Call me Ari. I met him, sure. They were friends."

I try not to seem too anxious, and wait for her to continue. She inhales deeply from her cigarette, studying me. She seems to be relaxing, and I realize it's the smoking. Finally, Linda says, "What do you mean by that? Allen's father died for your father?"

Ari begins explaining, surprised that I don't know this. Her father, Garvey, was about to be fired for some bad decisions he'd made, and my father intervened, although she isn't sure how. It seemed to work for a while, until her father suspected that Milian was messing with the books to make the finances seem better for the buyout.

"Do you know exactly what was going on?" Linda interrupts.

"No. After the lawsuit and the publicity, my dad was screwed up. He never talked about it." She goes on and tells us about Milian firing her father before her father could expose him, and Milian's campaign to ruin her father. To me she says, "Your father tried to stop Milian, basically blackmailing him into stopping, but you know what happened to him."

"The accident?"

"Accident? That was no accident. Not according to my dad," she says. "But it didn't matter. Milian made sure my dad was a laughingstock and destroyed his credibility. He had him blacklisted, so he couldn't get work. My dad just fell apart."

"What about his suicide?" Linda asks.

"Blackmail?" I ask, realizing what she just said.

Ari glances at me, but tells Linda, "It was his second attempt. That we knew of. He tried to OD on pills first." She grimaces at the memory. "That asshole Milian distorted everything, dug up his visits to a therapist and made him out to be a mental case. Everything he did and said was distorted to make him look like a nut. And the bastard got away with it."

"Did you say my father was blackmailing Milian?" I ask.

"Something like that. Had some dirt on him, as well as what my dad told him." She starts a new cigarette with the dying ember of the old one. "He might have even tried to get some money out of Milian."

I can't believe this. "My father?"

She tilts her head at me and almost smiles. "What, too messy for you to take?"

I draw back. "No, but I can't see him—"

"This is what I heard from my dad and mom yelling at each other. After the lawsuit, my mom took me to New York."

There's something about the word "blackmailer" that evokes for me a dark, sordid image, greed and cowardice driving the person who thrives on secrets. I can't reconcile this with my father, and picture him either sitting in front of the TV, exhausted, or toiling in the backyard, digging a hole for a pond. He seemed uncomplicated, unsophisticated, and this clashes with the idea of his blackmailing anyone.

Linda asks, "If you were in New York, how do you know the suicide was real?"

"He was completely out of it. He barely got out of bed. My mom had to send him money to eat. He was a mess."

I say, "So there's no doubt about suicide—"

"No doubt. Milian didn't have to kill him. He was dead long before the suicide." She sees someone she knows walking by and smiles, raising her cigarette hand at him. I glance at the man in a Berkeley sweatshirt. I'm not sure how much I should believe.

"Did your father have any proof against Milian? About the books or anything?" Linda asks.

"No. If he did have proof, do you think he would've let Milian destroy him like that?"

"Why didn't he hire a lawyer?"

"He did! But they kept quitting on him, so he finally took the case himself, which of course was disastrous."

"Did you meet my father?" I ask.

"Sure. A bunch of times. He seemed like a nice man. Very quiet." She studies me. "My dad pretty much lost it after your father died."

"But you don't know what kind of information he had to blackmail Milian with?"

"Other than what my dad suspected? No."

"Would your mother know?" Linda asked.

"No. She washed her hands of all this pretty fast."

"Do you mind if we call her?"

Ari holds up her hand and says, "Slow down. I just got up, and you're giving me a headache." She rubs her eyes and sips her coffee. She explains to us, "Late night."

We wait, and the drone of voices at the nearby tables settles around us. I'm still trying to understand her claim that my father blackmailed Milian.

Ari says to Linda, "Call my mother? Go ahead, but I haven't spoken to her in a while."

"Why not?"

She shrugs. "We were never close." She looks out onto the street, thinking about it. "I didn't like the way she left him like that. I can't blame her, but we were all he had." She takes another deep drag of her cigarette and says with smoke coming out of her mouth and nose, "He tried to do the right thing and everyone left him."

Linda says, "But they were divorced long before that."

"They were still friends. I spent the weekends with him, until my mom moved me East."

"So our fathers must have known each other well," I say.

"I guess. Didn't you know? Maybe you were kind of young."

"Weren't you?"

"I was in my teens. In high school," she says. "So why're you looking into this now?"

Linda turns to me. I tell Ari that my partner was recently killed, and everything keeps leading back to Milian. Ari shakes her head, trying to understand, so Linda adds, "The more we look into Milian, the more suspicious it gets."

"But why would he kill your partner?"

"That's what we're trying to find out."

She waves her cigarette and says, "Maybe he was blackmailing Milian. That seems to do the trick."

Her tone bothers me. "Are you sure my father was blackmailing him?"

"That's what I overheard."

"What exactly did you hear?" I ask.

"That John was using my dad's information and some other things to get money from Milian."

"John?" Linda asks.

"My father," I say, distracted. "His first name was John." I hear two women sitting behind me talking about a class. A cool breeze blows around us, lifting away Ari's smoke. She sees someone else walking by, waves, and the woman calls to her, "You finished already?"

"No. I still have five hours," Ari replies.

"You don't know what information my father had on Milian?" I ask.

"No, just what I said. Hey, I got to get back to writing a paper," Ari says. "Is there anything else?"

I shake my head.

Linda asks, "Your mother's phone number?"

"I don't have it with me. Call me at home."

We thank her, and she lights up another cigarette. When she grabs her bag and stands up, I notice that her navel is pierced. She walks briskly down the street. Linda asks me what I want to do now.

"Let's go."

My father was a blackmailer, and probably died because of it. I don't feel like talking, and Linda sees this. We return to my car. I drive to the South Bay in silence.

I drop Linda off at her apartment. She asks me what I'm going to do. Although I'm supposed to head up to Santa Clara now to check if Junil Kim showed up at church, I just don't have the energy. I'll call Grace Park later. Then I remember that I have to pick up David this afternoon, that I promised to practice tae kwon do with him. I tell Linda that I'll rest for a while, then see David. I'll call her tonight after taking David out to dinner. She says, "Be careful."

I return home and walk around my neighborhood, trying to reconcile what I've just heard about my father with what I know. Maybe it was out of anger: my father seeing what was happening to Garvey, and trying to get Milian not only to stop, but to pay. Was my father so calculating? And would he blackmail for money? I imagine this. He needed the money for medical school, and was having trouble saving. Milian was a convenient target. Maybe my father became greedy and demanded more. Maybe he saw an easy way up. Then Milian arranged the accident. I feel heavier with this knowledge, this possibility of my father blackmailing for money, and understand that I know almost nothing about him.

33

After spending an hour with David at my gym—we used the empty aerobics room—I take him out for some tacos and try to keep a conversation going. I'm preoccupied by what I learned earlier from Ari, and have trouble listening to David. He asks me twice about his form, and I reply, "You're a little rusty, and you need to get more flexible, but it's still pretty good. Do you stretch out every night?"

"No. Should I?" He squeezes extra hot sauce into his last taco.

"Yeah. Before you go to sleep, just do a quick routine of stretches. It might even help you relax. You know, splits, calves, thighs, back, and arms."

"All right. What about my side kick? How is it?" he asks. His cheeks are still flushed from the practice, and I notice that he moves in his seat with some stiffness, rolling his shoulders painfully. I'm impressed he doesn't complain. He adds even more hot sauce.

"Okay," I say, remembering the way he used his heel more than the knife edge of his foot. "As long as you practice in front of a mirror, you'll be fine. You can correct yourself."

"Do you practice?"

"Not that much anymore. I still lift weights, though, and I'm trying to run again," I say. "How's your mom?"

He looks down at his taco and shrugs. "She's okay." His long hair falls over his cheek, a few strands near his mouth. I want to tell him to get a haircut.

"What's she up to?" I ask.

"Working. She's been kind of busy lately."

"Why?"

"I don't know."

"You holding up?"

He grunts a yes, but doesn't say much else. I feel guilty for not calling him sooner. I say, "You miss your father?"

"A little."

"Are you still cutting classes?"

He grins. "No. Well, maybe just study halls."

"Did I tell you that my father died when I was young? A little younger than you?"

"No."

"Screwed me up. I had to live with my aunt, and had to move. It was tough."

"What about your mother?"

"She died when I was born."

"So, what happened when you moved?"

"I hated it. I didn't make any friends, and just holed up in my room. I went running a lot."

He waits for me to explain, then asks, "Running?"

I say, "Running. It helps me think. You should try it."

He considers this, and stares out of the window. He says, "What did you think about?"

"Back then? Everything. Sometimes nothing. I was having trouble with my aunt, and needed that time to myself. No one could bother me when I ran." It suddenly occurs to me how true this is. I told myself that it was for soccer, for tae kwon do, but really it was for the solitude.

"Did you think about your dad?" he asks.

I turn to him and nod slowly. "Of course. I think for the first few years I tried not to, but eventually I did. I still do. I've been thinking about him a lot lately."

"Like what?"

I study him. He's waiting, completely focused on me. I say, "I remember things about him, things I haven't thought of in years. You know, small things."

"Like?"

"Is this twenty questions?"

His cheeks turn red, and I wave my hand. "I'm kidding," I say. "I don't mind. I've been thinking about this garden he was trying to build in the backyard, with a small pond and little trees. He barely had time for anything because he worked so many hours, but he really wanted that garden."

"You mean like those bonsai trees?"

"Sort of. That's Japanese, though. He wanted a Korean garden, the kind he remembered as a kid in Korea. It's funny. He'd use his one day off breaking his back, digging and moving rocks, even though he spent the rest of the week hauling boxes all day."

"My dad hated taking care of the yard."

"Really? I thought he would've liked that kind of work."

"No way. He'd pay me to do it."

I smile. Now that David mentions it, I can see Paul becoming impatient with the pace of yard work. He would want to finish it all quickly. I imagine him getting frustrated with the weeds, and it almost makes me laugh. I glance at my watch. "Come on, let's go. Your mother said she'd pick you up at my place."

He sighs, and says, "Already? How about more of those videos?"

"Videos? Oh, right. ProServ. I've been suspended from there."

"Suspended? Like in trouble suspended?"

"Yeah. I got in trouble."

He is about to ask me something else, but I stand up and wave him along. I drive him back to Monte Vista. He tunes the radio to a rock station and opens his window. He lets his hair flip across his face. As we approach my apartment building he says, "You're not going to say why you got suspended?"

"I annoyed the wrong people."

"Oh."

I pull into my lot and see Sonia's car parked along the street. David also sees his mother and thanks me for taking him out. He asks if I'm going to say hi to his mother.

"Is she in a hurry?"

"I don't know," he says.

"Ah, I should let you guys go."

He shrugs and leaves my car. As he approaches his mother's car, he turns and waves to me, then opens the passenger door. I head to my front door, but Sonia then climbs out and calls to me. I stop.

"Hey, you weren't going to disappear without saying hello, were you?" she says, walking toward me. She's wearing a baseball cap, and she takes it off, mussing her hair with her free hand. A tuft sticks out near her ear.

"It looked like you were in a hurry."

She rolls her eyes and says, "Not for a hello."

I lean against the low railing on my steps. She sits next to me and says, "How are you?"

"Not that great. I've gotten into a little trouble at ProServ."

"Screw them. I've decided to sue. They've been holding up Paul's 401(k) and life insurance."

"When did this happen?" I ask, wondering if this had anything to do with my problems with them.

"Just this week. My lawyer's drawing up the paperwork."

"So Polansky doesn't know yet."

"Not yet."

"Well, I hope you get blood."

"You might be called to testify."

"Great. I look forward to it. But I've been suspended, so I don't know how good my testimony will be."

"Suspended?"

I sigh. "Long story. I'd rather not get into it."

"Don't worry. I'll get them."

"How about a drink?" I ask. "Maybe David wants something too."

"Okay," she says, waving for David to come over from the car. I open the front door, glad for the company, and lead them upstairs.

"It's kind of small and messy," I say. David is looking at the peeling paint along the hallway, and I add, "It's old."

"We don't care," Sonia says.

I let them into my apartment, and Sonia pulls off her cap, scratching the back of her head. David immediately wanders to my bookshelf, where I have a few martial arts books. I ask Sonia to get the glasses while I check how much juice I have. "I might only have water," I say.

I watch her cropped shirt ride up as she reaches into a cupboard for the glasses, the small of her back exposed. I look away as she pulls her shirt down. I pour the last of the orange juice for David and give Sonia and myself ice water. She holds up her drink and smiles. We clink glasses. She toasts, "Down with ProServ."

"All right."

"David," she says. "Come have juice."

My buzzer goes off and I glance at my watch, wondering if it's Linda. When I press the intercom button and ask who it is, the voice answers, "Is Allen Choice there?"

"That's me. Who is this?"

"May we speak to you for a moment?"

"Who is this?"

"The police."

Sonia stops drinking. I tell her to wait there while I go down to check.

I approach the front entrance warily and see two clean-cut men in suits standing there, one holding up a badge and identification card against the glass. "Allen Choice?" he asks, his voice muffled.

I nod, and open the door.

"We're with the Monte Vista Police Department," he says, pocketing his ID. He motions to his partner and himself. "I'm Lieutenant Hollis. This is Detective Ingram. We were wondering if you have time to come down to the station to answer a few questions."

"About what?"

"We'd prefer to get into that at the station."

"You can tell me what it involves."

He and his partner exchange looks. Ingram clears his throat and says, "We found . . . a deceased person today, and we'd like to ask you a few questions about it."

"What?" I ask, hearing Sonia walk down a few of the steps to see what's happening. "Who?"

"We prefer to wait until—"

"Who was it, goddammit?" I say. For a moment I think it's Linda and feel a strange weakening in my chest, my breathing shallow.

Hollis says, "We believe, pending further identification, it's a man named Junil Kim."

"Oh, shit," I say, rubbing my sternum. "How did he . . . ?" But I can't quite finish my sentence.

"Let's go to the station for this," he says. "There's no need to do it here." He glances up at Sonia.

"Allen?" she says. Her voice sounds thin.

"He was someone I recently met," I tell her.

"Mr. Choice, we really should talk at the station."

To Sonia I say, "I have to go. Sorry."

"Do you need a lawyer?" she asks.

I turn to the men. "Do I need a lawyer?"

"You're not under arrest," Hollis says. "We just want to talk."

"Am I a suspect? Was he murdered? How did he die?"

"Mr. Choice—"

"How did he die?"

"We're not sure yet."

"Am I a suspect?"

"You're not anything at the moment."

"Then why can't we talk here?"

Hollis sighs, and Ingram says, "You're free to have a lawyer present. But we need to talk at the station."

I ask Sonia, "Do you know a lawyer?"

"Yes. I'll call him. He'll meet you at the police station."

"Can you lock up?" I ask her. "I've got my keys and everything on me."

She nods, glancing at the policemen.

"All right," I say, stepping out with them. "Should I drive?"

I see them hesitate, and Hollis says, "No, we can give you a lift."

This worries me. I say, "You could've just called me, you know."

"We tried. You weren't home."

"So you showed up in person instead?"

"We saw you come in," he says.

This really worries me. They were waiting for me.

•

Part 4

The Sounds of
Solitude

34

Hollis and Ingram drive me to the Monte Vista police station off Shore Drive, which is adjacent to the fire department building. Two large red fire engines sit in the open garages. I ask them if they're still looking into Paul Baumgartner's murder. "Yes," Hollis says. The lead homicide detective for Paul's case, Detective McCall, is apparently investigating Junil Kim's death as well, and he recognizes me as soon as I come in. Although he was friendly with me at our last meeting, McCall walks by me without saying anything. Hollis leads me to the interrogation room, and I wait at the door. I'm still not sure how to play this—if I should try to be helpful immediately or should wait for a lawyer.

"Mr. Choice?"

I turn around. An older black man with a graying beard approaches slowly, wearily. He has large, heavy bags under his eyes and seems exhausted. He looks me up and down, thinks for a moment, then says, "I'm Sergeant Busch of the Santa Clara Sheriff's Office. Please come in." He opens the door to the interrogation room and motions me in. It's the same room I was in after Paul's death, with two video cameras stationed in the corners, a metal table with four chairs, and a phone next to the door. I remember staring up at the ceiling covered with acoustic white tiles, since it's similar to the ceiling in the basement of my aunt's place in Oakland. Once, as a teenager, I tried counting the tiny holes out of boredom, and gave myself headaches.

"Have a seat," Sergeant Busch says. He waits until I sit down, and he pauses, breathing slowly. I watch him fix his crooked tie. He then leaves me alone and shuts the door.

They make me wait for almost thirty minutes. The video cameras are probably taping, or at least transmitting a live feed as they watch me. I'm sure there's a microphone somewhere, though I can't see anything yet. I guess the telephone is rigged to listen in. I sit back, becoming more suspicious. I'm being treated like a suspect. Where is Sonia's lawyer?

Sergeant Busch and Detective McCall walk in. Busch sits across from me, exhaling when he settles into the seat, while McCall remains standing at attention, giving me a blank stare. They don't apologize for making me wait, and I sigh inwardly. Standard interrogation procedures. I say, "How can I help you?"

"We'd like to ask you about your relationship to Junil Kim and your whereabouts this past week," McCall says. His demeanor has changed completely since I last met him. Not only is he tense, but his body language—the way he tightly folds his arms now and looks down at me—is hostile.

"I'm glad you're still working on the Florentino's shooting," I say. I smell wintergreen, and am not sure where it's coming from.

Busch nods. "We are."

"Are you new here?" I ask him. "I don't remember seeing you."

"We'll ask the questions, if you don't mind," McCall says.

"I'm coordinating the investigation with the sheriff's office and the Monte Vista police."

"How do you know Junil Kim?" McCall asks.

I explain that he was an old friend of my father's and I have recently begun looking people up, trying to learn more. I then explain how I located him, through my aunt and Grace Park, and then tried to talk to him again, but couldn't find him. "I asked his neighbor to look out for him, but he didn't hear anything from Kim."

"Where were you this weekend?" McCall asks.

I think about the break-in at WestSun and become wary. "Can you tell me how Junil Kim died?"

"How do you know he died?" Busch asks.

"The lieutenant told me."

They glance at each other. McCall says, "We'll get to that in a second."

"Can you tell us where you were the past forty-eight hours?" Busch says.

I reply slowly, trying to determine if they have any evidence against me, "I was with a reporter, helping her on a story, then I was with David Baumgartner—"

"What's the name of this reporter?"

"Linda Maldonado of the *San Jose Sentinel*. Now, can you tell me what this is about?"

Busch says, "Junil Kim's body was found this morning in Moorfield Park. He had been beaten to death."

Moorfield Park is only a few blocks away from me. "Beaten to death?" I say.

"The coroner is doing the autopsy, but a . . ." McCall looks down at his notes. "A Mrs. Grace Park filed a missing person report today with the Milpitas police, which is why we were able to identify the body."

Busch says, "We'd like to know why he was here in Monte Vista. The only connection we have so far is you."

"Me."

"We already spoke to the victim's neighbor, who said you were looking around there on Thursday."

"I wanted to talk to him again, but couldn't find him."

"And why did you want to talk to him? When was the first time?"

"I met him at his church. You can ask Grace Park that. He knew my father and I had more questions."

"What kind of questions?"

"I wanted to know more about my father. He died when I was young."

They study me. McCall then says, "Do you see David Baumgartner often?"

"No. A couple times. I promised I'd practice tae kwon do with him."

"Did you know him before his father was killed?"

"Know him? I knew of him. I met him a few times when I visited Paul. Does this have anything to do with Junil Kim?"

"How about Sonia Baumgartner? Did you know her through Paul Baumgartner?"

I nod. "Same thing. We met a few times when I went over to their place for dinner."

Busch asks, "Can you tell us why ProServ fired you?"

"I'm on leave. I wasn't fired."

"Indefinite leave, according to your employer. What's the reason?"

"It's complicated."

"Tell us."

I'm pretty sure Charles or Polansky were tight-lipped about it, so I say, "It was too soon to return to work."

This hangs in the air for a moment. The smell of wintergreen is familiar, medicated lotion for sore muscles. It's coming from Busch. I turn to him, but McCall asks, "So what's your relationship with Sonia Baumgartner?"

The way he circles back to this question is suspicious. I say, "What exactly is this about?"

Busch says, "Mr. Choice, we're trying to get through this—"

"I'm afraid I don't see the connection to Junil Kim," I say. "Why all these other questions?"

"All right," McCall says. "Why did you search Junil Kim's trailer?"

"What? I didn't—" I start to say, but stop. "Oh, you mean when I visited. I wanted to make sure he wasn't home. The door was unlocked."

"What did you want to talk to him about?"

"I told you. My father." I wonder where that lawyer is.

"You said you were worried about him. Why?"

"What?" I ask. "When did I say that?"

"To the neighbor. You said you were worried about him and you wanted the neighbor to call you if he didn't show up."

I shake my head. "I was worried because he apparently never went anywhere but was then missing. I told the neighbor to give me a call either way, because Kim doesn't have a phone."

Busch looks up.

I say, "You didn't know that? That's why I had to visit him in person. That's why I had to call Grace Park. Junil Kim is hard to find." I watch him tug at his beard, and he turns to McCall.

McCall clears his throat. "Do you currently have a romantic interest in Sonia Baumgartner?"

"What? What the hell are you talking about?" I say, raising my voice. "What does this have to do with Junil Kim?"

"Well, do you?"

"The answer is no. I do not have a romantic interest in Sonia

Baumgartner." I look up at the camera. "Did you get that? Now how in the hell does this connect with Junil Kim?"

"We were just wondering why two homicides in one month seem to, well, connect to you."

They wait for my response, and I see now that they're trying to get me angry. I lean back in my seat and shake my head. "That's what this is? You have two unsolved murders, so you look for the easiest solution?"

Busch says, "The simplest solution is usually the correct one. Occam's razor."

"The simplest solution is usually the stupidest one," I say evenly. "At this time I am formally requesting the presence of my lawyer. I'd like to make a call."

Busch says, "You're not a suspect, you know."

"No, I don't know that. You're treating me like one."

"We just need some questions answered."

"About Junil Kim?"

"About you," McCall says.

"What does Sonia Baumgartner have to do with anything?" I ask, knowing the answer.

They don't reply, and I'm getting angry. I say, "What's with that case, anyway? Have you made any progress? I had to tell Paul's son today that the police aren't doing shit about his father." I see if this has any effect. "I had to tell him they're sitting on their asses."

McCall's face hardens. I realize that they are working on it, but probably aren't getting anywhere. I say to Busch, "Is this why you, Sergeant, were reassigned? Were the higher-ups not satisfied with the progress?"

McCall says, "Now, wait a minute——"

A look from Busch stops him. I sigh and repeat my request for my lawyer. "I hope he's not waiting for me out there. That would be illegal, denying me representation."

"You're not under arrest."

"You bring me down here, you make me wait for thirty minutes, you double-team me and throw everything you can think of at me . . . I'm a little disappointed, to tell you the truth. My friend and partner was killed, and now I learn that a family friend was killed, and the best you can do is treat me like this."

McCall is about to respond, but Busch stands up slowly while holding his lower back and says, "Get Hollis. We're done for now."

"What about—?"

But Busch shakes his head and leaves the room. McCall follows. I pace around the table, trying to figure out what exactly they want from me. They're just fishing for anything they can use. They're getting desperate. Two murders in their neighborhood.

Hollis opens the door and motions me outside. We walk to a holding-cell area with a pay phone, and he tells me to call my lawyer. I call Sonia at her house.

"Did you get that lawyer?" I ask.

"I did. But he just called. Where are you?"

"At the police station."

"But he was just there looking for you."

"In Monte Vista?"

"No! He's in Palo Alto!"

I sigh. "I'm at the Monte Vista police station."

"All right. I'll call him right back."

"Is he expensive?"

"I'm not sure. He's the partner of the lawyer who's taking care of my things."

I thank her and hang up. I think about how much money I have in the bank, and suppress the faint feeling of anxiety.

Fifteen minutes later, I discover that Stan Browning is expensive. Everything about him is expensive: his Italian suit, his Rolex, his gold pen. He glitters. He has pale, wispy blond hair, a dimpled chin, and bright, white teeth. He charges $150 an hour and requires a $5,000 retainer, but I don't have time to shop around, and I'm not sure what I am up against. When he arrives at the police station, I know he's the lawyer before he introduces himself to me by the calm, smooth demeanor with which he talks with McCall, who directs him to me. He's comfortable here, and smiles easily. We talk in a private office next to the interrogation room. I tell him what has happened and what I've already been asked; he wants to know more about Linda and a detailed accounting of where we've been the past few days. I explain as much as I can—leaving out the breaking and entering of WestSun—and then repeat some of the questions McCall and Busch have been asking. When I tell him about Linda and my suspicions about Paul's death, about Milian and Durante, he asks if I have evidence or any kind of proof. Except for vague warnings and the surveillance, I have none. I have been focused on my father's death, not Paul's. I tell Browning that

I've been looking into it, but have very little. I realize how weak this sounds. He frowns, then suggests that I might want to hold off on making any unusual and unsubstantiated accusations. He leaves me to talk to Busch and McCall, and arranges a brief interview period, to be recorded, with him present.

"What are they looking for?" I ask before we enter the interrogation room.

"Just information at this point. They're suspicious of seeing you here twice. I won't let you answer anything that's out of line."

The entire interview takes less than twenty minutes, with some of the same questions being asked of me, but this time Sergeant Busch does all the talking. The atmosphere is formal, and Browning objects to two questions about my relationship with Sonia and Linda, saying he can't see how that's relevant to their investigation and I don't have to answer them.

When it's over, Browning gives me his card with his cell phone and beeper numbers, and tells me to contact him as soon as anything else happens. He advises me to talk to Linda, since the police will undoubtedly contact her soon, and he also tells me to drop by his office tomorrow morning.

"Why?"

"The retainer. A check is fine."

"Oh," I say. I thank him and walk back to my apartment. Five thousand dollars. I have about seven thousand in my savings account. I have no job, no income, and two thousand left after the retainer. The rent is due in two weeks.

Then it finally hits me. Junil Kim is really dead.

35

I run. I return home, change into a sweatsuit, and head out. It's dark, and the neighborhood is quiet. Sunday nights are usually calm. I take the side streets along Main, weaving around blocks and deeper into the residential area, drifting farther away from my apartment in larger circles. The night air is cool, the perspiration down my back chilling me. My thoughts keep returning to Junil Kim, and I have trouble grasping that he might have been killed because of me. It doesn't make sense. I'm not that important, and I can't see my actions having any real effect.

Maybe that's the problem. I can't see my responsibility in this, but my role grows with each determined step I take toward Milian. When those two men attacked me in the alley, warning me away, I didn't really think about what it all meant; I simply reacted. They could have killed me, but didn't. Why? Because Paul had just been murdered, and my death would have raised too many questions with the police, who would begin looking into the connections. So, Milian could only warn me. When I didn't heed the warning, he tried to cut off my contacts, Stein and Kim. He was worried enough to eavesdrop on my entire life, and to kill Kim when threats failed.

This means I'm not finished with Stein, since he must know something that's worrying Milian. Linda and I should also talk to Mrs.

Garvey, who might have more background for us. The most obvious step is learning more about Milian himself.

I remember how pleased Junil Kim was when he saw me, his easy and friendly words a surprise. I suddenly worry about his trailer, his rice-paper drawings curling in the sun. What will happen to his calligraphy? I wonder if I can get some of them, but have to resist the urge to drive up there. I can no longer be seen anywhere near his place.

My knees start hurting, the usual sign for me to slow down, but I continue my pace. I hear Mrs. Bruno crying; she wails for her dead son, Chris, and the back of my neck prickles as it did over two decades ago. I never knew the details of Chris's accident, but always have imagined him running out into the street without looking. We used to play soda-can soccer, scoring goals in between parked cars, and we often paused the game while cars passed by. It would have been easy to be hit if he was playing alone. I see Chris kicking the can out into the street and running after it. I'm not sure where this image came from, and why I always have pictured the collision in such detail, though it was probably from my father telling me about the accident. He told me that Chris had been run over by a car, so I envisioned a terrible scene of the car knocking Chris down, then rolling over his supine body. Even the sounds of the thumping and screeching were vivid to me. I was a morbid kid, giving myself nightmares. I know my current spate of waking dreams has to do with the deaths around me.

Linda is waiting in front of my apartment building when I return. "The police called me," she says. "I have to talk to them tomorrow."

I lead her upstairs, sweating and panting. My legs hurt. In between breaths I tell her about my visit to the station. "They're going to check my story with you."

"So he's . . . dead?"

"That's what they say. He was found in Moorfield Park."

"Jesus. Why would they—"

"I don't know. I have the feeling they tried to warn him like Stein, but he wasn't the kind to be pushed around. He would've fought back. He looked pretty tough."

"And you're a suspect? Why?"

"I'm not sure. They're not sure. My lawyer—"

"You hired a lawyer?" she asks, looking up sharply.

"Yeah. He said the police are suspicious that two deaths somehow are linked to me."

"What did you tell them?"

"I've been looking into my father's past. That's all. They wanted to know where I was this week. I told them the truth."

"What about WestSun? The other night?"

"I just said I was with you, helping you with a story. They'll ask you about that."

"Oh, man," she says, sitting down. "I can't believe this."

The phone rings. Both of us tense. I answer it and Sonia asks me what happened. I tell her Browning showed up, and that this isn't over. "The police will probably contact you to check my whereabouts."

"What's going on? Why are you being questioned?"

I tell her briefly that an old friend of my father's was killed. The police are curious about me, since I contacted the victim recently.

"Allen," she says, her voice tight. "You're not getting me into any kind of trouble, are you?"

"No," I say quickly.

"You know I'm about to get into a lawsuit with ProServ."

"You mentioned something about it." I see Linda listening to me.

"All right," Sonia says. "I'll talk to you later."

We hang up. Linda asks me who it was. When I tell her she looks surprised. I say, "I've spent a little time with David, Paul's son."

"Are you okay?"

I nod, and tell her I'm going to wash up. She stares at me but keeps quiet. I limp into the bathroom, turn on the shower, and study my sweaty, pale face in the mirror. Startled by my anxious expression, a wild-eyed look, I sit on the side of the bathtub and breathe slowly, inhaling the steam rising from the water jets. Too much going on. I'm having trouble absorbing it all, and can't believe the police are suspicious of me. I haven't done anything. I'm just trying to figure what the hell happened to my father. I'm looking into my partner's death. Christ, I'm doing their job for them, and this is what I get?

There's a knock at the door. Linda says, "Allen?"

"Come in."

She peers in slowly and sees me sitting there in my sweatsuit. She waves the steam away from her and asks, "What are you doing?"

"I'm thinking."

"I guess I'll be going."

I sit up. "No. I'll be out in a second."

"Are you sure?"

"I want you here."

She fans her shirt and says, "What should we do?"

"I want to talk to Stein again. We should contact Mrs. Garvey. I also want to see Milian."

"See him how?"

"Visit him."

"Why?"

"We keep circling. We need to get to the source."

"What do you think will happen?"

"I don't know. I need to see him. I need to see the man who could kill so easily."

"It might make things worse."

"I know," I say. I think about Browning, how I have to visit him with a large check. "I'm already in trouble."

"Don't self-destruct on me now, Allen."

I look up. The steam has filled the bathroom, shrouding Linda. As she steps out she says, "We're getting somewhere. We're going to break it open soon."

I'm not sure I agree. I undress and climb into the shower, my thoughts heavy.

Later that night, as Linda and I stay up talking about what to do next, I confess that I'm overwhelmed and worried about money. "What started out as nothing, just me looking around, is now me without a job, an expensive lawyer, and Junil Kim . . ."

"Do you have enough for the lawyer?" she asks, sitting back in the futon and crossing her legs.

"For now."

"I can lend—"

"No way. Thanks, but I hate borrowing money." I'm struck by this offer and repeat, "That's very nice of you, but it's okay."

"I'm the one who got you into this."

I shake my head. "I did this because I wanted to."

"What about your aunt?"

"For money? I don't think so." Although I've already considered this, I can't see myself asking her for anything. We have had too many problems with that in the past. I tell Linda about growing up with my aunt and how cheap she was. "That's one reason why I dropped out of college and started working. I couldn't stand to depend on her anymore. Once she even gave me a hard time for wanting new socks."

"Socks?"

I explain to Linda that at one point most of my socks had holes, and I went to my aunt for some money to buy new ones. She looked at my socks and told me to keep turning them around to wear out the other sides first.

"But they're fitted to be worn one way," Linda says.

"I know. I'm definitely not asking her for anything."

"That money is supposed to be yours, the settlement for your father."

"It's possible. We don't know that for sure. Maybe I should ask Milian if it was for me."

"Maybe you should."

We look at each other, the idea making sense. I say, "We should just show up and see what happens."

"It's risky."

"I'd like to meet the man who killed my father."

"Allen," she warns.

"Don't worry. I'm okay." I sit back in the futon and ask her, "Don't you ever wonder about your father? The one who left?"

"No. My stepdad is my father."

"You're not curious at all? Don't wonder what he's like, what you inherited, if anything?"

"I don't care."

I turn to her, and she really doesn't seem to care. She rolls her eyes and says, "He just knocked my mother up, that's all. He's nothing more than a sperm donor."

I resist this. If I'm smart, I'll let all this go and ignore what I've learned so far about my father's death. I should roll my eyes as Linda just did and forget about Milian and WestSun and anything that has to do with him. Of course I can't. When I think about my father studying medical textbooks, struggling with English, and moving boxes and driving a rig when he wanted so much to become a doctor, coming home exhausted at night and watching TV silently, the weight of me sitting there, reminding him of his responsibilities and his dead wife, I brood over Milian, over my aunt, over everyone who fucked up his life. Including me. I killed my mother by being born.

"Are you okay?" Linda asks.

"You *keep* asking me that," I say quickly. I see her startled reaction, and add, "Sorry. I didn't mean that."

"You're a little touchy."

I nod. "Everything's a mess."

"You're probably tired. I'll get going."

"Wait. Hang out a little bit."

She hesitates, then says, "All right." She lies down lengthwise along the futon, resting her head on her arm, and curls her legs near the armrest. "How did he die?"

"My father?"

"Junil Kim."

"I don't know."

"I can find out," she says. "In fact, I'm sure the story will show up in tomorrow's paper."

"Shit. You think I'll be mentioned?"

"It depends on what the police want people to know. It'll probably be a short piece. There isn't enough information for anything longer."

"Can you check tomorrow?"

"I will," she says. "I'm sorry this happened."

"I'm not sure how to feel. I still can't get it."

"Does he have any family?"

"I don't think so. But I should call Grace Park, who goes to his church. She's the one who filed a missing person report." Linda's hair fans out by my leg. She stares at my bookcase. I pick up a lock of her hair and let it fall.

"Does she know? Have the police—"

"I think so, if she filed the report."

"Oh," she says. When I twirl some of her hair, she closes her eyes and lowers her head, sighing.

"This okay?" I continue, and spread her curls through my fingers.

She murmurs yes. After a minute she says in a sleepy voice, "Talk to me."

As I brush her hair with my fingers I tell her about Chris Bruno and how he and I used to play jokes on his mother. Once we placed a water-filled balloon on the top edge of a slightly open door, rigging it to fall as soon as someone pushed the door. I was worried about angering her, but Chris assured me that he did this all the time. We then pretended we were fighting, yelling "Take that! Ow! You can't do that!" and punching the sofa and stomping our feet on the ground. I heard his mother run down the hallway. She called out, "What's going on in there!" and my fear of what was about to happen was mixed with anticipation, and Chris and I grinned at each other. His mother burst through the door, and the water balloon jiggled, warped and elongated in the air, and fell onto her shoulder, breaking open but wetting only her arm and leg, most of the water splashing onto the carpet. Chris laughed, but I waited to see what she would do. Her expression moved from confusion to recognition, then she looked down at the water spot, crossed her arms, and said, "Very funny. You're going to clean that up, you know."

Chris kept giggling and saying, "You should've seen your face!"

She smiled, shook her head, and left.

I tell Linda that Mrs. Bruno's tolerant smile was something that amazed me, since no one I knew would have reacted so calmly. I look down at Linda and ask quietly, "Are you asleep?"

When she doesn't answer, I watch her breathe slowly, her nostrils flaring a moment. I place my palm on her forehead, wondering if she is dreaming. I draw a blanket over her, then stand up slowly and walk to my desk. I have to go over my bank account and figure out what to do about money. I glance back at her. She's curled up in a fetal position, resting her head on her praying hands, locks of her hair covering her eyes, her expression calm and quiet, and she is quite beautiful.

36

Writing the check isn't that painful, since I can always tear it up, but handing it over the next day to Browning's business manager hurts. I can't remember when I've ever written a check that large. Even my car required a smaller down payment. I watch the manager double-check the amount and log this payment into the computer. He thanks me, but I stand there.

"Something else?" he asks.

"Do I get a receipt?"

"If you'd like."

"I'd like."

He writes out a receipt. I walk out of the Palo Alto office. Browning and I spoke for a few minutes, but there is nothing new, and he'll keep me posted on the progress of the investigation. I calculate that those three minutes cost me $7.50.

When I return home, I listen to Linda on my machine tell me she'll meet me for lunch, and that I should get a copy of this morning's *Chronicle*. I walk down to the bookstore and leaf through the edition. In the Bay Area section, my headline is toward the bottom of the page: "Florentino's Shooting Bodyguard Questioned in Second Murder."

"Oh, shit," I say, and buy the paper. I skim the article outside. I am named, but the article states that I'm not a suspect at this time. This doesn't sound very good. It ends: "Choice has been suspended from

ProServ Executive Protection Services for what a spokesman for the agency cites as 'an unrelated matter.' " Charles is the official spokesman. Why did he reveal this? To shield themselves from bad press.

I call Grace Park, who is not happy to hear from me. I say, "I just wanted to let you know how sorry I am—"

"Because of you he's dead," she says.

"What?"

"Why did you bring this to him?"

"I didn't do anything," I say.

"He told me you were bringing trouble."

"When? When did he say this?"

"After you talked to him at church."

"Why did he say that?"

"He just knew. He never bothered anyone. Why did you bring this?"

"I didn't mean for any of this—"

"You can't call here anymore. You can't come to my church. I had to identify him! Why did you do this?"

"I'm sorry," I say. "I didn't know—I was just trying to find out more."

She hangs up.

I reread the article. The initial findings are that Junil Kim died from severe head trauma. I close my eyes and try not to imagine Mrs. Park identifying Kim's dead, beaten body. On my table next to the phone are scraps of paper with the different numbers I've called, and I search for WestSun's number. When I find it I call, and the receptionist answers. I ask if Mr. Milian has any openings today.

"May I ask who this is?"

I think for a moment and say, "This is Chris Bruno of Pinewood Investments."

"Oh! Pinewood. But aren't you going to see him tonight?"

"Tonight," I say.

"The party starts at seven. Your colleague Mr. Frankel said he'd be there."

I remember the name. "Right. Kyle mentioned that. Is it at West-Sun?"

"God, no. It's at Mr. Milian's house. Do you need directions?"

"That would be great."

After she gives me directions—Milian lives in Los Altos Hills—I say, "I don't seem to have an invitation. Will that be a problem?"

"We didn't send out invitations."

"Okay. I'll probably come with Kyle. Thanks."

I hang up. My palms are sweaty. A party to celebrate Pinewood's involvement? They are investing in the company, closing the deal. I begin to make sense of Junil Kim's death, of the warning to Stein, of bugging my apartment. Milian is ensuring success. I realize that this is probably what happened twenty years ago, when Sunrise Goods was merging with Western Imports. Garvey was railroaded out, and my father killed. I still don't know what exactly my father knew, what the source of the blackmail had been. I see patterns, everything arranged in logical order, and try to reach Linda at work and at home. She isn't in. I still have a couple of hours before lunch, and I need to do something.

I call my bank's automated account information and input Browning's check number, knowing that he wouldn't have had time to deposit it yet, but I want to hear the status of check 454. The recorded voice tells me no checks have cleared within the past five days. I remember my rent, and write out check number 455. I balance my checkbook, going over the math three times, and note nervously that my funds are rapidly approaching the one-thousand-dollar mark. I skim the classifieds in today's *Chronicle* and squelch the faint feeling of dread at the prospect of another job search. I have to update my résumé, and find people to be references. I have to practice my smile and my interviewing technique. Christ. I did this to myself.

By the time Linda arrives I've gone over the classifieds and am amazed by how unqualified I am for most good jobs. There are plenty of security-related positions open, but they're all entry-level uniformed gigs, armored car drivers, or mall walkers for $7.00 to $9.50 an hour, no benefits. I did that six years ago, but not anymore. I'll have to start contacting the agencies, Triumph and Black Diamond first, maybe check up on some old contacts. The possible problem: it's a small security community, and they'll have heard about my suspension by now. Hell, it's in today's paper. I'm not sure what the other agencies will think. I'll have to start making some calls soon.

"I was just talking with a detective," Linda says as I let her in.

"Monte Vista police?"

"They showed up at the *Sentinel*. It looks like they're very interested in you."

"How so?"

"They wanted to know everything about you."

"What did you tell them?"

"Everything safe. And the story I'm working on is an extended profile of you."

"They bought that?"

"Not really, but I didn't have to talk to them at all, you know. I was curious to see what they'd asked. It looks like they're trying to find a motive for killing Junil Kim."

"I have none."

"And they're also going back over Paul's death."

"They can't possibly think I had something to do with that."

She points at me. "They're very curious about you."

"They won't find anything," I say. "But I have some news for you." I tell her about Milian's party tonight and Pinewood's presence. "I'm thinking of showing up and seeing who's there."

"Why?"

"I want Milian to know that I'm not going to disappear."

"You'll antagonize him."

"I know."

She shakes her head. "It sounds foolish."

Hiding my irritation, I say, "Maybe. At the very least I want to see where Milian lives, maybe see who's at the party."

"I got Mrs. Garvey's number from her daughter," she says. "I thought we'd try to call her tonight."

"You didn't tell the police anything about WestSun and Milian, did you?"

"I thought about it, but no."

"Thought about it?"

"First, we don't have anything. Yet. Second, I realized that I'd be locked out if they found something. It wouldn't be my story anymore," she says. "Should we call Mrs. Garvey now?"

I hesitate, remembering that Mrs. Garvey lives in New York—an expensive long-distance call.

"What's wrong?" she asks.

"Nothing. Let's call."

Linda does the talking while I sit next to her, my ear pressed next to hers. Her hair tickles my neck. She changes her voice, softens it, and when she introduces herself to Mrs. Garvey, adding that Ari gave her the number, Mrs. Garvey seems pleased. "How is Ari?"

"She says hello, and hopes it's okay that I call," Linda says. She tells Mrs. Garvey that Ari is doing well in graduate school and is finishing up a round of papers. Linda immediately establishes a familiarity with Mrs. Garvey, and I know I could never do something like this. When Mrs. Garvey asks what the call is about, Linda says she's doing a story about WestSun, and her ex-husband's name came up in the research.

Mrs. Garvey immediately becomes quiet.

"I was wondering if you could give me a little background," Linda says.

"My ex-husband committed suicide a long time ago."

"I know, but I'm more interested in what happened around that time when he was fired. What was going on then?"

"God, you're not digging up all that, are you?"

"Well, a little."

"Did Roger tell you anything?"

"Roger Milian?" Linda asks, glancing at me. I quickly move back next to her to hear Mrs. Garvey's response.

"I think you should talk to him, not me," she says.

Linda pauses, then says, "May I ask what your relationship to Mr. Milian was at the time?"

"Wait a minute. This is for a story?"

"I'm looking into WestSun's history and possible illegalities—"

"I don't know anything about that," Mrs. Garvey says. "I was an innocent bystander. I had nothing to do with Noah or with Roger's problems with him."

"Of course not. I didn't mean to imply you did. But your relationship with Mr. Milian—"

"Wait, wait, you're twisting my words. I didn't have a relationship with Ro— Mr. Milian."

Linda is quiet. The line hums. I wonder briefly how much this is going to cost.

Linda finally says, "Mrs. Garvey, your relationship with Mr. Milian isn't at issue here—"

"Wait! I didn't say that! You can't quote me—"

"I already spoke to Krista Milian about this."

Another static-filled pause. "That bitch. I have nothing else to say." She hangs up.

Linda turns to me, her eyes shiny.

"Holy shit," I say.

"Holy shit is right. Milian must have had an affair with Mrs. Garvey."

"Are you sure?"

"Didn't you hear her?"

I nod. "I heard something. But she never really admitted anything."

"She didn't have to."

I consider this. "If she had an affair with Milian, that would explain Garvey's anger at Milian."

"But is it enough for blackmail?"

"Milian was married at the time."

"So?"

I say slowly, "The merger was going on around then. What would a divorce do?"

"Right! She could sue for her part of the company somehow. She could put an injunction on the merger itself until everything was resolved."

"We should ask Krista Milian about this."

Linda glances at her watch. "And I think we should visit Milian tonight."

"You sure about that?"

"I am if you are," she says, opening her day planner and flipping through the pages. "Her number is in here somewhere."

I try to figure my father's role in this. He must have followed Garvey's lead and continued blackmailing Milian after Garvey had been fired. Yet this doesn't sound right. Would Milian have murdered my father for that? Why not simply fire him? I just can't see how a potential messy divorce would have prompted Milian to murder.

Linda is calling Krista Milian. I sit on the windowsill and watch her work. I don't know where she gets the energy for this, and I try to reserve my strength for tonight. I prepare to meet my father's killer.

37

Linda drives us to Los Altos Hills, since she knows the area from attending extension courses at Foothill College. Milian lives up in the hills about a mile away from the campus, and as we wind our way off El Monte, through some twisting streets deeper into a neighborhood with large stone and iron fences hiding most of the houses, Linda and I continue to speculate about Milian and Mrs. Garvey. We haven't been able to reach Mrs. Milian, but Linda called a colleague to ask about divorce law. We learned that Mrs. Milian could easily have hindered a merger depending on how many of the corporate shares she owned and how much she had helped her husband in forming the company.

"What are we going to ask him if we get in?" Linda says.

"Anything we can." The houses here are getting larger and more hidden the deeper we drive. Huge hedges and low-hanging, leafy trees shroud entrances. "How the hell are you supposed to find a place?" I ask.

"I think that's the point."

"Oh."

She says, "When I was at Foothill I sometimes drove around here."

"Why?"

"Looking around."

"What classes did you take?"

"Computer work. Just beefing up my skills."

I see a woman wearing white tights and a fluorescent vest jogging on the sidewalk. Her sneakers glow, her ponytail flops side to side. It must be safe out here. Linda says, "You'll never catch me doing that in *my* neighborhood."

I nod. The affluence here reminds me of my critical money situation.

Linda asks, "What's wrong?"

"What? Nothing."

"You're thinking."

"About money."

She says, "Is this my fault? Did I pull you into this?"

"No. You just asked the right questions." I look up at the street signs. "This is the street."

"What's the number?"

"Five sixty-five. It should be coming up soon."

She says, "What are you going to do? About money, I mean."

"I have no idea."

"I think it's there. Where the cars are." She points ahead and pulls us toward the curb. She shuts off the engine and turns off the head-lights, and we sit quietly. Streetlights curve around the bend. Every-thing is still. We begin to hear faint music coming from the house. Linda says, "We should find out more about the Pinewood deal."

"Kyle Frankel will be there. He's the contact."

"Lot of cars."

"The bigger the better."

"If they all know each other, we're not going to get very far."

I nod.

We leave the car and walk through the front gate. The main house, a two-story Spanish-style sprawling building with orange tiles and a pale red facade, is lit up, voices spilling out of the first-floor windows. Dense rose bushes with red and pink flowers envelop the lower walls, and small path lights blink on automatically when we move near them. We stop, and I can't tell which is the front door, since there are three doors along this side.

"It sounds like a lot of people," Linda whispers.

A sports car glides in from the street and parks in the driveway be-hind other cars. Linda and I step off the path and hide behind a trellis. Behind us is a pool lit up from the bottom, blue shimmering light re-fracting and shooting up like flames against the walls of a changing room. Two men in suits climb out of the car and talk in quiet, serious tones. They walk to the middle door and ring the doorbell. A woman opens the door, greets them with a hug and a kiss, and lets them in. I say, "This might not be easy."

"We're underdressed," Linda says.

More voices and some music reach us from another part of the house, and we walk along a gravel path, low lights flickering on at our feet. We circle the pool, coming toward an open patio where two huge stereo speakers are propped on a table. About a dozen people, most of them with drinks in their hands, lounge in the kitchen, which opens up to the patio. More partygoers come in from another part of the house. The music stops for a moment, the warble of voices cutting through, then some saxophone jazz begins playing. Someone turns up the volume. A man's hearty, fake laugh rises up above the music.

"Just walk in?" I ask.

"Wait a minute. I think they're moving out here."

She's right. More people walk into the kitchen, and a few bring their drinks onto the patio. Someone calls out to turn the music down. The jazz softens. Linda nudges me. I see Milian talking with two other men. They stop in the kitchen, continue talking, then move outside. Milian wears a crisp blue suit, his beard short and trimmed, his hair combed back. He looks tired, however, and as he listens to one of the men, his face sags for a moment, then snaps back to attention.

A group leaves the kitchen and gathers on the patio, the conversations growing louder, drowning out the music. Linda whispers, "Shall we try?"

"Do you want to go straight to Milian?"

"No. Let's find that guy Frankel, and also let's see what we can learn about Pinewood. We'll split up."

"What if we're recognized?" I ask.

"I don't know. Maybe the danger of having a scene will keep it quiet."

"If something happens, let's meet at the corner by the car."

"Okay." She walks around the patio, trying to slip in behind the speakers where she might not be noticed. A few people glance at her as she moves slowly across the patio and into the kitchen. I want to follow Linda's lead, but pause when I realize that everyone at the party is white. I wonder if I'll be noticed. I try to see how Linda is faring, but she has disappeared into another room. I walk onto the patio, smile at a few partygoers, and pick up a glass of wine from the counter in the kitchen. Milian hasn't noticed me; I watch him from the kitchen. Shiny copper cookware hangs from a metal lattice above. I move next to the oversized stainless-steel refrigerator. Milian finishes his glass of wine and continues nodding to something the man to his right has just said. Milian looks like he's trying to concentrate, but is having trouble. His eyes are bleary.

I see a man my age with a crew cut nursing his drink by the window, trying not to seem uncomfortable. He fixes the jacket of his gray suit. He leans, then stops leaning. He looks around. I approach him and nod. "How's it going?"

He shrugs, but holds out his hand. "Frank Gaines."

"Chris Bruno," I say. We shake. "You're with Pinewood?"

"No. Brennan, Roth. I'm one of the associates at the law firm. What about you?"

"Indirectly with WestSun. What's your role in all this?"

"You mean the deal? We're handling all the filings and SEC junk. And you?"

"I'm just a friend of the family. So I'm not even sure—has it all gone through?"

"Just the first stage. Don't you know?"

"I don't know anything."

He smiles. "I know the feeling. I'm actually just a grunt. I don't even know what the hell I'm doing here."

This stops me, and I stare at him. He loses his smile, unsure if he has said the wrong thing, but shrugs and smiles again. Then I see it. He has the dis-ease. For a moment I'm tempted to ask him about his life, but I instead stick to my job here: "Do you know if Kyle Frankel is here?"

"Sure. He's out there." He points toward the patio.

"Which one is he?"

"The shark in the two-thousand-dollar Brooks Brothers. The one with the earring."

I look out the window, but can't see him. Gaines says, "You're a friend of Mr. Milian's?"

"My father was." I then see Milian walking alone into the kitchen and through a side door. I get a glimpse of a living room. I excuse myself from Gaines and follow the same route. Milian is greeting people but working his way to another part of the house. I am momentarily distracted by the opulence of the living room, a huge grand piano smack in the center, sculptures and paintings cluttering the walls. I see Linda talking with two men, and Milian notices her as well, though after a confused stare he continues walking down a hallway.

He goes into a bathroom, and I wait outside. When he steps out, he smiles at me, then stops, trying to place me. "Hello," he says. "Do I know you?"

"Mr. Milian. I'd like to talk to you."

"I hope it's not business-related. Are you with Pinewood?"

"I know what you've been doing, Mr. Milian. I think we'd better talk."

He looks startled. "Excuse me?" Something catches his attention over my shoulder, and I turn. Durante is hurrying toward us, unbuttoning his sport coat.

"Jesus, what the fuck is this?" Durante says.

"Vic?" Milian says. "What's this about?"

Durante grabs my arm. "This is the guy I was telling you about."

"Mr. Milian," I say, surprised that he doesn't know me. "My name is Allen Choice. You employed my father, John Choice, twenty years ago."

The name registers immediately. He says to me, his voice flinting, "You again. You are trespassing here. I should call the police—"

"And I should tell them about your killing my father, Mr. Milian. I should tell everyone, even Pinewood investments—"

Durante pulls me away, and I shake him off. Milian holds his hand up to Durante and says to me, "So you're taking after your father, I see. Are you going to blackmail me too?"

This catches me off-guard. "What?"

"Your family must smell money in your sleep," he says. "Sniffing around to see what you can get."

"I'm not here for money," I say. "I know what you did to Junil Kim."

Durante motions to some people down the hall. I watch Milian's reaction, but he keeps shaking his head. "You think this is a place for a handout? You're dead wrong." He turns to Durante and says, "This is what you're going to have to deal with, you'll see."

"I'll take care of him."

"Just call the police. They'll handle him." Milian doesn't even glance at me as he frowns and walks away. I want to follow him, but Durante steps in my way.

"You stupid fuck," he says to me. "You got no idea what you're doing, do you?"

"He doesn't know about Junil Kim," I say. "You killed him."

"I could've taken you out a dozen times. I let you live, and you just don't learn."

"What happened? Did you try to warn him? He wouldn't take your shit, would he? He didn't roll over, and something went wrong."

"You don't know nothing."

I stare. He's young: his facial hair hasn't fully come in yet, a wispy mustache only beginning to appear. His round, smooth cheeks are flushed. He's trying to be threatening, and gives me a dead stare. I say, "Running a business isn't like running your buddies in juvenile hall."

He tenses.

"Or running your cell block in San Quentin," I say. "Even the hint of crime will scuttle everything."

The three men Durante beckoned converge on me. I remember Stein's comment about "goons" and walk quickly in the other direction, having no idea where this hall leads and how I'll get out. They hurry after me, but no one seems to be in a real rush. I enter a bedroom, find myself trapped, then think, Why am I running? I open the door and walk toward the three men. They're surprised to see me appear.

I said, "I'll leave. But I'll leave through the front door."

"You leave where we throw you," one of them says.

"Do you want me to ruin this party? Make a big scene and wait for the police to break this up?" Durante hesitates, so I turn and walk toward the living room. Linda notices me moving through some party-goers, but she disappears into a crowd when she sees Durante and the others following me. I hope she's more successful.

Then I stop. I focus on a man in a suit who looks familiar. His weak chin triggers something. He stands by the wall, surveying the crowd, and I peg him as security. But that isn't where I've seen him. He is dressed differently, though I know I've seen his face before. He turns, our eyes meeting, then glances at Durante, and he stands up straighter. I know him. I know the angry eyes.

It's the man in the Raiders jacket at Florentino's, the one who was inspecting the Tank.

Startled, I try to determine why he's here and who he is. If he's working for Durante, then Paul's death was definitely connected to everything here. The man realizes I am staring, and after a moment of indecision, he turns to leave. I yell for him to stop, and go after him. He bolts.

He slips through the crowd and runs through the kitchen. I follow him out onto the patio, but he jumps across some bushes and keeps running. Someone tackles me from behind, and we go down heavily. I try to kick him off, and struggle to see where the other man went. "Son of a bitch," Durante says as I connect my heel against his neck. He rolls away. I scramble up and run through the bushes, searching for the man. Durante and the others are right behind me. I hurry along a dark path, cursing myself for letting him get away, and find myself running beside a high stone wall, scraping my shoulder and tearing my shirt. Durante is close behind. I begin limping. An iron rear gate has been left ajar. I run out onto the street, but can't see anyone, and run to the corner. I look around. No one.

Durante and the others throw open the gate, and I run down the street, still looking. After another block I know I've lost him, and I stop at a curb, bending over, panting and rubbing my knee. I hear the gate slam shut. Durante and the others are no longer after me. I limp around the block, toward Linda's car. That man called me a gook at Florentino's. I remember him clearly. I wanted so badly to catch him. I lean against a tree. My legs are shaking.

38

Linda learned from the party that Pinewood's offer to buy out WestSun is still in the works. Although they agree in principle, Pinewood's accountants are still reviewing WestSun's books, and Milian is in the process of selling off a subsidiary to lighten their debt load. "Here's the strange thing," she tells me as we arrive at my apartment. "They referred to Durante as Milian's son."

"Son, as in father and son?"

"Yes. Durante is going to take over for his father, is what they're talking about, and he's going to stay on for Pinewood if the buyout goes through."

"Milian said something to him about me. He said, 'This is what you're going to have to deal with.'"

"'When you take over?'" Linda says, finishing the thought. "It might be true. But how is he Milian's son?"

"Maybe he's adopted."

"Are you sure you saw the same man from Florentino's?" she asks again.

"Yes. And he ran."

Linda says with amazement, "Then it's connected."

"Milian—or more likely Durante—wanted Paul dead? Why?"

"Paul was freelancing for them. He must have seen something. You don't think Milian is behind it all?"

"It seemed like Durante was calling the shots. Milian didn't seem to know anything about Junil Kim."

"He's protecting his position. With Milian retiring, Durante can't have anything going wrong."

"But why kill Paul like that?" I ask. "Why'd he do it at the restaurant?"

"Durante is young, doesn't seem very experienced."

"I don't know."

Linda says, "And the man you saw, the decoy—he was part of it, to get you away from Paul."

If Paul's shooting was planned, then it didn't go well. Too much left to chance. I could've lagged behind with Sorenson, and I might've spotted the motorcyclist along with Paul. He could've stayed with Sorenson and I could've moved to the perimeter. What if that had been the case? What would I have done in Paul's place? I'm not sure if I would've spotted the motorcyclist in time. But Paul could've found cover easily near the Tank. The other security—Long Hair, Lawrence—could have drawn faster. There were too many variables, and a hit aimed at Paul like that was just sloppy.

Then I remember that Paul had switched our positions at the last moment. Paul had wanted to talk to Sorenson, tell him to stop blabbing about the Tank, and he had sent me forward as point guard. Paul usually took point, and if he had stayed in position, then *he* would have confronted the guy in the Raiders jacket. He would have been out there alone, and the decoy and the motorcyclist would have both had clean shots. By sending me out there as point, Paul had messed up their plans. I had confronted the decoy, who was forced to leave when Long Hair showed up next to me, and the motorcyclist was left on his own. Linda was right. If everyone had stuck to his positions and routines, it would have been a clean hit. Not the best plan, but viable if Paul had gone out first.

We stop before entering my place. I check the sliver of paper I wedged into the top of the door, in between door and jamb, a quick way to determine if a door has been opened. The paper is still there. We walk in and I check my windows. Everything seems okay.

When I tell Linda about Paul's last-minute switch, she says, "That's what must have happened. Durante's plan didn't quite work, but they still got to Paul."

"And they did it at the restaurant because everyone would think the clients were the primary targets."

"But we need hard evidence of all this. The decoy—he'd be able to identify the killer and Durante."

"But he's probably long gone," I say. "What about Milian? What about my father?"

"A twenty-year-old murder might be tougher to prove."

I don't like the sound of that, but keep quiet. Linda says, "Now that Durante knows how determined we are, he might take more precautions."

"I know." I think about my aunt. I'm not sure if Durante will try threatening her to get to me, but I can't take that chance. I'll have to warn her. I keep spotting weaknesses in my life. I turn to Linda and say, "You should be careful."

"I will," she says. "I think I have some leverage, though, being with the *Sentinel*."

"Are you going to tell your boss about this?"

"I don't know. I need more."

"More?"

"Something definite. Hard evidence."

I say, "I'm going to ask Stein about Mrs. Garvey. Maybe he knows something about a possible affair with Milian."

"And Ari too. I'll give you her number. She might know."

I nod. "What about you?"

"Durante. I did a search on the state courts, but I want to check the county."

"Why?"

"Sometimes the county court doesn't send its data to the state repository, and I also might get a better look at whatever misdemeanors he has. I also want to check Vital Records to see who his parents are, if I can. Sometimes that's tough."

"What about Junil Kim's death? The details?"

"That'll start coming out soon, I'm sure. I'll check on it." She sits down on the futon next to me and lets out a long breath. The evening's rush has worn us out. She glances at her watch.

"It's late," I say.

"I guess I should get going. I'm tired."

"You can stay over if it's easier."

She looks around. "Where?"

"You can have the futon. I'll take the floor."

"Really? You wouldn't mind?"

I shake my head. "And I sleep really deeply. I won't know the difference."

"How deeply?"

"Once I fell asleep at Tronics. I was on a break and slept in the lounge. Someone at first thought I was dead."

She laughs. "You weren't breathing?"

"Breathing very slowly, I guess. The guy, a janitor, kept shaking me. I finally woke up and he looked relieved."

She stares at me with a small smile, then stands up. "I'll wash up."

I change into sweats, my back sore from Durante's tackle, my legs still aching from the long run. A few years ago I wouldn't have even considered the pain, but everything seems to hurt more now. Is this what happens after thirty?

I'm only beginning to calm down, but I can't stop thinking about the man I saw tonight, the Raiders-jacket man. His expression when he recognized me was confusion, then shock. He hadn't expected to see me ever again. Durante or Milian hadn't told him anything; he's just a grunt.

Linda leans out of the bathroom and asks if I have an extra toothbrush. I tell her there's a new one in the medicine cabinet. I make the futon up for her and bring out extra blankets and a pillow. When I ask Linda if she wants something to sleep in, she says she does, and I hang an extra set of sweats on the bathroom doorknob.

By the time Linda is ready for bed, I'm having trouble keeping my eyes open. I wash up quickly, and find Linda sitting on the futon, leafing through her planner. She's wearing my old blue workout sweats, the fabric thin from years of use; her sleeves are pushed up her forearm, her feet are bare, and she curls her toes as she writes something on her pad. She hands me a slip of paper with Ari's phone number. "I doubt she'll know much, but it can't hurt."

"You don't want to call?"

"I think she took an interest in you more than me."

"What?"

"Didn't you notice? I'm not sure if it was because of your father, but she seemed to like you."

"No. She was cool to me."

Linda shrugs. "Still, I'm just a reporter. You're the son of her father's friend." She climbs under the covers and curls up. "You sure you don't mind me staying over?"

"No," I say, turning off the lights. "It's nice to have company." I rearrange the blankets on the floor and try to get comfortable. My shoulder blades and tailbone hurt on the hard floor. I roll on my side, but my hip is tender. I lie on my back again and raise my knees. The floor creaks.

"Are you okay?" she asks.

"Fine."

She sits up. "You can sleep here. Next to me. There's enough room."

My lower back aches. "Are you sure?"

"Oh, come on. We're adults."

I move my pillow and blanket next to her and lie down, the thick cushion under me a relief. I sigh and thank her. She laughs. I find myself getting excited, and I'm glad it's dark. I try not to touch her, but I feel her inches away, every movement—even her breathing—shifting the futon and the cushion a fraction.

She asks, "Did you notice that I was the only Chicana woman at Milian's?"

"Not many women there."

"There were six or seven others, I think, other than the help."

"You counted."

She says, "Didn't you?"

I smile and wonder how often I do that. It took me less than a minute to see I was the only Asian there.

Linda shifts her position, fluffing her pillow, and rolls over to her side. I feel her legs next to mine. She says, "By the way, my sister invited me to dinner. She said I can bring someone."

"Where is this, Walnut Creek?"

"It's a drive," she says. "You interested?"

I hesitate. "I don't know. Would I enjoy myself?"

"Probably not. I usually don't."

"Then why go?"

"She's my sister. Even if she tends to lecture me."

"About what?"

"My life."

"You have a good life."

Linda pats my arm. "That's why I'm going to bring you along."

I turn to face her, though I can only make out shadows. I say, "I'll go if you want me to."

"It won't be for a couple of weeks anyway."

I can't plan that far ahead. I know that tomorrow I have to send off letters to Triumph and Black Diamond, maybe some of the smaller agencies, and I want to look for Stein. I don't want to think about how much money I have left in the bank. I wonder if I can hit my aunt up for money in a pinch. No. I can't do that. I'd rather flip burgers than do that.

"Allen?" Linda whispers.

"Hm?"

"Just seeing if you fell asleep."

"Worrying about money."

"Is that what you do at nights as you lie in bed?"

"Yeah, pretty much."

"Can I ask you a question?"

"Shoot."

"And I want the most objective, cold-blooded answer, okay?"

"Okay."

She stops, then says, "Never mind."

"Come on," I say. "Ask away."

"Well, I was just wondering. Is there something off-putting about me? Is there something wrong with me?"

"What? What do you mean?"

"Just that."

"You mean your personality?"

"Yes."

"Of course not," I say. "Why are you even asking that?"

"I was just wondering."

"About Thomas?"

I feel her jolt. She says, "God, is it that obvious?"

"No, but it makes sense. You're wondering what happened."

"I wasn't in love with him, but I don't know what I did—"

"If anything," I say. "He might've just wanted to see other people. Maybe he had another girlfriend."

"Great."

"You're the most attractive and smartest person I know."

"You must not know many people."

"Ha," I say. "No, really. I never met this guy, but I know you can do better."

She's quiet for a moment, then says, "Thank you."

We fall silent, and I hope I haven't said too much. But I mean it, and

I can still hear her crying on the phone. *I really liked him. He was nice.* I should say more, tell her again that she can do much better. I can't see her expression. She's too quiet. I suspect she's thinking something akin to Christina at Tronics. She's worried that I might be falling for her, and she's probably thinking, Oh, no, I don't need this.

I'm about to say something else, just to change the subject, when she says, "Good night, Allen. Thanks."

I say good night, and hear her turn away and settle in. I feel foolish. I should learn to shut up. I try to think of something else, and focus on what happened today, my thoughts rushing by too quickly. Milian and the party. Durante must have been the one who sent the two men to warn me. He did that even before I started looking into anything closely. Of course, Durante got to Stein and then Kim. It's the way he works. That son of a bitch. I should have done more than just run from Milian's house, avoiding a confrontation. I should've started a messy one, showed him I couldn't be pushed around like that. The more I think of it, the more worked up I become. Now Junil Kim was dead, and had nothing to do with any of this; I caused his death. I'm not sure about Paul's involvement, but Durante was behind it. I was certain of this.

Paul's bloody face flashes before me. I shake it off. I imagine Junil Kim being beaten, and have to force this out as well. I'm in bed with a beautiful woman and all I can think about is death. I climb quietly out of bed and walk to my window, staring out onto the street.

Hell. I'd better calm down. I'm never going to sleep like this. I sigh deeply, and stare up at the quarter-moon partially shrouded in clouds. It's quiet out. I remember with mild surprise my father lighting fireworks with his cigarette. We were in some park—the Rose Garden in Oakland, maybe—and there was an empty fountain, streaked with dirt, the paint peeling. He found a half pack of firecrackers on the ground. I had never seen them before, and he told me what they were. "Cover ear," he said, motioning to his head with the two fingers still dangling his cigarette. He was wearing khaki pants and a short-sleeved polyester dress shirt, the top buttons undone. I saw sweat stains under his arms. How do I remember that? Maybe we had gone to a picnic, a July Fourth picnic. He pointed again to his ear with his cigarette. The smoke zigzagged. I covered my ears, and he lit a fuse with his burning ember, throwing the firecracker into the fountain. The explosion to me was overwhelming, my vision actually blurring, and I fell back, startled. My father looked at me and laughed. I was confused and wasn't sure what had happened. He asked me if I wanted to see another one. I shook my head. He laughed again and threw the rest of the firecrackers away. He tussled my hair and grabbed my neck with his warm, calloused hand. He smiled and shook his head. I could feel the calluses on his palm scratching my skin. The smell of gunpowder and cigarette smoke mingled around us. Rose bushes lining the path. Very much like Milian's yard. Milian. *Your family must smell money in your sleep.* He can fuck himself. I should've punched him right then. Damn. I have to stop going over all this.

"Allen?" Linda says.

I turn to her. My eyes now adjusted to the dark, I see her looking at me sleepily.

"What's the matter?"

"Having trouble relaxing," I say.

She pulls herself up slowly and leans on one arm. Her hair falls over her face. "Is it me?"

"No, no. I just can't stop thinking."

"Everything will be okay," she says. "Rest."

"I know," I say, though I don't believe this. "I'll be up for a little while more."

She lies back down, and I watch her fall asleep.

39

Linda is gone when I wake up, and I find a note lying on the table: "Had to go to work early." I've overslept by a few hours, though I remember that I don't have a job to be late for. Last night I stayed up past three, and even then barely fell asleep, my thoughts hovering near the surface even as I dreamed those waking dreams. They are getting more violent, these dreams, and I feel vaguely disturbed as I sit up and look at Linda's impression on the pillow. A strand of her curly black hair rests on it. I reach down to examine it, but the phone rings.

"Sung-Oh, what you do?" Aunt Insook says.

"What?" I say, still half asleep.

"I talk to Grace Park. She said you cause Junil to die."

"What?" I clear my head. "Grace Park?"

"She tell me you cause Junil to die," she says harshly. "What you doing! Why you doing this?"

"I didn't—I mean, it wasn't really . . ." I stop. "Maybe it was my fault."

"*Aigoo!* I tell you not to do this! Why you do this?"

"Did you know Mrs. Garvey?" I ask. "Noah Garvey's ex-wife?"

"Who? What?"

"Noah Garvey was my father's friend. You told me that. His ex-wife. Did you know her?"

"I don't know."

"Did you know she had an affair with Roger Milian?"

"What?"

"Roger Milian. He had an affair with Noah Garvey's ex-wife."

"He did?"

"So you do remember her."

"I don't know," she says. "Why you do this? Why you look into this?"

"I'm going to find out what happened to my father. I'm not stopping until I prove Milian's role in his death. That's why I'm doing this."

"Sung-Oh, you get trouble, you get danger. That man is danger."

"Milian? I know."

"No more, Sung-Oh. You stop. You forget."

"I can't. I have to know."

She is silent. I hear her breathing. She finally says, "You like your father. He never listen."

"To you he didn't."

She says something in Korean that I don't understand, and hangs up. I'm now completely awake, and put down the phone too hard, the handpiece cracking loudly. I feel a headache coming on from sleeping badly, and have aspirin and coffee for breakfast.

After showering, I can't muster the energy to write job letters, and I don't feel like driving out to Palo Alto to talk to Stein, even though I know I have to. I see Arianne Garvey's number next to my phone, and call her.

Five rings later, she picks up and answers sleepily, "Yeah?"

I apologize for waking her and tell her who it is.

She sighs. "What the hell did you guys say to my mom? She called and started yelling at me."

"We asked her questions she didn't like."

"Like what?"

"Well, we asked her if she had a relationship with Roger Milian."

"My father's boss? The guy who ruined him?"

"Your mother got very angry at us."

"Well, yeah. That was pretty stupid of you."

"She seemed to know Milian, and his ex-wife."

Ari is quiet. "Know him? How?"

"Just the sense we got. Familiar with him. Calling him Roger, for example, and knowing the ex-wife enough to call her a bitch."

"So what are you saying?"

"Do you know if your mother had some kind of relationship with Milian?"

"Jesus. Are you *joking*?"

"Can you remember anything that might point to this?"

She doesn't reply for a while, then finally says, "This is why you woke me up? With some bizarre theory about my mother?"

"It might make sense. Your father found out about Milian and your mother. He got angry and tried to do something about it. Milian ruined him."

"Why are you telling me this?"

"It connects with me. My father was friends with yours. He saw what was happening, maybe even started blackmailing Milian, and then got killed for it."

"So why are you calling *me*?"

"Can you find out if your mother did have an affair with Milian?"

"Christ. I don't need this now. I've got papers to write. I've got a dissertation to work on. I don't need this."

"Don't you care?"

"What the hell? This happened twenty years ago. Get a life, for chrissakes."

"This is important to me. Don't you want to know?"

She sighs. "Frankly, no."

"But your father—"

"Was a manic-depressive, probably, and my mother might have been a tramp. Big deal. This doesn't concern me."

"But it's your father . . ."

"Look, I sympathize with what you're doing. But I don't have time for this. I'd appreciate it if you left me out of this. I've got to run now." She hangs up.

I stare at my phone, stunned. She really doesn't care, and I wonder if it's me, if I'm the only one with this need to know. I hang up, grab my coat, and head out to my car. Stein is next.

I make a quick check for bugs or tracking devices, then drive toward Palo Alto. Almost immediately I mark a green car tailing me. It's a Ford Taurus, with one driver, and although he is two cars back, he keeps pace with me, turning at my turns, speeding up and passing a car to keep up when I start testing him. One of Durante's men? After last night, there's little doubt in my mind that they want to keep a close watch. There is too much at stake.

I want to test how close this man will stay with me, so I drive to the Stanford Shopping Center, park in the lot, and hurry through the main entrance. The man also parks and follows me on foot. I lead him through a few stores, circling around and through Macy's, and finally stop back at the lot. I turn around and walk straight to him. He's a young guy, too young to be a plainclothes cop, I suspect, and dressed in jeans and a blue blazer. He seems startled as I approach. He turns and is about to walk back into the store, but I say, "Excuse me. Do you have the time?"

He hesitates, then looks at his watch. "Almost eleven."

I say, "Who are you working for?"

"What?"

"You're a terrible tail. Who are you working for?"

"I don't know what—"

I grab his jacket and shove him hard against the wall. A few people glance in our direction. I feel a holster and tense up. "You're carrying." I slam my palm against the gun, making him cringe. "Who are you?"

He looks around and shakes me off. He walks away.

I return to my car, sweep it again, then drive in circles for a while, making sure I'm not still being followed. It must have been a Durante flunky. I make my way to Stein's restaurant downtown, parking a few blocks away, and walk to the back alley. The smell of broiling fish blows around me with each breeze. The rear door of Stein's restaurant is propped open with a crate. The kitchen, filled with sounds of sizzling and chopping, is empty except for an old bald Asian man in a dirty white apron slicing vegetables. He grabs a bottle of sesame oil, the label stained brown, then notices me.

"Is Stein in?"

He nods to the office across the hall and goes back to work, pouring oil into a dented metal frying pan. I hear the lunch crowd in the dining area growing louder. This kitchen is connected to the sushi bar by a narrow door, and the sushi chef sticks his head in, sees me, and asks the old man for something in Japanese. The old man raises his hand and continues chopping. A waitress rushes in through the same door and slips a green order form next to two others in a metal clip by a counter. She says to the man, "Come on, already. They're waiting."

The old man raises his hand again. He glances at me and smiles. He's missing a front tooth.

I walk across the hall and find Stein on the telephone. He looks up and freezes. "I'll talk to you later," he says into the phone. He hangs up slowly and says to me, "I'm going to call the police now. You're harassing me." He picks up the handset.

"You know that Junil Kim is dead."

He stops. "I know that you're linked to it somehow."

"You know that Milian is behind it."

"I know nothing of the kind."

"Did you know that Milian had an affair with Garvey's ex-wife?"

He thinks about this. "No."

"Did you know that Milian has a son? I'm not sure if he's adopted or what, but this son is taking over the business."

"Why does this matter to me? Why do you keep bothering me?"

I say, "You're my only connection to that time. Junil Kim is dead."

"And I will be too. Can't you see that?" His shoulders sag a fraction, and he puts the phone down.

"Did you know Garvey's ex-wife?"

He shakes his head slowly. "No. I told you everything I know about him."

"My father was good friends with Garvey."

"I didn't know that."

"My father was probably blackmailing Milian, which is what got him killed."

Stein blinks. "Your father?"

"Yeah."

He says, "A blackmailer? No. Your father was one of the most honest guys I ever knew."

"Milian himself confirmed it."

"And you believed him?"

This makes me pause. "You don't?"

"I knew your father. Not well, but enough to know that he couldn't even tell a lie. Remember, I was the third-shift manager. I had to deal with all sorts of drivers and shippers. They were liars, drug users, cheats, and thieves. Your father couldn't even fudge a timesheet."

"But something got him killed."

"It was ruled an accident. One that was hushed up, but it could've been a legitimate accident."

"The police said that?"

"The police weren't really involved. The insurance people said it."

"Insurance?"

"They had to look into it before paying claims."

"Why didn't you say this before?"

"Say what? That the company had insurance? Isn't it obvious?"

I realize that it is. Why didn't I consider it? I say, "Do you remember the name of the company?"

"Of course not."

"Where would I find out—"

"Leave me alone!" Stein says, his voice rising. "Get the hell out of my restaurant!"

"Mr. Stein, I'm just—"

"Out! I'm calling the police! Get out!" He picks up the phone and dials. I back away, holding my hands up, leaving his office, and walk through the kitchen. The old man in the apron watches me. I nod my head, and he shrugs. He returns to cooking something on the stove. I hear Stein cursing loudly to himself as I leave through the back entrance. The kitchen erupts with the sounds of frying, the cook jostling the pan. I walk slowly through the alley, not having a clear idea of what to do next, of where to go. I wonder if I'm cut out for this kind of work,

40

I spend most of my afternoon trying to find out what insurance company Sunrise Goods used. I don't get very far until I call Mrs. Milian again. When I reach her, I ask first what a divorce might have done to Sunrise Goods and its merger twenty years ago. She says, "It was my father's money that helped him buy Sunrise in the first place. I guess I could've stopped the merger, or dragged him and the company through the courts."

"When you finally did divorce him, what happened?"

"Part of the settlement was his buying out my share. I didn't want to have anything to do with him or the company."

I then ask her about the insurance company. Does she happen to know the name of it?

"I have absolutely no idea."

"How would I find out that information?"

"You're asking me?"

"Any ideas?"

She says, "You could contact other executives who worked there then."

"Do you remember any names?"

"You know I wasn't really connected with them. I had very little direct contact."

"How about names of colleagues? Another manager?"

"I'm sorry. Why don't you just look it up in the corporate records? They have to register in Sacramento. They'll have a list of the officers."

"Right. Of course," I say, "Thanks so much, Mrs. Milian."

My door intercom buzzes. I ask who it is, and a mailman says he needs my signature for a letter. Immediately suspicious, I tell him I'll be down in a second. I bring my gun, wrap it in a jacket, and walk downstairs. A man in a postal uniform is waiting outside the lobby door. I relax. I sign for the certified letter with a ProServ return address, and open it on the stairs. At the top of the letter is the heading "Notice of Termination." I sigh, and read the rest, which says in legalese that my employment at ProServ has been officially terminated, and that I will be paid a severance package of two months' salary. The letter is signed by Charles and Polansky.

When I call Polansky, he's curt. I ask him if this is a joke, and he says it isn't. I ask him what has changed. He asks me if it's all right if he tapes this call. When I say I don't care, he asks me again, this time with the tape recorder running. I say it's fine. He says, "We feel that the ongoing police investigation and your involvement in activities that might possibly jeopardize—"

"Wait a minute. Are you reading from something?"

"I'm reading a statement prepared by our attorneys—"

"Oh, Christ. Just tell me what's going on."

He shuffles some papers, then I hear a click. "I found out the police are getting more on you, Allen. We have to shield ourselves."

"What? What have they got on me?"

"Something about your relationship with Sonia."

I close my eyes and try not to sound surprised. I say steadily, "What about it?"

"What you do in your private life is none of my business, but when it brings the possibility of bad press and an investigation into ProServ, we have to go into gear. Allen, I don't know what you're doing, but you're fucking up."

"What?"

"That's all. We can't talk anymore. Don't call here. I'm sorry, but that's the way it is." He hangs up. I try to reach Sonia, but she's not home. I then call Browning and tell him what just happened.

"Yes. I want to talk to you. We have a problem."

"Don't tell me that," I reply. "You said all this would be straight-forward."

"I'm going to have to refer you to different counsel. There's a conflict of interest here that might hurt the firm."

I say, "Conflict?" Then I remember that Sonia uses the same firm. "You mean because of Sonia?"

"Yes. We didn't think there'd be one, until yesterday."

"What'd she say? What happened?"

He clears his throat, then finally says, "That's the point. My partners and I—we're in a bind. We can't advise each other on our cases if we keep both of you. So, I'm afraid I'm going to withdraw as your counsel. I can recommend one of the best criminal lawyers in the area."

"You're *dumping* me?" I ask. I can't keep the shock out of my voice.

"I'm sorry, Allen. We just didn't expect this."

"What exactly is Sonia telling the police? What the hell is going on?"

He says, "All I know is that she was advised to tell the complete truth."

I think quickly. The complete truth? That we slept together once? How can that affect me—unless the police believe that it's a motive? I feel an unsteadiness, a shifting of everything around me, and begin seeing what might be happening. The police are focusing on me. A relationship with Sonia would be a motive for killing Paul. But it was only one time, and well after Paul's murder. How can they tie that to me?

"Allen?" Browning says.

"Yeah. I'm beginning to understand this better. You could drop Sonia, you know."

"We took her on first."

"She also will be suing ProServ, for what I guess will be a lot. Does that have anything to do with it?"

"Not at all."

"Your cut will be huge if she wins."

"I can't comment on any of that."

"But I'm no one."

"I'm sorry, but I can't—"

"What about my retainer?"

He rustles something. "Yes, of course. We'll return that to you as soon as we figure out the billable hours and expenses—"

"Whoa, whoa. It's only been a week. How much could you have worked?"

"Quite a bit, actually. Especially today and last night, as we learned about this conflict of interest."

"Around how much?" I ask, trying to keep my anger in check.

"I don't know. Our business manager will figure out—"

"Estimate for me, will you? Around how much of the retainer is left?"

"I couldn't tell you—"

"Goddammit, just tell me how many hours you've worked on this, then. You have to know that. You have to keep records." I am sweating.

"I don't have my sheet with me here—"

"Then go get it."

"Let me get back to you. All right?"

"No, it's not all right. Get it."

"I don't have time right now. I'm in the middle of—"

"You're in the middle of screwing me over. Get the timesheet!"

He pauses. "I'll call you when you calm down." He hangs up.

"Oh, shit," I say. I pace my apartment. "Holy shit." I let out a strange laugh, and think, I am getting fucked. I stare down at my hands. I am so fucked.

I suit up and go for another run.

As I head toward Camino, hurrying through downtown and past Moorfield Park, where Junil Kim was found, I refuse to think about Browning or Sonia or ProServ. Instead I focus on what Krista Milian told me. I intend to find out who the officers of Sunrise Goods were. I'll start making calls when I return. I can do this. I can sort it all out. I tell myself not to worry, not to panic. I haven't done anything wrong, so I shouldn't feel this dread spreading through me. Breathe. Breathe. I pace myself with a phrase, You-will-be-fine. You will be fine. After a while I almost believe it.

An unleashed dog raises its head as I jog by. I expect a chase, since dogs always seem antagonized by me. Once I was even seriously bitten as a child. The dog stares at me, but I keep looking forward, and the dog soon puts its head back down.

I was bitten in my calf, the tiny jagged scar still there, and my aunt smacked the German shepherd away with a rolled-up newspaper. By that time my crying, the barking, and my aunt's yelling brought out the owner—a next-door neighbor—and she took the dog inside. I remember looking at my calf immediately after the bite, the fast chomp that stung for an instant and made me stumble. I had trouble standing, and as soon as I looked down at the bloody gash, I began shrieking uncontrollably. My screaming startled the dog, which stopped barking for a moment. There was no pain, just shock. I couldn't recognize my own leg. I had trouble believing that a dog had done this to me, and the blood terrified me. People ran out of their houses to see what was happening. A car stopped in the middle of the street. After I was stitched up at the hospital, and the dog tested for rabies, my aunt threatened to sue the landlord of the apartment building next door. Dogs weren't allowed in the complex, but this rule wasn't enforced. The tenant was eventually evicted.

I was impressed by the swiftness of my aunt's rescue, though afterward she was certain I had teased the dog somehow, which I hadn't. She was a cat person, and had an affinity for most animals. I was annoyed that she sided with the German shepherd over me. My father, who was still alive at the time, told me to start carrying a weapon. Maybe that was why I began looking for a walking stick.

When I return home and shower, I see that there are no messages on my machine, which means Browning is blowing me off. I'll deal with him later. I begin making calls to the state offices, trying to find out where to get corporate information. Directed to a few different places, I finally reach the Secretary of State's Corporations Unit, where I'm told that I can't make any requests over the phone. I'll have to mail it in, and pay four dollars per inquiry, six dollars per Certificate of Status, or five dollars for a Statement of Officers. "That's what I want," I tell the clerk. "The officers."

"Send in a written request, plus the fee, plus an additional five dollars if you want it faxed to you."

"How long will it take?"

"About a week."

"That's too long."

"You can come in and do this over-the-counter."

"Where are you?"

"Sacramento."

I sigh. "What if I fax you the request, with my credit card number? Can you fax the information back immediately?"

"Within a day or two."

I tell the clerk I'll do that, and take down the numbers and information. Although I don't have a fax machine, I can use the mailbox and copy shop down the street. They'll also hold any faxes for me. As I write out a request, I decide to pay extra to find out about Western Imports and the combined corporation, WestSun, in addition to the original Sunrise Goods. Three companies, thirty dollars. I'm not even sure how much of a balance I'm carrying on my credit card. I'm paying the minimum each month, and that's it. I try not to worry about it.

I go out to fax the request, then return to my apartment. Still no messages. I call Browning, whose secretary says he's in a meeting. Bullshit. I call Sonia, who still isn't answering her calls. What the hell is going on here? I call Linda at work. When she answers I say, "Well it looks like my lawyer is—"

"I can't talk now," she whispers. "We'll talk tonight."

"Why?"

"Don't call here. Meet me at my place tonight."

"What's wrong?"

"Can't talk. Tonight at six." She hangs up.

I still have a couple of hours before seeing her, so I go to the café, bringing ProServ's letter of termination with me. I read it over a few times, glad for the severance pay. Two months of salary, after taxes, comes to about three and a half thousand, and that will take care of rent and food, but what if I have to retain another lawyer? What if the police bear down on me? I feel the pull of the inertial deception, the desire to allow myself to drift, to be acted upon. The rate of acceleration is constant. I see myself as a meteor careening toward the earth, but I must resist this. I must act, I must do. I must not feel overwhelmed by the events around me.

I sip my coffee and stare out onto the street. Someone walks by my building, checking the mailboxes, and I tense. I watch the man for a few minutes until I realize it's a teenager, and then see that it's David. Startled, I hurry out and call to him.

"What are you doing here?" I ask as he approaches. I look around for his mother. "How'd you get here?"

"I took the train."

"From Palo Alto? Does your mother know you're here?"

"I had a fight with her."

I study him. His eyes are red and puffy, his long-sleeve shirt is inside out, the backside of an indistinguishable logo over his chest. He folds his thin arms and waits for my response. I say, "Come in and have a snack." I lead him back to the café, buy him a muffin and soda, and sit down with him. "What happened?"

"Nothing," he says, picking the walnuts from his muffin. He lets his hair fall over his face.

"Should we let your mother know you're here? She might be worried."

"Good," he says sharply.

"So what's this all about?"

"She's just getting on my case."

"About school?"

"About everything. It's like, with my dad gone she can only focus on me. I'm going crazy."

"Listen, let me call your mom—"

"No."

"Wait. Let me call her and tell her you're all right. Okay? She might be calling the police or something."

He looks up at this, then nods. "I didn't think of that."

"I'll use the pay phone here. Let me tell her that I'll drive you home as soon as we finish eating."

"I don't want to go home."

I stand up. "We'll talk about that in a second. What's your number?"

He tells me, and I go to the phone and call Sonia. Her machine picks up, and I say, "This is Allen." I remember that I just left a message earlier. "This is Allen, again. I ran into David here, and brought him to a café. I'll drive him back to Palo—"

The sound of feedback squeals as Sonia picks up. "Hello? Allen?"

She was screening my call. I say, "Sonia, why didn't you pick up earlier?"

"Is David there? Let me talk to him."

"He's at the table. I'm at a pay phone."

"Allen, which café? I can drive there—"

"He's kind of angry. I thought I'd buy him a soda, let him calm down, then I'll drop him off at your place."

"How did he get there?"

"Train."

"Alone?" she says. "Which café? I'll go right down—"

"Wait. He's angry. He needs to calm down."

She sighs. "All right. Bring him back when he's calmed down."

I ask, "What did you tell the police?" I look over to David, who is finishing his muffin.

"What?"

"You told the police about us?"

She's quiet. "Allen, I told them the truth."

"The truth? What exactly did you say?"

"I can't get into this now. I just can't. Put David on, will you?"

"I doubt he'll come to the phone," I say. David is tearing up his napkin into small pieces.

"Just bring him home then."

"I will." I inhale slowly. "Sonia, what did you tell them? You didn't lie—"

"I just told the truth."

"What was that?"

"You know."

"That we slept together? That one time?"

"Yes."

"So why did Browning drop me?" I ask. "Why did Polansky fire me?"

"I couldn't lie. Don't you realize that they thought that *I* might be a suspect? There was too much at stake—"

"You mean the lawsuit? Is that what this is all about? Money?"

She doesn't reply, then says, "Just bring David home, please."

"But why would they focus on me if we—"

"Allen. Bring him home."

I say, "All right. I'll talk to you then." I hang up and return to the table. David looks at my half-finished muffin, and I tell him he can have it. He takes a bite, and asks me, "What did she say?"

"That I should bring you home."

"Will you?"

"I guess. There's no rush, though. She knows you're okay."

"I heard her talking with her lawyer."

"Yeah?" I say.

He stops eating. "Is it true?"

I think, Oh, no. "Is what true?"

"That you and her . . ." His cheeks redden. He looks down and picks at the muffin.

"Oh, man," I say. I quickly consider lying to him, but then see no point. I say, "Do you really want to know?"

"Yeah."

"Then, yes. Once. It was stupid for both of us, but we were lonely." I wonder if he's too young for this.

"But did you and her . . . before my father died . . . did you—"

"Is that what your mother said? To her lawyer?" I ask, alarmed.

"I don't . . . I'm not sure. I was just wondering—"

"But did she say that to her lawyer?"

"I don't know."

"No," I say. "Absolutely not. I would never."

"You didn't when he . . ."

"When he was alive? Hell, no. No way. Your dad and I were friends. I'd never do that to him."

He looks uncertain, and says, "But why did you, it's like, he wasn't even gone for that long . . ."

I nod, and shift in my seat. "I know. It was a mistake. I'm sorry if it upsets you. Is this what you fought about?"

"With my mom? No. She doesn't know I know."

"Then what was it?"

"Everything. She wants to move. I'm in the middle of everything and she wants to move."

"To where?"

"Into the city."

"So you won't be far from friends—"

"I don't want to move. I . . ." He shakes his head. We sit quietly, and he finally says, "Whatever."

"I told you I had to move after my father died, didn't I?"

He nods.

"It's not that bad," I say, although this isn't entirely true. "You can start over."

"Whatever."

He seems beyond consolation. I say, "Should I drive you back?"

"I guess. Do you want to practice tae kwon do at your gym?"

"That sounds great, but I have to be somewhere at six."

"Oh."

"Some other time," I say, standing up. "Come on. My car's in the lot next door."

He follows me to the car. As I drive him back to Palo Alto, he doesn't say much, and I try to ask him questions about his mother's wanting to move, about what they were fighting about, but he is shutting down, and barely utters one-word answers. I tell him to call me in a few days, and we'll go to the gym to practice. "Actually, I'd better use that gym more. Once my membership is over, I'll have to quit." He turns to me, and I say, "I've been fired from ProServ, so my discount at the gym no longer works."

"Fired?"

"It's a long story. I've been getting myself into a little trouble."

He blinks, then looks out the window. When we arrive at his house, he remains still. Sonia looks out the window. She opens the front door and waits on the front steps, her hands on her hips. David glances at her, sighs, and climbs out. He ignores his mother. She just shakes her head and purses her lips.

"Thanks, Allen," she says as she comes to the car.

"You want to tell me what you told the police?"

She stops. "They kept asking about my relationship with you."

"And what did you say?"

"That we were friends," she says. "But they knew that you'd visited. They kept telling me that if I was hiding anything, it'd look really bad later."

"And?"

"And my lawyer told me that they could start interviewing my neighbors and checking phone records and all that, and it scared me. He said it would look like a motive for murder."

"Jesus."

"What else could I do? I told the truth."

"But what else?"

"That's all. They kept asking if we had a relationship before Paul died. I said no, but they kept asking about when we had met and times and dates."

"They suspect something."

"That's why I told them the truth. And the insurance company is also looking into it, now that I'm suing."

"ProServ?"

"ProServ, their insurance company, and Florentino's."

"The restaurant?"

"My lawyer says he has a case."

"Their firm dumped me. Conflict of interest."

"They told me."

"I feel like I'm getting screwed."

"I'm just telling the truth. I'm not trying to get you in trouble—"

"I hope you said that we didn't see each other until after Paul's death."

"But that's not true."

I don't move. I feel an uneasy chill up my back. "What are you talking about?"

"We saw each other. You came over for dinner with Paul. There was that Christmas party."

"But not alone. We were always with Paul. It's not like we saw each other alone."

"Well, no. But we were occasionally alone. When we talked."

"Innocently. What did you tell the police? You didn't imply that—"

"I didn't imply anything. I told the truth."

"But you can make it sound bad. You can make it sound like I was interested in you when Paul was—"

"I didn't do that. I didn't. I just told the truth."

"Wait a minute," I say, trying not to raise my voice. "If you make it look like I was pursuing you, then I'll have a motive, but you won't."

"Allen, I was told not to talk about—"

"Oh, shit. And your lawsuit! Pain and suffering, right? If they knew the truth, that you wanted to sleep with me, that'd screw up the lawsuit, so you're making it look like I took advantage—"

"I'm only doing what my lawyers—"

"What *exactly* did you tell the police?" I say. "What were the words you used?"

She straightens. "I don't like your tone. You have no right to interrogate me—"

"If you're about to frame me for Paul's death? I can interrogate you any way I goddamn want—"

"That's all," she says, holding up her hands and backing off. "This conversation is over."

"Sonia, don't lie to the police just to give your lawsuit more—"

"Go to hell. I'm telling the truth." She turns and walks away.

"There are different kinds of truth!" I yell at her. "Don't screw me over, Sonia!"

She slams her front door. David is watching me from his bedroom window. I take a deep breath, wave to him, and drive away. A car is parked farther down the street, two men sitting in it. One has a camera and takes pictures of me as I drive by. The fucking police. This is great. This is perfect. Goddammit. I cannot succumb. I cannot crash into the earth.

I show up at Linda's apartment, but she hasn't returned from work yet, so I wait in my car, going over what Sonia said. I can see what the police are thinking: I was in love with Sonia, having spent time with her and Paul, and I knew they were having marital trouble. Maybe the police think I knew about the hit, or in some way arranged for Paul to get caught in the crossfire. Maybe they even think I arranged the shooting. They know I don't have any money; all it takes is a glance at my bank records. Sonia's lawsuit and insurance claim will go a long way for the both of us. But Sonia is pretending she's a victim as well, a victim of my attention. Maybe they are also trying to connect me to Junil Kim's death.

Although this seems ridiculous, it looks easy and convenient to the police. They like connections. They like easy motivations. And the fact that the case has gone stale probably goads them on. I'm certainly under some kind of surveillance. Those men taking pictures were probably the police. Maybe that man tailing me was also the police, though I doubt it, since he was so careless. It was probably one of Durante's men. I sense all kinds of activity going on beyond my field of vision, my range of hearing, movement involving me somehow, and all I can do is sit here and wait.

I consider this from Sonia's perspective. She needs money. Paul is gone. She has a son to raise. Her lawyers are telling her how much she can make if she handles this right. Her one-night fling with me complicated matters, so by playing the victim, she directs the police toward me, and salvages her lawsuit. She says that I seduced her, took advantage of her grieving state. I can see it happening. Maybe she even begins to believe that I intended to pursue her all along. *I seduced her?* If it weren't so serious, I might actually laugh.

Then it occurs to me that Sonia could've arranged everything, including Paul's murder. Isn't that what Linda suspected at first? Sonia's marriage was deteriorating. Perhaps even a divorce was in the works. But there are inconsistencies: Durante had a role in Paul's murder—the Raiders-jacket man is connected to Durante—and there's nothing connecting Durante and Sonia. I just can't believe Sonia could be so cold-blooded, but I have to be smart. I have to think of all the possibilities. Christ.

Linda drives into her lot and parks her car. As I walk toward her, I see that she looks disturbed, her face flushed, her forehead shiny, and she apologizes in a distracted way for being late. Her eyes are wary. I ask her what's wrong.

"Come in," she says.

Her apartment is messier than usual, newspapers and magazines strewn on the floor and tables. She quickly disengages the doorknob alarm with her key, then, after closing the door, reactivates it. "It's working okay?" I ask.

"I forgot a couple of times to turn it off. It's really loud."

"Always keep it on. I don't know exactly what's happening, but I seem to be under surveillance."

"By the police?"

"By everyone."

She nods.

"Why couldn't you talk to me on the phone?"

She sits down on her sofa. "Because I was in the middle of being yelled at."

"Why?"

"For not going to the news editor with my information about you."

"About me?"

"The news of the police focusing on you leaked out. The fact that I knew a lot of what was going on and didn't say anything really pissed off the editor."

"What leaked out?"

"That you had a relationship with Sonia Baumgartner."

I keep very still.

Linda doesn't look at me. She says, "Tomorrow's *Sentinel* will have another story about you becoming not quite a suspect, but a target of interest by the police."

"You wrote it?"

"No. I should have, but I'm in the doghouse."

"Shit. I'm sorry."

"They think I'm about to jump to another paper or something. They're boxing me out. They thought I knew all about your relationship with Sonia."

"I don't have a relationship with her."

She stands. "You didn't have sex with her?"

I flinch and say slowly, "I did. Once. A huge mistake."

"Obviously," she says.

"I wanted to tell you—"

"Why? You don't have to tell me anything. I'm just helping you stay out of jail and find Paul's killer. That's all. I'm just a donkey getting all kinds of information for you and not getting paid for it and putting my job in jeopardy for you, that's all. Why should you tell me anything? Especially something like that?" She shrugs dramatically. "You slept with your partner's wife? Your partner who got killed? The wife who is suing everyone for a couple of million dollars? Once she gets it you two will retire in Maui? Why should you tell me that?"

"That's not true. I have—"

"Stop. Don't even try to explain."

"Please, wait. I know you're angry—"

"Angry? Jesus. How could you not tell me this? What else haven't you told me? Do you have a Swiss bank account I don't know about? Are you planning to run off soon?"

"Linda—"

"Do you know how stupid I looked? Here I am, supposed to be working on a story about you, an exclusive, and the *Chron* is scooping us with news about you every other day. Everyone already thinks I'm some dumb affirmative action kid, and now I look like you've been playing me along this whole goddamn time!"

I can't reply. I've never seen her this angry. She keeps pacing, and shaking her head. She says, "Dammit, Allen! Why didn't you tell me?"

"I was embarrassed. It was a stupid mistake."

"You didn't think it would get out?"

"I didn't think she'd say anything. It was a mistake. We both knew it."

"But now it means you have a motive."

"For what? Killing Paul? I didn't sleep with her until well after—"

"It doesn't matter. Maybe you were just waiting for the right time. Maybe you two had started something, but couldn't go on until Paul was out of the way."

"All right," I say. "I know how stupid it was. Do you think Sonia planned it?"

She stops pacing. "What?"

I motion around me. "Planned it all."

"Killing her husband?"

"Yeah. Could she have arranged that?"

Linda stares at me, then sighs. "I've been thinking about that, and no. She'd have to be pretty dumb. And Durante's hand is in all this. Durante and Milian."

"What if she's working with Durante?"

"On what? Killing her husband for money? She'd be the first suspect. I think she's taking advantage of her husband's murder. I think she's taking advantage of whatever she can. She didn't have a whole lot of insurance, and the lawsuit might not only fail, but cost her tons of money. So if she did plan it, it'd be the stupidest plan ever. No, she's just seeing an opportunity. But Durante and Milian have other concerns, their buyout, for one."

This makes sense. I'm thankful that Linda is here stabilizing me. "I really screwed up," I say. "I know I did. I messed things up for you too."

"I'm no longer working on this exclusive about you. The editors basically said, 'Stick to lifestyle.'"

"I'm sorry."

"Even if I get some kind of story out of this, they won't be interested, or they'll just assign it to someone else. I've lost whatever chips I've built up."

"Did you tell them about Milian and WestSun?"

"I told them everything, but they're just theories upon theories. Do you know how flimsy it all is once you lay it out?"

"Maybe," I say. "But it's not too flimsy for ProServ or my lawyer to dump me." I tell her what has just happened.

"It figures. It doesn't look so good for you."

I ask, "Did you get anything more on Junil Kim's death?"

"Yes," she says.

I wait, but she's still angry. She's looking down and shaking her head. I say, "I'm sorry, Linda. I didn't mean to get you in trouble."

"You made me look stupid."

I nod.

"You made me look like . . . like an amateur."

I don't reply, and rub my temples.

"Is there anything else you haven't told me?" she asks.

"About Sonia?"

"About anything."

I shake my head. "I wanted to tell you, but I was embarrassed."

"You can't do that again. Do you understand? You can't hold out on me."

"I know."

"I'm not going to get any help from the *Sentinel* anymore. I can't let my colleagues know I'm doing this now."

"What did you mean by 'affirmative action kid'?"

She waves this off. "Nothing. Someone once made a stupid remark to me."

"About affirmative action?"

"Just that there are a lot of white journalists out there struggling. He implied that I ought to be thankful for the position, that there were more deserving people out there."

"He said that today?"

"No. A while ago."

I start to apologize again, but she holds up her hand. "Forget it," she says. "What's done is done. Anyway, it just confirmed what I suspected."

"What's that?"

"I didn't go to the right schools, go drinking with the right editors, and work on the right stories." She waves this off, walks into her kitchen, and pours herself a glass of grape juice. She asks me if I want one.

I decline, but say, "You still have your job, though, don't you?"

"Yes, but my next story assignment is on high-tech electronic pets."

I'm not sure if she's kidding until I see her angry expression, her eyes still flashing. I ask if I can do anything.

"No. It'll pass, I hope," she says. She takes a deep breath, shakes her anger off, then sits on the sofa. She looks up at me. "Junil Kim died from blunt-force trauma to his head. His hands and arms showed signs of fighting, but there were also rope marks on his wrists."

"Any evidence of who did it?"

"Not really. The forensic evidence revealed that his body had been moved, and they found some fibers that might have come from a car trunk, but that's about it."

"What about Durante as Milian's son?"

"Nothing. Vital Records won't release that information. I was going to ask another reporter who has contacts there, but now I can't."

"Can't?"

"No one can know I'm working on this."

"Have they assigned someone else?"

"Not beyond the possible connection to the Florentino's shooting."

"They don't think there's a story?"

"Not yet. I even found a possible connection with Durante and a smuggling case two years ago. He was a witness in a CFC smuggling case—"

"A what?"

"CFC. The Freon in air conditioners and refrigerators? It's banned."

"He smuggled it?"

"Not directly, I don't think. He testified for the prosecution, the government, probably for some deal."

"People smuggle it?"

"Yes. I did a search and found that most machines still use it, but the ban is forcing expensive substitutes. But countries like Mexico and China still make CFC cheaply. Anyway, it's a dead end. An ex-con has criminal friends. So he testifies against one. Doesn't mean anything."

"So we haven't gotten anywhere," I say.

"What about Stein?"

I tell her what I learned from him, about a possible insurance company and my search for the old corporate records. "I'll know tomorrow. I'm hoping to—"

The doorknob alarm begins shrieking. We jump, and I kick her coffee table by accident, sending her grape juice across her carpet. We look at each other, and I pull out my gun as I rush to the door. I yell for her to turn off the alarm. My ears twinge from the pain. I try to cover one ear and open the door, but the deadbolt is engaged. I slap it open and pull the door ajar, my gun ready. A spiky-haired, wiry man stands there startled, and he leaps back when he sees me, assuming a boxer's stance, his fists raised. His eyes flicker toward my gun. I point it at him, checking quickly up and down the hall for more people.

Linda turns off the alarm, and there's a jarring silence. The man, faint acne bumps along the sides of his narrow, bony face, locks his eyes on me and the gun, and raises his hands, backing into the wall. "Whoa, whoa," he says. He cocks his head; his moussed, pointy hairs stay frozen. "Easy with that."

"Who the hell are you?" I look him over to see if he's carrying. He has on a loose windbreaker, but I can't make out any holster. His jeans are tight; he might have a gun in the back of his pants. "Don't move."

"Manny," Linda says.

The man glances behind me. He's quick, already shifting aside to see Linda, and lowering his hands. He turns to me, points a crooked finger, and says, "I'm her ex-husband. Who the fuck are *you*?"

"Never mind that," Linda says, her voice low. "What are you doing here? Why were you trying to break in?"

"I wasn't. I was just checking if you're home."

"How did you find me?"

"Just looked you up."

"I told you I never wanted to see you again. Ever."

He grimaces, his skin pulled tight around his face, and says, "I just wanted to say hello. I'm in the area—"

"What do you want?"

"Just to say hello and to see . . . Who is this guy?"

"Get out," Linda says. "Just leave me alone, and don't come back."

He takes a step forward, and I tense. I wait for him to do something. He glances at me and asks her, "Who *is* this?"

"I'm calling the cops," Linda says.

"Hey, hey, take it easy. I'll leave. I just wanted to say hello."

I watch him and keep my gun at my side. I'm beginning to calm down, my ears still ringing.

"Is this your trusty dog?" he asks.

"Just get the hell away from here," Linda says. "I don't know what you think you're—"

"Calm down, I'm leaving," he says, backing away down the hall. "No harm in checking up."

"You come by here again, and I'll get a restraining order."

He begins to laugh, but then hardens his expression as he stares at her. "For what, saying hello?" He turns to me slowly. I reholster my gun and try to imagine Linda with this man. I can't. He says to me, "Can't you speak? Are you the trusty dog?"

I remain quiet as he sizes us up, his composure regained. "I'll be in town for a few weeks," he says as he walks away. He stops, eyes her up and down. "Hey, you're not looking so good."

"Fuck you," Linda says.

To me he says, "Doggie-style. That's how she likes it."

"Asshole," she mutters.

He goes back into a boxer's stance, throws a few rabbit punches, winks at me, then turns the corner. I tell Linda to wait here, and I follow him. I watch him leave the building; he touches his hair with his fingers, checking the spikes, and walks to a small blue car, and with a jolt I wonder if this is the same car that I thought followed me on Camino. I'm not sure, but doubt it when I see how dirty and old it is— the car following me was well-kept, shiny and waxed—but I can't be certain. He climbs in and drives off, and I wait until his car is a few blocks away.

Linda has locked her door, and I knock, telling her it's me. She opens it. "Is he gone?"

"Yeah."

She closes the door behind me and sets the alarm, then continues wiping the purple juice stain from her carpet.

"Sorry about the spill," I say.

"It doesn't matter." She uses a new paper towel to blot the juice, then scrubs the area with a small brush, adding a little soap and water. The brush seems oddly familiar. Linda sits up and balls the pink soggy paper towels together. She stops and stretches out an empty hand. "Look," she says. Her hand is shaking.

"Hell. Should we call the police? Is he dangerous?"

"I don't think so. He's usually not that full of bluff. I think we— you—caught him off guard. That alarm and your gun. It was strange seeing him like that."

"What did he want?"

"I guess money. He didn't expect you."

"Has he done this before?"

"No. But I know him," she says. "He must have heard I was doing okay. This is the first time I've seen him since the divorce."

"He heard? From who?"

"Maybe my parents, or friends of theirs? I send them my clippings." She takes a deep breath and exhales slowly. "He is the last person I need right now. And great—now he knows where I live."

"Should we worry?"

"I should. You shouldn't. No need to bother you with my stupid little dramas."

"Let's get a drink," I say. "Let's go out."

She looks up at me, then nods. "First let me clean this. I can't let it stain." She scrubs the carpet with the brush, lathering the soap, while I go into her kitchen to get more paper towels. I see her shaking her head as she grinds the brush into the spot, her lips pressed together, her forehead creased. She says to herself, "Goddammit," and continues scrubbing the carpet; her arms flex and tighten. I watch her, then stare at the brush, and recall with a mild shock a similar one my aunt used on the carpets the night my father died.

42

I haven't thought about it since that night, but when the police came to my house to tell us about my father, they walked into the foyer with muddy shoes. They were two large men, towering in the small hallway in their blue uniforms and heavy, bulky belts that would've sunk me to the floor if I tried to hold them. My aunt had left me alone in the house for a while, then returned with tea, and was boiling water when the doorbell rang. I was in bed but climbed out in a feverish haze, curious. My aunt, dressed in slacks and a sweater, looked out the small window, checked her clothes, then let the police in. They tracked dirt onto the plush pale carpet, cakes of mud sticking to the fibers, and I stared in horror at the contrast between the light carpet and the dark footprints. My aunt didn't say anything, which alarmed me even more. This was my father's house, but my aunt, when baby-sitting me, kept it as clean as her own. I listened to one of the policemen mumble to my aunt, mentioning "sorry so late" and "accident." She let out a small cry, and her hand went to her mouth. I was startled and stepped out from behind a corner. The other policeman, the silent one, nudged his partner and motioned to me. They stared, then the first one squinted. "Chicken pox?"

My aunt nodded. The other one backed away and said, "Never had it. I better go out."

"My kids just had it," the first one said. To my aunt, he said, "But maybe you should put him to bed."

She led me back to my room, ignoring my questions. I shut up when I saw how pale her face was. I stayed in bed until I heard the voices ending, the door closing, then climbed back out and peeked around the corner. I saw my aunt scrubbing the carpet, using a brush and a Tupperware bowl filled with soapy water. The teapot began whistling. My aunt turned off the stove, then called a friend to watch me for the rest of the night. She continued to clean the carpet before her friend arrived. I still wasn't sure what was going on, and would only learn of my father's death the next afternoon, after my aunt had seen my father's body at the hospital and had begun the funeral arrangements.

I remember the sound of the scrubbing, the quick back-and-forth strokes. The brush, a wooden one with short, hard bristles, the corner dipped in the sudsy bowl, was stored underneath the kitchen sink. I was still feverish, and when I returned to bed unprompted by my aunt, who had not noticed me, the sounds of her scouring the carpet followed me into sleep.

The memory of this disturbs me as I sit with Linda in a corner booth at the Emerald Bar. We've been drinking, and listen to the jukebox on the other side of the room playing pop songs I don't recognize. A group of young techies in white shirts crowd around a pinball machine. I feel light-headed, and let the memories of that blurry night drift away. Linda is talking to me, and I focus on her. She's telling me about her brother. "He was spoiled, but now he's a mess," she says.

I nod, concentrating. "A mess."

"And the divorce screwed him up more."

"When was the divorce?" I ask. I shut out the music, the rowdy conversation two booths down. The floor is sticky.

"When I was nine. My brother was eight. My mom wasn't doing well for a few years, but then she met my stepdad."

"Was he still spoiled by then, your brother?"

"My mom let him get away with everything. My stepdad couldn't do much. And my brother was really slick, and soon had my stepdad snowed."

"You said that he steals their money?"

"I told you that? Well, me and Julie are pretty sure he's into drugs now, and we're just waiting for everything to explode."

"You haven't seen your father since you were nine?"

"Nope. He supposedly showed up once a couple of years after, at least that's what my brother said, though I'm not sure if I believe him."

"Why would he lie?"

"To make me crazy."

I don't understand the sibling relationship and drop the subject. I imagine it would be comforting to have a brother or sister around, but Linda seems to be getting more agitated with each question. I ask her about her ex-husband, and if he would ever try to break into her apartment.

She frowns. "I don't know. I guess that he heard voices, and checked the doorknob. I'm really glad I have that alarm."

"You should post a note in the lobby telling everyone not to let strangers in," I say. "Someone must have buzzed him in."

"I don't feel so good," she says, grimacing and holding her stomach.

"Too much beer?"

"Too much everything."

"You want to go back?"

She hesitates. "Not really."

"Let's get some air."

She agrees, and we work our way toward the exit, weaving around dancing couples. The music is growing louder. Outside, we walk slowly down the block, and pass her apartment building. She takes my arm as we fall into step together. She buttons her leather jacket. The cool air awakens me, and I check around us, the occasional car driving by keeping me watchful. I almost expect Linda's ex-husband to pop out of the shadows.

We eventually return to her place, and she resets the doorknob alarm. I say, "Hang on. I still have to get out."

"So soon?"

From the tone of her voice, I realize she's uneasy. "Are you worried?" I ask.

"Not worried . . . just . . ."

"I can stay over, if you want."

"That'd be good. Do you mind?"

I tell her I don't, and kick off my shoes. She prepares for bed, moving a few times from her bedroom to her bathroom in different stages of undress and cleansing. When she sits down next to me on the sofa, she's in her pajamas, her hair held back with a clip, her face pink from washing. Long wisps of curly hair dangle against her smooth, bare neck, and her pajama top drapes loosely down her neckline. I try not to look below her throat. She turns off all the lights except for the small lamp by the sofa. The quiet settles around us, and the first thing she whispers to me is, "I think the reason I was so upset was because I had to hear about it from the editors. Here I am supposedly working on a story about you, and I don't know a huge thing like that."

It takes me a moment to connect her remarks to Sonia. "It's not huge. It's nothing," I say.

"Why didn't you tell me?"

"I thought about it, then realized how bad it sounded," I say. "I actually called you that night. I left a message."

"I remember. When I called back the next day you said it was nothing."

"I was really embarrassed. I wanted to tell you."

"Do you still . . . like her?"

"Her last words to me were 'Go to hell.'"

"Why?"

"Because I told her not to lie to help her lawsuit. You're right—she's looking out for herself." The thought of this dazes me, people and events are conspiring against me, and I close my eyes. "I can't believe I'm in this mess."

"We'll figure it out," she says.

"You're no longer on the story."

"For them I'm not."

I open my eyes. "You'll still help me?"

"Of course," she says. "Tomorrow I'll try again to find out about Durante being Milian's son."

"How?"

"I'll find Durante's former parole officer, maybe check probate court or bankruptcy court records—"

"But what about your editors?"

"I'll deal with them." She rolls up the cuffs on her pajama legs, and she catches me looking at her calves. I pretend to glance at the carpet stain.

"Will that come out?" I ask.

"Yes. Don't worry about it," she says.

"You know, that reminded me of the night my father died."

She turns to me. "How so?"

I tell her about the visit from the police and the muddy carpet. "My aunt used the same kind of brush."

"I learned to use that from my grandmother, who cleaned houses." She looks down at the carpet. "Your aunt must have been in shock."

"I guess. It's all so unclear. I was dizzy with a fever that night. I wonder if I imagined any of it." I stand, and tell her I'm going to get ready for bed.

"You want to borrow some sweats?"

I do, and begin washing up. Linda remains on the sofa, curled up in front of the TV. She calls to me and says that she has extra toothbrushes under the sink. I find a toothbrush and also see her diaphragm case next to a tube of spermicide jelly. I stare at these for a moment, remembering what her ex-husband said. I close the cabinet.

Linda is still on the sofa, and raises her head drowsily toward me. Small wooden sculptures sit on the shelves behind her. A sandalwood dolphin arcs in front of a row of journalism books. Mahogany horses rear up next to a CD collection. On top of the shelves are scruffy stuffed animals: a penguin, a panda cub, and an elephant. I ask, "Where are those from?"

She looks up. "The panda and the elephant I've had since I was a kid. The penguin my niece gave me as a gift."

"And you've kept them all these years?"

"I almost threw them away a few times, but couldn't. A lot of memories." She yawns, and lowers the TV volume. "Actually, I think the panda was a gift from my father, my biological one. My mom told me that, but I don't remember."

I stare at her window, the light from a building next door shining through her blinds. She says, "Aren't you sleepy?"

"Not really."

"I'm beat."

"I know," I say. "I can take the couch."

"I'll get up in a second."

"Can I ask you something?"

She turns to me.

"Should we worry about him?"

She's quiet for a while, and I'm not sure if she has fallen asleep. Then she says, "I can handle him, I think."

"What's with the boxing moves?"

"What? Oh, right. What a joke. He did some amateur bouts and then started thinking of himself as a boxer. He's a scared kid, really. He's nothing."

"But you seem so . . . rattled."

She sighs. Her eyes are closed. "Yes. He throws me off-guard. He can do that. He's really good at provoking me." She yawns again. "When we fought and I started winning, he'd get ugly, mean. He always had to be in control."

I don't reply, and she goes on, more slowly: "I remember once when we were fighting about the car. We had one car. I was using the bus for my job and for school, and I wanted to switch off with him, since he only used the car to get to work and back. But it became clear that it was a macho thing, that he didn't want to be without a car since he'd look bad. I started making fun of him. I knew what I was doing and I saw how mad he was getting, but I couldn't stop myself. It was stupid. I was running myself ragged taking transfers and showing up late for things, and he could've just taken a direct bus, or I could've just dropped him off and picked him up. But still, he didn't want to be driven around, no, not by a woman. I let him have it. And I knew how to get to him. I taunted him, telling him if he was such a man worried about how he looked, then he should've been making more money to get his wife a car. Or he should be a real man and not be making me pay for my own schooling. He wanted to look like some kind of provider but he wasn't. I was doing a lot of the providing. He was such a fake. And he couldn't stand to hear it."

She curls up tighter, and I pull the afghan over her. She keeps her eyes closed, and continues quietly, "So I kept giving it to him. He was also drinking a lot. He was sleeping around. I just had had enough. I kept telling him to be a real man. A real man wouldn't care what other people thought, if he took a bus or was driven by his wife. He wasn't a real man. He was a fake man. He started getting mean, and did his usual routine of calling me fat and ugly and all that. Telling me he was all I had, things he said when I was younger. But I was getting smarter. I saw what he was doing. I laughed in his face. That's the best he can do? That's the best argument he had? And we were screaming at each other and I guess he couldn't stand to be made to look so dumb because that was when he punched me really hard in the face. God, he never hit me like that before. The only other time I've ever been hit like that was when I was a kid and got into a fight with Eddie Mendez, but this time everything happened so fast. I was bleeding in the mouth and I knew I looked bad because he looked so scared. The thing is, there I was on the ground, in shock really, looking up at him, and I couldn't help smiling. Bloody lip and all. I knew I had won. I knew I was out of there."

"So you left."

"Not right away, but yes."

"Not right away?"

"He's sneaky. He pretended to change. But it didn't last long."

"So you still fought."

"Yes. It got a little worse before I got a lawyer and moved out."

She's quiet, and I'm completely still. Her voice had thinned until it was almost a whisper, and now I hear her breathing slowly. I don't know what to say, but feel the rancor burning through me. The fact that I met him tonight makes everything tangible. I try to smother it, and find myself shaken. I lean down and stroke her hair, smelling lavender soap. She half-smiles, and whispers, "I'm . . . pretty . . . tired."

"Sleep," I say, and continue stroking her hair. She relaxes into the sofa cushion, pulling the coverlet up to her chin. After I'm sure she has drifted off, I kiss her forehead lightly and lean in next to her, keeping our arms touching. I want the contact with her. I lie back and close my eyes, listening to her breathe.

43

The fax from the Secretary of State's Corporations Unit is waiting for me at the copy shop. I pay the clerk at the counter and hurry home with it, reading the blurred listing of officers for the different corporations. Although I have a Statement of Officers for Western Imports and the merged WestSun, it's the Sunrise Goods list that interests me, and I see that only Roger Milian, CEO and president, carries over to the merged WestSun. The vice president, David Ernst, and the treasurer, Frank Villanova, of Sunrise Goods, no longer appear on the merged WestSun list, which means they left. I need to contact these two. I skim the other lists, and find Durante on the updated WestSun list, but his and Milian's are the only familiar names.

I begin calling information operators, asking for David Ernst and Frank Villanova. I don't have much luck—I find a few people with the same name but they have nothing to do with Sunrise Goods—and call Linda. I tell her what I have. She says she could do a quick computer search on commercial databases and Internet telephone directories. "It might take a while. I'll have to do it on my lunch break."

"That's fine."

"By the way, did you notice? The *Sentinel* killed the story about you."

"I haven't seen the paper yet."

"At the last minute the editor bumped it off for another short piece."

"What about the *Chronicle?*"

"I don't know."

"Why'd they kill it?"

"It wasn't enough news. They'll wait for something more."

"That's good. I'll get a *Chronicle* now."

"I'll call you back after lunch."

I hang up and walk to the bookstore. The story, less than three short paragraphs, is buried in the Bay Area news section, and just summarizes Sonia's lawsuit against ProServ and Florentino's. I am mentioned in the last paragraph. It says that the police haven't ruled anyone out as a suspect, and that I, former partner of Paul's, am still a "person of interest" in Junil Kim's death. I buy the paper and reread the story a few more times. It's not that bad. A person of interest. So I'm not officially a suspect yet.

Back at my place, while I continue reading the newspaper, someone buzzes me from downstairs. It's a messenger service, and I immediately think of ProServ, though they can't fire me twice. I go downstairs, sign for the envelope, and see Browning's law firm as the return address. Inside is a check for $2,450, a list of billable hours and expenses, a brief letter telling me this is the remainder of the retainer, and some legalese stating that he's no longer representing me. He lists a few criminal lawyers I might want to contact for further representation.

Less than twenty-five hundred dollars out of five thousand? I read through the itemized bill; he charged me for waiting at the Palo Alto police station, even though Sonia had sent him to the wrong place, and he charged me for research on my case, including photocopies and faxes. He even precharged me for the messenger service. Less than a week has gone by and half of the retainer is gone. What if I'm arrested? What if I have to go to trial? I don't have enough money for this.

By the time Linda calls back, I'm feeling bleak. I've read Browning's expense report a few times, then studied my bank statements and calculated how much time I have left. I know I have to start writing letters to Triumph and Black Diamond, but just can't right now.

"It took a little doing, but I got a few numbers for you to try," Linda says.

"Anything is good."

"There was plenty on David Ernst, who shows up in the business news every few years, but not much on Frank Villanova."

"What about phone numbers?"

"Based on where Ernst might live, since the companies he worked for are all in the L.A. area. Here, take these down." She reads off a half-dozen phone numbers and says, "It's a start. I've got to run. I'm in the middle of something else."

"Thanks."

I start calling the numbers in L.A. and reach different businesses. When I ask for David Ernst, most of them haven't heard of him, but I persist, telling them that he might have worked for them years ago. At one machine tool manufacturer, a secretary transfers me to Human Resources, who transfers me to a VP, who tells me that David Ernst hasn't worked there in eight years.

"Do you know where he works now?"

"No, but after leaving here he went into packaging."

I thank him, and continue calling the other numbers. This goes on for another two hours, the time moving quickly because I feel I'm doing something useful. I finally reach a corporate consulting firm, and the receptionist knows the name. "Mr. Ernst freelances with us. He used to work full-time, but is in semiretirement."

"I'm trying to get in touch with him. Do you have a number where he can be reached?"

"You can leave a message in his voice mail here—"

"This might be kind of personal, and I need to talk to him right away."

She says, "I'm not allowed to give out home numbers, if that's what you're asking."

"He used to work with my father, who died. It's really important."

"I can give you a beeper number."

"That's perfect."

She gives me the number and the code. "Punch in your phone number once you hear the long beep."

I thank her, hang up, then dial the beeper system and enter in my number. I place the phone down and wait, suddenly not sure what I'll say to him if he calls. I begin thinking of ways to bring up the death of my father. What if Ernst was involved? It's possible that Ernst, as a vice president, knew what Milian was doing to ensure the merger went through. Maybe Ernst even left afterward because of it. Or maybe he was paid off. I go through the dozens of possibilities.

The phone rings. I jump, then pick up.

"I'm returning a page," he says. His voice is gravelly, almost hoarse.

"Mr. Ernst? David Ernst?"

"Yes. Who is this?"

"I'm sorry to bother you, but I'm the son of a former employee of yours, and I'm trying to get more information."

He waits. "Yes?"

"You were the vice president at Sunrise Goods?" I ask carefully.

"Where?"

"Sunrise Goods. It was an importing firm in Oakland. This was about twenty years ago."

He laughs. "Twenty years ago? Do you know how many places I've worked since then?"

"This was in Oakland. You worked with Roger Milian, the CEO, and Frank Villanova, the treasurer. The company was merged with Western Imports."

After a moment, he says, "And who are you?"

"My name is Allen Choice. My father, John, was a driver for Sunrise. He was killed in an unloading accident."

"And why are you calling me?"

"Do you remember the company?"

"I do."

"I'm trying to find out the details of my father's accident. I'm trying to locate the insurance company that investigated the accident, or talk to anyone with more information. Do you remember the accident?"

"As a matter of fact, I do. The whole company was shaken."

"Do you remember who the insurance company was?"

"No, but I do remember that they raised our premiums once they settled with us, and we soon switched companies."

"You don't remember the name?"

"It was quite a few years ago. Isn't there an insurance commission that would have records?"

"I'm not sure. What can you tell me about the accident?"

"Something about unloading after hours, and without any help. Wasn't there a witness—no, a woman on the scene?"

"What?" I ask, feeling a jolt.

"An office assistant working late. I think she found the body or something. I remember that—" He stops. "Why don't you just ask Roger Milian?"

"He's not helping me," I say. "An assistant?"

"Why isn't he helping?"

"I seemed to have angered him somehow."

Ernst asks, "And how did you do this?"

"I crashed a party of his."

He says, "That might do it."

"Do you remember the name of the office assistant?"

"No. But the secretary who hired her, my secretary, might. Her name was . . ." He pauses. "She worked for me for six years. . . . God, what was her name? Janine. Janine Lapinsky. Yes, that's it. I guess my memory isn't that bad. Janine went with me to Dunham after I left Sunrise. But I stayed at Dunham for only a year, and came down to L.A."

I try to keep my voice even, and ask, "You wouldn't happen to have her number, would you?"

"No, but I have an address somewhere. She sent me a card when my wife died two years ago."

"You still kept in contact with her?"

"Off and on. She was with me at three different companies. Hold on." He leaves me for a few minutes, then comes back on. "Here's the address." He reads it off—she lives in Alameda—then says, "She's probably listed in the phone book. Tell her I said hello."

"I will. Thank you, Mr. Ernst."

He says goodbye, and I immediately hang up and call information assistance. I get Janine Lapinsky's number, and call her home. A young man answers.

"May I speak with Janine Lapinsky?"

"She's at work," the man says.

"Can I have the number?"

He gives it to me. I then call this number and reach her on the first ring. Mrs. Lapinsky is surprised when I mention David Ernst's name, and is even more surprised when I tell her I'm trying to find the office assistant who was at Sunrise when my father died. It takes a few minutes of summary to explain why I'm looking for her.

"She was older than me, a lot older, so I don't know if she's even still alive," she says.

"Do you remember her name?"

"Yes. Mrs. Loverro. I liked her name. She lived near Berkeley, I think Albany. She quit soon after that terrible accident. He was your father?"

"Yes. Do you remember her first name?"

"I think Lauren? No, it was Spanish-sounding. Lourdes?"

"Lourdes Loverro?"

"Yes, I think so. Definitely Loverro. But she was in her fifties at the time. She had just gotten a divorce and needed to work. No, she was a little older than that, maybe late fifties, even early sixties. She could've been my grandmother's age."

"Thank you very much. You wouldn't have an address or number, would you?"

"God, no. I haven't heard from her since then. I'm not even sure about her first name."

"Do you remember the accident?"

"Yes. Everything changed after that. It was a shock. I remember your father. He was a nice man."

I want to ask her more, but I need to contact Loverro. I thank Mrs. Lapinsky and hang up.

Finding Lourdes Loverro is more difficult, because I quickly discover that of the few Loverros in the Albany and Berkeley area, none is named Lourdes, and the Loverros who answer their phones have never heard of a Lourdes, a Sunrise Goods, or anything related to that. After thirty minutes of calling, I think this through more carefully, eliminating a random phone search. I consider calling Linda for help again, but stop myself. She's busy with work.

I telephone the Monte Vista library and quiz the reference desk about locating someone. The librarian asks me a few questions about Loverro and suggests an Internet search, checking through the library's phone book banks, and possibly a search for her relatives if I know them. I don't, but when I say she might be in her seventies or eighties, possibly even passed away, the librarian recommends I check with the Social Security Administration or retired groups. "What about retirement homes?" I ask. "Is there a list of Bay Area homes?"

"We have phone banks for every city in the Bay Area, including a business index."

I thank her and head out to the library.

44

I walk through the Redwood View Retirement Center in Novato, the sounds of TVs and radios in almost every room, acutely aware of the sense of human decline beyond the stark yellow-and-white hallways. The presence of carpets and plush furniture doesn't diminish the clinical feel of the home, glimpses of hospital beds and mobile medical equipment appearing through some doorways.

To get to Novato—in northern Marin—I drove three hours, stuck in traffic on 101 for most of that time. I honked at drivers trying to cut ahead of me, something I rarely do. This worries me. I'm in too much of a hurry.

I know this might yield nothing. Yesterday I began calling all the retirement homes in the Bay Area and found that Lourdes Loverro had been a resident at one in Richmond, but she had left it two years ago. I managed to talk to a supervisor, who reluctantly gave me the name of Loverro's daughter. I eventually reached her by phone this morning, and she told me where her mother is. I wanted to call Mrs. Loverro right away, but the daughter said that her mother is hard of hearing and her memory is failing. "She's eighty-six years old, you know," the daughter said. Visiting hours, she told me, were from four to six that afternoon.

A nurse scolds a resident as if he is a two-year-old. "Well, that's a naughty boy. Aren't you a naughty boy?" I watch the nurse shaking her finger at a man with a walker, who ignores her and continues moving forward. I try not to stare.

Lourdes Loverro has a private room in the west wing, and when I knock on her door, I remember that she's hard of hearing and knock harder. "What," she says.

I look in. "Lourdes Loverro?" A hunched-over, completely white-haired woman in a blue bathrobe sits at a small table. She's handling a deck of oversized playing cards. She glances at me. Her wrinkled, scrunched face is splotchy. The room is sparsely furnished with a low metal-framed bed, a desk, and a wooden bureau. Generic prints of sunflowers hang on the yellow walls.

"What?" she rasps.

"Are you Lourdes Loverro?" I ask louder. I smell mothballs.

She flips over a card which is twice the size of her hand. She looks down and frowns. "Who are you and what do you want?"

"My name is Allen—"

"I can't hear a word you're saying. You'll have to talk louder."

I raise my voice. "My name is Allen Choice, and I was wondering if you could answer a few questions about a job you once had."

"Why?"

I explain that I'm trying to find out more about my father's death. She looks up and stares at me. She says, "He died here?"

"No, this was twenty years ago."

"He died here twenty years ago?"

"No, he died at a place called Sunrise Goods."

She blinks, then looks up at the lights. She licks her lips. Folds of loose skin hang on her neck and throat, dark and spotted wrinkled flesh. She seems to be humming to herself. I wait for a few minutes, then wonder if she has forgotten I am here. I clear my throat.

"Quiet. Frank's radio is playing 'Mack the Knife.' "

I listen to the music coming from down the hall and say, "I thought you were hard of hearing."

"I said be quiet."

I'm about to sit on a folding chair next to the door, but she says, "I didn't say sit down. I said be quiet."

I stop in mid-motion, then stand back up. I wait.

She turns to me. "That's the one where Ella Fitzgerald forgets the words and makes them up."

"I thought you were hard of hearing."

"You're not a doctor, are you?"

"No."

"Or a lawyer."

"God, no."

She smiles, her face wrinkling. "You don't like lawyers?"

"I've only met one, and he screwed me over."

"My former husband was a lawyer. Watch your language."

"Sorry."

"That's okay. He left me. But that had nothing to do with his lawyering. He quit his job and ran off with some secretary."

I wait, then say, "I'm here because—"

"I'm afraid I poisoned my children against him. Now they don't trust anyone, not even me."

"Why wouldn't they trust you?"

"They think I'm going to give away my money. They feel like they deserve it. Do you think children deserve their parents' money? Just for being the children?"

"No," I say, thinking of the settlement for my father's death. "Unless the money was intended for them."

She glares at me. "My son didn't send you?"

"No."

"I worked very hard to make my money. And I put my kids through school. I fed them, clothed them. Why do they want more?"

"People are greedy."

"I know what they're thinking. When I die, the money should stay in the family. But it's my money, isn't it?"

"It is. Mrs. Loverro, I was wondering if you can answer—"

"When my husband left me, he took all the money."

I sigh. "May I sit down?"

She shakes her head. "No, you may not."

"Oh."

"So I had to go to work."

"What?" I say, snapping to attention.

"I had no money. My husband left me. My son was in the middle of dental school. I had to go to work. I should have been retired, but instead I had to find work."

"At Sunrise Goods."

She nods slowly and flips over another card. She purses her lips, and says without looking up, "I wondered if I'd ever see you again."

"Again?"

"You're the son, aren't you?"

I remain still, trying to determine what she is saying. "The son of who?"

"Of whom. Of your father."

"Who is my father?"

"You were a small, squat boy, weren't you? You had a terrible haircut, a bowl cut. Who cut your hair?"

"My aunt."

"Of course."

"You knew me."

"I knew you."

"I don't remember you."

"How could you? That was a complicated time. I remember watching you at the service. You had no idea what was going on."

"The service?" I ask.

"The funeral service for your father."

"The service was in Korean. You were there?"

"I visited. I wanted to pay my respects. You were wearing that terrible wool suit two sizes too small."

I'm surprised into silence. It *was* a terrible suit, though I remember hating it because it made my neck and arms itch. Of course, I can't really picture anything from that time, and I certainly don't remember her. "So you knew my father?"

"I saw him around."

"You saw the accident?"

She looks up, listening again. She says, "I heard it."

"The accident?" I ask, feeling an urgency in my chest.

She nods.

"You told the insurance investigator this? What did you hear?"

"What did I tell the investigator, or what did I hear?"

"You mean there's a difference?"

"There is."

I take a deep breath. "What did you tell the investigator?"

She flips a card, and I notice that the layout on the table is nothing like solitaire. She says, "I told him that I was working late, which I was. I told him that I heard a loud sound, then the sounds of chain falling, which I did. I went out and found your father dead."

"And what did you really hear?"

"Why do you want to know?"

"He was my father."

"Why now?"

I say carefully, "I need to know. I think it has something to do with things that have been happening lately."

She studies me. "I heard my boss . . ." She pauses. "What was his name?"

"Roger Milian."

She nods slowly. "Yes, he came in with a woman."

"Who?"

"I don't know. I never saw her."

I immediately think of Mrs. Garvey. "And?"

"And they were arguing."

"About what?" I ask, suspecting Noah Garvey was the subject. Maybe she was seeing her ex-husband crucified in the press.

"I'm not sure. I only heard the voices, his and the woman's. They were quiet."

"You didn't hear anything? Not a name?"

"Just voices," she says. "Your father drove in and began unloading. But he stopped."

"Unloading?"

"Yes."

"Where were you?"

"Filing in the back office."

"Did they know you were there?"

"Not at first."

"What happened?"

"There was more arguing, louder this time. Your father's voice. I couldn't make it out because the truck was still running. But I heard fighting, something breaking. The woman yelled for them to stop—"

"Them? Milian and my father?"

"I guess so."

My father must have been tightening the blackmail noose. Maybe he saw Mrs. Garvey and found another chance to get at Milian. "Then what?" I ask.

She says, "Then the voices stopped."

"Stopped?"

"Just the truck engine."

"Then what?"

"Then I heard the chain falling."

"What did you do?"

"I went out, and saw your father lying on the ground. The chains were on top of him."

"Where was Milian?"

"He was there. I surprised him. He saw me and told me to go back to the office."

"Was the woman there?"

"No. She must have just left."

"You went back to the office?"

"I did," she says. "And he came in and talked to me."

"What did he say?"

She exhales slowly. "I had no money. My son was in dental school, and my daughter wanted to buy a house. I had to think about my retirement."

"What are you saying?"

"He was at first angry that I was there, but then began to tell me what to do."

"What to say, you mean?"

"What to say. I was to wait until he left, then call the police. I was to tell them that I was working late and heard the accident."

"And he left?"

"And he left."

"Why would you help him? How much did he offer you?"

She says, "Ten thousand dollars if I did what he said, then another ten thousand if everything went well and quieted down."

"But he murdered my father. You knew that, didn't you?"

"I told myself that it was an accident, and he wanted to keep it quiet."

"So you lied."

"I lied."

"Then what?"

"Then I got paid, and I became an accomplice. He paid me the second half, and I quit."

"Then what?"

"I paid off my son's tuition, and helped with the down payment on my daughter's house. And I went to work at another company."

I need a minute to take this in. I have a witness and an accomplice right here in front of me. I say, "Why are you telling me this?"

"I'm not going to live much longer. I know this." She pulls herself up and shuffles to her bed. She climbs in slowly. "I'm going to rest now," she says as she tugs a sheet up. Her hands shake.

"Will you tell the police what you told me?"

"I don't care. If they ask me, I will tell them." She closes her eyes. "I'm very tired now. I haven't spoken this much in years."

"Mrs. Loverro, thank you for telling me what happened."

"I knew I would tell you someday. I knew it." She breathes slowly. I watch her as she takes a deep, unsteady breath, then sinks into her pillow. I leave her room, closing the door softly, and as I walk down the hall, I hear a scratchy record playing some jazz. I follow the music to a room three doors down, and look in. An elderly black man is sitting on his bed and listening. He turns his head slightly, but doesn't seem to register me. His eyes are glazed, a small smile on his lips. A horn solo finishes. The woman's voice on the record laughs. I say, "Is that Ella Fitzgerald?"

He blinks, then says, "What?"

I repeat the question.

He nods slowly.

I continue walking down the long hallway, listening to the scratchy, tinny recording bounce by the rooms, the sounds of solitude mingling with the warm air hissing through the ceiling vents.

45

The first thing I do when I return home is call Linda. When I reveal to her what I have just learned, she immediately asks, "Did you get that on tape?"

"No."

"I want to interview her. Will she let me?"

"I think so. She said she'll talk." I tell her where Loverro is and what the visiting hours are. "Is it time for the police?"

"Yes. We can break this open now. Wait. Is this Loverro senile?"

"I don't think so."

"Is she a credible witness?"

"Yes."

"I mean, why did she tell you this?"

"She's old. She's tying up loose ends."

"But will it hold up in court?"

"I don't know. What about Garvey's ex-wife? If she was there—"

"She could corroborate Loverro's account. Yes. It's clearer: Garvey's ex-wife was having an affair with Milian, and maybe breaking it off after what was happening with Garvey."

"Or maybe just fighting with Milian about what he was doing."

"Your father sees them, maybe demands more, or threatens them."

"More blackmail."

"And they fight. Milian kills him, and forces Mrs. Garvey to keep quiet."

"Because she's having an affair with him. She's involved."

"Maybe Milian breaks it off. She then leaves for New York, and she can't say anything because she's an accessory."

"Christ, it all fits."

Linda says, "We can get Milian. You should contact Mrs. Garvey again, maybe through the daughter. You need to get her to talk."

"Me?"

"You have things in common with the daughter."

"Why don't we try to meet her again . . . what's her name—"

"Ari. I can't. I have things to do tomorrow."

"Another story?"

"Uh, no," she says. "Just things."

I hear something change in her voice, a drop in tone. "Like what?" I ask. I can't imagine what's more important than this.

She pauses long enough to make me suspicious. She says, "I have to take care of personal things."

"Are you seeing that guy, Thomas?"

"No, nothing like that."

Thinking quickly of what she might be hiding, I suddenly remember her ex-husband, and say, "Oh, no. This doesn't have to do with your ex, does it?"

"What?"

"Your ex. Don't tell me you're meeting him."

"It's not like that. My sister will be there. It's the only way to stop him from bothering me."

"He's bothering you?"

"He keeps calling."

"What about a restraining order?"

"I know, but he's not exactly harassing me. He just wants to talk. What can I do?"

"It's a trick. He's seeing what he can get."

"You don't think I know that?" she asks, her voice rising. "I know exactly what he's doing, but I need to meet him once, and tell him in front of a witness not to bother me, even record it."

"I'm a witness. He tried to break into your apartment."

"We can't be sure about that. And you pulled a gun out. So he had reason to be hostile."

"Why can't you tell him to leave you alone over the phone?"

"I have, but I want do it in person first."

"What if he tries to—"

"Allen, I think I can take care of this. I know how he works—"

I say, "You told me how he works."

"Don't make me regret that."

I stop. I hear her breathing. I say, "I'm just worried about you, that's all."

"Thanks, but I can take care of myself."

"I know. I just . . ."

"I've got to go."

"Wait. I . . ." I want to handle this better. "Linda . . ."

"We'll talk later, okay? I've got to go." She hangs up.

I'm about to call her back, but when I tap the telephone hook a few times to disengage the line, I hear a faint clicking echo. I freeze, and a rush of adrenaline flashes through me. My face and neck burn, and I can't believe what I'm hearing. Not again. I continue listening while I press and lift the hook, listening for a tap. I do this a few times, and realize with panic that there is something on the line. I try to remember what I've been saying, and curse. Loverro.

Running out of my apartment and down the steps, I hope it's just another tape. I go to the basement and check the closet where the last recording device was. The hole is still there, but when I reach in I can't find anything. The clicks I heard sounded like a device triggered by the line voltage. It has to be a tap. I check again but still find nothing.

I follow the wall back to the telephone switch box, open it up, and begin searching. When I see a small circuit board buried in the clump of wires below, I yank it out, not caring what this will do. I was right. It's a parallel tap connected to a small VHF transmitter, which means that the transmitting range can't be that far—only a few hundred yards. I hurry out of the building and look around. Nothing. Either they aren't listening in or they left as soon as they heard me checking the phone. They could be anywhere—holed up in any of the apartments in the building, or even next door. I examine the transmitter closely, pulling out the central chip and reading the small numbers. I've never seen one like this.

"Shit!" I throw everything onto the cement and stomp on it. Goddamn careless. I grind my heel into the circuit board.

I run back to my apartment and call the retirement home in Novato, asking for Mrs. Loverro. The woman says that they aren't allowed to transfer nonemergency calls after nine o'clock. She can take a message, though. I tell her it's an emergency.

Mrs. Loverro answers the phone in a muffled, sleepy voice.

I tell her who it is, and she needs a second to remember me.

"I was asleep," she says. "Why are you calling me?"

"I want to warn you. Milian might send some people to keep you quiet."

"What?"

"To keep you quiet."

"Why?"

"He knows I talked to you. He might be worried about you telling the police."

"What can he do? I don't care. I'm tired. Let me sleep."

"No! You don't understand. He might physically hurt you."

She lets out a small laugh. "I am sick. Didn't I tell you? I'm already hurt."

"But—"

"Please, let me rest. If he comes, he comes. I told you what I did. I'm glad I did. I'm sorry."

"Mrs. Loverro, I need you to tell the police—"

"You can tell the police. You know now."

"It's not enough!" I yell, hearing her fumble with the phone. She mumbles something, her voice receding into static.

"Wait!"

But she hangs up. I call the receptionist again and tell her that Mrs. Loverro might be in danger. "Please tell the police that she might be in physical danger."

"Huh?"

"Can you do that? And don't let her have any visitors."

"I can't do that. What are you talking about?"

"Listen to me. Some people might try to hurt her. Do you understand? You can't let her have visitors, and you have to tell the police—"

"Why don't you tell them?"

"I can, but I need you to—"

Someone pushes open my front door, breaking through the lock. I haven't bolted it because I was in a rush to call Mrs. Loverro, and the lower lock barely holds as a man splinters the doorjamb. I jump toward my gun, which is on my kitchen counter, but the man who breaks through raises a revolver at me.

"Careful, now," a voice says from the hallway. Durante and another man walk in. The second man goes to the counter, takes my gun, and stands behind me. Durante points to the phone, and the man with the revolver hangs it up. Durante turns to me and says, "You're a fucking pain in the ass, you know that?" He nods to the man behind me, and for a fraction of a second I hear movement, then something crashes into the back of my head, my vision lighting up, everything blurring away.

Part 5

Lucid Dreams
of Dying

46

I wasn't knocked unconscious, but I'm dazed enough for them to hustle me into a van and drive off. My skull feels squeezed, and the pain in the back of my head blazes through me; my eyes water as I press my temples slowly. I curl up on the bare, rusting floor, and keep my body still. The muffler directly beneath me rattles. The van speeds over a bump, and I exhale painfully as I bounce, my arms protecting my head. We make a quick turn, and Durante says to the driver, "Slow down."

I look up and see Durante and the third man watching me. I recognize this pale, red-haired man with the revolver—he was at Milian's party and chased me in the yard. Durante lights a cigarette, glances at his watch. He seems unconcerned to be involved in a kidnapping. I say, "Where are you taking me?"

Durante looks surprised at the sound of my voice. "Did I say you can talk?"

"You didn't say not to."

He shakes his head, and I'm again surprised by how young he seems. His smooth face reminds me of an adolescent's. Even though it's getting dark, he has on his mirrored sunglasses that press into his round cheeks. I see my warped reflection. I ask, "Does Milian know you're doing this?"

Durante reaches up and touches the roof as he stands, then moves swiftly toward me, trying to kick me in the head. I cover myself and cushion the blow, but my forearms are forced into my face, and I roll back into the rear doors. My shoulder hits a door handle and I can't help grunting; the pain tightens my body. He kicks me again, this time in my chest, connecting with his toe, and I lose my breath. He says, "Now shut the fuck up."

I can't get any air down, and I keep still, trying to relax my diaphragm. I resist the urge to gasp for air, and attempt small, quick pants. The man with the gun is watching me with a smile. His teeth are gray. "Fuck you," I mutter to him, but it comes out strangled. His face tightens, and he moves toward me.

"Not now," Durante says.

"You're so stupid," I manage to say as I regain my breath.

"What?" Durante turns.

"You're so stupid. You don't think Junil Kim's death will be tied to you? And now kidnapping?"

"Didn't I just tell you to shut up?"

"And if I'm missing, you don't think this story is going to break real fast?"

Durante says, "What part of 'shut up' don't you understand? Don't you understand English?" He motions for the other man to give him the gun. I tense. But Durante takes the gun and says to the man, "T.J., maybe you can teach him English. Teach Bruce Lee here what 'shut up' means."

"Fuck yourself," I say to Durante.

The man named T.J. advances, but this time I'm ready. I wait until he's closer, then I spring up, ignoring the pain in my head and chest, and punch him hard in the solar plexus, immediately following with an upper elbow strike to his chin, his head thrusting back. I knee him in the groin and push him into the side door. The van rocks.

"What the fuck?" the driver yells.

T.J. staggers to the floor, his mouth bleeding. He holds his groin. Durante points the gun at me and says, "Sit down, Bruce Lee. I should've known you'd do the karate chops." He says to T.J., "You all right? You didn't see it coming from chop-saki, did you?" Durante smiles. "You're getting old."

"Motherfucker," T.J. says, hunching over and exhaling. He sits up, rubs his chin, and wipes away a small trickle of blood. His white face and neck are mottled red. "Let me break his fucking—"

"Later," Durante says. "We're almost there."

"At WestSun?" I ask.

"You just don't learn, do you?" Durante says.

"You're already known," I say. A shimmer of pain runs through my head. I close my eyes. "It's all going to come out now."

"What, you talking about that old woman? We'll get to her."

"You just can't kill everyone who might—"

"Who said anything about killing?"

"You killed Paul, then Junil Kim."

He looks annoyed, and says, "That guy Kim was an asshole who should've listened to us."

"You didn't have to kill him."

"Hey, he went apeshit on us. He busted up my guy's arm."

"So you killed him?"

"His fault."

"And Paul?"

He shakes his head and points the gun at me. "Shut the fuck up. Say one more word and that's it. One more word."

He aims carefully at my leg, and I stay quiet. We pull over a bump—probably the speed bumps in the parking lot of WestSun—and into a garage. I'm not as worried as I should be, partly because I know that if Durante wanted me dead, he would've killed me long before arriving here. The van comes to a stop, and the driver climbs out and opens our door. Durante tells me to get out.

We are parked inside a warehouse that I don't recognize—high crossbeams and dark cement walls—though I see some of WestSun's boxes and crates stacked by the entrance. The driver has already shut the garage door, so I look for a window, but they're too far up and translucent. T.J. climbs out of the van gingerly and says something to Durante, who nods. Durante turns to me and points toward a metal staircase leading up to an office. I walk up the steep grille steps. They follow, our heavy trooping echoing throughout the warehouse.

"In there," Durante says, pointing to the office.

I open the door and see Milian at a desk, typing on a laptop. He stops and looks up. "Why the gun?" he asks Durante.

"He wasn't willing to go."

"I wasn't asked," I say. "You should've just asked."

Milian frowns and says to Durante, "You remember what I said?"

"He was gonna make trouble," Durante says.

I turn to him, surprised. He adds, "I just wanted to make sure—"

"Put that gun away and stop acting like a criminal."

"But I had to—"

"Put that away," Milian says. He turns at me. "Have a seat."

"Kidnapping is a federal offense," I say. Durante gives me a lifeless stare, but shoves his gun into his belt.

Milian motions to the chair. "Please sit."

"What is this place?"

"A second warehouse we were renting out."

"Not anymore?" I ask.

He ignores this, and tilts his head, watching me. Although his beard and hair are meticulously well-groomed, his eyes seem more tired. That fatigued look has worsened since I saw him at his party. He absently taps his watch. Finally, he says, "How much would it take to get you to walk away?"

"What?"

"How much?"

"Did you kill my father?"

He blinks, his expression unchanged, and says, "What do you think?"

"I think you did. I think you and Noah Garvey's wife were having an affair, and my father was probably blackmailing you, so you killed him."

"Noah Garvey's wife?"

"Ex-wife. A divorce battle with your wife at the time would've ruined the merger."

He almost smiles. "Is that what you think?"

"And now that I can possibly stop Pinewood's buyout, you brought me here to pay me off."

"How can you stop Pinewood?"

"Why would they want to buy a company whose CEO and vice president will be going to jail?"

"And you have proof of this?"

"I do," I say.

"Lourdes Loverro won't talk to the police."

I try not to show any reaction. "Who?"

He smiles. "She loves her children too much."

I feel the fight draining. "What?"

"She might not like them that much, but she doesn't want any harm to come to them."

I don't reply.

He spreads his hands apart. "You can't win, you know."

"Garvey's wife?"

"You can talk to her all you want."

"But—"

"You're obviously way out of your league here. Like your father. How much?"

"Forget it."

"Your father wanted fifteen thousand. What's your price?"

"What if I refuse?"

"We'll deal with you another way. It doesn't matter to me. How much?"

I raise my voice. "Why did you have to kill him? Why did you kill my partner? What purpose did it serve? I don't understand."

"Who was your partner?"

"Paul Baumgartner."

Milian looks confused for a moment, and turns to Durante, who shakes his head and frowns. I say, "The one consulting on your security. The reason why I contacted you—"

"Him again. I'm not sure what exactly you—"

"It's no one," Durante says.

Milian pauses for a moment, shakes this off, then says, "I don't have time for this. Tell me how much. That's all I can do."

"You're going to kill me? You don't think that'll be connected to you?"

"How much?"

I say, "Fuck you."

He narrows his eyes, shaking his head slowly, then waves me away. Durante grabs my arm and pushes me up toward the door. I say to him, "You killed Paul, but Milian doesn't know, does he?"

"You should've taken the money."

"What happened? Did he see something he wasn't supposed to?"

"You're fucked now." He pushes me harder out the door and down the steps. T.J. is waiting for me with something wrapped in a large plastic bag. He has on gloves. I feel a surge of fear, and look for an opportunity to run.

Durante raises his gun. "Don't."

"The back?" T.J. asks.

Durante nods, and they push me toward a small boxed-off area at the other end of the warehouse. I try to see what's in the plastic bag, but can't make it out. My muscles are electrified, my shallow breathing raspy. I listen to Durante behind me, estimating where the gun might be, and am ready to make a break when the third man, the driver, appears holding my gun.

"You said I could," T.J. says.

Before I can turn around, something slams into the back of my head, exploding my vision, and I fall forward, unable to see. Something turns off. I can't feel my legs as I stumble to the ground. They are going to kill me. I roll away, trying to get on my feet, thinking, Run, but I hear T.J. approaching quickly, saying, "You think I was just gonna forget . . ." He gives me a running kick to my face, though I try to protect myself with my arms; I am flipped by the force of it, the muscles in my neck straining as I land in a twisted position. I let out a wheeze, breathing hard. I try to pull myself up, but he gives me another kick, this time to my midsection, and I don't have the energy to block it; I feel my ribs crunching, the shock of the impact blinding me. I see red lights. I can't breathe. He grabs me and pulls me up. I can't stand. He says, "You fucking piece of shit." He draws back a gloved fist and smashes my mouth, but I don't feel it and see myself falling back, everything spinning and red, and I think I hear myself slapping onto the cement ground, but I can't be sure. I know he's kicking me again; I hear his grunts and the sounds of his boot hitting me, but I can only see the red dirty concrete floor with oil stains and sawdust or sand ground into it, the cement moving underneath me as I am kicked again, and I wonder why this is happening if they're going to kill me. Why don't they just shoot me? I realize I am almost resigned to die, and I flash to one of those waking dreams I've had, one in which I see myself dying and I suddenly see that this is what those dreams meant, that I am witnessing my own death, and I hear Durante tell T.J. to stop. T.J. says, "Wait, one more." And I hear footsteps shuffling back for another kick, and I don't care because everything melts away, and I hear T.J. say, "Come on, just one more." And he runs toward me.

But I feel nothing.

47

The smell of vomit wakes me. No, it's the pain that wakes me, but the smell of vomit startles me, and I need air. I can't escape the smell, which seems to be everywhere. I then realize it's my own vomit, soaked and drying in my clothes, mingled with blood and dirt and dead grass. Dead grass? Dead grass surrounds me. I'm curled up in a ball, the full moon directly above. I turn my head away from the smell, and the pain is so excruciating that I start moaning and cursing. I lay my head back down. I throw up again and don't have the energy to move. It dribbles down my cheek. I pass out.

I wake up to a strong breeze chilling me. I'm alive. It doesn't make sense. Maybe they knew they couldn't kill me. There is too much connecting them to me. I try to sit up, and my entire left midsection flares with deep, cutting pain. I lie back down, and take shallow breaths. I'm stunned by how much everything hurts, and suddenly wonder if I've been shot, left here to die. This scares me, and I begin checking myself, touching my chest and stomach, looking for any bullet wounds. I feel my head, and find a large wet bump in the back. Blood. I touch the bump again, this time a little too roughly, and stifle a cry. I don't think I've been shot.

I lift my head, but something's wrong with my neck, and I struggle to straighten out the kink. I have to stop and rest every few seconds. The pain comes in waves now. My chest aches. I relax into the ground and lie still. I'm not sure what happened: all I know is that at one point I awoke for a moment as I was moved from the cement floor to the van, but then I faded away.

I'm getting dizzier just lying here, and I don't want to lose consciousness again, so I force myself to breathe more deeply, the ache in my chest and ribs spreading. I hear cars in the distance, the sounds of a highway, and am comforted by this. I'm near other people.

After what seems like a half hour of breathing, I pull myself up, stopping and waiting for each spasm of pain to pass. When I sit up, I feel the nausea rising and have to gulp the air to calm my stomach. My chest is still damp with vomit. I'm shivering. I look around. It's a small field, litter strewn around me, the freeway about a hundred yards beyond a broken chain-link fence. I don't think I'm far from Burlingame, and look toward the row of buildings a half-mile away. I've been dumped here by Durante on his way back to the freeway.

I was definitely kept alive by him. I'm not sure why. I worry about Linda, unsure if Durante has any plans for her. I have to warn her. I have to tell her about them getting to Loverro. Shit. I look again toward the row of buildings, and attempt the long, painful process of bringing myself to my feet. I raise my knee up, but need to balance myself. My ribs tighten, and I stop. I remain in that awkward position until the pain subsides, and I start thinking of revenge. This clears my head.

With one foot planted squarely in front of me, I stand slowly and totter to the side, the lights from the freeway blurring. I make it to my feet, hold my ribs, and stand unsteadily as the back of my head throbs. I begin walking—shuffling—toward the row of buildings, my head clearing in the cool night air, but every muscle and joint in my arms, back, and chest feels as if it is ripping open with each step. I have to stop and rest every ten feet.

I remember Milian's lack of concern with my threats, his supreme confidence in his position over me. Was it just because of Durante being there, or did I miss something? His affair with Garvey's wife meant nothing to him, or seemed irrelevant. Maybe he was a good actor. Maybe with Loverro quieted, he felt he had nothing to worry about.

And he didn't know anything about Paul. I'm certain of it. Durante was involved in something outside of WestSun. Linda has been right all along: my father's death might have had nothing to do with Paul's murder, but my looking into Paul's death crossed over and began messing everything up. I can't make sense of this.

I stop to rest. Durante will get his turn. I promise myself this.

I wipe dried blood off my lips and chin. The punch to my mouth has swollen my lower lip. My teeth are aching. I could've been beaten to death. I could've been shot. Yet I feel no real relief, no thankfulness, no joy.

I continue walking. I am alive. I should be relieved. I could've ended up like Junil Kim. Why am I not relieved? I wonder who would've missed me had I been killed. I can't think of anyone except Linda, and even then I'm not sure. I know I'm a story for her, a few extra inches in the newspaper, but I hope there's more. Wishful thinking. This depresses me.

I reach the buildings. Most of them are commercial warehouses and storage facilities, two- and three-story buildings made of windowless concrete. Everything is closed. I search for a pay phone, ready to break into one of these places if I have to. Adjacent to a self-storage garage is an architect's office, and I find a pay phone in the doorway. I call Linda collect, and she accepts the charges.

"Listen to me carefully," she says, before I even speak.

"Wait—"

"No, listen to me. The police have focused on you as their prime suspect for Junil Kim's murder. They are at your apartment right now searching for evidence. There is a warrant out for your arrest. I am being watched and my phones will probably be tapped, all calls traced, by tomorrow morning. They received a tip about you earlier, and apparently found something in your car. Do you understand?"

"What could they have—"

"The murder weapon."

I say, "I'm being framed. I was just with Milian and Durante. They did this."

"You need to get a lawyer, you need to—"

"Can you come pick me up?" A breeze blows around me, and I shiver.

"Allen, I'm being watched."

"I need . . . I need some help. They roughed me up," I say. "I'm somewhere in Burlingame." I remember the man, T.J., holding something in a plastic bag. Could that have been the evidence, the murder weapon? "What time is it?"

"What?" she asks.

"What time—"

"Past midnight."

"I've been out all night," I say. "I am so fucked."

"Should I find you a lawyer? What do you need?"

"I need clothes . . . I need . . ." I can't focus. Everything is moving too quickly. I say, "I need clothes."

"I'll get someone to bring you some. Where are you?"

I hesitate. "Your phone isn't tapped now?"

"I doubt it. All this broke a couple of hours ago."

I look up. "I'll be in front of Anvil Self-Storage. I think it's Burlingame, but it's right off 101."

"I'll get the address. Are you okay?"

"No," I say. "I'm a little . . . messed up."

"They hurt you?"

"Yes."

"God, Allen. Okay. Don't move."

"The police think I did it?"

"They found something in your car. What did Milian say?"

"He got to Loverro."

"We need to sort this out. Wait for the clothes."

"Who will come?"

"I'll send my sister."

Before I have a chance to ask what her sister looks like or how long I'll have to wait, Linda hangs up.

I cross the street shivering, and huddle behind a garbage Dumpster. So that's why I was allowed to live. They didn't want to kill Junil Kim, but he fought them. Broke someone's arm. More than anything I've done. I remember his smile when I mentioned my fight. I said there were two men, and he was amused. The guy at the trailer park called Kim an iron man. He was a fighter and wouldn't be pushed around. Once he died they needed a scapegoat, and when I refused to deal I became the perfect candidate. The police and press machine are now at work, my name going out to everyone as a prime suspect. I feel a grip of panic and force it down. I have the urge to run, to disappear. I begin coughing uncontrollably, and each breath shocks my ribs. I cover my mouth, then look at my palm with surprise. It's speckled with blood. Jesus. This scares me more than anything else. I curl up against the Dumpster. I almost want to weep, but I tell myself to get a grip. Stop fucking whining, I tell myself. Stop feeling sorry for yourself. Get a goddamn hold of yourself.

I can't believe how stupid I've been. I was stumbling around while they were covering up their weaknesses one by one, shutting me down point by point. Then they took care of me. Stupid! I'm just a screw-up, and I'm soon going to get what I deserve. My father had done something like this; he saw an opportunity to blackmail Milian, but was outdone at each step. He finally died for it. I still can't see this—my father a blackmailer. At least he had something against Milian, some kind of leverage. That was why he probably got killed. Too much leverage. That's what I need, something to fuck up Milian.

Then I remember the buyout. That might be leverage. He is doing everything he can to keep me away from it, to keep everything on track. Kyle Frankel. Maybe Frankel is a weak spot. I can get to Milian through Frankel.

I'm getting colder, and can't stop shivering. I have nothing with me—no wallet, keys, or money—and I remember that Durante has my gun. It doesn't matter if he has it, uses it for a crime, and lets it get traced to me. I'm already screwed. It doesn't matter that the police are searching my apartment, probably finding more evidence planted by Durante. It doesn't matter that everything, even Paul's death, might be blamed on me. The more I think about it, the more I begin to shut down. This is beyond me. What can I do? Who will believe me besides Linda?

I lean against the Dumpster, shielding myself from the wind. A stray dog, a thin spotted mutt with an ear missing, trots across the street. I close my eyes and rest.

I have no idea how much time has passed when I finally hear a car approaching. I'm unable to move, my body numb, and my thoughts are confused as I try to remember what I'm doing here. I force myself to get up, ready to run if it's the police, though I know I'll never get far in my condition. I grab onto the cold Dumpster and pull myself toward the edge, my ribs burning, and suppress a moan. I look across the street and see a minivan parked in front of the self-storage building. The headlights are on, the engine running. I can't see the driver that well, and search along the street for cops. After a few minutes, the driver turns off the engine. I wait. The driver rolls down her window and calls out, "Allen Choice? Are you here?"

The woman is blond, plump, very Anglo, and I hesitate. I then recall that she is Linda's stepsister, so they don't have to look alike. I walk out from behind the Dumpster, and she notices me, her expression fearful. I hold up hands, which hurts my chest. "I'm sorry I'm a mess. I was beaten up."

"Allen Choice?"

I nod.

"I'm Julie, Linda's sister." She has a moon face with a small double chin.

"Were you followed?"

She looks startled. "Oh, I don't know. Linda didn't tell me—"

"It's okay. Did she call you?"

"Yes. I drove in from the East Bay. That's why it took so long."

"Do you have clothes for me?"

"I do. I'm supposed to give you clothes, and some money that she'll pay me back, and take you where you want to go. I hope you're not getting her into any trouble."

"I know," I say. She is wearing a UCSB sweatshirt and her hair is held back with a headband. "It's late," I say. "I'm sorry."

"She said it was an emergency."

"Can you hand me the clothes? I smell pretty bad."

She nods and climbs into the backseat. She opens the rear doors and steps out with a bundle. "It's my husband's old clothes," she says, handing it to me. She looks at me carefully. "What happened to you?"

"Linda didn't tell you?" I take off my shirt slowly, sucking in the pain, and put on the T-shirt and a faded blue sweatshirt. It's soft and warm. I'm about to pull off my pants, and she turns around abruptly. I change, and throw my old clothes into the Dumpster. The jeans that she has given me are too large. I climb into the back of her minivan and shut the doors. She gets into the driver's seat, starts the engine, and puts the car in drive. She turns around. "Are you going to stay back there?"

"I can't be seen," I say, sitting on the floor. Candy wrappers, a sock, and an empty tissue box are stuffed under the seat.

"Why not?"

"The police want me."

"What?" She shifts to park. "Wait a minute. Are you a criminal?"

"Linda will explain everything. I'm being framed."

She stares at me, then says, "She doesn't need more hassles."

"I know."

She turns to the road and begins driving. "Where do you want to go?"

I can't go to Linda's, and I definitely can't return home. Will the police know about my aunt? I say, "How about Mill Valley?"

She sighs. "All right."

It's warm in here, and I lower myself against the door, out of view. I ignore the ache traveling up my midsection. I need to distract myself. I ask, "You came from Walnut Creek?"

"I'd just gotten back. This is my second time down here tonight."

Second time? Then I remember. "You were with Linda and her ex."

"How did you know that?" she says sharply.

"She told me."

"Who are you? What's going on here?"

I don't answer.

"You're not connected with Manny, are you?"

"No," I say. After a moment I notice that she opens her window a crack. I must really smell. I say, "How did it go with him?" I feel dizzy from the rocking car movements, and lie down.

"You're not going to pass out or something—"

"No."

We are quiet as she pulls onto 101 North. I take shallow breaths. I ask again, "How did it go with her ex?"

"I heard you."

I wait. I'm feeling more queasy, and ask, "Can you turn off the heat, please?"

She does, and opens her window farther. Cool air swirls around me, and I immediately feel better.

"Why did she meet him?" I ask. "He seems a little dangerous."

"A *little* dangerous?" She snorts.

"So you were there—"

"Of course. I wouldn't let her see him by herself. And I *told* her that it was a mistake."

"Something happened?"

"Nothing that we didn't expect."

"He wanted money."

"You know about him?"

"A little."

"What's your name again?"

I tell her.

She sighs, then says, "He does something to her. He knows how to set her off, or wear her down. She's out of practice, dealing with him.

She's . . ." Shaking her head and muttering to herself, Julie changes lanes and speeds up.

"He wanted money?" I ask.

"Of course. He found out she's doing okay at a good newspaper, so he climbed out from under his rock."

"What did he say?"

"Typical things. He mentioned making her life difficult, jeopardizing her job, that kind of thing."

"She can get a restraining order."

"No kidding."

"So how did it end?"

"It's not for me to say. You have any more questions, you ask her."

"Okay."

"I don't know what you're doing, but if you get her in any trouble . . ."

"I won't."

"You'd better not," she says, then adds under her breath, "Like she needs any more losers in her life."

This stings, but I'm too exhausted to reply. I close my eyes. I hold my ribs and rest.

48

Her voice pulls me out of my haze of pain and drowsiness, and I look up with confusion at the roof of the minivan. ". . . hello? You have to tell me where to go. . . ."

I can't seem to move my body for a few seconds, nothing responding, and I say, "Where are we?"

"Mill Valley. Where should I drop you off?"

"Do you know where the high school is?"

"Tam High? Yes."

"Right there is fine."

"It's the middle of the night."

"I know," I say, still trying to sit up. I want to watch my aunt's house first, make sure the police aren't waiting for me.

"How much money do you need?" she asks, her voice tightening.

"Forget it."

"Linda said to give you some money." Her eyes lock on me in the rearview mirror.

"I don't need money," I lie.

She shrugs.

I say, "So is she okay, after meeting with him?"

"With . . . oh, yes. She's okay. She's a little mad at me."

"Why?"

"I got on her case afterward."

"What do you mean?"

"I told her she should never have met him."

"She probably knew that."

"I know she knew. That's why I'm helping her."

"You mean helping me," I say.

"Yes."

"So what happened with him?"

"You'll have to ask her that," she says. She pulls in front of Mount Tamalpais High School. A scrolling electric sign with red-bulb letters casts a crimson haze across the sidewalk. "Congratulations to our Merit Scholars," it reads before rotating up.

"What should I tell her?" Julie asks.

"Tell her?"

"I'm supposed to call her after I drop you off."

"Tell her we'll talk tomorrow. I'll try to call her at work." I climb slowly out of the van and shut the door. She drives away, the only car on the quiet street, and I move through the school grounds, student body election posters taped to fences and tacked to trees. Bicycle locks hang empty from a rack, and I stop to catch my breath. I cut through the student parking lot and walk along a still street adjacent to the football field, the houses dark; the only movements here are my steps on the dirt shoulder. My jeans keep slipping, and I have to hold them up with one hand while trying to keep most of the pressure off my left leg. I stifle my growing dread. I can't think about the police out there looking for me.

The road to my aunt's house is dark. I search for any activity, any surveillance, and look inside each parked car along this road. I don't see anyone, and begin to feel better. I work my way up to my aunt's, climbing the steep hill, and feel the strain in my legs and back.

At the front door, I knock quietly and wait. I knock again. I ring the doorbell. After a minute I hear movement inside, the wood floors creaking. The light above the door flickers on, and I step back for her to see me through the peephole.

Aunt Insook opens the door and says, "What you doing here?" She's wearing a threadbare robe, the sleeves frayed. Her bloodshot eyes blink rapidly. The left side of her hair is matted down, her face red and puffy from sleep.

"Sorry to bother you. I need a place to rest."

She squints, then steps back, startled, looking me up and down. "You have accident? You look hurt."

"No. Some people beat me up."

She frowns. "You have fight? It's three o'clock!"

"I'm sorry."

She opens the screen door and lets me in. She says, "You in trouble?"

"Why?"

"You tell me, not ask why."

"I might be, yes."

"With who?"

"The police."

She stops. "Why the police?"

"They think I killed Junil Kim."

"Did you?"

"No!" I say. "I didn't have anything—"

"But why police think that then?"

"I was framed."

She seems to age in front of me, her face sagging. "Frame? Who frame?"

With little energy to explain, I say, "It's complicated. They didn't mean to kill him, but once they did they needed to point it at someone. Roger Milian and his son are using me. . . ." I'm exhausted and wave it off. "I'm really tired—"

"You wake me up at three o'clock! It's three o'clock in morning!"

"I know. I'm sorry. Can we talk later?"

"I told you it's danger. I told you to listen to me."

"If I had listened to you, I wouldn't have found out that my father was blackmailing Milian, and that my father's 'accident' was probably murder, but Milian covered it up."

"What?"

"That's right. And that insurance settlement you got from Milian—that was a payoff, wasn't it? For you to keep quiet. You suspected what happened."

She steps back. "I don't know what you mean—"

"My father probably told you what he was up to, and so you knew exactly what was happening. That's why Milian had to pay you off."

She shakes her head violently and says, "No one pay me off."

"And how much was it, by the way? How come I never saw any of that money? Wasn't it intended for me in the first place?"

The sound of a car outside stops me. I wait as the car continues revving up the hill. My aunt watches me, then glances out the window. She says, "My neighbor with Jeep. He goes up all the way."

"At three a.m?"

She shuffles toward her bedroom. "You sleep on sofa. It's late."

I realize I raised my voice, and I say, "I didn't mean to yell."

She pauses in the hallway. Without turning, she says, "You yell the whole time I took care of you. Tonight the same." She continues walking and shuts her door. I hear her easing herself slowly onto her bed, the mattress creaking.

I wash up quickly in her bathroom, shocked by the size of the pink gash on my lip, the interior flesh exposed. I examine my bruises, and from the pain I know my ribs must be fractured. I wipe myself down with a damp washcloth, and make sure I clean out my cuts. Dozens of small lacerations and scrapes cover my body. I've bled into the T-shirt. When I finish I sit down on the sofa, but know I shouldn't sleep yet; I'm sure the police will check here as soon as they realize I'm not returning to my apartment tonight. They might be on their way right now. What I need is money and clothes.

Then, as I consider checking her purse for money, it strikes me how deep I am in this. I need a lawyer. I need thousands of dollars. Loose change won't mean shit. Panic flutters in my stomach, a queasiness I am beginning to recognize, and I stand up and tell myself to think. Don't panic. Think.

I need to talk to Linda, find out what's going on. I need to rest. I need my strength back. I decide to look for some clothes, and search for a basement or an attic. A door in the kitchen leads to a basement, and I walk down quietly, waving my hands blindly as I search for a light. I flick on the wall switch and look around: it's a small concrete room filled with moldy boxes next to an old green washing machine and dryer. The air is cold and damp, the smell of mildew mingling with detergent. I open a box and discover a dozen old Korean Bibles, the covers worn, the pages dog-eared. Another box contains pots and pans. When I find a box of clothes, I drag it out and look through it slowly, setting aside a polyester sweatsuit and a small blue jacket. Beneath the clothing the box also contains books, and I stop when I read a title: *Human Anatomy*. It's an old textbook, speckled with mold on the edges, and I stare at it for a full minute without touching it. When I pull it out, the spine cracks. Underneath are more textbooks—*The Endocrine System, Pathological Basis of Diseases, Principles of Internal Medicine*—that have warped, the covers arched, the pages curled and wavy. I go farther down into the box, pulling out textbooks with titles like *Pharmacology* and *Osteology,* and open one up, seeing my father's name scribbled inside the cover. He printed his name carefully, "John H. Choice." I flip through a few pages. He underlined and starred passages, and scribbled illegible notes in the margins. I ignore the moldy smell and pull out all eight of the books and stack them on the floor.

My father went through all of these textbooks carefully, even copying some of the diagrams into the back blank pages along with notes to himself in Korean script, which surprises me. Did he have to translate everything to understand it? What language did he think in?

It's cold down here, and I put on the jacket. I see a textbook titled *Allergic Mechanisms* and pull it out. Car brakes squeak outside, tires crackling on the dirt road. I immediately turn off the light and hurry back upstairs. I look out the window and see a patrol car. I don't know if they have a search warrant or if they are just warning my aunt, but I can't stick around. I hurry to the sliding door facing the porch, and slip out quietly. Climbing down onto the rocky hill, I listen to the police ring my aunt's doorbell; they left their car lights on. The radio squawks.

My footing slips, sending some gravel down the slope. I stop and wait, then continue down, heading into a neighbor's yard. I listen to my aunt's doorbell ring again faintly. The living-room lights flash on; a white glow spills onto the trees. Ready to run farther down the hill and toward the high school, I watch the shadows moving slowly in the curtained windows as my aunt and the police talk in the living room.

But then the house shudders with the front door closing tightly. Footsteps return to the patrol car. After two muted car door slams, the car backs down the hill instead of doing a U-turn, the brake lights going on, then off, on then off. That's it? I hurry back up the slope and onto my aunt's patio. I push open the sliding doors and climb back in.

The living room is empty, but I hear her moving the boxes downstairs. "Hello?" I say from the top of the staircase.

"What you do here? You leave a mess."

I walk down to her, and ask, "What did the police want?"

"They tell me you might come. I have to call them if I see you."

"They didn't want to search the house?"

"I don't care. I tell them to come in. They look around, but see that I don't care."

"What if I was hiding down here?"

She turns to me. "Then you might be caught." She sees my frown and says, "What you want me to do? Not let them in? Then I get in trouble."

"They need a warrant to search the house, or even to come in. You didn't have to let them in."

She shakes her head. "You know nothing about police. And why you bring this to me? Why you bring trouble?"

I point to the textbooks. "I thought you said you gave away everything."

"I forget about this. It was too expensive to give away."

"What else you have in these boxes? Anything of mine?"

"I don't remember. Some of this is very old. I forget all about these books."

"Can I have these?"

"Why?" she asks quickly.

"Because they're just sitting here getting moldy," I say, bending down and picking up the allergy textbook. I flip through the pages and see more notes. "I'll hold on to them."

"Where you read them, in jail?"

I turn to her, startled. "Jesus. You must really hate me."

Her eyes focus squarely on me. "I don't hate you."

"What did I ever really do to you? I was a difficult kid. So what? A lot of kids are difficult."

"I go back to bed," she says slowly, turning away.

"Yeah, go on. You're an old woman, you're very tired," I say.

She stops, her back straightening. I'm ready for an argument, but she remains still, then walks back upstairs. She moves across the living room above me, and into her bedroom. How could she mention jail so easily? I try to push this away, surprised that she let the fight go. Not too long ago she would have stopped, turned around on those steps, and marched back down toward me. She would've pointed her finger at me and raised her voice.

On the inside back cover of the allergy textbook, I see a list written out in Korean, but at the top is my name scribbled in English. I can't figure out what this is until I read the word "pollen" in English near the bottom, then realize it's an allergy chart for me. I hold on to the book and return upstairs. I sit on the sofa and flip through more pages, a stale smell coming from the paper. Cigarette smoke. It appears as if my father read this textbook a number of times, some passages underlined twice with different-colored inks. His notes in Korean fill up the margins. I read a heavily marked page with a passage starred: " . . . the reserve of antibodies interact with the antigen and cause an antibody antigen reaction. This reaction releases mediators such as histamines . . ."

I fall into a fitful, light sleep, waking up often with the textbook on my chest. I jolt awake at one point with the startled thought that the last person to flip through these pages was my father, his dense fingers turning the same page, jotting notes. I drift off. I keep hearing noises outside, and my heart seems tuned to a permanent rapid beat, pulsing against the textbook and filling my ears with rhythmic warnings.

49

My aunt is gone when I awake. I call out to her, and pull myself up. My head immediately pulses and I get dizzy; my ribs
flash in pain. I lie back down slowly, a sheen of sweat breaking out over
my body. I call out to my aunt again. I roll out of the sofa onto my
hands and knees, then stand up with just my legs, trying not to use any
of the muscles around my ribs and back. A slice of sunrise cuts through
the living room. The morning air is fresh and cool. I check her bedroom, but see no sign of her. Not until I look for coffee in the kitchen
do I see a note from her: "Money for you in the closet. Check money
belt and take it all. Go far away and hide." That's all it says, and I puz-
zle over it for a minute before searching through the two closets—one
in the living room and one in her bedroom. I find the money belt—a
thin canvas pocket that straps under a shirt—hanging behind her
dresses, and pull open the Velcro pocket flaps. Inside are hundred-
dollar bills, at least fifty of them neatly overlapping one another so that
there isn't one bulky section, but a uniform thickness along the length
of the belt.

I stare. Go far away and hide.

Wrapping the belt around my abdomen and securing it with the
straps, I find that it helps ease the pain in my ribs, softening the movement of walking and turning. A money bandage. I use the bathroom,
first washing up, then staring with shock at my pink urine filling the

toilet. I flush quickly. I blame all this on Durante. Go away and hide? I can't.

I sit down next to the telephone and dial Linda's number, but hang up before it rings. Her phone is probably tapped and ready to trace any calls. I'll try her office from a pay phone. I get Pinewood Investment's number from the information operator, and then call and ask for Kyle Frankel. After insisting it's urgent, I persuade the receptionist to pull him from a meeting. He answers his line with an annoyed "What is it?"

I tell him who I am. He's silent, then I hear rustling. "Didn't I just read about you in the paper?"

"Maybe. I'm wanted for murder."

"Murder," he says. After a moment he asks, "What's this about?"

"I wanted to warn you. When I'm arrested, I'm implicating Milian and Durante and WestSun."

"What?"

"Milian was involved in a murder twenty years ago, and a cover-up. They are both involved in two murders that I know of recently, including that of Junil Kim, which I'm being framed for."

"Is this a joke? Who is this?"

"Mr. Frankel, the *San Jose Sentinel* will be breaking the news of this soon. I am warning you because of your buyout. Your company might get some bad press."

"Do you have proof of this?"

"I have an eyewitness to the twenty-year-old murder," I say. "And more evidence keeps appearing every day."

"Why should I believe you?"

"It doesn't matter to me. Go ahead with the buyout." I hang up.

That should slow things down for WestSun. Frankel would be stupid to move ahead without looking into my claims, and he is certain to stall in order to confer with his partners. I have to get at Milian in any way I can.

I am about to leave the house, but remember Frankel's statement about the newspaper. Maybe that's why my aunt left; she read or saw the news. She left me the money, but didn't want to be involved. My photograph has probably been published. I go into the basement and search through the boxes of clothes, certain that I saw a baseball cap here last night. I find it: a blue mesh cap without a logo. I then return to my aunt's bedroom and find a pair of sunglasses. I also pocket a handful of quarters.

I look in the mirror and am surprised to see a badly dressed, over-grown teenager, with baggy jeans, an oversized T-shirt hanging out underneath a jacket, a baseball cap, and sunglasses. My lower lip is still swollen. The bruises on my cheek and around my eyes are partially hidden by the sunglasses. I move toward the front door but stop when I see the open allergy textbook on the sofa. I consider taking it with me, but leave it on the coffee table.

Hurrying from my aunt's house and through the high school campus, I receive a few looks from students. I cross the street and find a pay phone at a Safeway. I watch for police cars. I hunch next to the phone and use my aunt's quarters to call Linda at work.

"Is this line okay?" I ask when she answers.

"I think so, but let me use a different phone."

I give her the number and hang up. A minute later she calls back. "Where are you?" she asks.

I tell her, then say, "I won't be here long."

"It looks bad. They found a crowbar with blood on it, possibly the victim's, in the trunk of your car. They're checking for fingerprints."

"Shit." The plastic bag must have contained the crowbar. "They'll find them," I say, and tell her about being beaten up. Durante could have put my hands on the crowbar when I was unconscious. "They planned all this out."

"You're in the papers."

"Front page?"

"No. They're still testing for fingerprints and blood. Once it comes through, you'll be bigger news."

"Did you talk to Loverro?"

"I did by phone. She's denying everything. She's obviously scared."

"Denying everything she told me?"

"Everything. She's claiming she doesn't remember you. She's playing senile."

"Jesus. What the hell am I going to do?"

"Calm down. It's not as clear-cut as it seems. There are too many loose ends showing up: Loverro, Garvey's wife, even Junil Kim. I mean, think about it. What motive could you possibly have?"

"They'll come up with something. What about Mrs. Garvey? Milian didn't seem concerned about her at all."

"Maybe he knows she won't talk?"

"It seems more like I was wrong. He said she has no role in this."

"Of course he would say that."

A police car drives by. I look down, and let my cap shield my face. I say, "I have to get out of here."

"Get into the city. Staying up there is dangerous. My sister said you didn't take any money."

"I have a little."

"From where?"

"My aunt."

"Your aunt?"

"She gave it to me," I say. "We need to plan. Do you know any lawyers?"

"Yes. I know a good one in the city."

"I'll find a way out of here. We should talk, but you have to be careful. They'll watch you."

"I know."

We agree to meet at a restaurant in Union Square at noon, and I hang up. I see a Golden Gate transit bus passing in front of the school. It's still early enough for the commuter buses to be going into the Financial District, but I'm wary about being recognized. I buy three papers from a row of newspaper kiosks, then wait at the bus stop across the street. The story about me is still in the Bay Area sections: evidence was found possibly linking me to Junil Kim's murder, and I am wanted for questioning. I'm now considered a suspect, and anyone with information about the crime or my whereabouts is asked to call the Monte Vista Police. However, there are no photographs of me.

Another bus arrives, and I board it, asking the driver if it's going into the Financial District. He nods. I empty most of my quarters into the machine and walk to the back. A few commuters glance up at me. I take a seat, lower my cap, and begin reading the other sections of the newspapers. I feel the money belt digging into my waist. Maybe my aunt is right. Maybe I should disappear. I can go into the city, take a train anywhere up or down the coast.

But I can't let Milian and Durante win. Eventually I might have to run, but not until I pay them back. I think about all the people who Durante seems to employ, at least four or five that I know of, and wonder what would happen if they were faced with jail time. Would they turn on Durante, who would then turn on Milian?

Then, in a moment of jarring clarity, I remember that the other security at Florentino's, the one with the long hair—what was his name?—spoke to the man in the Raiders jacket. That's a connection. Lawrence. The PI. He can identify the man, and that might be a link to Durante. It's not strong, but it's a start. I'm focusing on Durante and Milian when I should be thinking more broadly. And I have to get to Mrs. Garvey. If she is subpoenaed, will she reveal everything in court? Why wasn't Milian worried about her?

I mull over all of this while the bus crosses the Golden Gate bridge. The morning fog shrouds most of the water and the view of the city. A man in a business suit behind me listens to his Walkman too loudly, the music hissing from his earphones. I continue reading my newspapers, and look for Linda's byline in the *Sentinel*. I can't find anything, and wonder if she's working on my story, if the new evidence linking me to Junil Kim has given her more clout with her editors, or has gotten her in more trouble.

When the bus finally enters the Financial District, I get off and walk a few blocks to Union Square, the tourists already beginning to clutter the streets. The restaurant where I'm supposed to meet Linda is on Geary. I'm over two hours early. The breakfast crowd is thinning out, and I'm able to find a booth near the back. I haven't eaten since lunch yesterday, though it seems longer, and I order a breakfast. After three glasses of water and two glasses of orange juice before my food arrives, I feel better, and begin thinking more calmly. I haven't been checking if anyone recognizes me, if I've been followed. I wonder if my picture was shown on TV; someone could've spotted me by now. I must be more careful.

What to do next: I have to contact Mrs. Garvey again. She's the key. Maybe Milian wasn't worried about her because she was involved in my father's murder and had no choice but to remain quiet. She was upset when Linda and I called her, immediately denying everything and refusing to talk.

All this is so messy, so unwieldy, and I sit quietly, trying to figure out how to salvage this. I keep thinking about my aunt's note. Go far away and hide. Where the hell would I go? I could probably disappear in L.A.

I shake this off. The impulse to flee is growing. I have nothing holding me here. The idea of a normal life is incomprehensible to me.

Linda walks in at a quarter to twelve.

"Were you careful?" I ask.

"Yes." She stares at my face. "God, Allen. Have you seen a doctor?"

"Not yet. But thanks for sending your sister."

"Let me look at that," she says, leaning in closer. She touches the side of my face, her fingers cool. "Allen . . ."

"It's okay. I'll have it looked at later."

She nods, her expression still concerned. She says, "I just got a call from Milian."

"When?"

"Before I left. He was pissed. Really pissed. What did you do to Pinewood?"

I smile, which hurts my lip. "So Frankel must have stalled the buy-out. I told him that I was going to implicate Milian and Durante."

"Good thinking. Milian was cursing you out. He wants to meet."

I shake my head. "No. I've had enough meetings with him."

"He's going to call my cell phone at noon."

"You have a cell phone?"

"It's the paper's. I'm officially working on this story."

"Congratulations," I say.

"I think he might want to make a deal. Maybe you back off Pinewood, and he'll help you with Junil Kim."

"How could he? The evidence is there. I'm screwed unless I prove I was framed."

"Maybe he'll let one of his employees take the blame."

"No. I don't believe it. He won't be satisfied until I'm in jail or dead. I'm screwed."

"I don't think so. It looks bad, but the evidence isn't as clear as you think."

"Why?"

"Your trunk lock was broken, and they're also testing the fibers. I'm guessing that the fibers on Junil Kim won't match the fibers in your car, or whatever they'll find on the crowbar."

"His blood. That's all they need," I say.

"No, we have a chance. Milian sounded desperate."

I stare. Is this just a game for her? I could go to jail for murder. I don't know what to say.

Her phone chirps, and she answers it quickly. She says, "Yes, hold on." Holding up her phone to me, she nods and mouths, "Milian."

"Yeah," I say into the phone.

"What exactly did you tell Frankel?" he asks.

"The truth." I'm aware that cell phone calls can be intercepted.

"That's unlikely," he says. "Do you think this is going to change anything?"

"Maybe not. But at least I messed up your plans."

He is about to say something but stops himself. "I want to meet and talk."

"Sorry. My last visit didn't go so well."

"Your aunt is here."

I tense. "What?"

"Your aunt . . . is visiting." Static on the line breaks up his voice so that the word "aunt" splits in two, the signal returning quickly with static blanketing the silence. Could one of his men have been watching my aunt's house? Why didn't they tip off the police?

"Did you hear me?" he asks.

"I did." I try to think what this means. My aunt?

"I want you to call back Kyle Frankel."

"Why would I do that?"

"Because your aunt wants you to."

"I would still be wanted by the police. Framed. Why would I help you?"

"We could fix that."

"How?"

"Give them the real murderer."

"With my prints on the murder weapon?"

"We can find a way," he says.

"And if I don't?"

"Your aunt will be very disappointed." I hear the phone being shifted in his hands, and after a brief pause my aunt says, "Sung-Oh, just go away. Don't listen to—"

Her words are muffled, and Milian comes back on. "You see? She advises you to listen to me."

"You've got to be shitting me," I say, raising my voice. "You think you can do this?"

"Do what? You should take your aunt's advice."

I can't find the words. Linda is watching and trying to figure out what's going on. She points to the phone and gives me a questioning look. I try not to stutter as I say, "You can't be . . . This is insane."

"We'll meet then, to talk. Come by my house."

"So the police can—"

"Are you slow? After what you've just done with Frankel, I can't have you caught. Yet."

"I don't know."

"You don't know? Well, think of something. I'll expect you in an hour. If not, well, that's . . . that's all I can do." He hangs up.

I close the phone. Linda says, "Well? What was all that about?"

I explain quickly what he wants, and she cries, "That's ridiculous! It's a setup."

"I know, but what can I do?"

"Don't go."

"What about my aunt?"

She shakes her head. "And how can you change Frankel's mind? That doesn't make sense."

"I can call him and say I made it up just to stop the buyout."

"But . . . why go there? I don't get it."

"My aunt's there, Linda."

"You don't think he'd actually do anything to her?"

"Christ, think of Junil Kim."

"What if he just wants to kill you?"

I nod. "I know. But I have some leverage—you're going to break this story if anything happens to me."

"Is there a story?"

"Not the one I want, but there is one."

"So I go with you, and tell them that the story is set to go if anything happens?"

"No, you shouldn't go. But I tell them the story is about to run."

"That Milian is involved in your father's murder—"

"And they're implicated in Paul's and Junil Kim's death."

"Are they?"

"They will be," I say. I tell her about the man in the Raiders jacket, how he might be a connection between Paul's death and Durante.

She takes the cell phone, her eyebrows knitted as she thinks this out. "I don't know," she says. "It's all so sketchy."

"My aunt is there," I say. "What else can I do?"

50

The first time I went out on group work with ProServ I worried about making a mistake and embarrassing myself. I worried about my appearance, my demeanor, even the way I was walking. I wondered if I looked like I belonged there with the others, all security professionals or ex-cops or ex-military who had probably done this kind of thing hundreds of times. I, however, had rusted behind a console in a computer company lobby for years, getting slow.

Paul was in the group, though he wasn't the team leader for that job, and he grew agitated with one member of the team, Sean Rodale, who kept kidding around with Brodie. Rodale, who would leave ProServ a few months later for a rent-a-cop job in the city, was telling Brodie a story and imitating a voice, which Brodie listened to with half a smile. But I could see that Brodie was distracted. Our client was supposed to arrive at this meeting point ten minutes ago, and we were getting impatient. Every time a car drove by the parking lot, we looked up. Paul finally said to Rodale, "Keep it quiet."

Rodale stopped in surprise, then looked around with a what's-with-this-guy look on his face. He turned to me and shrugged. I didn't respond. I noticed that Paul was watching me. We had never said more than a perfunctory hello to each other at that point, and I knew he was trying to figure me out. Later, he would tell me that when he began to lead a team, he chose me because of that moment, when I could have been sympathetic to Rodale, but kept focused on the job. I didn't tell him at the time that I had been too worried about everything to care what Rodale was doing or to respond. When Rodale had shrugged at me, I had been thinking of where exactly I should be standing when the limo arrived.

Sometimes I wondered if I hadn't been so nervous, what would I have done? The truth is I probably would have shrugged back, since I tend not to like the authoritative tone. Moreover, Paul hadn't been the team leader and was on the same seniority level as Rodale. It wasn't really Paul's job to reprimand him.

And yet Paul and I worked well together. I remember this as I approach Milian's front door. What would Paul do in a situation like this? Probably not go in alone. Linda has driven off, heading back to her office; she is my only defense if anything happens to me. She can run the story. On the way down here she told me that she'll start working on what she has. She can talk to Lawrence. She can get to Mrs. Garvey. She can hammer away at Mrs. Loverro. At the very least, she can report on my investigation of my father's death.

I have no idea what to expect. Milian might shoot me, then say that I came here seeking revenge for my father's death. But that will raise questions about Milian's role. He might say that I was obsessed with him, but Linda will be reporting why. I can't see how Milian is going to save his deal with Pinewood and shut me up. Would he really hurt my aunt? Does he think I'll ignore the murder charge leveled against me?

Durante opens the front door and looks me over with a smirk on his face. My ribs and back ache, and I feel a rush of hatred. I push him aside with my shoulder, forcing him out of my path. He lets out a small laugh and moves ahead of me into the main living room. Milian is sitting in a leather recliner, drinking something with ice, and looks wearily up at me, his eyes haggard. He glances at my clothing. "Where is your reporter friend?"

"She's going to run her story until I tell her to hold it. If I tell her." I look up at a clock. "You don't have much time. Where is my aunt?"

"She's fine. She was never in any danger."

"I'd like to see her."

"Why are you doing this?" he asks. He waves his hand in the air.

"For my father, and my partner. For Junil Kim, who did nothing."

He sighs and said, "I did not kill your father. He was blackmailing me—he grew to hate me, in fact—and I paid him when I really didn't have to. But I did not kill him."

"You're lying."

"Junil Kim—I still don't know how that happened." He turns to Durante, who is standing in the doorway. "My son assumes responsibility for that, since one of his men made some mistakes in judgment. His men confuse violence with power." He continues staring at Durante, and says, "My son needs to learn the art of management better."

"And my partner, Paul Baumgartner?" I ask.

He shakes his head. "I have no idea who that is."

I point to Durante. "Maybe you should ask your son, since Paul worked for him. He probably found out too much about your son's business." Durante turns to me. I say, "When Paul was murdered, one of your son's men was there. It all connects."

Milian's face shows almost no expression. His eyes, though, stay focused on me, appraising me. He raises his voice without turning, asking his son, "Is that true?"

Durante clears his throat. "No."

"I have an eyewitness," I say to Durante. "Someone who talked to the decoy you set up. A lot of people saw him. Even the police know about him. It's only a matter of time before the police find him, and he points to you."

"You don't have shit—"

"Enough," Milian says. "Is what he's saying true?"

Durante suddenly looks uncertain, and starts to reply, but stops. I say, "What happened? Did Paul find out what you're smuggling or stealing? Why did you kill him? He had a wife and kid. He didn't have to die."

Milian stands up slowly, the cushions beneath him inhaling. He turns and faces his son, and repeats his question, his voice lower, softer. "Is this true?"

I watch Durante struggle with this question; he frowns, then glances at me. He turns quickly to his father and says, "Can we talk about this later?"

"My God," Milian says, putting down his drink and squeezing the bridge of his nose. "It's all falling apart."

"No," Durante says. "We can smooth—"

"This has to do with that sideline of yours, doesn't it? Didn't I tell you that it would end up like this? Didn't I warn you?"

"Nothing's gone wrong—"

"You ruined this deal, you know. There is no way that Kyle—"

"I can fix this!" Durante says. "It's not ruined!"

I clear my throat. "This is all very sweet, but I'd like to see my aunt."

Durante says, "You fucking piece of shit—"

"Enough," Milian says.

"—goddamn son of a bitch. I'm going to make sure I'm watching when you get—"

"Enough!" Milian barks. Durante stops.

I turn to Milian. "The story will still run. You and your son will go to jail. If my aunt is hurt, you can bet—"

"The story won't run. We won't go to jail," Milian says.

I'm taken aback by his confidence, and I ask, "Is this the art of management? Do you really think you can get away with murder?"

"You'd better call your reporter friend and tell her to stop the story."

I stare. "Are you joking? What are you going to do, kill me? You don't understand— "

"No, *you* don't understand," he says. "If that story runs, your aunt will go to jail."

"What?"

He sighs at me, then calls out, "Insook."

I'm not sure if he's talking to me, and say, "What?"

He turns toward the hallway leading to the other rooms, and raises his voice: "You should come out now."

We wait.

My aunt enters the room, her expression frightened. She says to Milian, "You said you wouldn't tell—"

"I had to. He was going to let the story run."

"Aunt Insook?" I ask, a coldness settling in. "Are you all right?"

She barely looks up, and her eyes flicker away.

Durante says, "Course she's all right. She came here on her own."

Aunt Insook turns to Milian, waiting for him to say something, but the silence grows, and I slowly understand what's going on. I say to her, "You're with him." She tenses, and begins to shake her head.

"I told you go away," she says. "I told you forget about this."

"If the story runs, you'll go to jail?" I ask.

"Why don't you listen to me!" Her face is red.

Milian says something that I can't understand, and it takes a moment for me to realize that he is speaking Korean to her. I whirl toward him. He finishes what he is saying, then smiles at me. "I think it's shameful that you can't speak your mother tongue."

"You speak Korean?"

"Fluently."

"How?"

"I was a translator during the Korean War. Why do you think I went into this business?"

I say to my aunt, "How are you involved in this?"

Durante laughs. "She's the one who killed your old man, you stupid fuck."

"No, no, it was an accident!" my aunt cries.

"You killed my father?" I say. I turn to Milian. "It wasn't Mrs. Garvey with you that night my father died."

He shakes his head.

"It was my aunt."

He nods.

To her I say, "You were having an affair with him, and my father tried to stop it."

"Your father blackmailed me," Milian says. "He hated us together, but he profited from it."

"I didn't mean to hurt him," she whispers. "He fight with Roger."

"What did you do? How did you kill him?"

"No," she moans. "I just push him away. I just push."

"He fell off the loading dock," Milian says. "He hit his head."

I continue staring at my aunt, who refuses to look at me. For the first time in my life I see fear in her expression, and she keeps checking with Milian, glancing at him, then looking down. I've been so stupid. She was involved the entire time. She knew all this ever since I started living with her, and, of course, she resented me because I reminded her of everything she had done. I'm having trouble grasping this. Twenty years of knowing this. I ask, "You've been with him all these years?" I motion to Milian.

She shakes her head. "We don't talk or see each other after that."

"Until you started looking into it," Milian says. "You caused your aunt quite a bit of anxiety."

"Shit," I say to her. "I can't believe this."

"Don't curse."

I blink. "What? Did you just tell me not to curse? Are you kidding me?"

She balls her hands into fists, but keeps her arms pressed to her sides. She says, "You don't speak to me that way."

"You killed my father?" I say, still incredulous.

Milian says, "So you see why you have to call your reporter friend. I don't know what sort of evidence you think you have, but your aunt will be the first one to be exposed."

"I'm still wanted for Junil Kim's murder."

My aunt moves toward the doorway. She says to no one in particular, "I go home now."

Milian nods to Durante, who walks with her to the front door. I say to her, "This isn't over, Aunt Insook."

She stops for a moment, then continues.

Durante says to Milian, "I'll get Sal to drive her back up."

But Milian is watching me. Once Durante leaves with my aunt, Milian says, "He's young, impulsive, and impatient."

"I'm not going to jail because of his stupidity. Junil Kim and my partner shouldn't have died. What's he doing, dealing drugs or something?"

"Absolutely not."

"Smuggling, then? Using those Asian contacts for smuggling?"

"That's unimportant. I'm sure we can find a way to clear your name."

"How?"

"You'll have my best lawyer. We will get my son's employee responsible for the deaths to confess."

"I doubt you'll do that."

"Anything is possible."

I hear voices outside. I say, "He's not Krista's son."

The sound of her name startles him; he shakes his head. "No. He's the result of an affair I had."

"Not my aunt."

"No. I didn't know he was my son until a few years ago."

"He's got quite a criminal record."

"Will you retract that story?"

"It's not mine to retract."

"But you can deny everything, and stop helping the reporter."

"You're beginning to sound desperate," I say.

He lets out a slow breath and says, "You would let your aunt go to jail?"

I see how frail he seems, how old he really is, and am surprised by my thoughts: I can kill him right now, just snap his neck. We are alone. I'd have to move quickly, but there wouldn't be any sounds. Could he implicate my aunt if he was dead?

"You hate her, don't you?" he says.

I stare at him, not having really heard his question.

He says, "She gave up her life to take care of you. She had big plans, you know. She didn't want to be a bookkeeper all her life."

"When she killed my father, she had to take care of me."

"Your father . . ." he begins, but shakes his head wearily.

"What is it?" I demand.

"Your father was a petty, vindictive man—"

"Careful, now," I say, holding up an imaginary piece of thread. "I'm holding your future up with this."

"I have very little future left. This is for my son," he says. "Your father wanted to get back at me because of the business with Noah Garvey. And he couldn't stand the thought of his sister with me."

"So he blackmailed you."

"Not at first. He just demanded we stop. But how could he? He was just a flunky. I could've fired him, if it weren't for your aunt. But once the merger was in the works, and he found out about my ex-wife's shareholder power, he had a little more ammunition."

"That's all it took? The threat of your ex-wife knowing?"

"No. There was more. Some of my contacts in Seoul and Hong Kong weren't completely legitimate."

"And Koreagate was going on."

"But I didn't have to pay. I could've ruined him more easily than Garvey, but your aunt intervened. Only after your father became greedy, wanting more money, did I stop paying."

"What happened at the warehouse? Why did my aunt . . ."

"Your father had a short fuse when it came to me. I told him I wasn't paying him anymore. He threatened to tell my wife, but it didn't matter. The merger was finished on paper by that time. He had nothing then. Your aunt and I had won. He attacked me."

"And my aunt pushed him?"

"She pushed him. He fell off the dock and hit his head."

"And you made it look like an accident."

"I wanted to protect your aunt."

"And your company. All that bad publicity. You were an accessory."

He waves this off. "We're wasting time. What is your decision?"

"I'll do what I can to help my aunt, but I'm not going to let this go."

"If that's true, there's nothing you can do for your aunt. You'll destroy her."

I don't reply.

"Cold-hearted, aren't you?" he says. "An emotionless man. I remember what it was like. The stone look at everyone around you. But nothing is that simple. Your father could've learned that and led a happier life."

"What the hell does that mean?"

"He didn't think about how your aunt felt or what shades of gray there were in our relationship. He didn't care that Noah Garvey was an unstable man. Your father wanted to stop me, and that's all he considered. You are about to repeat the mistakes of your father."

We hear more voices in the foyer, and Durante walks in with Linda. He holds her arm and jerks her forward. I freeze. Shit.

"Who's this?" Milian asks.

"This is the reporter. She was across the street."

"Is Insook—"

"Sal drove her home."

Milian turns to me with an astonished expression. "You're even more stupid than your father."

Linda pulls away from Durante. "Don't fucking touch me again."

Milian says to me, "You couldn't have had enough information to go with the story yet. So, I have everything here."

I think quickly. "We have enough to start the investigation against you and Durante. If anything happened to us, especially her, you'd be the immediate suspect."

Linda says, "Most of my story is filed. I also have a partner at the newspaper who is following up."

Milian studies her. He asks Durante, "You still have his gun?"

Durante pulls out my SIG.

I ask, "Did my aunt know everything? Did she know about Junil Kim?"

"After the fact," Milian says. "And she couldn't do much about it."

"She knew she was leading me into a trap, though."

"Trap?" Milian says. "We felt you'd go along with us once you knew everything."

Linda turns to me in puzzlement.

Milian adds, "And we didn't expect the reporter to be here."

I feel strangely calm. Am I going to die? I say, "Killing us won't solve anything. It'll just raise more questions."

Linda adds, "My partner and the police will be very interested."

Milian is staring at me thoughtfully.

"Kyle Frankel is not going to change his mind just because I turn up dead. He'll immediately suspect you."

"Yes," Milian says slowly. "It looks like you've irrevocably damaged the buyout."

Durante says, "What?"

"Unless," Milian continues, "you go to trial for Junil Kim's death, and don't name us in any way."

"Why would I do that?"

"Why indeed," he says.

"Oh, fuck," Durante says. "The deal is dead?"

Milian nods slowly, still watching me.

Durante points my SIG at me. "You stupid fuck. You goddamn—"

"How much was the deal for?" Linda asks.

"You shut the hell up," Durante says.

"The interesting thing is that your aunt is a shareholder of West-Sun," Milian says. "She would've benefited from the buyout."

"What?" I say.

"When WestSun was formed, your aunt received quite a bit of the private corporation's shares."

"Why?"

"She helped me. And it was part of the settlement for your father's death. I'm sure she would've given you some of the gains."

Durante laughs. "So you just screwed yourself over."

There's a small beeping coming from the front door. I see a red light flashing on a security panel, and Durante rushes over to it. "Someone opened the front gate," he tells Milian.

"Get Sal to—"

"Sal took the car."

"Where are the others?"

"At the warehouse."

Milian nods and opens a drawer, pulling out a .38 snub-nose. "Check what it is," he tells Durante. To us he says, "Sit down."

I ask Linda, "Why didn't you go?"

"It's my job," she says quietly. "And I couldn't just leave you here."

Voices outside. Someone curses. As they enter the house I hear a familiar voice say, "What the hell is going on here?"

Linda sits up. We watch Manny, her ex-husband, wearing the same windbreaker, now torn and dirty, walk in. Durante trails behind, his gun drawn. Linda says, "Oh, man."

"He broke the gate," Durante says to Milian.

"Who is he?"

Manny looks at Linda. "What is this?" His jeans are muddy and wet, his spiky hair at odd angles. He takes us in, surveying the living room. Durante shrugs at Milian's question, and they watch Manny shake his head at Linda. He says, "Who are these people?"

"You followed me?" she says, standing.

"And you again," he says to me.

"What's the meaning of this?" Milian says.

Manny says to him, "I just wanted to see her." Then he turns to Linda. "What are you up to?"

"Look who has the guns—"

"Shut up!" Durante yells. "Who are you?"

"He's my ex-husband," Linda says.

"You think a call from your lawyer's going do anything? I didn't touch you. I didn't even shake your hand."

"That's it," Durante says. "Shut the hell up." He pushes Manny toward the sofa.

Manny whirls around. "What is this?"

Milian says to Durante, "Keep him quiet."

Durante swings the pistol quickly at Manny's head, and connects. Manny curses and staggers back, holding his forehead. "Ah, shit."

Durante says, "Punk-ass little piece of crap. Keep your mouth shut."

"What the—"

"Enough of this," Milian says. "We have to decide—"

"It's perfect," Durante says. He looks us over. "The ex shows up for revenge."

"What are you talking about?" Milian asks.

"Check it out. Those two are together. The ex shows up, kills them both because he's so pissed, then kills himself."

Milian shakes his head. "No more killing."

"I'm getting the hell out of here," Manny says, pulling himself up.

Durante aims his gun at Manny, continuing to talk to his father. "Don't you see? We get rid of three in one, and then we just drop them off in her car. It's perfect."

Manny stands up and says, "No fucking way—"

Durante whips the gun even harder against Manny's face. The sharp snap fills the house.

"Stop!" Milian yells. Manny's eyelids flutter; he staggers back and falls into the sofa. He tries to sit up, but swoons and his head falls back. He presses his palms on the sofa, and leans away, moaning.

Durante keeps the gun aimed at him. "We should start with this guy."

"Stop," Milian says quietly. "Stop that."

Durante looks up. "I should make him eat the bullet. That's more like suicide."

"Son, calm down."

"You're crazy," I say.

"You don't have a prayer," Durante says, turning to me and aiming the SIG at my chest. He's close enough that I think about trying to take him down.

"Stop," Milian says. "Please calm down."

"If he wasn't such a fucking pain in the ass, none of this would've happened."

"Calm down," Milian says.

"I can fix this. I can make it work. I can think of something."

"No. Stop. We'll figure this out—"

"I can't believe this stupid chink son of a bitch—"

"We just have to plan—"

"—could fuck up everything—"

"Oh, Jesus," Linda says, staring at him in disbelief.

Durante moves toward Linda, aiming the gun at her, and Milian says, "Son." Linda looks up, her eyes startled. Without thinking I jump toward Durante, who has just noticed me moving, and as he turns with the gun I dive at him, tackling him but making sure I grab the gun, locking onto it and pushing it aside. We fall onto a glass coffee table, which shatters, and we roll across the floor as I try to keep the gun aimed away, but Durante pulls the trigger and the gun goes off, the heat blasting near my fingers, but I hold on, the barrel hot. I see in my periphery Linda diving for cover, and I begin punching wildly at Durante's face and neck, trying to stop him from shooting again, and I suddenly realize that I am stronger than he is, that each punch and each twist of the gun pulls it freer, and Durante can't hold on; I'm twisting the gun away from him, and he can't seem to twist back, and his eyes widen as I squeeze his hand tightly, pulling at the gun. He grunts and goes berserk as he starts kicking and clawing at me, even trying to bite my hand away. I jam my elbow into his neck a few times, making him choke, and I slowly twist the gun into his chest. He realizes what's happening and reaches down toward his ankle, loosening his grip on the gun, and I'm not sure what he's doing until I see a flash of steel, and he tries to stab me with a small knife, a pocketknife really, but the angle is wrong and the blade hits the money belt I'm wearing, stopping and skipping off it. I then grab that hand, and force the gun into his chest with my other hand, and he lets out a wheeze as he tries to scramble away, still struggling with the gun, letting go of the knife, but now trying to get out of the way, and our eyes meet and I know I have him and he does too, and he says, "Fuck you, chinko." I pull the trigger and the kick of the gun is muffled in our grips. Blood spurts from his chest. He keeps staring at me. "Fuck you," he says again. He looks down and lets out a small whimper. His grip loosens, and I yank the gun away.

He searches for Milian, who rushes over to him, saying, "Oh, Christ. Oh, Christ."

I aim the gun at Milian, remembering his .38.

Durante tries to speak, but saliva dribbles from his mouth, and when he touches his lips and sees blood on his fingers, he makes a warbling, clotted moan, his eye fearful and uncomprehending. I move quickly toward Milian and pull the gun out of his hand. Milian barely notices as he stares down at his dying son, his hand resting on Durante's forehead. He whispers something inaudible, and strokes his son's hair.

Linda says, "I'm calling the police." But she remains still.

Milian whispers something else to his son, and lays him back carefully. He pulls himself up slowly, his knees and back cracking, and he turns to me. "You . . . you killed him."

"He was trying to kill me."

"You didn't have to shoot him." He advances.

"Whoa, hold on," I say, raising my SIG. "Don't do anything stupid."

"He was so young. You didn't have to kill him." He keeps moving toward me, and I back up.

"Stop. Just stop."

"It doesn't matter. Shoot me. I was doing this for him. He didn't have to die."

"Neither did my father. Neither did Junil Kim, or my partner. Mr. Milian, stop right now." I raise my gun higher.

"Your father died crying like a baby," he says.

I'm not sure I heard him right. I stop and say, "What?"

"He didn't die right away. In fact, he stood up after Insook pushed him off the deck. Then he sat down. Then he began crying. He looked at Insook and cried."

"What're you talking about?"

"It was the most pitiful sight I've ever seen. He knew he was beaten. We tricked him at every turn. He was stupid, slow, and weak."

I take two quick steps toward him, and glide into a jumping round-house kick to his head, hopping off my right leg, then swinging it up and connecting with his ear. The momentum of the kick snaps his head to the side and throws his body to the floor. He holds his ear, but stays on his side. He breathes heavily for a few moments, then collapses. For a moment I think I might have killed him, and go down to check his pulse. No, he's still alive.

Linda says, "Allen . . ." She is looking at everyone around us. "Allen . . ."

"I want to go after my aunt."

"We have to call the police."

I give Linda the .38, and say, "Let me have your keys. I'm going after my aunt. Keep this on Milian when he comes to."

"Your aunt? Let the police—"

"Please."

She hesitates, then digs into her pockets. She hands me her keys, but seems numb. She glances at her ex-husband, who is still dazed on the sofa, then she stares at Durante on the ground.

"Linda, will you be okay?"

She nods absently.

I ask again, "Are you okay? Look at me."

She does, and slowly focuses. She shakes her head clear. "I'm . . . I'm okay."

I run out to her car.

51

On the way up 101 I keep thinking about my father crying, and know on some level that Milian was trying to get to me, but it feels true, and I can't stop the image from repeating, and I end up angering myself. My fucking aunt knew all about it ever since I was a kid, and no wonder she hates my guts, since every time she looked at me she'd see my father and remember what she did. All those fights in Korean she had with him, fights I couldn't understand, must have been related to this. And the money. She must have had plenty of money, and yet she acted as if there was nothing, making me feel guilty for every dime I spent, even for a pair of goddamn socks. The money came from my father's death, which she had caused. She was profiting from it and made me feel guilty. Goddamn all this.

I reach down into my torn shirt and touch the slice in the money belt. I feel a few cut bills inside the pouch. My aunt knew I was getting closer, circling in on the truth, and it frightened her. She tried, in her strange way, to bribe me, to send me away with five grand. The money belt is damp with sweat. I wonder what would've happened if the knife had made it through.

I drive over the Golden Gate, only ten minutes from my aunt's house, unable to sort out what exactly I'll say or do. The more I think about it, the more I begin to see that she left me at Milian's house to die. How could she have known what he would do, since Milian himself seemed unsure? She didn't even want Milian to reveal her presence. She was hiding in another room.

Still bewildered by her role in this, I try to trace back every reaction, every word she said to me about my father and Milian. She kept saying all that had happened many years ago, and she couldn't remember, baldly lying to me. She was very good at lying, and I was stupid to believe her just because she was my aunt.

I drive into Mill Valley and take Linda's car up the hill, parking on the side of the dirt road in front of my aunt's house. The shades are drawn. I knock on the front door, but no one answers. I doubt that I could've beaten her here, so I try the doorknob, and find it unlocked.

"Are you home?" I ask, opening the door.

I immediately see her carrying clothes to an open suitcase in the living room. The lights are off but the sun fills the room from the bay window. Her shadow stretches onto the ceiling. She stops, a bundle of blouses in her hand, then continues to the suitcase, which is almost full. I walk in and say, "Durante is dead. Milian is about to be arrested."

She nods without looking up and stuffs the blouses on top. She closes the suitcase and locks it. She then moves to the dining-room table, where I notice a pad and pen, scribbles filling the page. She sits down and writes. "What are you doing?" I ask.

"Go away, Sung-Oh."

I approach and see that her letter is already two pages long, in Korean script; she's adding a postscript at the end. On the table next to her is a red rice bowl with two white pills sitting at the bottom. "What're those?"

She ignores me.

"Why did you lie to me?"

"I couldn't tell you truth."

I say slowly, "You left me there to die."

She pauses. "I told you to go away."

"You knew that they were going to kill me."

She doesn't answer.

"Why did you do it?"

Her hand shakes. She puts the pen down and rests her palms flat on the table. She stares straight down and says, "I'm very sorry about your father. My life is ruined because of it."

"Ruined?" I survey her house. "It doesn't seem ruined to me."

"I was very . . . I love Roger very much back then. We wanted to get married."

I almost laugh, but say, "Oh, please. No sob stories. You were fucking Milian, and my father didn't like it. Milian paid him off for a while, then you killed him. It's not very romantic."

She flinches.

I continue, "You killed him. At the warehouse he was fighting with Milian, and you chose Milian over him, your brother. You pushed him and he died."

"He hurt Roger. He was stronger than Roger."

"But you killed him. After you two covered it up, you couldn't stay together because it would look suspicious. But why not later? Why did you stay apart after enough time—"

"Because of you! I couldn't go to him! You hate me because of what I did!"

"I didn't know what you did. I had no idea."

"You hate me. I see how much you hate me."

I study her, and say, "If I resented you it was because you didn't want me around. I was a burden to you and knew it."

"My life ruined because of you. I couldn't do different because you there. I couldn't be with Roger because of you."

This startles me. Inertial deception. She felt unable to change her trajectory, and blamed it on me. I say, "You could've seen him if you wanted to. I wouldn't have known—" I stop. She's faulting me for her separation from Milian? I've never even heard of him until recently. Then it hits me. Durante. Milian admitted Durante was his son. I say, "Wait a minute. Durante was from an affair. Milian said that. Milian was seeing other people."

She is motionless.

I say slowly, "He had other women. Even a baby—Durante—with other women. He dumped you, didn't he? He ended it after my father died. He paid you off and dumped you."

"It was because of you!"

"Because of me?" I say. "I doubt I had that much pull as a ten-year old. Jesus Christ. You're blaming me, but he just got tired of you."

She cries silently, covering her eyes and turning away. I feel nothing. I say, "Why couldn't you just move on?"

"I kill my brother!" she says, her face contorted, her mouth drawn down. "I kill my only family!"

I step back. She seems shocked by her own outburst, and presses her palms back down on the table, steadying herself. She looks at her letter, and says quietly, "Go away, Sung-Oh. Leave me alone."

"What're those pills?"

"Cyanide," she says, pronouncing it *cy-night*.

"Where did you get cyanide?"

"Roger. His son smuggle chemicals."

"Durante smuggled chemicals, from Asia? That's the sideline?"

She stares straight ahead and picks up her pen. "Go away, Sung-Oh," she says with exhaustion. "Please."

"What are you writing?"

"I write confession. Complete confession."

"I don't know if that's admissible in court."

She shakes her head, then says, "Not for court. For me."

I watch as she finishes writing, signing her name at the bottom of the page. She begins reading it over, and I look at her suitcase. "What's with that? Where are you going? What are you doing with the pills?"

"I don't know."

I remember her advice to me, to go far away and hide, and I ask, "Where would you go?"

"I don't know."

"Then what's with these?" I say, reaching for the rice bowl. I pick it up and examine the two pills.

"Give back."

"He wanted to go to medical school, didn't he? He wanted a better life. He was going to use Milian's money to pay for it."

"Give that back!"

"What . . .what was he like? How come he would blackmail someone? I don't understand."

She walks back to the living room, checking her suitcase. She says, "Roger break down Noah Garvey, so your father think it's okay to get back at him. But he also get back at me for being with Roger."

"You were with the enemy."

"Not enemy to me." She sits on the sofa and rests her arm on the suitcase. The look in her eyes is spiritless, but the wrinkles in the corners and around her mouth seem smoothed by fatigue, and I see for a moment a younger woman, attractive to Milian, maybe even in love. Her life was filled with disappointment in the men around her, including me.

"You know, if the police want to find you, they will."

Her eyes sharpen for a moment. "I'm smart woman, Sung-Oh."

"I should call the police right now. Maybe they're on their way."

"Good."

I hold up the rice bowl. "Were you really going to take these?"

"I don't know."

My anger has dissipated, and I no longer have any idea what I should do, why I even drove up here. I see the allergy textbook on the coffee table, and I pick it up. "Who gets that letter?"

"I give to Grace Park to give to police."

"If it's true that my father's death was accidental, you don't have to run."

"I can't . . . I can't face everyone." She stares down at her suitcase. "Go, Sung-Oh."

Dropping the pills into my pocket, I say, "I'll take these."

"I have more."

I know this is an empty threat. I point to her suitcase. "Will you leave the country?"

She shakes her head and says, "I don't know."

I look down at the allergy textbook, and turn to leave. I think for a moment about my allergies and how my father studied my symptoms. I was allergic to everything, and then I think of my aunt's cat. I stop at the doorway. "Do you remember that cat you used to have?"

She turns to me slowly. "What?"

"Your cat. Do you remember it?"

She nods.

"What was its name?"

"Sammy."

"Sammy?"

She says, "My friend give it to me. Already name is Sammy."

"Did you know I killed that cat? Accidentally?"

She nods. "I know."

Startled, I say, "What?"

"I know."

"How did you know?"

With a sad smile, she says, "You think I can't tell? Sammy missing for three days, so I look around yard. You don't think I can see the fresh dirt? The fresh grave? You don't think I dig up? And I see the dirty hammer in the garage from digging?"

"Why didn't you say anything to me?"

She shrugs. "Sammy dead. You killed him. I don't know what to say to you. I don't understand you."

"It was an accident."

She folds her hands in her lap and says quietly, "He was gone. Accident or not." She looks down at the empty rice bowl, and blinks. "Goodbye, Sung-Oh." She doesn't raise her head as I back out of her house. My last view of her, before I close the door, is of the shiny floors bouncing the sunlight around her, her hands clasped, her head bowed in prayer.

52

The police move quickly and find Durante's hired men, most of whom are still working at WestSun the evening their boss dies. The police even find the man in the Raiders jacket, positively identified by Lawrence, the long-haired PI who saw him at Florentino's. The man immediately begins cutting a deal as soon as he realizes that he is now a prime suspect in the conspiracy to murder Paul Baumgartner. He details Durante's role in Paul's death, offering evidence that Durante was smuggling industrial chemicals. Paul's accidental discovery of this led to his murder. The man points the police to T.J., Durante's second-in-command, who killed Junil Kim in what seems to have been a warning gone awry. They pulled Kim into the van to warn him away from me, and to find out what he'd already told, but Junil Kim fought back. Three men had to take him down. As soon as this is revealed, and the list of charges grows, all of Durante's men begin working out deals, confirming that Durante and Milian are the leaders.

Milian starts fighting everything when he is arrested, and has with him some of the best lawyers in the state. Linda tells me that he might actually get away with quite a bit, since Durante was running his smuggling operation without Milian's explicit knowledge. The men who worked for Durante answered only to him.

My aunt has disappeared. The police tracked her as far as Guam, but after that she no longer used her passport or bought any tickets in her own name. Linda tried to find a trace of her in Seoul, and a Korean American colleague at the *Sentinel* made a few dozen calls, but has come up with nothing yet. The interest in my aunt by both the police and the *Sentinel* seems to be in her eyewitness accounts of Milian and Durante—her role in my father's death has become almost irrelevant to everyone but me. Grace Park, who is handling my aunt's donation of her house and belongings to the church, denies knowing anything except her final instructions: she has my aunt's power of attorney (granted to her the day before my aunt left, the timing of which points to my aunt's realization of the approaching end) and is required to give everything of value to the Santa Clara Methodist Church, with one exception. Mrs. Park recently shipped me a box of textbooks and two photo albums. The church receives the house. I get books.

Aunt Insook's confession was translated into English and printed in some newspapers, including the *Sentinel*, but I haven't read it yet. I've been avoiding most newspaper and TV reports. I did, however, see Linda's appearance on PBS as a guest on *This Week in Northern California*, a roundtable discussion of local events, where she played up the twenty-year-old-murder angle. She is getting a promotion, a raise, but seems subdued by her success. We finally meet at my apartment almost two weeks later, when the initial wave of press and attention has died down, though if Milian has a trial, the activity will undoubtedly begin again.

"Will he have a trial?" I ask Linda. She sits on my futon and drinks a beer. It's almost midnight, and we finish a quick late dinner while she updates me.

"His lawyers are trying to work out a plea bargain."

I look up. "Will it happen?"

"To a degree. He'll probably get time at a minimum-security prison."

"That's it?"

"A long time, but yes, that's it."

"Unbelievable."

"Well, he still has to deal with U.S. Customs Special Investigations, the Justice Department, and even the EPA."

"Because of the smuggling."

She says, "It's going to drag on for a while."

She has told me this before. I look out my window and say, "I'm sorry, you know."

"For what?"

I turn around. "For leaving you there alone. I had to see my aunt."

"I know." Linda puts down her beer and takes a deep breath. "It was strange being there with them. I've never been so close to . . . to all that."

"I'm sorry."

"But that's not what bothers me."

I wait.

"I was there with the gun, and began thinking—and I actually found myself thinking about this—what would happen if I shot Manny and said Durante had done it."

I'm not sure if she's serious, but when I see that she's completely still, waiting for my reaction, I ask, "Was he conscious?"

"Barely. And what would've happened? It was obvious that Durante could've done it anyway—"

"He wanted to."

"It would've been so easy."

I shake my head. "But you're not like that."

She looks up sharply. "Don't think he wouldn't have deserved it."

"I'm not saying that. Why didn't you?"

"I couldn't. You're right. I'm not like that." She rubs her eyes and stretches her back. "I think all this scared him away for a while, but I can't help thinking what it'd be like if I had done it." She stares at me. "I wonder if he'll ever really leave me alone."

I wish I knew what to say.

"How are *you* doing?" she asks.

I sit down next to her, imagining her poised over her ex-husband with the .38. The strange thing is that if I were her, I might have done it. This alarms me. I feel nothing over Durante's death. I shot him point-blank and watched him die, and yet I feel no regret or remorse. It doesn't seem like that much of a leap to become a killer like Durante.

"Allen?" she asks.

"I'm okay," I say. "Just thinking."

"It's getting late." She glances at her watch.

"You can sleep here tonight."

After a long silence she says, "Did Lawrence contact you?"

"The PI?"

"He wanted to call you. I think he wants to offer you a job, or become a partner or something."

"You're kidding."

"No. You're getting all kinds of offers, aren't you?"

"A few. Polansky, Black Diamond."

"What are you going to do?"

"I don't know."

"Would you go back to ProServ?"

"No."

"Maybe you should start your own agency."

"Maybe."

She smiles. "You'd rather not talk about it."

"I'd rather not think about it."

She sits up, kicks her legs over the armrest, and lies down with her head next to my legs. She stares up at the ceiling, and says, "Have you heard from Sonia Baumgartner?"

"She left me a message. She apologized, but it looks like her lawsuit might be dismissed."

"Because ProServ and the restaurant aren't at fault."

"Right. And it's not like she'll get any money from Durante. Or even Milian. He's ruined." I turn to her. "It wasn't clear from your article how Paul found WestSun."

"That's because it's not clear to me. It looks like he started avoiding high-tech firms because he was worried about overlapping ProServ and others who might connect him with them."

"Violating his contract."

"Yes, and having Polansky find out. So he started going after shipping firms, warehouses, places that needed security but weren't connected to the tech industry."

"And he went after the wrong firm with WestSun," I say. Her articles detailed Durante's industrial chemical smuggling, which he was trying to finish off before the buyout, and Paul, in his usual thoroughness and rigor, not only stumbled across this sideline but immediately recognized the danger to himself. He quickly withdrew from WestSun, but by that time, Durante had already decided to eliminate his mistake, which Paul clearly was. Durante couldn't have anything jeopardize the buyout. WestSun was about to become his company, after all. He arranged to kill Paul while he was on duty, which was risky, but Durante knew the suspicion would then fall on the client's enemies.

"Are you going to call her back?" Linda asks.

"Who?"

"Sonia Baumgartner."

"No," I say. Her eyes flicker toward me. "No. I learned my lesson."

"What about her son?" she asks.

"David? I should talk to him again, but his mother was going to screw me over. I'm not too happy about that."

She says, "Hmm," and relaxes into the cushion. I reach down and play with her hair. She smiles to herself, her eyes closed, and nods. She says in a sleepy voice, "My sister thinks you're trouble."

"I can see why. I didn't make a good first impression."

"No, you didn't," she says.

"But it must be nice to have a sister worrying about you. She was so . . . protective that it made me like her."

Linda hums an agreement. I continue playing with her hair, running my fingers through her curls, lifting up strands and letting them fall slowly. Her breathing slows, her body settling into sleep. I'm not sure if I should wake her—she's in an awkward position—and decide not to. She's probably exhausted.

I stare at Linda's tranquil face, and rest my hand on her warm forehead. I slowly pull away from her, and stare again out the window, watching cars at the stoplight. I won't be able to sleep for a few hours. My ribs ache. The doctor said I had massive bruising and a small fracture in one rib, but it wasn't too serious. I had trouble believing all that pain came from bruising. He was more concerned about my kidneys, but after a series of tests, he told me I'd be okay. Still, my back is tender.

I have medical terms bouncing in my head—my reading material before I go to sleep is now my father's textbooks—and I wonder what would have happened if my mother hadn't died giving birth to me, if my father had been able to go to medical school, and if he and my mother had lived together as a family. I wonder what I'd be doing now, this very moment, if I had never lived with my aunt and was leading a normal life.

My father was a blackmailer, a vindictive, angry man. He didn't choose his friends or enemies very carefully, and it ended his life. I can't feel much for him, except some sorrow, since I didn't really know him. He is a faint memory. He watched the TV news with me. He showed me photos of my mother. He helped me carve my walking stick.

I can't stop thinking about my aunt, who harbored her secret for so long, seeing in me the constant reminder of her crime against my father. One of her last statements to me was that she had killed her brother, that she had killed her only family, and I realize only now that she hadn't thought of me as her family. I lived with her for over seven years, and she baby-sat me for longer than that, and I was her nephew, but I was not her family. I was instead a burden, an unexpected and unwelcome reminder. A punishment for her betrayal.

I sigh.

Linda stirs. I turn and see that she's awake, and staring at me. I'm surprised, and tilt my head questioningly.

She sits up slowly. "You okay?"

I nod. I say, "I never really thanked you."

"Thanked me."

"For everything."

She waves this away.

"And for coming back. For not leaving me at Milian's."

She leans forward, still watching me closely.

"If you hadn't come back, and your ex hadn't followed . . ."

"I didn't want to leave you there alone."

I shake my head. "I still don't know why you took such a risk."

"You don't?" she says. In the semidarkness around us I notice that her expression is different—curious, a slight smile emerging—and when she stands, it seems all sounds around us stop.

"You don't," she says, this time a statement.

I remain frozen, and she takes a step forward, waits, then takes another step. She moves across the floor this way, inching toward me. Some of her hair falls over the left side of her face, shadowing it, and I can no longer see her expression. I remember how she looked that day in Palo Alto, when we were searching for Stein's restaurant, the way she leaned back against the railing with one leg hooked behind her, her throat exposed, her hair falling back. When she saw me and waved, when I realized she was happy to see me, I felt a twinge of joy that embarrassed me. Now, as Linda moves up to me, a breath away, and studies me, all I can think about is that moment when it seemed we were both glad to see each other. This makes me anxious, uncertain, since I know I will mess everything up. I always do.

She moves even closer to me, her legs touching mine, her eyes probing.

I say quietly, "Do you know that you're the only person I trust?"

She answers me by reaching up with her hand, touching my cheek lightly. Her fingers are cool. She rises on her toes and kisses my forehead, her hair brushing over my eyes. Her fingers graze my neck and rest on my shoulder. Then, slowly, we lean in and kiss, pulling each other closer, the hint of her faded perfume unwinding around me. I feel the small of her back. I hold her tightly. I mumble something about her being great, and I feel her laugh. She pulls back, grins. Her eyes are bright. I am about to say something else, but she puts her finger to her smiling lips. We move closer and kiss again.

Epilogue

Here is a true story: my father never gave up his dream to be a doctor. Even in his forties, a widower with a ten-year-old son, out of school for twenty years, his English skills poor and his bank account empty, he read and reread dense, obscure textbooks with the hope of someday using this preparation for medical school. He made margin notes in messy Korean script, he tried to connect what he read to the world around him—to me—and the pages stained with coffee and smelling of stale cigarette smoke revealed a life of my father's that I did not know existed. When I used to think of him I thought not of dreams deferred or dreams dying, but of the palpable world of physical work, of gasoline smells and blackened fingernails, of exhausted evenings in front of the TV news. Now I think of him yearning for more.

I have begun running every evening, ignoring the faint pains and stitches throughout my body, reveling in what was once a routine as a teenager in Oakland, zipping down noisy streets but hearing only my heartbeat and my heavy breaths. The spring rains have arrived, and I find myself pushing through sharp downpours that begin and end with a blink. I used to run as an escape from my aunt and my life with her, but now I run toward something indefinable, something that's around the next corner, hoping to shake my dis-ease, hoping to find engagement. Is it possible? I don't know. My philosophy of remove-ment is a work in progress.

When I run I think about all these things. I think about Linda, about my father, about my aunt, and I think about the two pills I took from my aunt, which I now keep in a jar labeled "Poison," a skull and crossbones crudely penciled in. I'm not sure why I keep them, but I can't seem to throw them away.

I remember the folktale Junil Kim told his class, the one that Grace Park translated for me about the crying blue frogs. When a sudden cloudburst explodes over me, and I splash through puddles and my shirt pastes to my back, I hear Mrs. Park's voice punctuating Junil Kim's droning Korean, the two languages melding over me. But through the rain I don't hear the lament of the mournful frogs near the river, wailing at the rising water and the washed-out graves. I don't hear the cries of regret and pain and melancholy. What do I hear? I hear my quick and deep breaths. I hear the splashes and soothing sheets of rain around me. I hear my heart pounding into my sore ribs. I hear the faint booms of distant thunder that sound like deep, robust laughter.

ACKNOWLEDGMENTS

I'd like to thank the following people for their help: Carissa Evange-lista for her faith and encouragement; Eloise Klein Healy for bring-ing me aboard at Antioch; Dave Smith and J.A. for their security knowledge and contacts; Julie Cooper and Dan Halpern for their ed-itorial expertise; Judith Weber for her critical eye; and a special thanks to Nat Sobel, whose confidence in me and perseverance on my behalf were remarkable.

ABOUT THE AUTHOR

Leonard Chang is the author of two previous novels, *The Fruit 'N Food* and *Dispatches from the Cold*. He was born in New York City, raised on Long Island, and studied at Dartmouth College, Harvard University, and the University of California at Irvine. In addition to novels, hc writes short stories, essays, and book reviews, and his work has appeared in numerous literary journals, including *The Crescent Review, Confluence,* and *Prairie Schooner.* He currently teaches in the graduate writing program at Antioch University in Los Angeles and lives in the San Francisco Bay Area.